LYNN MARIE HULSMAN

I'm a writer. My mother's death brought an epiphany. "Life is short," said my inner voice. "Thanks, I.V.," I replied. "I know what I have to do." In short order, I got an agent, co-wrote two books, ghost-wrote another, published an article, and sold a novel.

Kentucky-born, tall tales and hyperbole are in my bones. I love story. My real jobs? Equity actor. Ad copy writer for casinos, ("Loose slots!") Stand-up comic. Pharma editor. Cheese cube passer-outer (admitted low point). I'm an Ideation Agent (sounds fake, right?) and run an improv company in NYC. My favorite, favorite thing to do is write Romantic Comedy.

I live with my family in Hell's Kitchen, and am seen around town auctioneering for charity, hosting gay men's fashion shows, and calling bingo games.

You can follow me on Twitter @LynnMarieSays.

Thornton Hall

LYNN MARIE HULSMAN

Harper*Impulse* an imprint of
HarperCollins*Publishers Ltd*
77–85 Fulham Palace Road
Hammersmith, London W6 8JB

www.harpercollins.co.uk

A Paperback Original 2014

First published in Great Britain in ebook format by HarperImpulse 2013

A catalogue record for this book
is available from the British Library

ISBN: 978-0-00-759165-7

Automatically produced by Atomik ePublisher from Easypress

For my dear friend Kate Bushmann.

Chapter One

"Juliet, it's Phillipa from The Gastronome's Trust. Big stuff. I hope I'm not calling too early," she said, not sounding sorry at all.

I held the phone with one hand and stroked the still-warm, empty space next to me in the bed with my other, drinking in the sensation of being a grown-up.

I seriously cannot believe I'm me, I thought, suppressing a manic giggle. *I'm in my boyfriend's Mayfair apartment – which he owns! – answering a phone call from my agent who's about to offer me real money for my very much in demand culinary skills to put in my – wait for it! – savings account. A savings account which now has enough for me to go back to college and complete my sociology degree. Who would have thought it? Juliet Hill – back on track. Certified Grown-up. Even my mother would have to agree.* My mind was racing, even though my body hadn't quite caught up, yet.

I'm on the brink of a new beginning, I'm moving back to New York to complete the studies I'd dropped all those years ago. And I'm moving back with my successful boyfriend…successful and athletic, I thought, wincing as I stretched out my aching limbs. After recent work trips to the States, then New Zealand, Ben seemed determined to make up for lost time: he was like the cat that swallowed the canary. Absence had certainly made his body grow fonder, and his heart, too, I hoped. So maybe, if I'm honest with myself, my world hadn't been properly rocked last night… but then he'd practically just stepped off a plane, for heaven's sake, I couldn't expect nirvana. We'd have plenty of time this holiday season to get back on the same page in the old sex department.

Where is he, anyway? I peeled one eye open to check the clock on his night table. 6:55 a.m. My agent, Phillipa, certainly was getting the worm, as it were.

"Juliet," she said sharply. "Are you listening to me? I asked if I've awakened you."

"No, Pips, it's fine," I lied breezily, forcing myself to sound alert, "I've been up for ages." Phillipa Burton, owner of London's top agency dedicated to placing chefs in private households, expects everyone's full-on attention. I've always thought of her as one of those British school-mistressy types. She scares me a little, but I pretend she doesn't. I'm a favorite because I've always behaved like a soldier in her army.

"Darling," she said crisply, "I've just had a specific request come in for you to work over the Christmas holiday. I explained that you blacked those dates out with us, but the client insisted I ask, and here's the kicker…You'd need to be there tonight." She paused. "The housekeeper rang and said if I could send Juliet Hill, they'd pay a fee for the late notice, and a holiday bonus. The call came at six, and I'm sorry to say the offer's only good until eight o'clock this morning."

I let her talk, knowing I'd be turning the job down. I'd tell her about my plan to move back to New York with my soon-to-be fiancé and having to leave the business altogether once the holidays ended. No need to stir up emotions and spoil the joy right now. While she tried to sell me on the job, I let my mind wander to thoughts of caroling around the piano with Ben's cousins and uncles, mugs of warm mulled wine on the sofa, and smiling faces peeking over a crispy roast goose flanked by massive tureens of root vegetables. This Christmas was going to be special – a real family celebration. Impeccable Ben, in his well-cut suit, standing possessively with his arm around my shoulders, welcoming me into the fold, and for once in my life, I'd be wearing the right thing. Nothing too slutty, or cheap. And certainly no stains on my starched, white blouse. His family would murmur among themselves about what a perfect match I was for their Ben.

I was determined that all would go according to plan. When I'd phoned him last week to firm up this year's holiday plans, he'd been kind of quiet on the phone from his office in New Zealand – he's on location there for a film his firm is representing. I'd chalked his lukewarm mood up to exhaustion. Poor Ben, I'd thought. He's lost without a girl like me to loosen him up. After all, he is English. He can't help it if he's tightly wound.

He told me he had something important he wanted to talk about with me. Once he said that, I'd changed the subject, fast. I hadn't wanted him to spoil the big surprise, hoping he wouldn't discuss logistics until after the thrill of the engagement wore off. I couldn't help grinning and giving myself a little hug just thinking about it.

Anyway, back to the present. Focus on Phillipa. I would never act like a diva with my agent so I let her ramble. "Keep your head down, do excellent work and don't cause trouble," is a roadmap I try to stick to. Well, for the most part, if you don't mind turning a blind eye to the whole Paris debacle.

"Juliet!" Phillipa barked, snapping me out of my daydream again. "Did you catch that? I said eight a.m."

"Of course, sorry," I said, stifling a yawn. "Who requested me?" I asked, though I pretty much knew.

"So you're interested? Are you changing your mind?"

I wavered for half a second. Of all the food-forward, over-the-top, gourmet meals I'd created, I'd never once done a traditional Christmas feast at an English hall. My wheels started to spin, planning menus and visualizing the tabletop in full cinematic Technicolor. The chance to design a dinner that would simultaneously hearken back to childhood roots so different from mine, while putting a surprising, modern spin on conventional favorites like sage and onion stuffing, roasted Brussels sprouts with chestnuts, a flaming Christmas pudding, drew me in – quite against my will. My cells started tingling, just thinking about the chance to put my signature all over a meal that jaded guests thought they knew inside out and backwards. I bit my lip.

"I'm sorry, Pips," I said, honestly. "I want to, but I just can't." I was surprised to feel my eyes beginning to well.

"Well, if you change your mind, you know where to find me," she said crisply. "If I don't hear from you, I hope you have a happy Christmas and check in with me in January."

"I definitely, definitely will!" I said, pushing the "end" button on my iPhone with my left thumb. I looked at my naked ring finger. *And when I do call, you'll be stunned to hear that not only am I moving to New York, but I'm also engaged to be married.*

So, I'm a chef, but not a chef like you'd think. I'm a chef who makes my living cooking not in any restaurant where a regular person – or a rich, powerful or famous person, actually – could book a table, but behind the legendary "green baize doors" of some of the most posh private residences in the world. I've made it to an apex in my career. All the meals I cook now are invitation-only.

I eventually escaped upward from testosterone-fuelled kitchens in France, and the early days of the London restaurant scene, but not before honing my culinary skills, growing a T-bone-thick hide, and a tongue like a sushi knife. Nothing else has ever come as naturally to me, and I have to say, so far, it's given me a pretty good life. I've done more traveling than most people do in a lifetime, and I've stood in rooms with princes, war heroes and TV stars. And, indirectly, it led me to Ben. Handsome, funny, swaggering Ben in his well-cut suits.

In my wildest dreams I'd never thought I'd attract such a catch. He was the type of man who simultaneously made office interns swoon, while garnering nods of approval from mothers and grannies. Sexy, but respectable.

Rolling over onto Ben's pillow, I put my phone down on the night table, on top of his *Financial Times*.

"Ben? Good morning!" I called out, propping myself up on an elbow and craning my neck to look around the corner into the bathroom. "Are you making coffee?" I really had to pee. We must have had a bottle of wine each last night. I'd talked a little about how giving up The Gastronome's Trust – Phillipa's agency – made me sad, but he just told me again, firmly, that going back to The States and finally getting serious about my life was the sensible thing to do. Deep down, I knew I didn't have a leg to stand on in that department, after dropping out of college to chase a man to Paris – and look how that turned out.

So I let Ben have the last word, and wrap up the conversation. Anyway, he wasn't much in the mood for talking, if you follow me.

I got up off the bed, and pulled the sheet around myself, just to be safe, even though I was pretty sure now that he had already left the flat.

Where would he have gone at this hour? He didn't say anything about an early client. I walked to the bathroom using tiny geisha-like steps since the bottom of Ben's sheet was winding itself tighter and tighter around my ankles, practically hobbling me. Stupid, maybe, since Ben saw me naked on a semi-regular basis. Then again I've never been a flaunter or the parade-around-naked type, whereas my best friend Posy would happily drink tea and read the morning papers without a stitch on, all the while chattering about the weather. The combination of growing up with servants and living at girls' boarding schools had cured her of modesty.

Posy Wase-Bailey is my closest friend on earth and why I live in London now. You've no doubt seen her in the papers, attending this gala or that premiere. Owing to the fact that her dad is that charismatic airline owner – the one who took himself to outer space – she has spent her life in the limelight. It doesn't hurt a bit that she's a fearless trendsetter, often spotting the next "it" designer, and that she's always good for a controversial quote. We're like chalk and cheese in that way, but under the surface, where it matters, we're soul sisters separated at birth. I cannot imagine what my life would be like had she not spotted me crying into my coffee that day in Paris. I might have fled home to the States, or worse yet, begged Stephen for one more chance.

Anyway, back to the present! Memo to self, must not dwell on the past.

Normally, by this hour of the morning, I would have mainlined caffeine. Being an addict is a job hazard. In every kitchen where I've ever worked, there's been a top-shelf espresso machine and we staff pound coffees all day long. I had the briefest fantasy that Ben might bring me a cup, then sighed. I was the coffee bringer in this relationship.

I dropped my sheet and eased, undrugged, into the trickle of tepid water the English insist on calling a shower, beginning to suds my hair with the Jo Malone Lime, Basil and Mandarin shampoo sitting on the ledge, delighted to find that there was a matching bottle of conditioner. It smelled heavenly and his thoughtfulness warmed my heart. It more than made up for not bringing me a cappuccino. Normally, there was only a sad jug of Boots brand baby shampoo.

He never said so, but I could tell Ben wasn't wild about my keeping toiletries here. He's a neat freak, so I made it a point to carry out whatever I'd carried in, like my travel toothbrush and trial-sized toothpaste. I'd left my gold drop earrings on the sink once, and the next morning, after he left for work, I found them on the kitchen table in a creamy, business-sized envelope with my full mailing address on it. I smiled thinking about it. It's habits like uber-organization that got him a place as a solicitor at Thompson Loyal, his logical stepping-stone to his goal – being a real New York lawyer. What a mature quality. It would make my mother drool. Posy on the other hand once said she thought Ben was a bit OCD.

Did he leave for work? I thought to myself, rinsing the last of the conditioner out of my hair. Ben's usually like Pavlov's dogs when he hears shower water running, sprinting in and stripping along the way. He loved shower sex. Me, not so much. "Where's your sportsmanship?" he'd ask me, winking. "It's a challenge when I'm slippery." Usually, I was glad to give him what he wanted as, let's face it, most females of the species would kill to be with Ben. I could see it in super-hot girls' eyes when Ben and I were out for drinks or dinner. And I could practically hear them thinking, "He's a solid 9 and, she's, well…not."

Clean, I stepped out of the shower and grabbed a white Turkish towel off the towel warmer. English people are so weird about bathrooms. They aren't interested in ambient heat or water pressure, but they'd rather die than press a room-temperature towel to their bodies. I could forgive the quirks, though, since being converted to full-on Anglophile. I'd lived here long enough that England felt like home, and there was no denying that Ben being an Englishman was part of the turn-on.

It had been over a year since I'd met Ben at the London Aquarium benefit. I guess you could say we went from zero to sixty, fast. I think I called him my boyfriend the first day we woke up together. If I was honest, I'd have to admit it stung that he still hadn't introduced me to any of his family, except for one sister over a quick after-work drink.

Well, the tide was about to turn, and I had big plans to make it all turn out like in the movies. Maybe his mother would invite me to call her "Mum"? Could I say that without feeling like a poser? Or would it be "Mother Flannery"?

I was determined that this Christmas would be perfect, especially since the last one had been a major disappointment. He had invited me to his family's home, but at the eleventh hour, he'd called from the New York office. He made a thousand apologies and cancelled the whole holiday plan, explaining that he'd have to stay in the U.S. through New Year's, while I was stuck in London alone.

"I'm crushed, Darling," he had cooed transatlantically into the phone. "And so's my family. Dad especially. He said he wanted to get a good look at my girl to see if she fit in with the Flannery clan. Please try to understand."

I remember the squeezing feeling I'd gotten in my stomach. At the time, I'd sensed a whiff of Stephen. *Don't catastrophize, Juliet. Ben is not your old boyfriend.*

"You do wish you were here with me, don't you?"

"Don't be an idiot," Ben had replied impatiently. "Of course I want to be with you. It's just quite impossible at the moment. Be practical, Juliet."

It sounded like something my mother would say, and I was embarrassed. I was being selfish, wasn't I?

"Any man who wants to put a little money in the bank, maybe raise a family someday has to get ahead, right?" Ben asked. "It's torture to climb the ladder at Thompson Loyal, but those who can't stand the heat should get out of the kitchen. I am proving my worth. If my boss says jump, I have to ask how high? Being abroad at Christmastime is just one of the many small sacrifices I have to make while I'm junior."

I chose to ignore the fact that Ben had called me an idiot, and focus on how my heart sizzled at the word family. *Oh my god, does Ben want a baby? Wait! Do I want a baby? Would we have more than one? 28 isn't that young, after all and…*

"They call work *work* for a reason," he'd lectured on. "I have to be on location in the Big Apple because old Martin Loyal has us representing that film production studio in Soho – The New York Soho – and it's all hands on deck here. Contracts for directors and film stars, insurance riders for the special effects…you know, boring."

"I'm sorry you have to work," I had told him. At that point, I'd started feeling dumb. Who wouldn't rather be wined and dined and taken to bed than stuck in a boring law office discussing contracts and insurance? This was proof that he was good husband material.

Don't fight him on this one, Juliet. Support him, and soon, you'll be working in the kitchen to prepare holiday dinners for your own little family, not for strangers.

"Sorry, Ben. Of course you're right. Just making sure you don't have something cooking with The Statue of Liberty," I'd said, trying to laugh it off.

"You're the only absurdly tall woman who carries a torch that I'm giving it to," he'd flirted.

"What'll you do for the holiday? You won't be in some diner eating pressed turkey and instant mashed potatoes alone, will you?"

"Don't worry about me, one of my mates from the office here has claimed me. I'll be seen to…Look, I have to run. I miss you like mad and can't wait to get a handful of your…Yes, Bob? Right! I'm just hanging up! Bye, Jubes," he whispered, "Happy Christmas. I'll call when I can."

Today would be more about getting back to normal as a couple than about fantasy land, though. We had trip plans to solidify, details to discuss about scheduling. I was tired but running on twitchy excitement. *With Ben gone already, I could have slept late,* I thought, wrapping myself in his waffle robe ("It's a dressing gown, Jubes, I'm not a judge," Ben would have scolded me). I went into the kitchen, still harboring a tiny glimmer of hope that he might be sitting at the table going over briefs and sipping a cup of coffee.

No such luck. No Ben…and no coffee. My brain felt like lead. I didn't think I could make it to the *Pret* around the corner to buy one before getting dressed, so I grabbed a bag of ground espresso from the freezer. I twisted off the portafilter and saw that there was no filter basket inside. Urghh! I'd asked Ben a dozen times to tell his cleaner to leave the machine alone. First, she washed all the parts with soap, which ruined the taste of the lovely pure Kona coffee I kept here, and second, she never put it back together properly.

Irked and jonesing for my java, I held onto the kitchen counter with a tight grip, plotting out my next move. Go out for coffee, or look for the missing piece. *Just be methodical,* I told myself. *It can't have disappeared. Just look one place at a time, and you'll find it.*

I'll admit to feeling a bit smug as I worked from top left to bottom right, searching the cabinets. I was thinking how adult it was of me not to flip out just because I'd been awake for this long with no coffee. And wasn't I grown-up for not wishing that Ben's cleaner would be deported before her regular Wednesday shift so she could never touch this espresso machine, ever, as long as she was alive?

As I rifled through each cabinet and cupboard, I grew more and more frantic. Agitated, I moved on to the drawers. Rubber bands, twine, and scissors in this one. Potholders, tea towels, and sponges in that one. Soon I was ripping through the deep drawers all the way over by the table, where, realistically, no coffee filter would ever dwell. Still, I was on a mission.

A tiny, distant voice tried to tell me that I'd crossed a line. I had the vague sense that if Ben walked in, he wouldn't be amused at my ransacking his flat. But that didn't stop me. Another drawer. Place mats, table cloths, and candlesticks, but no filter. A cabinet. Photo albums, maps, and board games, but still no filter. Deep in my rational mind, I knew that the filter wouldn't be around the corner in the lounge, but my rational mind was deeply asleep and my coffee-addicted animal sense was propelling my body.

I flung open the double doors of the cabinet below the television set, and pulled out a stack of file boxes. That's when I saw the corner of the padded envelope sticking out of *The Economist*, on top of a pile of folders. My body beat my brain to the panic. Blood roared through my ears as I eased out the envelope and held it in my hand.

Amanda Selmont
39 East 79th Street
New York City, NY 10075

Amanda, the 5' 2", ice-blonde from Manhattan? The one who called the cocktail dress I'd worn to the company party "appropriate"?

I watched my hands tear it open like I was watching a movie of someone else's hands. I slid out a thick, creamy slice of stationery and watched a tasteful pair of platinum hoops fall to the floor. Amanda's earrings.

Is that who had *seen to him* last Christmas?

I flashed back to the cream-colored envelope that had once held the earrings I'd left overnight. The envelope that had my full mailing address on it. The one I'd been naïve enough to be charmed by. Ben wasn't a neat freak! He was a son-of-a-bitch liar who walked around behind me cleaning up any proof that I'd set foot in his bachelor pad.

Tucked inside the large envelope I now held was a thinner, smaller envelope. I pressed it between my fingers and thumb. Whatever was inside crackled against the paper. My heart was clawing at my ribcage, skittering and wild. I knew I didn't want to see what was in there, but my eyes couldn't convince my hands to stop tearing paper. To my horror, I reached in and pulled out the world's scratchiest lace thong, dotted with rhinestone studs. I held it up to find that one side of it was ripped, threads dangling.

That goddamn son of a—He'd lied about his flight! To my face! He'd gotten back a day early and holed up in his love cave with Amanda. Right here in London. Had that bitch been in his bed – the bed that I'd just crawled out of – the night before I was? Did he leave early this morning to meet her for a quickie before work?

Oh my God, did I just use her shampoo?

I had to get out of there…I was wearing nothing but silk underwear and a trench coat when I'd shown up last night (on Posy's advice), so I tore into Ben's bedroom and grabbed a pair of his gym pants, rolling them up at the waist, and his black Ralph Lauren cashmere turtleneck. I stepped into my high heels as I was running, leaving the door to the flat wide open in my wake. Dramatic maybe, but after what I'd been through with Stephen, there was no way I was going to be made a fool of again.

Out on the street, I pulled my coat tightly around myself and marched towards the tube station. The wind was bitterly cold, but the air was dry and its sting felt harsh on my face, like a slap. I welcomed it. It cut through my numbness.

I was a girl without a plan. Suddenly single, obviously there would be no wedding in my future. Without Ben to encourage and support me, would I be able to finish my studies and become a therapist? A small voice inside asked if I'd even want to. I felt as though I were filled with helium, hovering.

It was only 7:45 a.m. and the street was busy with commuters. Eyes brimming, I stopped dead in the middle of the sidewalk, where many a worker bee slammed into me or swore at me under his breath.

As far as I could see, I only had one option. I dug in my bag for my phone and stabbed in the number for The Gastronome's Trust.

"Pips, Juliet Hill here. I'll take that job. Where do I need to be and when?" Although I didn't really need to ask. There was only one client who I knew would play a card like a two-hour deadline – Jasper Roth.

"Oh, my dear, that *is* good news," she trilled. "Fab, just fab. You report late tonight, I'll text you the details. You'll be working at Thornton Hall."

Chapter Two

Numb, I pointed my elderly Golf in the right direction and drove out of the city of London. I'd been to Thornton Hall enough times to know the way. Although, I have to say I was surprised that Jasper Roth, America's wealthiest tycoon, was invited to his wife's ancestral home this particular Christmas. It had been all over the Daily Mail and other rags that he and Lady Penelope were suffering trouble in paradise. Based on what I think nearly happened between him and me in the drawing room at the Hall last time I catered for the family, I figured she'd finally caught him cheating. But then that whole incident between him and me was kind of a gray area. And we were drinking that mellow port, the one that slid like silk down the throat and left you thirsty for more. And he was so sincere when he confessed that despite his success, what he really wanted was to feel a part of someone's life.

Was he really about to kiss me, or was it just a weird moment of connection between us? Maybe I imagined the whole thing. That's probably the real truth. Face it, I couldn't be trusted to separate the good guys from the bad guys, could I? I'd been duped by both Stephen and Ben. Whatever. Fucking men. No wonder Mother had opted out.

Oh, God…Mother. I nearly swerved off the road, thinking of how my mom was going to react to my news of my break up with

Ben. I think she saw Ben as a guide toward sense and stability. It was no secret that she held out hope for my giving up "being a cook", to go back and complete my studies, the plan Ben wholeheartedly supported.

It was hard to believe that, as of last night, I'd been ready to do exactly that. To start a life that Mother was excited about. Thinking about disappointing her made my head split. Or maybe that was the hangover. I concentrated harder on the road, lightheaded with hunger and the starkness of my new reality. If I had moved to New York and gone back to school, Ben in tow, Mother would have had to admit I wasn't flighty. That I did have direction. Of course, flighty to her was switching from math camp to science camp my last year of high school. But marrying Ben would have given me gravitas. Or I hoped she'd see it that way. On the one hand, a successful lawyer, he's a highly sensible choice, I thought, looking for a turn-off. On the other, although she approved of his profession, he is a man. And who knows if she could approve of any member of that gender.

Men didn't exactly play a starring role in my childhood. My grandmother, a surgeon and lab scientist in Chicago, divorced my grandfather when my mother was little. When she visited us, she flew solo. And my father, by the way, is a sample cup. Mom made sure I knew all about the science of conception, and what a sperm donor was, from the time I could toddle.

"Juliet," she told me time and again, "I wanted a child, not two children. Men, my dear, are children. Besides that, they cloud the brain. Take it from me, solidly establish who you are before you try blending with someone else. That way, you don't get lost."

Her personal philosophies were sensible, well thought-out, and written in stone. She expected me to benefit from her experience and buy in hook, line and sinker. Growing up with my mother, *good enough* had never been good enough. She's not a barrel of laughs, Mother, but she gets the job done and she taught me to do the same. I got A's in school, and sacrificed dating and boys to do it. That suited her fine. I followed her directions until graduation, all the while gazing wistfully at the artsy crowd who smoked clove cigarettes, and even at the stoner crowd who smoked pot. At least they looked relaxed. When it came time for college, I got accepted to Duke, Vanderbilt, Penn and Cornell. Mother was horrified to the point of dumbstruck when I chose Bard, a liberal arts college near Woodstock, New York. She knew I wanted to be close to my aunt, who I may as well tell you is Suze Wyatt, the life coach you've seen on *The Eva! Show*.

Everyone who ever lived has dreamt of being interviewed by Eva, the most famous and altruistic self-made woman on the planet. The woman who singlehandedly made book clubs cool, and started schools for girls in every remote corner of Africa. The woman who revolutionized daytime television. Everyone except for Mother. She hated Eva.

To this day, I cannot believe I had the strength to defy Mother and go to Bard. It was like a little compass in my head directed me away from the life I had lead up to that point. Had the college not given me a full ride, Mother would have blocked my going.

"What are you going to do, Juliet?" she had mocked. "Cruise through university taking basket-weaving? Next you'll be telling me you're studying to be a life coach! Why not skip college, seek an apprenticeship with Dr. Phil, and get your own *TV show*." A thinly-veiled dig at Aunt Suze. She practically gagged when she mentioned television. She owned one solely for research purposes. An irrational thorn in her side, reality TV sent Mother into paroxysms of soapboxing. How many times had she ranted "Project Runway! Don't the sheep realize that it's not a competition, it's a show *about* a competition? The producers get those kids drunk and they hide their scissors, all so we can watch them throw punches and scratch each others' eyes out! And don't get me started on the worst of the bunch, *The Food Channel*"?

"Just because I love the food channel, it doesn't mean my brain is soft," I'd told her. "I happen to like Prunella Paulson."

"I wrote a journal article on that woman entitled 'Images of Breasts: Conflating our Desire for Flavor and Nourishment with Sexuality.' She sells with her boobs."

"What about Piers Conley-Weatherall?" I asked, naming another well-known TV chef. I smiled just thinking about him. "How can you not love that guy with his outrageous, curly hair and accent?" I mimed throwing a handful of spices into a pot. "Who's your daddy?" I shouted in a gleeful Yorkshire accent. I never missed an episode. I know lots of people are like this with celebrities, but I felt like I really knew him. I followed him on Twitter because I loved all the sweet tweets he sent about his kids and the normal life his family seemed to have. They ate dinner, they went camping, the kids were allowed to believe in Santa Claus – something of which Mother didn't approve. "He just draws you in."

Mother scowled. "Him."

"I think he's adorable," I said. "He's the kind of man you'd spontaneously hug." Mother raised an eyebrow. "Well, maybe not the kind of man *you'd* spontaneously hug, but the kind normal people would. Admit that you like my apron with his face on it! It's really cute." I'd won it in a Facebook contest.

"The apron that asks, 'Who's Your Daddy?' No, the man has a *catchphrase*, Juliet. He sings to *food*. He lives life in a dream. I don't want to discuss him." She took a long, hard look at me. I was a little uncomfortable under her gaze. "Really, sometimes it's hard to believe you're my daughter." That stung. I wanted to be her daughter. She was my mother, and we all worship our mothers, don't we? I vowed then and there that I'd become the kind of woman she would admire, someone she'd see as a scholar and a colleague. Become the therapist she wanted me to be.

But I still loved Piers.

I didn't bring it up again, but I watched his show, even reruns, every night with the sound turned low, before falling asleep. Something about him soothed me.

Mother is the most respected psychiatrist in Louisville, Kentucky, where I grew up. She divides her time between her elite clinical practice and teaching at the university. For kicks, she writes science articles. I like to think I'm more fun than she is, but I did inherit her work ethic. If she could succeed, I could succeed.

A car blared its horn, startling me out of my reverie. *Focus on the job at hand,* I told myself.

I glanced at my dashboard clock. I was making good time. Jasper Roth told the agency to have me arrive before the early guests were going to bed so that I'd be on deck to make midnight sandwiches and still be up early to lay the elaborate and excessive breakfast he always demanded.

The hours at Thornton Hall were long and brutal, but at least Rose the housekeeper would be there. Just thinking about her nearly made me cry. The pure kindness she beamed was so unfamiliar: I think Mother skipped parenting school the day unconditional love was taught.

I rifled around in my purse for a breath mint, remembering I hadn't eaten all day and hoping to take the edge off my hunger. On the passenger seat beside it, among the many bags of groceries, was a sack of Welsh blue potatoes from Sainsbury's. Roth reveled in having the best and most expensive of everything, so in the morning, I'd roll the potatoes in some dirt from the driveway and wrap them in brown paper. That way, when my boss came to micromanage, he'd assume I'd gone to the market and purchased them from a farmer. I needed a shortcut or two. *I'm doing the best I can,* I thought. *And that's good enough.* Aunt Suze told me to repeat that to myself as often as possible.

Thrown next to the potatoes was a pile of wrapped gifts for Ben's family. I'd almost chucked them, but my frugal side put the brakes on that. If nothing else, I could pass them out to the staff at Thornton. After last year's cancelled Christmas, I'd made sure to shop in advance for all Ben's relatives, including the family spaniel. I'd even asked Posy to "style" me for the evening I was sure he'd pop the question, though without telling her why. From the beginning, she'd never been Ben's biggest fan.

I finally saw a BP station. I was bursting, and I hadn't eaten a thing all day. Was the queasiness in my stomach only hunger? Or dread? I felt so disenfranchised. I hit the loo, then bought myself a Lucozade, a packet of crisps and a pork pie in cellophane. Sitting under a street lamp in the parking lot, I took huge, greedy bites. I knew I was eating for comfort, but didn't care. I deserved any pleasure I could get at the moment. This ersatz meal was a lurid example of what chefs eat when they're not working, and I inhaled it with gusto.

With the heat off in the car, I was freezing. It was the bone-deep damp that can't be escaped here. Why does England have to be so cold? My cottage on the grounds was likely to be as freezing inside as it was outside when I arrived. Had taking this job been a panic choice or the right thing to do?

Slugging back my Lucozade (which was making me even colder…why in God's name didn't I get a cup of tea?), I wished I could beam myself back to before I'd even met Ben. I longed to be in Posy's lavish Parisian apartment, where she'd taken me in for nearly three years. She rescued me in Paris after I'd followed Stephen there, although she'll tell anyone who'll listen that I rescued her.

Given my start in Paris – struggling junior chef barely earning enough for rent – that level of luxury was something I never dreamed of. Well, to be honest, given my middle-class suburban ranch house growing up, being in Paris was something I never dreamed of either. Like a lot of things before I'd met Stephen. Like being stone-cold dumped in the most romantic city in the world.

Stop dwelling, Juliet. That's "anti-luck thinking" according to Aunt Suze. Positive visualization will manifest positive results. God, Mother would have a field day if I said that out loud. I secretly subscribe to "Suze Wyatt's Make Your Own Luck" e-newsletters. My aunt also authored the book *Follow Your North Star to Happiness*. Following her lead, I created my own "Heart Phrase". Goofy, I know, but when Aunt Suze explains that we should all pick a mantra and proclaim our truth, it sounds so right.

"Food is my new passion." I'd tested that out on Mother from Paris, when I'd started working my first kitchen job at Chez Henri. After being humiliated in the city of love, I couldn't go crawling home, so I took the only job I could get, and made the best of it.

"I'm sorry," she'd said. "Did you just say, 'Food is my new passion'?"

"No," I'd answered quickly. At this point, most people could say, "Put Dad on the phone." I imagined a jolly father who would say, *"Don't mind your mother. You know she loves you. I'm proud of you for following your dream."* Although, unfortunately, there is no jolly father.

Back in Paris, Posy introduced me to Charles, an American, and his lover, Luc. They opened my small-town eyes. Charles threw legendary parties, during which he draped the apartment with red velvet swags and rigged up champagne fountains from fish-tank pumps and vintage birdbaths. His motto had always been *I know it's too much, but is it enough?* Luc got me that first job at Chez Henri, as a hostess and busser, lying wildly about my French. I was a spectacular failure at front-of-house. My first night, I insulted the local *commissaire de police* by seating him next to the kitchen, and delivered an expensive bottle of port to a restaurant critic's table, calling his mistress by his wife's name. I forced myself to suck it up. In my halting French, I apologized and told the chef and owner Henri that if he wanted to send champagne to make up for my blunders, I'd work the hours to pay for it. Impressed, Henri told me something in French that sounded like, "You are a man, and I like that in certain women." Instead of a pink slip, he gave me an apron, and sent me to the kitchen where I learned to cook through trial by fire, under Henri, that exceptional chef with a mercurial temper. To this day, when people ask me where

I trained, I tell them, "In Paris, at *The School of 'Not Like That, Stupid!'*"

After living through the shock Stephen had handed down, I needed a purpose. Henri pissed me off enough to want to show I could win. So far in Paris, my only goal had been not to curl up and die. Now I had something to master. It was weird, because it was the opposite of intellectual, but I worked better when I turned my brain off.

And I was enchanted. I cooked my way through a variety of restaurants in Paris, took weekend courses and did short stints in France's other regions, always staying just long enough to learn the best of what each chef had to teach me. And that was my life in France. Work, sleep, an occasional free day, when I went to museums or bought cheap seats at the ballet or theatre. I was happy socializing with Posy and my new gay best friends, or curling up with a good book. I had a good run there. Until London. Until Ben.

I started the engine, cranked up the heater, and checked my phone. I was both furious and relieved that there were no messages from Ben. I imagined him sitting at his huge desk. Smug and satisfied, he was probably having an office drink about now, gearing up for the holiday. I supposed he hadn't yet realized I was gone. There was only one text:

Call me anytime, day or nite. need ur advice urgently P xx

Fumbling with my earpiece, I had a brief thought that I probably shouldn't drive and talk about stuff that upsets me, but I needed to hear her voice.

"Are you sitting down?" Posy demanded. "I'll bet you're lying down, you right old slapper! I suppose you couldn't be troubled to ring Posy back because you were on the receiving end of an epic shagging. You American girls," she teased. "When the boyfriend shows up, it's all 'Bye-bye, Bestie, I've got a ride to climb aboard…'"

Normally, I'm delighted at this send-up. I'd never worn the "bad girl" label, and it made me sound sassy. Part of me dreamed of donning thigh-high boots and false eyelashes, and falling into bed with strange men who smoked. Between slow drags, they'd slide their eyes up and down me and say, "Juliet, you are one hot slut." Anyway, um, back to the present!

I'd never admitted to Posy that Ben and I weren't exactly chandelier-swingers. Ben's only the second man I've been with, in fact. And now, I wasn't with him. My throat closed as I choked on a giant sob.

"Hello? My little tartlet? Aren't you speaking to Posy? I've called to tell you I've been proposed to!"

"What?" I sputtered. "By whom? Oh God, not Baz! I mean, it's Baz, isnt it? I mean, what?"

I'd been tiptoeing around confessing that I wasn't a fan of Posy's latest boyfriend. Trashing someone's love interest is dangerous territory. One minute a couple splits up and you're pointing out that the guy has bad breath and talks with a whistle, and the next thing, they're having a baby and you're not invited to the christening.

"I'm lying. It's a joke!" Posy exclaimed. "I called to tell you I gave Baz the boot!"

"Really?" I asked, relieved.

"Too right! He may well murder in the sack, but hadn't you noticed? He's a bit of a wang! All he ever cared about was having the latest Gucci sunglasses to wear on that yacht of his. We were aboard that thing every weekend, and he mostly just got plastered with his mates and yelled 'I'm king of the world!' whilst peering off the bow. We broke up just in the nick of time, too. You know that uber-sexy, silver fox author of *Get Fit the Yogi's Way*? Well, after his book launch party, he took me to his flat and showed me how to bend in ways I'd never dreamed possible, if you catch my drift."

"Isn't he kind of old?"

"Who cares, as long as he's hot and fit. There are lots of older blokes I fancy. Like the new James Bond, you know, what's-his-name. And your man Piers Conley-Weatherall."

"Eew, I don't think of him like that."

"Maybe I have more of an open mind. He's cute and he can cook."

"Posy, I have to tell you something," I said.

"Don't say it, I know. I can't commit, and you're halfway down the aisle, Mrs. Bridey MacWeddingband. Where are you, anyway?"

"Driving," I said, remembering that I was. "Listen Pose, Ben cheated on me." My hands were shaking so badly, I had to pull over and put on my hazard lights while I told her everything. She punctuated my story with interjections of "That bastard!" and "That bastardy *bastard*!"

"So that's it," I finished. "It's not a direct dump, like Stephen, but once again, I feel like a fool." I looked out the windshield at the dark countryside, feeling very alone.

She paused, then said, "Thank God, Jubes. I am so happy for you."

"Happy? My heart is broken, I'll never be loved, I'll die old and childless and, once again, it proves that Juliet cannot follow through on a plan, just like my mother always said." I fished for some tissues to wipe my runny nose.

"Plan, my arse! Come on, then. Plans are for old fogies, and schoolmarms, and, and, city planners!"

"But how can you say you're happy we broke up? I thought I got it right this time. Now I'm alone!" I practically wailed.

"Nonsense. You've got me."

"I don't want to go back to the States on my own. You know, without Ben."

"So don't go back to the States."

"Then what would I do with my life?"

"Um, you'd live here and work as a chef like you have been doing! And love it! You get hired by the coolest clients. Liz Hurley calls you 'Sister,' for eff's sake! You're at the top of your game. It's what you do. You're brilliant at it. Screw being a boring old therapist. You're a hot chef. Chin up! You could be me, with my boring ex-boyfriend and my crap job," Posy scolded me.

"In what way is your job crap?" I asked. I didn't question the ludicrous boyfriend.

"Well, it's not as good as yours," she replied stubbornly.

"It's apples and oranges. Besides, don't you think going the therapist route is the right thing to do? Food is just a stopgap to pay the bills for now."

"You've been saying that for years, and when you do, I hear your mother talking. If you want to know what I think, I'll tell you—"

"You always do." I interrupted.

"—Here's what I think: You're mother wants you to be her mini-me, so she puts down your career as a chef. I think you're avoiding the issue. Hey, listen to me. Maybe I should be a therapist!"

"I wouldn't give up the day job just yet: your job's awesome. You work at a sleek, sexy publishing house, surrounded by brooding, bookish young sexpots who wear glasses and corduroy, and seduce you at launch parties when the cheap Chianti is flowing."

"As an assistant! And they only keep me because I speak French, and keep reeling in richies and B-list celebs from Dad's world to-do memoirs and cookbooks."

"Well of course that's why they keep you," I told her. "You're a star. There's no shame in leveraging your assets. Admit you love your job!"

"I'll admit I love my job when you admit you love your job. Say it! Say you love being a chef."

My mouth started forming the words, then I hesitated, tapping the steering wheel. "It's not that simple."

"It looks simple from where I'm sitting! Embrace what makes you happy, even if there's no guarantee. You're trying too hard for the sure bet, and your mother's like a siren calling you back to her version of stability. You gambled by taking a chance with Stephen and you've been beating yourself up ever since. You grabbed what made you happy, then it was gone. So what? You're still alive, and you had a bit of good fun. Nothing lasts forever. Speaking of taking a chance, what about that scrummy resident chef Edward at Thornton Hall?"

"What about him?" I shifted uncomfortably in my seat. Suddenly, I felt claustrophobic. I undid my seatbelt and wrestled off my hoodie, phone pinned between my shoulder and ear.

"You could have had him for twenty pence and a slap on the arse."

"I was with Ben!"

"Not at first, you weren't."

"Anyway," I said, rebuckling, "you witnessed how Stephen diverted me off course. And then Ben. It'll be a cold day in hell before I go looking for another man to rain down chaos on me."

"Why go looking? Won't Edward be doling out the goodies this Christmas?"

"Posy, Thornton Hall is where I work! There's a quaint saying in America, 'Don't poop where you eat.'"

"Oh, I know that one!" she squealed, like she'd won a prize. "Only we say shit."

"Why won't you let me be a good girl?" I asked, exasperated.

"Because deep down, you're not," she said.

"Just you watch," I said. "I'm going to learn from my mistakes, like a mature woman should. I'm almost 30!"

"No you're not!"

"I'm 28."

"Well that's positively ancient! Better start saving for vaginal rejuvenation surgery."

"Vaginal what? Never mind! I'm about to start the next chapter of my life, and you'll see how making sane, adult choices leads to contentment. No Edward. No drama."

"Right. Maybe your mum's satisfied to bed down with her psychology journals, but I predict you won't be wearing socks to sleep in for long. Besides, thirty is the new *hot*. Let's neither of us sign our death certificates just yet. Once you've had true love, you can't very well settle for a substitute."

"When have you had true love?" I asked.

"God, is that the time? Forget stupid, bastard Ben and ring me when you get to Fancypants Manor. Love you loads. Byeee!"

I cautiously pulled back onto the highway, tires crunching through the gravel in the thick darkness. I put Posy and Ben out of my head and kept my eyes focused on the black road ahead. It's amazing how remote this part of the country can feel, given its actual proximity to London's bright lights. Music of the season blared from my speakers. "*I'll have a bluuuuuue Christmas… without youuuuuu…*" I didn't feel blue or even angry. I felt nothing, and was glad to be headed for a job, where the preparation and clean-up would propel me forward. There was always something to be done in the kitchen of a full house. I longed to sleepwalk through my days. I welcomed the loss of myself.

Chapter Three

I finally turned off the last shared road onto the mile-long private drive on the estate. Thornton Hall, arguably one of the grandest estates in the Cotswolds, is an eighteenth- century number featuring countless wings and annexes. I'd worked in lots of grand houses, but The Hall was by far the most imposing. It was old and draughty, never silent, even at night – I always heard creaking, settling and the scratching of mouse claws. Nevertheless, it had every creature comfort one could imagine, and everyone inside its walls was pampered to a tee.

This is the area where anybody who thinks he is anybody has a weekend home. Highgrove, Prince Charles's place, is right down the road, and you're likely to run into "serious" film stars and models who've married rockers while you're shelling out six pounds for a baguette at the local bakery or buying artisanal goat cheese, made in-house by a former Britpop band's bassist. Think The Hamptons, but with thatched roofs.

I stopped the car at the gate that was the entrance to the main house, got out and punched the code into the security panel, and got back in. The gates eased open. Putting on my brights, I drove slowly and carefully over the cattle grid. Even though I expected it, the loud machine-gun fire of the grate always stopped my heart, and tonight, it slammed me back into reality. For a while there,

I'd forgotten about how I ended up here on December 22nd.

Sighing, I drove slowly around the circular drive toward the former stable that was now a garage, and paused in front of Thornton Hall's massive front door. With the elaborately decorated wreath and other festive touches bedecking it, the ivy-covered stone mansion was more breathtaking than usual. Fairy lights were twinkling all over the façade, and candles were burning behind shuttered windows. The people who lived here were gearing up for a yuletide filled with beauty and cheer, surrounded by friends and family. While I was working over the holidays having just been dumped. Wow, my life blows.

Immediately, Aunt Suze's voice rang in my head: *"Failure is an opportunity to reinvent."* I sat up a little straighter, continued to pull my car around and blinked the last remaining snow flurries out of my eyelashes. *There, that's better, now I'm not even thinking of Ben and Amanda.* Until I was. And how *she* was probably at Ben's parents' right this very minute. She and his family would all be merrily gathered around the piano, singing Christmas songs and remarking that they'd "never thought Juliet was right for Ben". Amanda would be gliding gracefully around the fire-warmed room in three-inch heels, fully at home in the scarlet-red velvet evening dress and white fur stole she'd worn for the occasion. A distinguished uncle would comment on how clever it was for Amanda to be of an appropriate height for a woman. Ben would ring for servants to take away the mulled wine, and bring champagne, then he'd get down on one knee and…

Suddenly, I heard a sickening metal crunch as I smashed my car into the estate's riding mower, parked right outside the garage. "Aaaah!" I moaned weakly, as my head bounced off the side window. I quickly backed up and my front bumper fell to the ground. I killed the engine and lay my head down on the steering wheel.

"Really?" I said out loud. "Story of my life. The minute I get where I'm trying to go, I crash and burn." Unbuckling, I eased myself out of the car, just as Rex, the Earl's favorite retriever, came barreling toward me, charged up by the now-falling snow. Jasper, my boss and the Earl's son-in-law, wasn't a big dog person. But he hadn't much room to complain, as it was the Earl's estate, however much Jasper had his eye on it. I wondered if the poor beast had been "accidentally" let out in the cold.

"Hey boy," I called, happy to see a friendly face. I squatted down and opened my arms, and he knocked me off balance, on my rear in a slushy puddle. "Ho, ho, ho," I said, as he licked me heartily. "Merry Effing Christmas to me."

Rounding the house to the back entrance, I was met by Seamus, the estate manager, the most senior of the staff. He took my hand warmly in both of his, his genuine smile making his eyes crinkle. "Welcome, welcome again, lovely Miss Hill," he said, bowing with mock formality. "We're so glad to be working alongside you, especially in this joyous season!" He had on a scarf but no hat, and his thin, wispy, black comb-over was blowing comically in the wind. I gave him a peck on the cheek, and he chuckled, pleased. "Having you and Edward cooking will be a grand thing, indeed." He nudged me aside gently and picked up my luggage to take to Dove's Nest, the cottage in which I always stayed. He made pleasant chitchat, but my mind was miles away. *Oh, man, Edward is here*, I thought. The Gastronome's Trust hadn't told me that part. I fished in my bag for a lipstick.

****

My first ever job here had had me training with the Hall's permanent chef, Edward. Before I'd met him, I'd heard through the grapevine that he was well liked by the staff and family – except possibly Jasper Roth. I'd also heard from a couple of the maids and another chef from my agency that he was sex on legs. And they were not wrong. Since that training stint, on occasion I'd been brought on as sous-chef to assist Edward with an especially large party or event, and to fill in when Edward was on vacation. The Earl and Countess were endlessly hosting weddings at The Hall for extended family. This was the kind of house that was staffed up at all times.

The first time we were introduced in the kitchen of The Hall, Edward had turned around from the stove and smiled. His face was so handsome. Not hard, but not pretty in any way, edged with the faintest 5 o'clock shadow. I sucked in my breath and blurted the first thing that came to my mind, "I love your Crocs!" I'd been told he was good looking, but that simple fact didn't begin to paint the picture. It wasn't just about his looks. It was more his essence. I felt like an animal, pulled in at cell-level by whatever invisible scent or sound it was he gave off that made me want him. When he locked eyes with me, I embarrassed myself by thinking that he had decided right then and there to take me to bed.

"I've never seen them in white!" I blathered. "Are they comfortable?"

"Like walking on air," he said slowly. His voice landed right below my belly, and vibrated there.

"But I've worn Danskos like yours, too," he said easily. "Now I've got my foot problem solved, maybe you can help me manage my 'chef's arse.'" He laughed a velvety laugh, and his eyes twinkled. Against my will, I laughed, too.

Chef's arse is the insider term for the occupational hazard of moving constantly in a sweaty environment, causing your pants to chafe, which might be the reason for chefs' fabled tempers. It was a bold thing to say to a stranger, very un-English. I took a step closer to him.

"I swear by cornstarch," I told him. "But a friend in New York told me about this ointment called Boudreaux's Butt Paste." I realized I was flirting, but couldn't stop myself. It felt like jumping off a cliff. "And it leaves you smelling sweet like a baby."

"Sweet is good," he said, smiling at me with his wolfish, lopsided grin.

"Everything in moderation, I suppose," I'd said. I heard my own voice and it sounded hollow and echo-y, as if I was hearing someone else talk down a long tunnel. I was alarmed at the attraction I felt. *For heaven's sake, Juliet,* I said to myself. *Keep it in your pants.*

"Well, fun's over," I said briskly, pulling myself back together. It was time to behave like a professional chef, instead of a starry-eyed fangirl. "This food isn't going to cook itself."

"Don't worry, we've got loads of time."

"I'll hold up my end, Chef," I told him, pulling out a cutting board. "No need to baby me."

"Ah, don't be one of those," he'd told me, with soft, amused eyes. "Life's too short."

****

"Seamus, but you really don't have to wait on me," I told him as he carried my bags to the back entrance of the Hall. "I'm just staff, remember?" I said, making a feeble attempt to stop him. "If you set a precedent like this, you'll be carrying me around on a litter like Cleopatra before Christmas comes."

"Nonsense. You're not 'just' anything. We're all so pleased that it's you assisting Edward. It might have been that grumpy old Frenchman who pretends not to understand English spoken by Irish folk. Now, take yourself to the kitchen…My dear Rose put the kettle on when she heard you come over the grate, and I'll wager she's laid out biscuits and some sherry to go with the tea."

Seamus and his wife Rose, the housekeeper, live in Rose Cottage, the largest on the grounds. It was built when Rose was new in service to the Earl, and she was the first to dwell in it. Seamus had already been working on the grounds when she was hired. Eventually, she and Seamus married and raised their son, Isaac, in the cozy abode. She'd lived there so long I doubt anyone could remember whether the cottage was named after her or the flower bushes that surrounded it.

Seamus and Rose, both from Ireland, are somewhere in their late fifties. Rose stands around 5' tall and is nearly that wide. Seamus is around 6'4" and lanky as a beanpole. Rose usually cuts through the shock when they're introduced as a pair by saying, "There's a cup for every saucer, isn't there?"

Trudging along the dark path, I started feeling a little better. I ached to be near Rose and her warm kindness, like a mum to the whole world.

"Ah, here we are, go on through and join the others," Seamus said as he peeled off down the path to carry my luggage to my cottage. Walking in the door to the pantry that lead to the kitchen, I wasn't surprised to first see Terrence, the butler at the hall, wielding a bottle as he turned.

"Look what the cat dragged in! Merry Christmas Eve Eve Eve," he said as he jumped up to slip my coat off and hang up my shoulder bag. He took a quick moment to slide the purse onto his own shoulder. He was wearing a long, silk smoking jacket and, oddly, a kerchief around his head, tied at the top with a rabbit-ears-like bow.

"Oooooh, Prada! I wouldn't have thought a sensible girl like you would be hauling around something this glam! Does it go with my dress?" he asked, cat- walking across the kitchen.

"It's a hand-me-down from Posy," I told him.

"She's a poshie, isn't she? I saw that photo of her in that trench coat in the *Daily Mail*. Supreme! If I were her dad, I'd put her in every advert for that airline of his. Maybe she'll rub off on you."

Rex came barreling through the kitchen, trying to find traction on the slick, wide beam wooden floor, sliding into the table and yelping.

"Not much chance. I'm just me. She was born to be fabulous."

"Could someone lock this beast in the laundry room?" Terrence asked, nodding toward Rex. "He nearly knocked over my glass!"

"Oh, hello there," I said to a smallish young woman sipping nervously at a glass of wine. She had a very plain face, but even underneath her modest black maid's uniform, I could see she had a pin-up girl, hour-glass body. "I'm Juliet."

"Hello, Juliet." I turned my attention from the girl to Edward, who was standing in the corner near the bookshelf, and froze.

"Glad to see you here," he said slowly. He reshelved the book he'd been flipping through.

All I could manage back was a slightly brusque, "Edward."

Thankfully, no one seemed to notice my temporary inability to speak.

"I've got big plans and they involve you. Hey, your head's bleeding." He continued. I reached up and felt a small, wet trickle near my hairline. Edward pulled out a handkerchief from his pocket. He cupped my chin in the palm of his large hand, and I could feel the roughness of his skin. He pressed the cloth to the side of my head. It hurt, but I didn't want to tell him to stop, to lose contact. His breath was warm on my cheek, and I felt dizzy. Was it Edward or the wound? Suddenly aware that all eyes on the room were on me, I took the cloth, and pushed his hand away.

"Oh, I guess I banged it when I wrecked my car just now."

"That's a thrilling conversation starter," Terrence interrupted, plopping down into a chair and slugging back half a glass of red wine. "One might think you're Dorothy Parker! I'm all ears. Mind that you don't blurt shocking remarks in the presence of our *underbutler,* though. We certainly wouldn't want to dislodge the stick from his bum."

"Terrence…" Rose cautioned as she got up and made her way toward me and enfolded me in a warm hug. "Welcome, my Juliet!"

"By the way," Terrence plowed on, ignoring my reunion with Rose as he held up a copy of *Tips for the Homefront: A Domestic Guide to Wartime Cookery and Making Your Rations Count,* "did you know we could make our own furniture polish out of turpentine and shredded beeswax?" The kitchen's south-wall collection of books was well visited by Terrence. "I'll bet Chisholm remembers doing just that! Don't let the half-inch of pancake make-up fool you. He's 95 if he's a day."

"I apologize for Terrence," I said, turning to the girl. "He's not happy unless there's full-on drama in the room. I'm sorry we got interrupted." I darted a glance at Edward, who was looking right at me, drinking from his cup of tea. "Um, like I said before, I'm Juliet, the chef. That is, the sous-chef, this time around."

"I'm Daphne," she said. "You can call me Daffy." She seemed to think for a minute, then burst out in almost a full voice, "You're so clean!" She saw that we were all looking at her strangely, and blushed. "I just mean that you're really fresh and, you know, pretty, for being, you know…your age."

I was taken aback and laughed out loud. It was a fact, but not something a stranger would normally comment on. I was dressed very simply in a red velour hoodie, jeans and my good leather riding boots, which had been a stretch for my budget, even on sale. But she was right, I was very clean. I'd scrubbed myself raw in my own shower after having awakened to Ben's betrayal, trying to rid myself of the anger and hurt. And also the smell of that whorey Amanda's shampoo. I didn't have a stroke of make-up on my face, aside from the lipstick.

"Don't mock the poor dear, you old cow," Terrence said to me. "Take the compliment. Sure, I've seen better, but beauty is in the eye of the beholder, they say."

"Ignore Terrence, Daphne," said Rose, and to me, "Juliet, dear, I've missed you like mad." She was still hugging me, a real squeeze, rocking me back and forth and it made me suck in my breath to keep from crying. Rose was a cuddler, and her warm touch brought all my sadness to the surface. I wanted to tell her all about Ben, but now wasn't the time. I bit the inside of my cheek and concentrated my attention on the napkin holder.

"Our Terrence is bent out of shape because he'll be sharing his territory with *the esteemed* Mr. Chisholm from Mr. Roth's Chelsea house. Also, he's in his cups. Terrence," she said loudly, as if to a deaf person, "perhaps it's time to slow down on the drink for the night. As for Mr. Chisholm, leave him to his corner. There'll be plenty of work for everyone and we'll all be minding our manners, won't we?"

Terrence waited till Rose turned her head and made wanking motions. I shook my head at him. He crossed his arms and scowled.

"Now then, Juliet, I'll pour you a nice glass of sherry." She set a glass in front of me. "Edward, will you have some too?" Rose asked. Edward nodded, and sat himself down in the chair next to mine. I couldn't relax.

"How's your fella, Juliet? Shame you're not with him at Christmas," Rose said, opening a cabinet and taking down a fresh bottle.

I glanced at Edward. "Well, to tell you the truth, uh, Ben… Ben's great." *Way to live your least secretive life,* I thought to myself.

"Chizzy had his teeth whitened, you know," Terrence burst in, cutting me off again, still preoccupied by his dislike for Jasper Roth's London butler. "Makes him look like a Las Vegas hooker!" Whenever they had to work under the same roof, an electrified friction crackled between Terrence and Mr. Chisholm. They were both egotistical, high-status, gay, and middle-aged. It was unlikely that either of them would be playing the part of "underbutler" this Christmas weekend. More like a duel of the divas.

"The American's my puppet," Terrence continued, referring to Roth, "billionaire investment banker or not. I think we've proved that time and again. Mr. Chisholm, Mr. Schmisholm…that big old Mary's no threat in *my house,*" Terrence said moodily. "I'll kill or die to defend my territory."

"My goodness, Terrence, you should be treading the boards with all that theatricality," said Rose. "No one's killing or dying on my watch."

Rose's son Isaac was seated at the far end of the table with a cup of milky tea and a plate of tiny mince pies.

"Hello, Isaac. How are you?" I asked. Just being near him calmed me.

"Well. I'm glad to see you, Miss," Isaac said, beaming.

"Isaac, it's Juliet. There's no 'Miss' with me," I told him, resisting the temptation to muss his goldy-blond hair. Even though Isaac is older than I am, his child-like simplicity invites those kinds of gestures. His hair was getting long – he had two modes of hairstyle: cropped extremely close to his head in a Caesar, or overgrown like it was now. Unintentionally, either one gave him the look of a surfer dude or rock star. His near-drowning as a child, when he fell through the ice on the estate's pond, had left him…well, not exactly slow, but different. I've never had a psychological pigeon-hole to wedge him into, so I just accept him at face value as a pleasant and kind person who is very uncomplicated.

"Wait till you see the gingerbread house I made," he said to me.

"It looks good enough to eat!" Daphne said. "But then a ginger-bread house would, wouldn't it? It's food, I suppose." She poured sugar into her cup of tea.

"It really is quite something," Edward said, looking at me over the rim of his sherry glass, green eyes twinkling. "I couldn't have made it." He put his feet up on the empty chair across from him. That was kind of him to say. Edward had a real artistic bent and it showed in his ice sculpture, spun sugar construction, and cake decorating. When there was a wedding on the grounds, he pulled out all the stops.

"There'll be time enough to see it later," Rose said. "It's quite a wonder, though…Isaac did all the design and embellishment. I just baked."

"Where's Jane?" I asked Isaac about his wife.

"Bed," he said, gathering up several cookies and mince pies in a paper napkin and taking his teacup to the sink. "She's sick so I'd better go home. G'night!" Isaac, said, his mouth full of pie. He rose and started out the pantry door.

"Make sure some of those mince pies get to your missus, Isaac!

She didn't get one from this batch. I hope her stomach's not still delicate, poor lamb. And make sure she has a cup of tea or some broth before she goes to sleep…Sweet dreams, don't let the bedbugs bite," Rose called as a blast of cold air rushed into the cozy kitchen from the pantry leading to the garden and the servants' housing, and the door swung closed behind Isaac. He'd be going to Stable Cottage, where he now lived. No one had ever expected Isaac to marry, and the whole staff had pitched in to fix it up when Isaac had married Jane and moved out of Rose Cottage.

I was aware of Edward's stillness and his glances in my direction. Nervously, I groped for something to say. I suddenly felt so ugly and conspicuous. "I didn't expect to see anyone. I thought I'd be heading straight to bed. I didn't bother trying to look nice." Now Edward was looking straight at me, listening hard. My face felt like it burst into flames, it was so hot. *Shut up, Juliet. You're babbling.*

"You have a smile on your face, my dear, that's all the adornment a young girl needs," said Rose.

"That's damning with faint praise," I said, laughing, trying to be a sport about myself. It only made me feel more under the spotlight.

"I'd take the 'young' compliment and run with it, if I were you," whispered Terrence loudly. He went back to chattering with Daphne.

I was hotly conscious of looking dull in Edward's eyes. Suddenly, I just wanted to get out of there and go to bed. I stood up, knowing I should say a big goodnight and hoof it out of there. My feet wouldn't move and I didn't know what to do with my arms. I wound up leaning over the table with both fists planted, like I was about to filibuster. All eyes turned to me, magnifying my discomfort.

"Rose has got a point," Edward said. He was very still. "You look beautiful."

"Well, then thank you, Edward," I said, turning my full body toward Rose and away from him. I couldn't even look at him

"That's very nice of you," I said, twisting awkwardly to block out the whole view of my attractive colleague.

"I guess they say there are different levels of attractiveness," my mouth continued, against my brain's will. My voice sounded like a recording. *Why won't you stop talking?* I screamed to myself. "There are visually attractive people and then interesting people," I said. I couldn't lift my fists off the table. Edward was listening to me with a small smile on his face, eyebrows raised. "People are striking internal responses," I babbled, not entirely following what I was saying myself. *Shut up, shut up!* I told myself. *You are losing control of your syntax.*

"With status, like Mr. Roth, maybe in the scheme of things," I barreled forward. My mouth kept forming words, and my brain seemed to be kicking back in a lounge chair, spectating. What *was* I trying to say? They all waited patiently for me to stop talking or to make some sense. Eventually, Terrence started making a "get on with it" rolling gesture with his hand, wineglass clutched death grip- style in the other.

"Mr. Roth is so…" Daphne finally piped in. She shook her head back and forth slowly, mouth hanging open. "Well, I mean he's you know, sexier than like, the Earl's mate from up the road. You know the one. That old bloke he hunts with, Lord Ambridge. Whatever. Know what I mean?"

After a pause, Terrence spoke up. "If you mean that even a burlap sack of oats is sexier than Lord Ambridge, then yes, I do know what you mean."

Edward laughed a big, open laugh, eyes shining. *Did he have to sit all splayed out, with his legs apart, looking so relaxed?* I thought irritably.

"The Ambridges are coming to stay, you know," Terrence said. "They're on the list."

"They are?" Daphne asked. "But they live a stone's throw away."

"Ah, the rich are different from you and me," he replied. "Who can explain anything they do? Especially out back, behind the riding stables, if you follow me."

"Right," Daphne said, eyes darting. "I'd better get to bed. I have to stoke the fires first thing." With that, she slipped from the table and disappeared up the stairs.

"Daffy indeed! Rose?" I asked.

"Well, she's a maid brought in by Mr. Roth to 'assist' me this holiday," she said haughtily. She bustled about the kitchen wiping and cleaning. "Seems he thinks this party is more than I can handle. She's in the small room in the attic. We tried to put her in Deer Cottage, but after one night she claimed she thought it was haunted. That certainly tried everyone's patience. She's a dim little thing who's hardly said two sensible words since she's arrived. I hardly know what to do with her, so I mostly have her tending the fires."

"That's good!" I said heartily, trying to keep the conversation rolling. "I've always wished it were hotter around here." The corner of Edward's mouth turned up. I shot him a stern look and he held up his hands in surrender.

Mr. Roth was obsessed with having a roaring fire in every fireplace at all times, whether the room was occupied or not. Being American, he liked to keep every room in the stone house hovering at about 80°C, baffling the staff and suiting me fine. In that respect, he and I were two peas in a pod, hence my predilection for flannel pjs.

"So did you know the Ambridges were here?" asked Terrence.

"No," I said loudly, relieved that the conversation had shifted focus. Suddenly I could move my legs. It was just in time, since my locked knees were cutting off blood to my brain and I felt like I might pass out. "Are they?

"They're above," Terrence said. "Lady Ambridge just got back from touring organic farms in The States. You know that one – she's not happy unless she's prowling fields, wellies covered in cowpat."

"She's a regular farmer, Lady Ambridge," Rose said. "It's a breath of fresh air that she works for a living, given her background."

"She'll get no complaints from me," Edward said. "She always brings truckloads of fresh fruits and veg. Between what she brought and what MacGregor might leave us, we'll eat well."

"Why isn't MacGregor at my welcome party?" I asked, finally relaxing a bit after a glass of sherry. I sneaked a look in Edward's direction. He looked good. Really good. He was wearing dark-wash jeans, and a white waffle-weave thermal shirt under his open chef's coat. I couldn't help noticing how it pulled nicely across his broad chest.

"He told me to give you a kiss for him," Edward teased, twinkling. "Shall I?"

My face went hot.

McGregor, the gamekeeper, was notoriously solitary, and mostly kept to the grounds or to The Pond Cottage. He was quiet and straightforward in the way a man who could live off the land often is. On occasion, he ate staff meals with us, but he preferred to eat in his cottage.

Rose said, "Be kind. I've known MacGregor for over 10 years. Sure he's a private soul, but he never gives anyone a moment's trouble. He comes out for Mass. I see him of a Sunday morning, and don't repeat this, but he almost always has a dozen eggs and a bird for Father Francis."

"He's a good bloke," Edward agreed. He took a bite of a buttered brown roll from a saucer near him. I locked eyes with him for a moment and thought, *I don't owe Ben a thing anymore. I could have Edward.* My arm involuntarily twitched and knocked over my glass.

"Oh, whoops, sorry…" I stammered, jumping up to get a kitchen towel from the hook. I brushed past Edward, and wound up knocking my hip into his shoulder. He reached around with his other hand to right me, and wound up pressing his muscular arm against my pelvis. "Oh!" I squeaked, jumping away like I'd been burned.

"Uh, is it a full house?" I asked Rose, wiping up the spill with a bar towel.

"It is, as a matter of fact," Jasper Roth said, pushing through the swinging door from the hall, "it is."

In a split second, Rose was on her feet, with Terrence right behind her. "Is there something you need, Mr. Roth? A cup of coffee? Some warm milk?"

Edward remained seated.

At the sight of him, I'd crossed the kitchen, without thinking, putting myself on the other side of the table from Edward's chair. Roth ignored Rose and her questions.

"Hello, Juliet."

"Hello, Mr. Roth." The corner of his mouth turned up, and he raised an eyebrow. Well, what did he expect me to call him? Jasper? In his robe, pajama bottoms, and slippers, he looked cozy and far more casual than usual. His hair was rumpled. Had he gotten out of bed when he heard me drive up? I looked at the floor. Even without seeing him, I knew he was looking at me. He stood in silence.

Uncomfortable as it was, we had to bear it. The ball was in his court. Everyone waited for him to make a move, to explain why he'd crossed the invisible line between the house and the servants' domain.

Edward stood up slowly, and spoke. "Mr. Roth, how can we help?" His tone was that of the perfect soldier. Undeniably respectful to his superior, but rich with the confidence and strength of someone who could kill and defend. He was stretched tall, to his full height, and his jaw was tilted slightly upward. This was clearly muscle memory from his days in the military. I was embarrassed that I found it so sexy. His eyes were trained on Roth. I wondered if Edward realized that even at proper attention, those eyes told a secret. Was he challenging Roth? Scorning him? Was I the only one who saw it?

"I'm making sure everyone knows what's expected," he replied, meeting Edward's eyes. "To meet the guests' needs, of course," he added, flicking his eyes over me, and smiling at Rose.

"Everything is in order, Mr. Roth," Rose answered, smiling back. "Your guests won't want for a thing, isn't that right everyone?"

"Of course. We intend to satisfy desires before people know they have them," Terrence said. "Isn't that right, Juliet?"

I was furious at Terrence for putting me on the spot with his obvious little joke, but I could hardly react with a room full of people staring at me.

"Of course, sir."

"That's what I like to hear," Roth said, looking at me. "Do you have everything to make that happen?"

"I've done all the ordering for the menus you've requested," Edward cut in, "and for the general running of the house. If you have any questions, I'll be happy to go over the plans with you." He looked Roth in the eye. "Sir."

Roth met his look, and smiled an easy smile. "I'll let you know if I think of anything I require. Goodnight all," he said, turning and pushing through the door.

We all waited a beat to make sure he was truly gone, as staff always do, then we relaxed, taking our chairs and going back to our drinks.

"Right then. As we were saying, Juliet, we've already got guests… Dr. Dearden is in the Oak Room. The whole Dearden clan used to come every year for Christmas, before Mrs. Dearden passed. With the children living abroad now, the good doctor comes alone. Hard to believe I've known him since his hair was dark and she was slim as a rail. I'm surprised he didn't come down for his midnight roast beef sandwiches. His missus used to get after him for eating red meat."

"Never punish a man for eating meat, I always say," purred Terrence.

"Lovely couple," Edward said. "There's a lot to be said for a long and happy marriage." He leveled his gaze at me. "Did you get engaged yet, Juliet?"

"I'm, well, expecting it on New Year's Eve," I lied. *What are you up to, Juliet?* I thought frantically to myself. I couldn't bear for Edward to think I'd been rejected by Ben. I felt like I was wearing a t-shirt that said, "Unwanted."

"Good on him, then," Edward said, face placid. "I'm sure you'll be very happy together."

"To tell you the truth…"

"And Lord and Lady Ambridge are in the Heather Room, of course," Rose continued. "Mr. Roth had them come tonight so they could join us for breakfast, then go bird spotting." Rose was putting lids on the last of the storage dishes and wrapping mince pies in foil.

Why didn't I come out and say that we broke up? I hated lying. Lying just meant extra work. Now I was going to have to keep it going, operating in a state of paranoia and exhaustion.

I poured myself a second glass of sherry, and filled it so full I had to slurp some over the rim to keep from spilling it. I needed it badly. Edward raised an eyebrow and smiled.

"Actually, the truth is, Ben and I…" I started, but my voice was so soft, Rose didn't hear me.

"The Ambridges arrived around the same time as the Deardens for cocktails and dessert, and I must say Edward outdid himself," Rose nattered on. "Lady Helena made a noise about watching her waistline, but she ended up having two plates. The chocolate cake was an idea off of that Conley-Weatherall show…you know the one, *Piers's Family Table*, I believe it's called."

"The 'Who's your daddy?' bloke, she means," said Terrence. "I like him. You can just tell he drinks while he cooks."

"He's my hero," I said. "I couldn't get his show in France, and I know it's weird to say, but I missed him."

"You feel like you know him, that Piers. He's been married to his wife for over 25 years," Rose said. "But Edward did some of his own recipes, as well. He offered an assortment of gorgeous treats, including that rich chocolate gateau and a fruit platter."

"Did you cut the strawberries properly, according to Our Master,

Jasper Roth?" I asked.

"Never tip to stern!" Edward laughed. "You'll get a spanking for that round here," he said, and winked at me. My insides turned to warm jelly. *Is he flirting? C'mon Juliet,* I said to myself. *Stop looking for signs. You're the one who put the brakes on. Since then, he's been the model of propriety and professionalism.*

The first time I worked at The Hall, Mr. Roth had stood over me, lecturing, as I scraped an Eton Mess for twelve into the trash because "the berries were vertical." I bit my tongue till it bled, all the while thinking that he could pretend he came from an English boarding-school background to the others, but I had his number. It took one to know one, and I was American. I saw how hard he worked to fit in and hide his nouveau manners. He didn't know any more about Eton messes than I did.

Roth was jealous of the real English, especially those who'd inherited peerages. The Earl of Gloucester, Lord of Thornton Hall, and his best mate the Baron of Hinckley, who owned the neighboring estate, had something Roth couldn't compete with. Try as he might, Jasper Roth would never be listed among the titled in *Debretts.* He could buy land and houses in the old country, but he couldn't buy status. It baffled me that he wanted to. He was practically Donald Trump. As a "celebanker", he was always on camera or in print. It made no sense to me that he was chasing down acceptance in some caste-driven society whose rules didn't come naturally to people like Roth and me.

The Earl was an artist in addition to being a British blue blood. Below stairs, we usually called him The Painter. Somehow, that vocation rang more true to us than his having been born titled. Hanging on the walls of this grand house, along with the countless gloomy, dark, heavy oil paintings of his ancestors, were vibrant, fresh, and sometimes shocking modern works by the Earl himself. The art world knew him as Hugh de Audley, Hughie to the insiders.

Born into the peerage, he could certainly have lived a gentleman's life but he worked hard instead. In his youth, he studied in Paris, the States, and extensively in Spain. He'd apprenticed himself to some famous Modernists and developed a smart style of his own, influenced by a mix of the Spanish masters Picasso, Dali, Joaquin Sorolla, while still drawing heavily from painterly English artists like Millais and Turner. I was no expert, but I knew Hugh de Audley was the real thing.

The Painter is one of Britain's most beloved and celebrated modern artists. And, in the social media age, it doesn't hurt that he's a one-hundred percent, grown-up English lad, with a fairly fit and youthful body, big wooly sweaters, and a full head of wavy and still golden hair – even in his late sixties – flopping appealingly over one ultra-blue eye.

Aside from some health issues and some noticeable thickening around the middle – inevitable with age – he lead a robust life. I liked him a lot. He treated me well and wasn't above coming into the kitchen on his own to prepare a cup of tea (which we, of course, never allowed, though the pretense was kind).

"You know," Terrence said to me, refilling his glass of wine dangerously close to the top, "you really missed it. I was asked to bring champagne to the drawing room the night Roth 'surprised' The Painter by announcing he'd host Christmas and handle all of the guest lists 'as his Christmas gift' to him and the Countess. His Christmas gift!

"He's lucky he's still allowed round here, given what the rags are all saying about the state of his marriage." Terrence took a deep draught of his drink. "Anyhow, his Lordship leaned over as I was pouring and said, 'He may not have noticed, but I'm not dead, yet' just a hair too loudly. He then thanked his son-in-law for his 'imaginative generosity in gift innovation' and pointedly asked me if I had the time, as his Patek Philippe watch seemed to be broken and would need replacing. I nearly wet myself on the Chinese rug."

"If anyone can put Jasper Roth in his place, it's The Painter,"

I said.

"I'd say you do a fair job of it, yourself," Edward remarked, twirling his wine glass by the stem.

"No, no!" I blurted, blushing faintly. "Not like The Earl."

The Painter got Roth's goat. He'd make a big show of standing at the head of the table until his son-in-law was compelled to stand and hold the old man's chair for him, underscoring his rightful place at the seat of honor. Despite Roth's bales of money, his father-in-law's status always trumped him in this Medieval-rules country. On one of my last engagements at The Hall, the Earl had delighted in winding Roth up by refusing a priceless bottle of Petrus in favor of a Californian Chardonnay, even though the main course was Porterhouse steak.

"I don't know who'd be happier to see His Lordship gone to the grave – Roth or Chizz."

"That's rough, Terrence. Old Chisholm's just trying to do his job and stay out of trouble, like the rest of us," Edward said.

"Well, he'd be much happier doing it in a manor house than a London townhouse."

"Juliet, take a look at the guest roster," Rose said, opening a folder of papers on the table.

"Oooh, let me see," said Terrence. "If that 20-year-old Earl of Glastonbury's coming, his room assignment is 'Meadow Cottage, my bed.'"

"You'd better watch your step with that," I cautioned. "He's not even gay."

"He will be after one night with me," Terrence retorted, thrusting his pelvis forward. "Let's see, Dr. Dearden…aged Scotch, dry sherry, doesn't like cilantro blahblah – rank 5 – Lord and Lady Ambridge, already here…no red wine, Ketel One martinis, she's allergic to strawberries, organic produce, yadda yadda – also rank 5. Oooh! Kaylie Hart and her escort Jaques Lacoste…sizzling brunette and her froggy food critic lover! Rank 4? I'd go higher than that, myself. Roth's put them in the Regent's Room and Tapestry Room, very sexy indeed, with that adjoining bath and dressing room. Did anyone see her latest flick, *Remembrances of Autumn*? Art film, that one. She shows full bush."

"Language!" gasped Rose.

"Well, it's nothing you can't see every night at dinner, here at The Hall," defended Terrence. "The broad above the dining table's starkers from where I sit. She's a real piece…I'd probably let her have it if I went that way."

"Take it down a notch, Terrence," Edward said quietly.

One of The Earl's most famous paintings, a nude called *The Veiled Madonna*, hung in the dining room, opposite the head of the table's chair.

Rose threw the baking sheet she'd been scrubbing into the sink with a clatter. "Excuse me! I'm going to the ladies'."

Just then, Seamus came in through the pantry, brushing snow out of his hair. "Where's Rose?" he asked.

"She's gone to the toilet," Edward told him. "Terrence was being a boor, going on about the nude above the table. Some people wouldn't know art if it sneaked up and bit them."

"He could use a trip through The Tate or The Cheltenham Art Gallery," I agreed.

"Does anyone listen to me?" asked Terrence. "I said the naked babe was *hot*. That's high praise coming from my tribe. No need to get your knickers in a twist. I'll tell Rose I'm sorry for being rude. Quel sensitiva!"

Seamus' face closed up and he busied himself making a cup of tea. "In fairness, Terrence," he said, clearing his throat, "you take things one step too far, too often, for my taste."

"Back to the guests," I said, trying to lighten the mood. Rose and Seamus were, after all, Catholics. Not to mention from a different generation. "Who else?"

"All that's left is a cancellation! Looks like we're minus one Mr. Famous Member of Parliament and his boringly appropriate wife – Rank 4 – from The Crown Room. No subpar view of the horses' rear ends for them, then." The bedrooms were named individually and were allocated in strict accordance with an unspoken hierarchy The grandest rooms were The Oak Room, The Regent's Room or the Heather Room. If you were placed in these rooms, you were either the only guests or the Posh and the Powerful – Rank 5. A bit lower, and you were taken to the Crown Room or the Hunt Room, for those slightly further down the social pecking order – Rank 4. If you were given The Chinese Room, The Blue Room or the Princess Room, you'd better suck up and laugh loudly at all Roth's jokes, because you barely made the cut. In short, if your room had rugs from this century, singing for your supper was advisable.

"Roth hates plan changes," Edward said, neck craning to read the list upside down. "Expect a foul mood out of him. Better yet, just expect a foul mood out of him. He rarely disappoints."

"Edward!" I said.

"Are you defending him?" Edward's jaw was set hard.

"No, but, is he really that bad?" I asked. I felt shaky. Something told me I should drop it.

"It's not for me to say. To me he's just another boss. It's different for you, though, isn't it?" he asked, staring hard at me.

"I don't know what you mean," I said, starting to breathe a little faster. I didn't want to be having this conversation. "Like you, I'm just here to serve the guests."

"Of which there are very few!" Terrence jumped in. "So you see, we don't need an underbutler."

"We don't really need a second chef, either," I said, crossing my arms.

"Sometimes we get what we want, even if we don't need it," Edward said, softening. "Whatever I think of Roth, in this case I'm glad he's throwing his money around wantonly."

"I say we pinch a few pennies and send Mr. Chisholm home on the next motorcoach," Terrence said.

"Terrence," I counseled, "just find a way to get along with him. He's here to stay."

Before long, Rose came back through the kitchen door, amiability restored.

"It's getting late, you lot. Juliet, you've had a long journey, you'll need your rest…and Terrence, I'd recommend stopping at the two bottles you've had if you hope to hold a candle to Mr. Chisholm tomorrow."

"Drink doesn't affect me," Terrence announced. "I've a high tolerance for spirits and pharmaceuticals. I'm like Roth's wife, the esteemed Lady Penelope of the Manor, in that respect…I could drink a case alongside a bottle of Percocet and still buttle circles around Mr. Chizz."

"Terrence, don't bite the hand that feeds you," I said.

"If you're talking about Roth, Juliet, I'd advise you not to bite anything of his," Edward said.

"I mean Lady Penelope, and you know it. Terrence, we all our have dirty little secrets. There are things we don't need to know about her private life."

"I'll bet there are private things you'd like to know about her husband," Terrence said, poking Edward in the ribs, and looking at me slyly from under his lashes.

"What? No! God, Terrence. God!"

Edward fixed his gaze on me, settling back in his chair.

Rose declared, "Bedtime, my pets. Time to stop torturing Juliet. Out of the kitchen, now, so I can finish cleaning!" She took Terrence's glass away, opened the door to the pantry and literally shooed Terrence and me through and out the back door.

"Edward's still here!" protested Terrence.

"I just have to bring a few things up from the store room." Edward offered.

"What about Seamus?" whined Terrence. He hated to see a party end. "Why does he get to stay?"

"I'm here to see my best girl gets home safe. Think of me as her knight in shining armor. Now off with you," Seamus told him.

"God save England," mumbled Terrence to me as he split off,

weaving in a serpentine pattern into the darkness, toward Meadow Cottage.

Chapter Four

I headed for Dove's Nest. I took my keychain from my pocket, and turned on my tiny flashlight, following its tight beam through the dark and the falling flakes. I opened the door – doors on the estate were almost never locked – and saw that Seamus had recently lit a fire and placed all of my things neatly on my bed. It was so nice to be cared for by a decent man. I wondered if I'd ever have one of my own.

I pulled my phone out of my bag and checked it. Five calls from Ben. Fuck Ben. A year of devotion and all I got for Christmas was another woman's panties.

I set my trusty wind-up travel alarm clock and put on my red plaid, flannel pajamas and a pair of fuzzy socks against the chill. But I was feeling agitated and too keyed up to sleep. I cursed myself for not bringing anything to read. Kicking my jeans aside, I saw Edward's handkerchief fall out of the pocket. *Rose can help me get the blood stain out tomorrow*, I thought. *Or, I don't know, maybe he needs it. It is his handkerchief, after all. I could just give it to him tonight. And. And maybe borrow a book.*

Edward and I were friends, I believed, even though we were so very different. He was a favorite of Lady Penelope, the Earl and Countess's daughter, and she'd taken him from house to house before she'd married Jasper Roth. She always requested that he personally bring her tray when she took meals in her room, which was remarkably often, much to the annoyance of her husband. This was a breach of protocol – in a grand house, only the highest-ranking maids and butlers go into family quarters. Chefs remain in the kitchen. The nuances of English manners still manage to baffle me, but I do my best to play along. But Lady Penelope is a wild card. If she wanted to have a chef in her pocket, it was her prerogative.

And Edward's skills were undeniable, so no one could say Lady P hired him just as eye candy. He'd started in the military, which he'd joined after his mother died, and once his stint was over, he'd been accepted at Le Cordon Bleu, London. On the strength of his training and admirable military record, he was cooking in fine English houses in no time. His haute-cuisine skills passed Roth's muster, but Edward's heart was plainly in his everyday cooking. Whenever MacGregor presented him with a goose, a wild turkey, or venison from the grounds, he made magic. When I'd first cooked at the hall, Edward introduced me to the kitchen library that Terrence loved so much. That whole south wall, shared with the laundry room, was lined with built-in bookcases and featured a collection of all the standard, rare, and antique cookbooks that attested to his wide-ranging curiosity. The shelves also featured guides to wild game and fish, scientific books on herbs and botanicals, and food photography. Edward pointed out all the family's favorites, and his, too.

I use recipes as a guide and improvise from there, and that's how I got really good, I think. Once I was out from under the thumbs of head chefs like Henri and that asshole from The Ivy I started to find my voice. When I got the chance to wing it, I felt exhilarated, and I did exactly that when I was cooking for myself or for friends. When I had employers with a more casual attitude, I got real job satisfaction from experimentation. And I'll just say it straight – it felt good to have a tableful of diners who'd eaten all over the world fawn over me and tell me I'm the best. I'd never tell all that to Edward, though. I already felt vulnerable with him, like he could see right through me.

Although I enjoyed working with him, I wouldn't say it was easy for me as I was always in a state of high emotion around him, either on the cusp of a laugh or irritation. He threw me off balance. It wasn't like that with Ben. With Ben, I'd been grounded and alert, and I could keep my feet planted. I always knew what to expect with Ben. That is, right up until the moment I'd found another woman's underwear in his flat. Instead I felt floaty around Edward, as if I wasn't Juliet, but just an idea that hadn't fully taken shape. *Boy,* I thought, *if I admitted that to Mother, she'd have a phalanx of analysts tackling me and tying me to a couch.*

Like one time, I'd been making a North Carolina-style brisket at Mr. Roth's request, with molasses and white vinegar. It had to slow roast for seven hours in a huge Dutch oven. Without asking, Edward poked his head in the oven, lifted the pot lid and threw in a cup of brown sugar.

"Why would you do that?" I asked, angry. Roth wanted what he wanted, and I was supposed to give it to him.

He smiled devilishly. "Why not? Don't you like it sweet?"

"Because opening the pot alters the cook time and the recipe doesn't call for brown sugar! And how about because it's *my* roast?" My blood was boiling and I couldn't see straight. I was usually more level-headed than this in the kitchen. In fact, I had a reputation for being the very opposite of a temperamental chef.

"What's the big deal?" he said amiably. "It's good to stir things up a bit." He was wearing a pair of oven mitts printed with winged, pink pigs on them. I was doubly infuriated by that whimsical touch. The kitchen was done in slate and mineral colors. All of the dishtowels, potholders and other linens were gray or black. Jasper Roth had had a heavy say in the recent renovation. Jasper would hate those mitts.

"The best surprises in life happen when you just say yes in the moment." He either couldn't see he was winding me up or he didn't care. "What else?" he asked. "Do you think maybe a little scotch bonnet?" he added, grabbing a pepper off the counter and making toward the oven.

"No!" I shouted, reaching for the pepper, which he was holding high, just out of my reach. I'd promised Jasper Roth this specific dish and my name was on it. "Stop it, Edward, I mean it. Seriously, I mean it." My voice was a bit too loud and I could feel I was red in the face.

"Does it always have to be 'seriously' with you, Jubes? Can't it ever be fun?"

Lady Penelope poked her head through the swinging door just then. She looked from me, to Edward.

"Am I interrupting something?" she asked Edward directly.

"No, Your Ladyship," I answered, steadying my breath in an attempt to appear calm. "What can we get you?"

"Edward, if you'd be so kind," she said, ignoring me, "I'd like a Nescafe in the dining room." I could feel him glancing at my face, but I busied myself smashing the pits out of olives with the broad side of a French knife.

"Of course," he said to Lady Penelope. He boiled the kettle and spooned coffee crystals into a cup, and set a tray while she stood watching. As he carried it out, I expected her to follow him. Instead, she walked up closely behind me.

"On second thought, put the tray on my vanity, will you Edward?" she called to him through the door. And then she said into my ear, "He's not for you."

"I beg your pardon?"

"What I mean to say is, he's an excellent chef, but he's rumored to be a Lothario. Just a word to the wise. You're best to leave him alone."

"There's nothing between Edward and me, Your Ladyship." *As if it's any of your business*, I added in my head. "I have a fiancé."

She glanced at my naked hand, and said, "Oh, don't you wear your ring at work?"

Stammering, I said, "Well, we're kind of… um… pre-engaged. Anyway, I have a boyfriend."

"Ah, well, that's a relief. For you, I mean," she said.

Edward came back through. "I've set up your hot drink, Your Ladyship."

"Thank you," she said, turning and walking out the door.

I wiped my hands, picked up my French knife and got back to work. I couldn't look at Edward. I felt foolish that I'd gotten that upset.

After a few beats, he said, "Don't mind her. That's her way." And then he was very quiet for a while.

"It's her house," I said, impersonally.

"You know, Jubes," he'd said to me, "it'd be nice if you'd loosen up – in the kitchen, I mean. Rules are meant to be broken." He was a bundle of contradictions in appearance and manner. His hair was still cut in military style but he had a thick tribal tattoo on the top of his left forearm that peeked out of the sleeve of his chef's coat. His uniform was always starched and spotless, but he sported unorthodox accents such as a heavy silver wallet chain or a thick, brown leather wrist cuff with an antique barn nail wrapped around it. And well groomed as he was, the shadow of a beard was always threatening to appear on his square jaw.

"In my book rules are meant to be rules. That's why they're called that. Rules." I listened to myself talking, wondering why I was being such a prig. I sounded like Mother, a wet blanket on any hint of fun. I'd broken the rules in search of fun with Stephen, and I'd been left with egg on my face. Once bitten, twice shy. Better to be safe, I told myself. Still, a little black ball of longing was curled up in my stomach.

For the rest of that evening, we cooked, cleaned up and made our way to our cottages with very little conversation, and I'd slept like the dead. After any tour of duty with Edward at the Hall, I always returned to London exhausted. I decided that being in a heightened state all the time didn't suit me. Better a calm routine, like the one Ben provided me.

Sometimes, though, I did find relaxation at The Hall. Sometimes, after dinner was cleaned up, we staff all sat together in the kitchen, cozily drinking wine and watching videos. I had a fine time doing jumbles, sudoku and crosswords with the others. Since Ben, I'd rarely passed the time this frivolously in my off days in London, the way I had with Posy, when I was single. There was always a biography to be read or a gallery to be visited. And I certainly never watched films like *The Terminator* or *Airplane*. At home, Ben and I took in documentaries, or French films, or Woody Allen. Edward teased me about wanting to be the "smart girl with my ducks in a row" and delighted in flustering me.

Edward and I took an occasional run together on the grounds. He'd pretend it was boot-camp, military style, and he always kicked my behind. From time to time, Lord Chinnerton, the Baron of Hinckley, would gallop by, enjoying the freedom to ride on his own land, and the land of his best friend alongside it. He was genial and casually friendly.

"Good afternoon!" he shouted on one occasion. "The rain has left us behind, at least for today. Fine day for some exercise."

"It certainly is, Sir," Edward had replied. "I'd venture Thunder thinks the same," he said, approaching the horse's muzzle and giving it a stroke. "Gorgeous!"

"Not as gorgeous as your pretty companion," he tipped his riding helmet to me. "'To love and be loved is to feel the sun from both sides,' as the quote goes," he said.

"Oh," I responded, coloring. "It isn't like that, Your Lordship. You see, we both cook at Thornton."

"I'm sure you do, my dear," he said wickedly. "See that you enjoy every minute of it." He nudged Thunder on and galloped away, kicking up mud.

Sadly, it was all-too rare that we could find the time to sneak away to exercise, which was tragic, as Edward was an excellent baker and was always making double-batches for us staff… which we naturally gluttonously accepted. "You have to stop tempting me, or I'll gain ten pounds," I protested. He knew I found it impossible to say no to his sugary treats. Ben didn't care for sweets and I didn't really like to indulge when I was with him.

"More of you to love," Edward had shrugged. His saying that made my heart hammer.

"A word of warning, Miss Juliet, if you don't mind," Seamus had said to me toward the end of my first stint at Thornton.

"Course I don't mind," I'd told him, worried that he was going to tell me that everyone in the drawing room was gagging on the cocktails I'd just sent out. I knew pairing hibiscus and mint was risky but hadn't thought of it as a deal-breaker.

"I think Mr. Roth has his eye on you and the young chef," Seamus said, busying himself by making a cup of tea.

"Thank you, Seamus, but there's nothing to keep an eye on," I told him. "Do they like the drinks?"

"Yes, yes, everyone's oohing and aahing about the color and the flavor. Back to the point, though, Mr. Roth doesn't like to know that those of us in his service have earthly wants and needs, like for food and water, and romance…or air, come to think of it," he said, chuckling at his own joke.

"Don't worry. I have a boyfriend in London. I don't need romance."

Back then, I was just getting a foothold as a chef in this world and didn't want to jeopardize it, so Seamus's words niggled at me. Plus, there was Ben. Even in the early days, I found myself defending Ben to Edward. Like that time we were making a multi-course Indian meal.

Washing lentils at the sink, I told him how we made sense as a couple – how Ben was working to make partner, how he and I were intellectually compatible, how his law degree and my undergraduate degree in psychology made us both analytical, how we had similar views on financial independence. "We split all expenses now, and I suspect we'll have separate accounts when we marry,"

I said smugly, feeling like one of the smart-woman financial advisors from *The Eva! Show*.

"You go Dutch at dinner. So he's a cheapskate?" Edward asked. He measured out jasmine rice into a pot.

"No! We're simply both autonomous," I told him.

"That sounds hot," he'd replied, getting under my skin again.

"Do all relationships have to be hot?" I demanded. At the very mention of the word hot, I became aware of Edward's shoulders under his close-fitting t-shirt. The family was out for the afternoon, so he'd taken off his chef's coat and hung it on a chair. That's Edward in a nutshell – a maddening combination of rule follower and risk taker.

"Hell yes, relationships have to be hot. That's part of it, anyway. A big part, if you ask me," he said, turning from his pot and shooting me a look. Anyway, you can't see much of him. How can you, when you're always here with me?" He smiled.

"Well, I'm trying to earn a good reputation in the business, in case you hadn't noticed. That's why I'm here, of course." *Not to be near you*, I said in my head.

"Or maybe you're just holding out for someone of higher rank?" He tossed this out casually, rhythmically chopping onions while he spoke. "Crossing the invisible line has its appeal. I mean, that's what I hear," said Edward.

I thought about Jasper Roth and flushed deeply, not waiting for an answer to my question. "Look, if you're implying that I have some kind of crush…"

"I'm just asking if…" his knife stopped. "Nothing."

"What were you going to say?"

He didn't answer. He lifted a pot lid, and began measuring out different colored powders into the curry he'd been making. I watched, pretending to be interested in the dish, but really wanting to hear Edward say more about Jasper. I reached around him to take the ghee off the stove, grabbing the hot handle of the iron pot without a potholder.

"Damn!" I cried, letting go immediately.

"Slow down, Jubes. There's no rush." He took my hand in his, and eased my clenched fist open. He kissed my injured palm, very lightly. "Let me wrap that hand up with some aloe gel," he said.

The tenderness set off a longing in me that I didn't want him to see. "That curry's going to be too spicy," I said, pulling my hand away, pretending it didn't hurt. "The tastes in this house are particular, you know. That combo will be too much for them, they're not The Rolling Stones."

"There's a saying in India, 'Spice wakes the sleeping.'" He looked directly at me, his emerald green eyes with the gold flecks holding me in his steady gaze. Then he took my hand again, pulling against my resistance. "Open up for me," he said. "You must be in pain. Let me look after you."

My hand did hurt, and I did need looking after. I imagined leaning forward and kissing his full lips. He always smelled like cinnamon to me, and I could almost taste it in my mouth. After a moment I said, "I'm here to do things by the book," and I turned away.

"That's a shame," he'd told me, letting me go. He waited a long time to speak, not saying anything until I checked in, looking at his face. "You know, Jubes," he said, "I don't chase after women. They usually come to me." I opened my mouth to call him arrogant and he put up a hand to stop me. "I'm not building myself up, it's just that most women I can take or leave, so I don't make the effort. If they show up, I say yes." A quick, hot jealousy flared up in my sternum and I involuntarily imagined him in bed with a faceless woman. *Stop that*, I told myself. *He's not yours.*

"I'm not a monk, you know," he said. "If you'd respond to what I think have been my *considerable* efforts," he said softly, "I would gladly turn a blind eye to the various offers around me."

I wondered what offers he meant…he rarely left the grounds. "Who…?" I began to ask, then thought better of it. *Stop the drama*, I told myself. If I was going to be with Ben, I was going to be with

Ben. I'd invested so much, the ship had sailed. It was the sensible thing to do. *And you love Ben*, I reminded myself.

"Sorry…" I whispered and I genuinely meant it. "If it weren't for Ben…"

"I get it. You can't blame a man for trying," he said, twisting his mouth into a wistful smile. He stirred his curry.

"Edward," I began.

"Let's just change the subject," he said, cutting me off. "You should always try for what you want, and if that falls through, readjust. Learned that in the military. Let's stick with the cooking."

Edward and I continued to work together, but became very careful with each other after that. Gentle, even. It worked for a while. But then came the stint when I was engaged to help at yet another of the Hall's weddings…

We'd had a wonderful morning together. It was a clear June day, and we'd sneaked off together to get fresh eggs. I'd seen very little in my lifetime that was as picturesque as the grounds of Thornton Hall when the weather cooperated. The grass was electric green and, the sheep beyond the fence looked so white and fluffy, I wouldn't have been surprised if they'd been shampooed and blow-dried.

"Race you to the barn," Edward had shouted, tearing off into a sprint.

"Totally no fair!" I screamed back, chasing him. "You had a head start!" I burst into a run, but I caught my shoe on the jutting root of an oak tree and went down, face first. I felt the wind knocked out of me, and by the time I caught a deep breath, Edward had doubled back and was helping me to my feet. My cheekbone was throbbing where it has smacked down on a flat rock.

"Maybe we should take you to Dr. Dearden." He looked concerned.

"No, this is nothing. But I bruise like a peach, and know in advance, I'm blaming it on you," I said, laughing it off. We ambled the rest of the way to the barn, and wound up talking, of all things, about how much we both wanted to see the Aurora Borealis someday.

Later that day, we were goofing around making a practice cake for the wedding, which we'd feed to the delighted staff. At one point, Edward shoved a slice of the trial wedding cake into my face while we were mock-fighting. It smarted where I'd hit my face in the fall. Involuntarily I cried out, "Hey!" Rose had come in at that moment and said, "Oh, look at the bride and groom, quarreling already."

"Mark my words, it won't last a week!" I'd joked, joining in. "My mother warned me about his type. Told me to marry a lawyer."

After that, Edward became very cold with me, and wouldn't look me in the eye. That day and the next passed with such tension that I thought our days of being able to work together were through. He ignored all my little jokes and refused the sandwich I put in front of him, even though he always said that sandwiches taste better when someone else makes them for you. I brooded about it, then eventually threw myself on the grenade.

"Edward," I'd said, the first moment I could get him alone. "I'd like to offer you the option of hiring another assistant. I'll give notice, and make my excuses."

"Unnecessary, Juliet. I was in the RAF Regiment. I've endured far worse than idle flirting from a woman who doesn't know her own mind."

"Listen…" I interrupted.

"There's nothing more to say. The fault is entirely mine. Now, if you'd be so kind as to wash and mince the parsley, we can get on with it."

Chapter Five

Snapping back to the present, I realized I'd let the fire die down in my little cottage. I tossed a log onto the dying flames and gave it a jab with the poker. Blame it on the cold and the darkness, but alone was the last thing I'd wanted to be right then.

Forgetting about Edward and all our history together had been easy enough when I was in London and didn't have to lay eyes on him. But being here at Thornton, with him standing in the flesh before me, right in the kitchen where we'd met, a million moments we'd shared together came back to mind.

Something knocked softly up against the old wooden door of Dove's Nest. A branch? Or was it just the wind? I walked over to the window, and pulled the curtain aside, but it was too dark to see. I heard the knocking again, louder and deliberate. Someone was at my door! Edward? My heart skipped a beat as I turned the knob.

"Juliet, I need to ask you something," Jasper Roth said, pushing past me and closing the door.

"Now?" I couldn't think of anything else to say. I could count the number of times people had come to my cottage while I was in it on one hand.

"I know it's late. I can see you're ready for bed." He looked me over. "I was going to catch you up at the house, but you slipped out the back."

I was keenly aware that we were both standing there in our pajamas. Alone.

"I didn't slip out. I just came to my cottage, nothing wrong with that." I felt weird, like he'd read my mind, because I'd just been thinking about slipping out to take Edward his handkerchief.

"Anyway, I had to wait until everyone left the kitchen before I could come."

"Why?" I asked, though I knew full well. "You're my boss and you just came to ask me a question, right?"

He raised his eyebrow, and gave a wry smile. "It's past midnight. People will talk. Speaking of which, what was Terrence getting at in the kitchen tonight?"

"Do you want to sit down?" I asked, gesturing to the little table, with its two ladder back chairs.

He crossed past me, and sat on the bed. I let myself imagine, for a second, how it could be if things were different. But things *weren't* different. He was my boss. More to the point, he was married, for better or for worse. "I can't stay long."

"Obviously."

"So what does Terrence know?"

I pulled a chair out from the table, and sat on the edge, taking care not to relax. "What is there to know?"

He sighed. "Nothing. There's nothing to know. Of course." He looked at me very seriously, and then smiled. "Tell me what he thinks he knows."

I hesitated. "Well," I began slowly, "he saw us. The last time I worked here."

"Saw us what?" His eyes were amused.

"He saw us drinking together in the dining room, the night we had the port."

"Ah."

"But I told him nothing happened! I mean, we didn't even kiss…" My cheeks were getting hotter and hotter, despite the chill of the room. Why did I say the word "kiss"? He sat listening, like he had all the time in the world.

Was he going to admit to his part in that moment that was so intimate, even Terrence could spot it, or was he going to leave me twisting in the wind? I felt like he knew I wasn't telling the whole truth, which was fair enough, because I wasn't. When Terrence had grilled me the following night, I'd caved under his expert interrogation …and half a bottle of wine. I'd filled Terrence in on the whole story of Nantucket the year before, and how Roth and I had blurred the line between servant and master, dining together, walking on the beach, and that…embrace. How he had confided in me during his wife's nervous breakdown.

"That's true."

I waited for him to elaborate, to add to the story. He just sat there on the bed, relaxed and confident, looking like he owned the place. I felt something slowly rising up in me, maybe anger. Or was it humiliation? Wasn't he going to admit to his part? I might not have proof, but I knew he'd wanted me. Didn't he? I scanned his face for a clue. Feeling foolish, a distant alarm bell was reminding me that I didn't know how to handle myself around men. My Achilles' heel was reading how they felt about me. This discomfort was more than I could bear. Was it better to die old and alone with a hundred cats?

A few minutes ago, I'd desperately wanted company. If you'd offered me Jasper Roth dressed for bed, I'm sure I would have answered, "Yes, please!" Now I wanted nothing more than to throw him out.

"All right then," I snapped, standing up. "I guess there's nothing more to say." I crossed to the door, and swung it open, letting in a blast of cold air.

He rose from the bed, and walked over to where I was standing. "If you say so." He turned from me, and walked toward the house. "Goodnight, Juliet," I think he said, but it was hard to tell because he was facing away from me.

Moments later, I had shut the cottage door behind me and looked around to make sure no one was around to see anything they shouldn't. The lights in the main house were off, but it looked like Rose and Seamus might still be awake. Losing my nerve, I considered retreating to my bed to lick my wounds in private. Damn Jasper Roth! As a matter of fact, damn all men! I'd give Edward back his handkerchief right now, and then my ties with all of them would be severed. Clean and simple.

The damp air enveloped me. Was it really twice as cold here as in London, or did it just feel that way? I wasn't wearing a coat. I had pulled on a robe over my pajamas and slipped my kitchen clogs over my wooly socks. In my domed hand, I carried my tiny keychain flashlight, letting out only as much beam as I needed to find my way. If I shined it any brighter, people would notice me. The ground was lightly dusted with snow and the air was dead silent. The frozen twigs and sticks sounded like bullets as they shattered under my feet.

I rounded the back of the big house and saw only a dim lamp-light in Edward's cottage. *Turn back, there's your sign, Juliet. He's already in bed. Leave well enough alone.* I have to admit, I was a little relieved. Better to sever the ties without a face-to-face confrontation. I crept up to the handmade wooden platform that served as a porch, laid the handkerchief near the saddle, and weighed it down with a rock. The door opened, and I found myself staring at Edward's bare feet.

"I thought you might be Father Christmas come early," he said as I stood up. "But even through all those red flannel layers, I can see curves the likes of which the old man never hoped to aspire to." I said nothing, trying Jasper's trick. I was hoping he'd fill in the gap by talking, but he was too clever for me. He crossed his arms, and leaned against the doorframe, head cocked, smiling.

Finally, I caved. "I brought you back your handkerchief."

"Good job, too. I don't know how I would have survived the night without it," he twinkled.

A light cut through the blackness and I saw that it was from Terrence's window.

"Mind if I come in," I said, pushing past him, over the threshold. "God knows what kind of gossip Terrence will be spreading if he sees me here."

"What kind of gossip should he be spreading?" Edward asked, in his coffee-rich voice, crossing to the open-plan kitchen and turning on the flame under the kettle. I shook my head, involuntarily. Is there some law in the British books that cups of tea must be forced on all visitors, regardless of the time or occasion?

I walked past the sofa where there was a pile of bed pillows, with some rumpled quilts spread around. A hardback copy of the novel *The Privileges* splayed open on the sofa's arm. There was half a bottle of red wine and a glass on the coffee table. Aside from that area, where he'd obviously been relaxing, the cottage was tidy for a man's house. His shoes and boots were lined up in a row by the door and dishes were in the drainer. Through the open door, I could see that his bed was made.

"Well, he could tell people I'm a liar, and he'd be right. I'm embarrassed to admit this to you, but I don't know if Ben is fine or not. I should have told you in the kitchen: we broke up. I caught him cheating on me, this morning."

He looked right in my eyes. "Did you come to bring me my handkerchief or did you come to tell me you broke up with your boyfriend?" I took him in. He had on a hunter green ribbed turtleneck over a pair of Black Watch plaid pajama pants. On his head was a wooly cap, which looked hip and youthful in a way I hadn't expected from Edward. The impulse to slide myself into his arms was so strong, I practically swooned. "Or," he said softly, "is there something altogether different you came to tell me?"

I clutched the back of a barstool. A breakfast counter separated the kitchen area from the entrance hall. "I…I suppose I came to apologize for lying." My face was growing warm.

"Is that another lie?" He leaned across the counter, his face inches from mine.

"Yes," I whispered.

"Your Ben story seems less a lie and more a sin of omission. Anyhow, your secrets are your own to keep." For half a wild second, I thought he might lean in and kiss me, but he stepped back into the kitchen. Reaching into the cupboard above his head for a mug, he said, "I was making tea, but would you rather have wine?"

Turn your body toward the front door, and walk out of it, Juliet. Coming here was a bad idea. Mother always counsels her patients who've ended a relationship not to start another for one year.

"I've already had a lot to drink, on a relatively empty stomach," I told him, my feet carrying me around the bar, intending to head for the door.

"Is that the excuse you'll give for kissing me?" he asked, taking a wine glass off the shelf and crossing to the sofa. With his back to me, he settled into the cocoon of blankets and poured my burgundy. I stood there, wondering what to do next – although we both knew what was going to happen. I'd known the minute I had made up my mind to give him his handkerchief back tonight.

After taking his time, Edward flipped back the corner of the quilts, holding them aloft. "You have to admit, it's cold out there, alone." I hesitated for a split second. "Come on then," he said very gently. "Who're you kidding?"

Live your least secretive life. Most of all, don't keep secrets from yourself. My aunt's voice rang in my head. Since the first conversation I had with him, I have wanted to press my body up against Edward, to cover his mouth with mine, to attack him without any of the shyness or reserve I had with Stephen or Ben.

"No one," I admitted, sliding into the warm envelope of blankets, and onto his lap. "Ah," I breathed out involuntarily. Even though I was terrified of where this might lead, I couldn't help myself. I'd been waiting so long to press against him that the first thing I felt was something like relief.

He wrapped me in his arms and I tilted my face up to his,

aching for a kiss. He looked into my eyes as we sat melting into one another, breathing the same air. "Please," I whispered.

He reached around, stroking the back of my neck with his big, strong hand. Tangling his fingers upward, into my hair, he teased me, holding my head still. Brushing his lips slowly across mine, he moved back each time I tried to drink him in.

"Edward, please," I sighed.

Clamping his mouth down hard onto mine, soft firm lips parted, and he turned my sigh into a moan. The only thing that existed was the warm lushness of his kiss. I was drunk. Our mouths moved together for what might have been minutes or centuries before I surfaced, becoming aware of all the sensations pulsing below my neck.

Underneath all of our fuzzy, wooly clothes, I could feel how tight and hard his body was. I was frantic with desire. Before I could think, I was straddling him, with my mouth still on his, my hands caressing the short, velvety hair under his cap. "Oh my good God," I sighed, pushing myself against his lap. "Edward. You feel amazing."

"There's my girl," he said quietly into my ear, as I was sliding my hand up his sweater, stroking past the down on his chest, up to the muscles of his shoulders. "I knew you were in there somewhere." He managed to untie and pull off my robe without casting off the quilts. I literally couldn't wait for him to unbutton my pajamas. The need for his hands on my skin was loud in my head. I pushed his hand under my top, and to my surprise, boldly showed him how to touch me. I could feel how aroused he was, but he followed my lead, all attention on my body, teasing me exquisitely until teasing wasn't good enough. I knelt over him, pushing his hand down into my pajama bottoms, panting "yes, like that," and "no, do this," until, with him looking right into my eyes, I rocked and shook the way I never had with any man.

We disentangled and I gingerly lowered myself to his side, putting my arms around his neck, laying my ear on his chest to avoid looking at him. I could hear my own heavy breathing and I was embarrassed by how forward I'd just been.

"I'm sorry if…" I began.

"Don't be sorry. That was beautiful," he said to me, his voice vibrating through his sweater. "I've missed you. I didn't know if you'd take a job here again, after our row." He pulled back and took a long look at me. "You're amazing, you know that. Promise you'll let me do that again."

I started to say what a bad idea it was to fool around with your co-worker, and what a mistake it had been, but who was I kidding. I knew I'd crawl ten miles to let him.

"Let you?" I said. "How about beg you?" I already felt starved for him. Inside my head, it felt like my brain had been replaced with warm, swirly, golden caramel. I couldn't form a logical thought.

"I have wanted that since the first minute I laid eyes on you," I said, matter-of-factly. "When we met in the kitchen, I wanted to put my hands under your clothes and feel your bare skin." My mouth was saying whatever it wanted, unedited. My body was in control; my rational mind had lost the battle.

"That's what I wanted," he said simply.

"Well what're your thoughts on letting me do a few things to you?" I whispered into his ear, gliding my hand across his lap to check his mood. Signs pointed to a positive outcome. And with one fell swoop, he picked the pile of blankets and me up, knocking over one of the wine glasses in our wake, and ferried me easily to the bedroom, even though we were pretty evenly matched, height-wise.

"My thoughts on that are impure," he said, pulling his top off, exposing his calisthenics-shaped torso. "Filthy, in fact. Are you down with that?" In a split second, he was poised over me in a push-up, waiting for an answer.

Well, Juliet, whatever plan you were supposed to be sticking to seems like it's out the window. Who knew I was so fickle? But with his mouth, and his hands on me, and the feeling of his…

"I have never been more down with anything in my life," I said, rising up to meet him.

Chapter Six

I woke up, face down on an unfamiliar pillow, to the rattle of a dropped pot lid. Disoriented, and too tired to lift my head, I took in a deep breath. I smelled cinnamon and the faintest, musky scent of a man's sweat.

"Morning, Princess," Edward said, padding toward me.

Oh dear God, I'm in Edward's bed. Is my brain broken? Am I missing a judgment gene? Instinctively I tried to mash myself further down into the mattress so as to go unnoticed. I tried to pretend I wasn't there, but images from last night flashed across the IMAX screen in my head: running my tongue over the sleek muscle over Edward's pelvic bone, the top of his head as he kissed a line down to my navel and below, his expression after he'd pulled me on top of him and I slowly lowered myself down, making him moan low and deep. I squeezed my eyes shut. "Um, Princess might be too strong a title. After my, uh, behavior last night, I may need a stint in finishing school."

Laughing, he said, "Proper ladies are dull. I'd rather be with you."

"Thanks. Maybe."

He leaned down, slid his hands under my shoulders and flipped me right over. "There's my sexy girl," he said. Before I could open my mouth to speak any kind of words that might justify my unrecognizable behavior from the night before, his soft warm lips were on mine. Instinctively, I felt myself tilting my chin and propping myself on my elbows to reach closer to him, unwilling to lose the lush sweetness of his mouth. When he stood upright, breaking the contact, it was excruciating.

"Nooooo," I heard myself whine. I snapped my eyes open to see Edward smiling and looking appreciatively at my naked breasts. I snatched the sheet upwards. Thank goodness it was still dark in his bedroom.

"Not much point in that," he teased. "I'm afraid the horse is out of the barn. I've seen every inch of you now." I started to turn my head away, but he held my chin in his strong hand, forcing me to meet his eye. "Every inch. And you're breathtaking." He ran his hand from my jaw, over my throat and stopped in the middle of my chest, pinning me to the bed with a gentle pressure. "Besides, why would you want to hide two of the seven wonders of the modern world?"

He released me, sliding his hand downward, pulling the sheet with it. My hands flew up to cover myself, but he caught them in both of his, holding them while he arched over, languidly kissing one of my breasts. My eyes closed, and I lay backward onto the pillow. He pulled his mouth away very slowly, the tip of his tongue the last part of him to lose contact with any part of me. Involuntarily, I cried out in protest. In a split second, his mouth was on my other breast sending an electric shock to the lower part of my belly. My hips rose up, and he pinned my body to the bed with his torso.

Easing his lips off of my tingling skin, he whispered, "Are you hungry?"

Oh, my god yes, famished, I thought, my eyes still closed. *I could eat you alive.*

"I'm starved to death," I said huskily, putting my arms around his neck.

"Good, because I have pancakes with Nutella and cream started."

"Oh!" I said, mortified. "Yes. Breakfast. Yum!" I sat up, and tried to look like the kind of girl who might sit properly at the table, discussing the weather and politics, instead of the sex-crazy succubus I felt like inside. "Pancakes. Very kind of you."

Eyes dancing, he was already peeling his sweater over his head and kicking off his slippers. "Bad luck, breakfast has to wait now." He slid his pajama bottoms to the ground, exposing his marble-hard thighs. "That little taste of you really whet my appetite," he rolled onto the bed and threw back the sheet. "It's all your fault for being so delicious." Straddling me, he said, "Now I'm starving too." He leaned over me brushing his stubble against my cheek, and whispered into my ear, "And pancakes aren't what I'm looking for."

****

With my cheek resting on Edward's broad bicep, and my arm draped across his chest, I began falling into a post-coital nap. For just that moment, the rest of the world fell away. There was no Stephen, no Ben, no Mother, no advanced degree to earn, no new career to get started on, and no empty kitchen waiting for me.

This must be what Aunt Suze means when she talks about being fully present. If the roof caved in and killed me right now, I could die happy.

"Much as I hate to move, I'd better get up if I'm going to send you off with a proper breakfast," Edward said, gently moving my head to the pillow. "It's 5:30. You'll want a minute to go back to yours and dress so we can get to the kitchen on time. I don't think Roth will accept 'caught up in the throes of passion' as an excuse for tardiness."

My stomach turned over when he mentioned Jasper Roth. "He can't know about us!" I said. Edward tilted his head quizzically. "I mean, of course, no one here can know. I mean, really, it's none of anyone's business."

"That's true enough," Edward said, walking into the galley kitchen. "What's between us is between us."

77

Why do you care what Jasper thinks? I asked myself. I didn't like the question. *Shut up, Juliet.*

"What I'm trying to say," I stammered out loud, "is that there must be rules against…you know, fraternization or whatever." I waited for a response and got none. "It's just that we have to think professionally, right?" No answer. "Can I use your bathroom?" I called.

"Go right through. You don't have to ask any more," he answered.

By the time I got back from the bathroom, he had a steaming cup of foamy coffee sitting next to a gorgeous plate of chocolatey pancakes.

"Sweets for the sweet," he said, leaning over and nuzzling my cheek.

What was I doing? I had just been preaching to Posy about sticking to the plan, and as of yesterday, hot sex with my co-worker under my boss's nose, and a ten-thousand calorie breakfast had definitely not been part of it.

"Edward, listen…"

"Shh," he said, putting his finger to my lips. "Not this time, Wordy Girl. This time let's just enjoy our day, and not talk it to death." He looked at me long and hard, with something like appreciation in his green-gray eyes. "All I know is this – I just made earth-moving, mind-twisting, bone-dissolving love with a woman who really means something to me. That's a good thing. Now eat your pancakes. We've a long day ahead of us."

Chapter Seven

"Edward, why in God's name is there a carton of orange juice on this list? If you don't want to squeeze orange juice every day – and I mean *every* day – before breakfast, you don't want to work at Thornton Hall," barked Jasper Roth as he burst through the swinging oak door leading from the dining room to the kitchen. "Oh, it's you."

"And good morning to you, Mr. Roth," I said, cheerily. I'd seen his moods before, plenty. No doubt he was feeling the stress of hosting holiday guests. He thought he'd take it out on Edward, but even this bad-tempered greeting couldn't pop the balloon in my chest and slam me back to earth. I all but forgave him for his bad behavior in my cottage last night. Anyway, after my blissful night, those feelings of anger were a very distant memory.

"Oh, it's you."

"Yes, we did establish that. And I did, indeed, sleep very well, thank you for asking," I said evenly, as I turned my back turned to him. I monitored a cast-iron pot of steel-cut Irish porridge, trying to appear busy. I felt him staring at the back of me, and I started to get uncomfortable.

The hairs on my neck prickled. Did I have missionary-position bedhead? I tried to think back to whether or not I'd thoroughly brushed my hair after skulking back to my cottage. *You're fine,*

Juliet. Keep it calm and easy, I counseled myself. *He can't read your mind.* Nothing could blacken my mood today. After the things Edward had done to me, relaxed wasn't a strong enough word to describe my state.

Sneaking a look back at my employer, I noticed he looked good this morning...really good. He was very casually dressed in a black, half-zip cashmere sweater and khakis. His dark curls were gleaming and his skin was a high color. He'd probably just come off the treadmill.

I smiled inwardly, after a night of perfect sex, does every man have to look like a meal? *It's bad enough I've just slept with a colleague, don't even think about what it might be like with your boss.* Especially not this boss. This married boss. Still, my mind wandered without my consent. Just because the familiar smell of his aftershave piqued my interest, it didn't mean I was going to act on it.

I couldn't wait to call Posy. It had been too early to call her when I'd left Edward's cabin in the dark, and I'd had to hit the kitchen before sun-up. My cell doesn't work on this vast expanse of land they call the grounds of Thornton Hall. When I want to communicate, I have to use the house phone in the laundry or the kitchen. There wasn't much privacy to be had, so I always had to plan calls strategically. Maybe I'd even tease her and tell her I'd been eyeballing stormy Mr. Roth, thinking about him right before I'd succumbed to Edward. She was always after me to stop being such a prude.

This morning, though, I thought it best to stay above Jasper's games. I'd seen his moods at the ski lodge, I'd seen them in the south of France and I (along with his neighbors Mr. Oscar-winning Hot Guy and Ms. Rockstar's Daughter Fashion Designer) had seen them on the patio of his Flood Street penthouse. I'd found that the best course of action was to ignore his tantrums. Luckily, or maybe not, I'd also seen his softer side in Nantucket. *And in the dining room, over port,* I thought, my knees going a little weak.

"About the shopping list," I explained in the manner of a preschool teacher, "we buy orange juice in a carton to baste the hams. You're always telling guests that there's no ham more juicy or rich than the ones served at The Hall." I kept my voice steady during this teeny tiny fib. Butter, as Rose was fond of saying, would have melted in my mouth.

"Oh. Yeah…O.K. He plonked a cardboard box on to the table and motioned for me to open it. Inside, wrapped in sturdy parchment and silver foil, was a truffle the size of a softball. "Ha! Show that to Edward. I want you to tell him to shave it finely over the scrambled eggs. I won it at auction last week. Charity benefit at Ambridge Dairy…my wife thought I should let it go, but I goddamn won it…sixteen hundred pounds I paid for it! Where is Edward, anyway?"

"We agreed I'd start the day, then he'd go late," I said, covering. The truth was I didn't know why Edward wasn't in the kitchen yet. I'd left him in the shower, and told him to go back to bed if he was tired, that I could take the early shift. *Must have needed his rest*, I smirked inwardly. "I have everything perfectly under control, Sir." As if.

I fired up the Nespresso machine and made myself a cappuccino. My nerves were already wired, but I thought I needed a jolt to keep me on track.

He scanned the list again, stood up, and walked over toward the range. I had my eye on the clock. I had not yet begun the batter for the buttermilk and blueberry waffles, which had to be cooked to order, on demand from the guests. This task required the use of an ancient stove-top waffle iron as opposed to a plug-in, because Mr. Roth liked the pattern it imprinted. *He may be a spoiled snob, but he does smell really nice,* I thought, inhaling deeply. *Focus, Juliet!* I had to pull out the food processor, prepare the strawberry butter, and grate nutmeg. I got to work, measuring ingredients into a large, earthenware bowl. As Mr. Roth peered over my shoulder, I did yoga breathing and tried to appear normal. On the inside, I felt anything but.

"Did Barry run to the fishmonger and get the lump crabmeat?"

"That's my next project," I said evasively. I had no idea what was in the fridge or who was supposed to do what, as Edward was the number one on this job. I hated being in the dark, but I guessed I'd have to improvise till he showed up this morning. It was a small price to pay.

Roth hovered behind me. "I'm gonna go get showered. Send me up a misto, will you, and send a filter coffee for Lady Penelope. If she whines for instant, tell her I ordered the coffee and just leave it. She doesn't get it. Coffee, I mean. The English don't know anything about coffee." He glanced at my coffee mug. "Not like we do, right?" That "we" tipped me off balance. For half a second, I envisioned the two of us sitting at a foggy, outdoor Seattle café, sipping lattes and reading novels together. *Edward, Juliet! You'd be drinking coffee with Edward.* I forced myself to take cups down from the cabinet. I felt like a puppet in my own body, like I couldn't predict what crazy act I might commit next.

"I certainly will," I declared, trying to sound normal. There was a pause and I could feel him standing there, waiting for something. I stood still, my hands clutching the china cups. *That sounded weird,* I thought to myself. *He knows everything.*

"Hey, Juliet," he said, in a softer tone of voice. "About last night…"

Here it comes, I thought. *He's going to fire me for sleeping with Edward.* I cut him off, saying, "I can explain…"

"No I want to explain," he said. "I botched that conversation. I wanted to talk to you about what happened in Nantucket, and more to the point, what happened here in the drawing room, well…it meant something to me. I know I'm…I'm married. At the moment, but…" He walked up behind me and put his hand on the small of my back. Just then, Barry, the gardener came in through the back door of the pantry, his arms laden with boughs and boughs of holly branches. Mr. Roth turned and strode out the swinging oak door, leaving it flapping on its hinges. I watched the door close, then turned back to my Aga. I heard creepy Barry laughing with a nasty cough as he walked through.

Did Jasper just say "at the moment"? I wondered, turning my attention back to my pot. After last night, pretending nothing had ever happened. Or, oh my God, was he going to confess something? Surely not. After all, he was married, and that made him the bad guy. But maybe he was. *Or maybe that's all in your head, Juliet.* I chided myself. *You've been attracted to him since that night at the Aquarium. Oh shut up!* I told myself, but my body was remembering how dynamic Jasper Roth had been the night I'd met him. The night I'd also met Ben.

****

Back while I was still working at The Ivy, Posy had whisked me to a benefit for the London Aquarium, an event with a capital E… surprisingly well attended by nobility, glitterati and money men, and for that night only, I let loose and practically hosed myself down in the free champagne. Posy dolled me up in a shimmery, form-skimming Zac Posen gown that looked alternately silver or aqua depending how the light hit ("It's like the *ocean*," she'd squealed, jumping up and down and clapping her hands at the sight of me emerging from her en-suite dressing room). Posy was done up in a pale, seafoam green gown concocted from a fabric that made it look painted on. On her head, she wore a tiara with a trident, suggesting that she was the daughter of Neptune himself. On anyone else, it would have looked like a cheap costume. On Posy, it was the perfect marriage of fantasy and royalty.

"You're gorgeous," I told her in the car. She'd brought a bottle of wine and two plastic glasses. It was like surfing, trying to balance the glasses, walk in heels and not spill anything on my dress.

"We're practically twins. If I am, you are." The wine and the cheerleading made me feel a tiny bit sultry. At first I'd been self-conscious in the tight dress, but I soon found myself mimicking Posy's flirty confidence.

Her father's driver dropped us at the door and we (or should I say she?) got a lot of attention with our entrance. We walked into a lavishly staged room filled with tanks of various sea life, giant screens projecting live feeds from the Aquarium itself and wave-like lighting designed to make us feel underwater. That was where I first laid eyes on Jasper Roth.

One of my favorite things about a do like this was checking out the food. Tonight's theme was Miniature Feasts, which meant that the food was all hors d'oeuvres and canapés, with everything cleverly served in shot glasses, on endive leaves or as "lollipops" on sticks. Often, you'd also find bite-sized delectables served on oyster or scallop shells, but since this was an Aquarium event, I noticed that catering seemed to be a "no fish zone." I would have been more comfortable in the kitchen than out on the floor. In fact, I was dying to sneak a peek behind the double doors to see how they pulled all this off from behind the scenes. This was without a doubt the fanciest party I'd ever been to. I just kept repeating to myself, *You were invited. You belong here. You're a guest.*

As I wobbled tipsily over to a canapé station on Posy's absurdly elevated and spiky Jimmy Choos (she cannot understand why I wear Dansko clogs in the kitchen) to check out what was being offered in order to mentally file away and steal recipes and presentations, I overheard a low, growly voice saying "…Andover, then Yale, then Harvard." The deep, rich tone of it sent a little shiver up my spine. I only saw the back of the man speaking. He had a full head of thick, curly dark hair, and a compact but solid and proportionate body. It was the classic upside-down triangle shape of broad shoulders, trim waist and tight bottom. He was clad in an unparalleled navy blue wool suit (Savile Row?) that was simultaneously a bit too uptight and made him stand out as more important than any other man in the room.

As I was peering over his shoulder to inspect the greenish sauce on the beef slices in the Chinese ceramic spoons on the table in front of him, my ankle gave way and I had no choice but to grab him by the shoulders from behind in an invasive bear hug to avoid going down like the *Lusitania*.

"Oh, shit…I mean, darn. Wow, sorry," I stammered, righting myself and almost knocking him off balance. He braced himself against the table with one hand, and pushed my hip hard with the palm of his other so I'd be upright again. I must have looked like one of those tall-haired, vinyl blow-up dolls waving wildly outside of car dealerships. "Oh, man, I'm just so sorry. Seriously… just, well, apologies," I said as I turned on my heel, slinking off to look for Posy.

As I turned to make my getaway, he expertly caught my wrist in his hand and spun me gracefully back around to face him as though we'd been taking pre-wedding dance lessons together for months. It left me breathless. I pretended it didn't.

"I'm not sorry. Who are you?" he demanded loudly in his broad-voweled Mid-Atlantic accent, Grecian-blue eyes boring into mine like he owned me. I got the feeling he thought he owned everything he laid eyes on. Those same eyes then took the liberty of skimming my cleavage, (hoisted up and presented in an Agent Provocateur bra), my hips, and the outline of my legs in the filmy dress, only to come back up to rest on my lips. He was still holding my wrist tightly, and the edge of his wedding band pressed into the bone. After Stephen, I'd been working hard on never again letting a man control me. Sure, I could be a servant, but I had tonight off.

That didn't stop my body from betraying me. When his eyes left my lips and came back to meet mine, they were searching for an answer to more questions than "Who are you?" *Oh my God.* My brain ricocheted off the inside of my skull. *He wants to have sex with me.* I hadn't had sex since Stephen. In fact, I hadn't had sex before Stephen, so imagining a strange man wanted me for sex and sex only sent me reeling. My belly dissolved into hot liquid and my breathing went shallow and quickened. *For God's sake,*

Juliet, I admonished myself. *Pull it together.* He was the worst kind of man in my book and the champagne had obviously clouded my judgment. *To him, you're a cross between a cater-waiter and a call girl. He must be ten years older than you are. Just like Stephen.* Angry with myself, I directed it at this American and answered him.

"I'm really nobody. Nobody you need to know," I said flatly, extending my spine ballerina-style and making a point of looking down at him. He's slightly shorter than I am. I felt like I was in a play that I hadn't rehearsed. "Again, very sorry. Goodbye."

With all the concentration I could muster, I turned and walked away without tripping or wavering. This was a monumental feat considering A) I was drunk, B) I was hopped-up on pheromones, and C) the waves of light projected over the floor made me feel swimmy. I could feel him watching me leave and was careful to keep my behind in check, with no hint of swishing or swaying. From the corner of my eye, I saw a man pull himself up from a violently red love seat shaped like a pair of fish's lips, lankily extend himself to full height and cross the room to fall in step with me.

"Have a nice trip?" the stranger teased.

I was in no mood for laddish pranking. Wanting to get out of there, I searched the room for Posy. I spotted her holding court in the far diagonal corner near a tank of sea turtles. There was a teenage boy, and old man, and a Fran Lebowitz lookalike, all hanging on her every word. I arrowed toward them, the stranger still walking shoulder-to-shoulder with me.

"Go away," I said, not even turning to look at him. I had dropped my party manners a while back and since he wasn't being nice, I didn't feel the need to be, either.

"You're American?"

"None of your business," I said.

"I saw the whole thing back there," he said, cornering me against a shiny, chrome room divider. It was cool on my bare shoulders. "You have to admire the old Casanova. And I suppose, you, too. I'm tough in the courtroom, but I don't have the bollocks to put

Jasper Roth in his place."

Jasper Roth, I thought to myself, filing away the name. *I've read about him.* "Don't you have anything better to do than watch me?" I asked my pest. "In some circles, you'd get arrested for that."

"'Fraid not, my ladyfriend has abandoned me for the social climbing, leaving me to the Miniature Feasts. I was told there'd be a meal…I've popped about 200 of those little bites into my mouth and I'm still ravenous. All the waiters know my name and I believe their managers have given them instructions to stop feeding me. I'm like one of those seals on the flat-screens behind you, barking and clapping for morsels. Nothing bite-sized about a nice big girl like you, though, is there?"

I raised my hand, thinking of giving him a slap in the face when I realized he wasn't criticizing me, he was eyeballing me with appreciation. "I love a woman my height," he said sincerely, though in fact, he was about two inches taller than I was, even in my heels. "I also like a bit of meat on the bones. There's something cold and hard about these rich, skinny chicks." He nodded in the direction of a pinched-looking stickbug in a gown that cost more than my car, whom I took to be his *ladyfriend*. "Like bedding down with a bicycle."

Despite myself, I relaxed and took him in. Nice smile, slim, in a well-cut suit with crisp white shirt and no tie, Gucci loafers, hair thinning a bit on top but appropriately cut, very short with perfectly fashionable sideburns, and…his eyes. One was brown and the other was blue. I'd never seen anything like it except once in an Australian herding dog and I couldn't stop staring.

He leaned in and whispered, "I'd kill for a massive plate of pasta bolognese, smothered with an unseemly amount of grated Parmesan cheese." Face to face, he had the nerve to push his knee ever-so-slightly in between my legs. Looking back on it, it wasn't exactly a promising start if I was looking for a stable, marrying type, since he was there with a date. Maybe it was all the French wine, or possibly the residual humming in my cells left over from the electricity between Jasper Roth and me. Or, maybe a small part of me had wanted a one-night stand with a powerful married man, but this seemed more honorable. None of it mattered. I looked him straight in the eye and said, "You're in luck. I'm the best chef in London. Your kitchen or mine?"

****

"Still deckin' the halls," Barry said to me, coming back through the entrance from the pantry to the kitchen with a fresh armload of branches. I didn't turn around from my pot. "If you have anything that needs deckin', let ol' Barry know."

I turned around and started after him with my spoon. He swung through the oak door, quickly. That swinging door played a huge role in my life at The Hall. When it opened, there was a corner of the vast, cherrywood farmhouse kitchen table that those in the adjacent dining room and hallway – namely the family and their guests – would get a glimpse of. Whatever was on the corner of the table would signify what was going on in the kitchen. Therefore we staff "planted" items there as a comfort to our employers, a sign that all was well and under control in the kitchen.

I took the pasta machine from under the counter, and clamped it to the corner of the table and reached for the flour container. Sprinkling flour over the machine, the table and – why not? – the front of my apron, I ensured that the family would be filled with smug pride when I presented freshly made, but bought-from-the-supermarket, pasta later. I picked up one of the phones that served as an intercom for the palace in which we worked and called for Rose. "The soufflé has risen," I intoned, code for Mr. Roth has gone above stairs. "Bring the juices."

I busied myself with two frying pans sizzling with meat and a vat containing a warm stew of seasonal fruit. Opening the oven door, I slid out a sheet of cranberry-walnut scones and put in a pan of oversized, Southern-style buttermilk biscuits that were, as

88

they say, "as big as a cat's head".

I surrendered to the process of preparing the 23-item buffet that was demanded at every breakfast taken at The Hall when Roth was *en famille*, regardless of whether or not the family had guests. It's a wonder I could think straight on so little sleep, but as I worked I watched the door for Edward, taking advantage of the solitude to replay highlights from last night in my head. A stroke up the thigh here, a flick of the tongue there. I remembered when Aunt Suze had said, "I'm afraid he doesn't get you," when I'd left school for Stephen. She was right, of course. The verdict was still out on Ben. In four hours, however, Edward showed me that he "got me" in at least one arena.

Four of the twenty-three breakfast items were sausages – all of which came from different butchers. I pulled them out of every nook and cranny of the Sub-Zero. As Mr. Roth said frequently and with the fervor of a religious zealot, "More is more!"

The sausage directives from my employer were exacting – the chicken and apple sausage, made with organic fennel, was to be fashioned into patties and fried separately from the beef and pork sausages. The word "fried," however, was akin to an expletive to Mr. Roth. We, in the kitchen, gently referred to the process of heating and browning the meat in a heavy skillet as "pan searing".

The kielbasa, acquired from Krzysztof's butcher's shop, located an inconvenient two shires away, had to be done outdoors, on the grill, à la Bobby Flay…regardless of the weather. My boss is the type of man who equates grilling with masculinity and never lets a session go by without having handled the grilling tools for at least a couple of minutes.

"Now that's a sausage!" he would exhort to his duly appreciative breakfast guests as they clucked over the meaty *pièce de résistance*, held aloft. "The casing is ovine, which in my opinion gives it the extra 'snap' when you bite into it. And the filling is ground pork and lamb, mixed with onion and a little dill. I send my chef specifically to the Polish guy for it. When I'm at the ski chalet, I have it flown in." This was a speech I'd heard so many times, I could recite it in my sleep.

With Roth, it was about appearances. It made me feel sad for him, in a way. The pressure to always come off as the smartest and the most in control had paralyzed Mother. I wondered what it did to Jasper Roth. He must sense that I see the man behind the curtain, as they say in Oz. Why else would he have ever talked so personally, or crossed a line with one of his staff? It went against his whole philosophy of looking perfect and proper.

I assumed that's why he married the dull but titled Lady. They'd been wed nearly five years, and people were beginning to whisper about her aging past her fertility window. "She's getting a little dry in the husk," Terrence once exhorted, never one to whisper. "They'd better get cracking."

Although she didn't bring youth or beauty to the match, she brought her status, her father's notoriety and presumably, in the future, Thornton Hall. At any given cocktail party, movers and shakers certainly perked up when Roth casually recounted tales of his stepfather-in-law, England's most celebrated modern painter. This pumped up Roth's ego and countered The Lady's blandness. On occasion, she overcame her own blandness, unfortunately with unexpected doses of crazy.

To broadcast his deep affiliation with the family, Jasper Roth had spent buckets of money buying up portraits of The Lady's ancestors, along with The Earl's current works, loaning some to museums and lining the walls of his many homes with others, setting them among his Hirsts, Warhols, Twomblys, and his sarcastic Rockwells. Involuntarily, I glanced up at a still-life of a fruit plate by Cezanne that hung beside the kitchen window. *Who hangs a Cezanne in the kitchen?* I thought, shaking my head a little. I saw the clock, too, and started to worry about falling behind.

Breathe, Juliet, I coached myself. *You're good at this.* Back in Paris, determined to make it without help, I cooked my way through a variety of restaurant types – a method for pan-seared scallops here, the secret to perfect consommé there, and the swiftest, cleanest and most efficient ways to make it all happen. I remember calling my mother from Posy's apartment, brimming with excitement.

"I'm working toward becoming a chef!"

After a long pause, she said, "So you're kitchen help." I could almost hear the wheels turning in her head. "Come home. I'll bail you out of this mess. We'll get you into med school, one way or another."

"I don't want to be a psychiatrist," I'd told her.

She sighed. "OK, if you want to get your Masters in psychology first, we can look into that. I'd prefer you were a real doctor, but we have to start somewhere. It's not my top choice for you."

"You don't get a choice for me!" I'd yelled into the phone.

"You are not on point, Juliet. Do you think I achieved what I have by flipping a coin, or by seeing which way the wind blew me? First you get to point A, then B, then C until you can take care of yourself. Look where following your heart has gotten you so far. You're a short-order cook in a foreign country. Life's not all about laughter and orgasms and fine food. You're every bit as foolish as Piers Conley-Weatherall!"

"Why would you bring him up?"

"I'm just saying you should go to med school, so you can get a job."

"I have a job."

"Sure and with a little work, you could climb the ladder all the way to Taco Bell."

I'd hung up on her. Her *and* her crisp pantsuits and tightly pulled bun. *Why can't I have a family who cheers me on and makes cardboard signs to welcome me when I fly into my home airport and who thinks I'm "just swell" the way I am?* I fumed. *Or a horde of brothers and sisters so I could get lost in the crowd?* I remember that old hole in my heart as my anger melted into longing. *Or at least a dad.*

Tending to the stovetop, I shifted my thoughts to Edward. *Maybe life is all about laughter and orgasms and fine food,* I thought, grinning. Freud would have a field day with my renting brain space to my mother after rolling out of my new lover's warm bed. *My new lover!* Normally, I cringed at the word lover, but in this case, it seemed to describe every nuance of the situation. *Lover!*

I heard the back door open and footsteps walking through the laundry room and the pantry. I knew instinctively that it was Edward. I kept my back turned and my eyes on my pans and pot, trying to look nonchalant. I heard him walk across the kitchen, and felt him stop right behind me. Without my consent, all the parts of me he'd touched in bed began tingling with the memory of it.

"Who does a fella have to sleep with to get a cup of tea around here?" he whispered into the back of my neck, the length of his whole body pressing against the back of mine. He had morning voice, husky and deep. My knees weakened and I leaned back against him for a split second, luxuriating in the firm support of him.

One of the sausages split and popped in the pan, startling me back to reality. I leaped sideways, wielding my spatula. "Me," I whispered, "but that's our little secret, right?"

I avoided touching him as I circled around to flip on the electric kettle and pulled down a box of tea bags. "As you can see, Edward," I said angling my face toward the oak door, "most of breakfast has been started."

He walked forward, arms open, and circled them around me, comfortably cupping my behind. "Why are you talking like that? No one's up yet." He leaned in and brushed my cheek with his. It was warm and damp and smelled like balsam shaving cream. I melted into his chest for a few seconds.

"Edward," I said, my mouth close to his ear. "Mr. Roth was down already." I felt guilty saying his name, but that was stupid. "Barry was just here."

"Roth's in the shower by now," he said, kissing me full on the lips. What seemed like a week later, he pulled back to say, "And sod Barry, I'm having my breakfast." He gave me another slow, deep kiss. I relaxed and started kissing him back, marveling at how good he was at this. Every nibble was a welcome tease and every move of his tongue left me wanting more.

The kitchen timer went off and I jumped backward, flinging his arms out to the side. "The biscuits!" Grabbing an oven mitt, I pulled out the tray. "Edward," I whispered urgently. "We cannot do this. Not here. Not now."

"You're right," he said, contritely. "Here is a bad idea."

I let out my breath, relieved. "Good, this is good. I'll just get breakfast laid out." I switched off all the burners on the stove. I'd need to transfer everything to the chafing dishes in the dining room.

While I was talking, he'd crossed to the corner of the kitchen, opening the door to the giant larder with the marble shelves that could easily house a family of four. He strode purposefully back to me, turned me around by the shoulders and frog-marched me into the larder, shutting the old, heavy door behind us with a click.

Pinning me up against it, he knelt down in front of me and pushed up my chef's coat, kissing my belly.

"No," I whispered. "This is crazy."

"Hush, they'll hear." He eased down my chef's trousers, deftly untying the cord in the semi-darkness and urgently yanked down my panties. I could feel the cold air on my body, and I was electrified. I gripped his head with both hands.

"Edward, no," I protested weakly. He pulled back and I could see him looking up at my face. "Shh…"

He kissed a line all the way down, and without warning, his tongue connected with the precise spot that was aching for it, and I moaned. I was vaguely aware that maybe I should hide the fact that I'd gotten so excited so quickly and how now I wouldn't say no even if the vicar walked in.

"Don't stop," I heard myself saying. My voice sounded two

octaves lower than normal. "Oh, Edward, yes, oh my God."

His strong hands were gripping my hips, holding me still, so hard I was sure he'd leave fingermarks, but I didn't care. I closed my eyes, spirals of color whirling behind them, and lay my head back against the hard wood, surrendering to the pleasure. Finally, my body relaxed and went calm. Like magic, Edward was standing in front of me, tying my pants. *When did he manage to pull up my underwear and my pants?* I wondered vaguely, as he wrapped me in his arms.

"It's not fair," I said. "I didn't do anything for you." My eyes were used to the dark now and I looked into his, worried.

He gave a soft laugh. "That *was* for me. You still don't get it, do you? I'm mad for you." He pulled me to his chest, and held me there. After a while, he said, "We'd better get back to it," and gave me a squeeze. When he reached behind me to turn the knob, the light blinded me. I blinked and looked around the kitchen. It all looked different.

"We'd better hurry," he said, pouring the water into his cup. "Time's ticking." He poured in the milk. "No matter though," he said, taking a sip and letting out an "ahhh". "We can just tell them you got waylaid."

To my relief, Rose and Daphne rushed in with trays balancing three large carafes of juice – one blood orange, one pink grapefruit and one regular orange juice. Technically, these should have been squeezed fresh before breakfast, but given the early hour and sheer number of dishes expected, this was a place to cut corners. They were a mix of store-bought and pre-squeezed, kept across the cobbled courtyard, in the fridge at Rose Cottage, out of the sight of prying American eyes.

Daphne and I took the juice through to the dining room, where Barry was up on a ladder, fastening holly to the frame of *The Veiled Madonna*. He was one servant who lived off the grounds, in town. That suited me fine, because he was a creepy old lech. I ignored him and got to work arranging the juices on the sideboard. On a card table in the corner of the room sat Isaac's replica of St. Paul's Cathedral in London, constructed from gingerbread. It was magnificent with a snow-covered dome, beribboned wreaths on the windows, tiny evergreens and bare oaks in the courtyard, and it was all made out of food, down to the winter trees fashioned out of chocolate Twizzlers and the piped frosting "snow". There was a magnificent green and red skirt on the table, brocaded with gilt thread, and probably hand-sewn by some indentured servant's wife from hundreds of years ago. If you looked up Christmas in the dictionary you should find a picture of this display. Massive as it was, I wondered if they'd move it to the table for the Christmas Day lunch centerpiece.

High on his ladder, Barry was draping garlands of fresh greenery on the crown molding. "*Cuisse de nymph*, eh?" he said, nodding sideways at the painting, raising his eyebrows at us. I looked at the painting.

The Veiled Madonna is a compelling portrait of a fully nude young woman, who is ripely pregnant. In fact, many have said that the famous *Vanity Fair* cover photo of Demi Moore that caused such a stir was a blatant rip-off of it. In *The Veiled Madonna*, the subject wears a black mantilla, entirely covering her head, but nothing else. She's standing, and on a console beside her sits a bright, blood-red envelope with an orange wax seal, with an elaborate letter G swirled into it. The woman in the painting covers her breasts with a clutch of laurel leaves and her lady parts with a rose.

"*Cuisse de Nymph*, get it? The breed of the rose what's between her legs. Thigh of the nymph, eh?" He leered, alternating between Daphne and me, and the portrait. He took a swig from a small, silver flask from his hip pocket.

"Yes, I understand. I studied in Paris," I said coldly. I situated my body between his and Daphne's. I focused my attention on arranging the food I'd been setting on the sideboard all morning.

"Oh, gay Par-ee," he said, cackling knowingly. "I'll bet you learned a trick or two there..."

"Yes, at La Marmite I learned to make a salad of goat cheese and *rognons blancs de coq.*"

"What's that when it's at home?" he asked, chuckling.

"Rooster's testicles," I told him crisply, stabbing a cheese knife into an oversized wheel of firm Huntsman. Daphne, letting out a tiny squeak, skittered through the south door into the library.

Pocketing his whiskey, Barry oozed past Terrence, who was coming through the swinging oak door, and disappeared.

"There she is," Terrence sang, carrying in a tray of polished silver, "and from the looks of that beard-burn, I'd say she has a lot in common with that basket of eggs I found on the back landing."

A feeling of dread landed in my gut. "What do you mean?"

"Freshly laid this morning!"

"*Shut up*," I whispered, ashen. "Whatever it is you think you know, you don't need to tell the rest of the house."

"I don't just think I know," he said, casually laying the silver in its drawer's velvet tray. "I know I know."

"Right, Miss Marple," I scoffed bravely. I carved a wedge out of the cheese wheel, and began to lay slices on the plate. "Just because I have a little breakout and my hair needs a brush, you think you've uncovered a secret."

"No," he said matter-of-factly, "it's because I saw you sucking the face off the head chef before bolting across the courtyard at sunrise."

"Shh! Shh! Shh!" I hissed. "Keep your voice down. What, were you spying on me?"

"Believe me, I wasn't. You in your nightclothes was the last thing I needed to see before I've had my tea. I woke up to have a wee."

"*Outside?*"

"I believe I'm the one passing judgment at the moment. What's it to you, anyway?"

"Your cottage has a bathroom," I said, putting serving spoons in pots of jam. "Why didn't you use that?"

"Your cottage has a bed. Same back to you."

"Terrence!" Jasper Roth said pushing through the door to the dining room. "Just the man I needed to see!"

I begged him with my eyes not to spill any beans.

"When you check the picnic hampers, make sure the chocolates I got from Belgium made it in. I want the ones with Meyer lemon and pine nuts and put in the ancho chile and cinnamon ones, too. Did someone get those out of the cellar?"

"I believe Juliet went down just this morning," Terrence said, with mischief in his eye. I gave him a pleading look.

"As long as someone's on top of it," said Roth.

"Oh, Juliet is on top of it," Terrence said gleefully. "In fact, I'd say she's been bending over backwards since well before sunset." I couldn't take the pressure. I had to bolt.

"If you'll excuse me, I have to start on the mince for more pies," I said edging out the door.

"With your permission, Mr. Roth," Terrence said, following me, "I'll just help Juliet. Even with her experience here at The Hall, I'm not sure if she can handle those huge sacks of nuts on her own."

Outside in the hallway, he doubled over, soundlessly laughing, as tears formed in the corners of his eyes.

"Very funny! You've had your laugh, but remember, I'm the one who controls where the leftover French pâté and Russian caviar go at the end of the night. Shut your trap or you'll be eating like a peasant for the rest of the holiday."

"Have it your way, but you might want to check your guild's handbook," he whispered, ascending the staircase. "Last I heard, trollops were supposed to have a sense of humor."

Chapter Eight

"Those flurries have become a light snow, and lovely it is. I thought of asking Jane to help in the main house today, but she's too weak, poor thing. I told her to stay wrapped up in bed. Isaac agrees. He's a good husband to Jane," Rose said, bringing in a round of dirty dishes from the dining room. Breakfast was being slung and inhaled in full force. I was doing some basic side work – chopping herbs, refilling the pepper mills, washing lettuce. "She's been sleeping round the clock, and can't keep anything down. Good job she already took this week off from the Post Office, or she'd be calling in sick."

"We don't need help," I told Rose. "I could do breakfast blindfolded and Edward should be here any minute, he's just popped out," I said, glancing at the clock. He wasn't in the kitchen when I'd come back in – which was lucky because I could feel my chest breaking out into a flush at just the thought of him. I was glad I had on my mandarin-collar jacket. Just to be safe, I pretended to stir a pot of boiling water on the stove, so I could excuse the red face. Part of me wanted to spill the beans about Edward to Rose, but I hadn't told her I'd broken up with Ben yet. However motherly, she was still a church-going senior citizen. I'd have to dole it out in teaspoons, if I didn't want to give her a coronary. And God forbid I asked her thoughts on Jasper Roth's behavior. Even thinking I'd had a mild flirt with a married man would have her dragging me to confession by the hair. *And maybe it should, Juliet, I warned myself. Lust-crazy behavior with single men is one thing, adultery is crossing the line into madville. You've dipped your toe into brazen tart territory, but let's stay away from being a homewrecker.*

Just then, Lady Penelope pushed through the oak door into the kitchen, wearing her dressing gown. She marched over to the kettle to flip on the switch, but saw that it was already on the boil. I did nothing at Thornton Hall if not make endless cups of tea.

"Good morning, Lady Penelope," Rose said.

"Good morning, Your Ladyship," I said, nervous that she was in the kitchen. It always rattled us when one of the family crossed into our territory. "Can I get you anything?"

"I've come in to make myself a cup of Sanka. There was filter coffee on my tray," she said archly.

"Why not rest in your room?" Rose asked her. "Juliet will make it."

That phrase was like nails on a chalkboard to me. I'd worked for an American family who'd gotten rich quick in the stock market. Every time the husband so much as reached for a glass to fill with water, the wife would scream, "Put that down! What do you think we pay her for? Juliet will make it!" In that moment, however, I'd have endured being called a slave if it meant Lady Penelope would leave.

"Excuse me?" she said sharply to me. "Are you even listening to me? Surely Edward told you I prefer Sanka?"

"He didn't mention it," I skirted, popping back to the present. *Your husband happened to, though, and he forbade me to give it to you,* I wanted to say, but I was already afraid she could read my mind and knew about the drawing room. "Please, allow me," I said, taking down a china cup.

"Oh dear! I see there are prawns on the counter, there. Were you informed of my shellfish allergy?" she asked, in a slightly hysterical voice.

"Yes, Your Ladyship. If you recall, I've worked for your family on numerous occasions, and I'm always scrupulously careful. As instructed, I separate it from other foods, plate in on special serving platters and only serve it from the sideboard."

"Hmph," she answered. "As long as you're aware. You'll need to keep track of our needs and preferences now that you're head chef for this holiday," she told me.

"But Edward's head chef, Your Ladyship," I said.

"Are you listening to me? You're head chef, now. Edward's car's just pulled out of the drive. He won't be in service this holiday. It's just as well. With the guest cancellations, having two chefs wasn't sensible. Poor Edward, he was quite distressed, saying he had to get out of here on the next train, so naturally I gave him the time off, no questions asked. We spoke early this morning, and he seemed keen to pack and move out right away."

My brain reeled and dipped like an eagle swooping after a sparrow. I grabbed the counter for support.

"Edward left? I…I don't understand…" I stammered.

"Before I left his cottage," she said, looking at me sidelong from under her lashes, "he mentioned that he needed to go home to clear his head."

"When were you at his cottage?"

"Juliet, dear," Rose cut in, pushing me toward the pantry, "please look for that jar of coffee I need." She was protecting me.

"That doesn't make sense," I mumbled, allowing myself to be guided . *What could I have done to make him bolt?* "Did he say…?"

"Now, Lady Penny, don't trouble yourself. We'll bring you your hot drink," Rose interrupted. "Juliet, never mind the coffee" she said pushing me over to the kettle, "will you boil the water?" I opened my mouth again, but Rose cut me off. "I'll bring it up the stairs and you can enjoy it with a bit of privacy." Rose lead her by the shoulders to the door.

"Normally, Edward brings it directly to my room," she said, turning back around to face me. "But thank you, Rose. That would be lovely. It's just as well he's taking a break, really. From the start, I thought it was frivolous to have two chefs, but Jasper insisted we hire Juliet." She looked at me with extreme concentration but seemed to have trouble focusing. "I mean an extra chef, of course, not you in particular."

"But, wait! I mean, excuse me, Your Ladyship. Did Edward say…"

"I'll have your coffee up in two shakes, Ladyship," Rose said, gesturing to the door, and encouraging her to go out. "That's right then, go have a nice rest," Rose said, as Lady Penelope left the kitchen.

Rose shook her head at me, whispering "Stay clear of her, that's my advice."

I couldn't help myself, "Does she go to Edward's cottage?"

"Not that I know of, but she doesn't report to me, does she?"

"Was she there this morning, or did Edward come here to ask for time off?"

"I'm sure I don't know, Juliet." She sounded exasperated. "If Edward comes back you can ask him, if you're so keen to know. Last I saw of him, Mr. Roth was putting him in a car with Barry at the wheel. Now you know as much as I know."

As she swung out the door with the Sanka on a tray, I tried to stay nonchalant. I picked up the peck of apples I'd nearly tripped on as I came up the stone steps to the kitchen this morning. At country houses, you never knew what would turn up, foraged or shot on the land. I dumped apples into the sink to wash. I'd have to thank Seamus or Isaac or MacGregor the groundskeeper, or whomever it was who'd left them there. On autopilot, I started peeling the fruit. I'd sugar them and set them aside. The Countess and the Lady never ate chocolate, due to their migraines, and preferred fruit desserts. There were enough apples to make pies for them, and the staff as well. I was grateful for something to occupy my hands.

"Did she say any more about Edward's leaving?" I asked Rose, when she swung back through with her empty tray.

"No, she didn't! The only other thing I remember is that he asked for the holiday off ages ago, and Lady Penelope pushed him to work. His father's been taken ill, has been for awhile. Maybe that's it," she said, picking up a towel and hand-drying the crystal flutes in the dish rack.

"Well, it doesn't make sense."

Rose gave me an assessing once-over. "Keep to your own business. You heard Lady Penelope. He asked again, she said yes. Case closed. She's very protective over Edward…" She moved a kitchen step and began carefully placing flutes on a high shelf.

"Now don't mind about Edward being gone. Are you nervous taking over? You've handled this many guests, and more, a number of times. Oh my, look at that," she said, pointing to the window above the sink, "snow's picking up. I'd say the birding party had better bundle. After I do the crystal, I'm going to look for warmer boots for the Countess. I'll get her lined Barbours. She's been busy with the guests all morning and won't think of it herself."

Rose fulfilled her function as lady's maid to the Countess impeccably, but there's a distance in their relationship. Often, ladies and their maids become thick as thieves, enjoying a sisterly relationship that crossed the class boundary. Forty years of knowing the Countess had given Rose a second sense about her needs but the Countess was nothing more than cordial.

"Did Edward ever mention a girlfriend?" I was desperately searching for answers, and trying not to be obvious.

"Not that I can recall. Some have gossiped that he had a girl back home, but you can't believe what you hear unless it comes from the horse's mouth. I suppose life in the military taught him how to be on his own and keep to himself." She turned and peered at me closely, a warm, assessing look in her eye that made me nearly blush. "If you weren't with your Ben, then I would have wished Edward for you. But it's not meant to be. Ah look, is that the time?" She gave me a quick squeeze and swept out of the kitchen without waiting for an answer.

She was a softie and a romantic, but Rose wasn't always hearts and roses. When she was protecting the weak, especially her son, Isaac, she was as fiery as her scarlet-dyed hair, teased and sculpted on top of her head.

It was nearly impossible to look away from Rose's hair. It's the kind of thing you don't get used to. A disturbingly unnatural shade, it teetered between purplish-magenta and apricot. Years ago, we'd been shopping in the village, when she'd pointed to a gorgeous young girl with alabaster skin and long, wavy auburn hair, gleaming in the sun like a polished copper pot, and said to me, "She's the spitting image of me at her age…" Much as I love Rose, it was hard to imagine the stout housekeeper as a ripe milkmaid.

Generally easygoing, on the rare occasion when Rose got truly angry, she clomped around like a fishwife, shrieking and muttering. It was usually Jasper Roth who got her dander up.

"I'm so livid, I swear the color has drained from my hair! That man is an, an…*arse*," she'd whisper, "and I don't say that lightly!"

Seamus, the perfect yin to her yang, was always the portrait of even-handed calm. "Of course he is, my dear. No one here has ever doubted it for a minute. Now, have a cup of tea to calm yourself." And, giraffe-like, he'd steer her to a kitchen chair and lope over to switch on the electric kettle. To this day, he behaves as if they were courting and there might be a chance he'll lose her. I really can't imagine anyone ever treating me that way. But in the back of my brain, there's still a tiny, pre-verbal, lizard-simple part of me that wants it – that stupid clump of neurons that conspired way back when to put my butt in an Air France seat to chase down Stephen.

****

My last semester of college, Stephen Schechter came to Bard to teach a seminar on female archetypes in American television, and, aspirant culture-hound that I was, I drank in his persona like a nectar. In Louisville, men and boys alike wore pleated khakis

104

and golf shirts as dress clothes, watched college sports and went to church with their families. Sex, politics and God were not discussed, but it was assumed that sex was had with opposite-gender partners, good citizens were fiscally conservative and didn't believe in big government, but everyone did believe in God. Needless to say, my mother fit in like a zebra on a farm there, but I went to school with these people. I had to make an effort. They were my milieu. And frankly, even though the boys were conserva-tive, cookie-cutter preppies, they might have been nice for a few practice swings, if Mother had ever stopped hovering over me.

Stephen's worldliness made my head thrum. Six-foot-four, with John Lennon glasses, he had a wry smile and a killer vocabulary. He'd published an arty novel as a Harvard undergrad, he curated and traveled with a vintage collection of Warner Brothers cartoon cells, and was a jazz drummer. I kid you not. He spoke fluent French and wrote television and film reviews for the American newswire in Paris, where he lived most of the year. He may have been a professor, but he was not an academic. I couldn't believe my luck when he beamed his light on me, ten years his junior, so I did anything and everything I could to keep his interest.

"Miss Hill," Stephen said as class was breaking up one day, "walk with me." It was not a request. I sensed something risky and exciting in this man and my pulse quickened. At Bard, no one called anyone "Miss" or "Mr" anything, so it was clearly a game, a flirt. I picked up my things and fell into step with him. He was leading me off the path, into the grass, toward his car. "I need a work-study student to catalogue my media clips. Are you interested?" His long, oxblood leather duster was billowing open, making him look like a futuristic cowboy or a super hero. Only really, really tall men can get away with full-length coats. And only if they're wearing boots. Which, of course, he was.

"Um, I'm already using my allotted work-study hours in the psych lab, setting up for trials and clinical studies." I rushed to keep pace with him. His strides were twice as long as mine. By the time he opened the driver's-side door of his hybrid Toyota Highlander, I was breathless. "I don't think they'll approve payment."

"Hmm, we're two intelligent people. Surely we can figure this out." He got in the car, reached across and flung open the passenger door. He motioned for me to climb in, and I did, shutting the door. "I've got an idea," he said leaning over and kissing me on the mouth, "why don't we do it under the table?"

I sold my car to buy my plane ticket to Paris ("It would infantilize you if I bought it," Stephen had told me). The day I arrived at the door of the flat in Le Marais where Stephen had been house-sitting for a few weeks, I expected a heart-fluttering, romantic reunion filled with glasses of *rosé* at outdoor cafes, visits to the Louvre, and, of course, long hours of alternately tender and bone-bruising sex. It had been nearly a month, and now that I knew what I was missing, I missed it. I dreamed about how we'd discuss current events and pop culture, and there would be pillow whispers about how he'd missed me. And maybe, there'd be a ring.

What I was greeted with was a whiny, self-absorbed "artiste" in a dirty bathrobe, who couldn't stop complaining about his allergies and the pollution and the overcrowding in Paris in the summer. My first night there, we stayed in and ate half a stale baguette and some wilty asparagus vinaigrette out of the half-sized fridge for dinner. After some world-weary and distracted lovemaking on his part, I rolled over and tried to sleep, my mind racing, hoping it would all seem better in the light of day. In the morning, he sent me out for milk.

"This antique bed's too small for two people. Those eighteenth-century Gallic bastards were homunculi! I wish we had a king...I didn't sleep at all last night. I'm too irritated to write. How am I supposed to finish my screenplay with people everywhere...it's making my skin crawl." He'd been working on his screenplay for five years. I declined to ask him why he expected to finish it this week. "You used to live in New York," I pointed out. "It's pretty crowded there."

He paced around the kitchen. "I need *protégés*," he said. "I feed off the collective energy, the youth."

"I'm here."

"I can't even set foot in a jazz club," he continued, ignoring me. "It's too close, and everyone smells. And the second-hand smoke! Everyone *smokes* on the sidewalks." He looked out the window, gesturing. "Look at the park. Everyone's smoking! Honestly, I cannot breathe."

"It's Paris," I told him.

"I'm just saying, I can't *breathe*," he said. After five more lackluster nights, he broke the news. He was going to Amsterdam. He was the last-minute replacement for Larry David to teach a television-writing class made up of promising young women from around the globe.

"Maybe there's a psych course there I could take. Everyone speaks English. Or I could be your assistant."

He looked at me hard. "I didn't force you to leave school, you know."

"I know that. I never said you did. It's just…"

"Hey, it's not like I planned this," he said. I watched him putting salt in a glass of water and gargling. He spit it in the kitchen sink. "What?"

"Nothing," I mumbled.

I wanted to call Aunt Suze for advice so badly, but I was ashamed. She'd often warned me that you can't change people's nature. And I couldn't call Mom. Obviously. *So this is what taking a risk is like,* I thought to myself. *Awesome.*

The day he left, I vacated the apartment and took the metro to no place in particular, wandering around and carrying everything I had to my name. Exhausted but percolating with panic, I parked myself to think. Sitting in *Au Carrefour*, surrounded by my luggage, I remembered Stephen's bloodless goodbye.

"It's like the end of *The Graduate*," he had told me, packing his computer in a box, carefully padding it with dishtowels that belonged to the apartment. "We made grand, sweeping gestures, now it's unclear how it will all turn out."

"Is it unclear?" I asked him, tilting my head. "Is it?"

"Will they stay together, or won't they? Where is that bus headed? Who knows?"

"Well, don't *we* know?" I asked.

"Yes," he said, doing a fist pump. "You get it!" He was practically manic in the way he was dancing around the apartment, shoving his things into bags. "We're in charge of the plot."

Suddenly, he stopped all movement and bored into my eyes with his, putting his hand on his heart. This was the signature gesture in the classroom that had made me, and many others, both male and female, swoon during his lectures.

Oh, thank God, I thought, breathing out, *he was just warming up for the giant "You were the one all along" speech like in the movies. This was just a phase. I complete him, of course. We're going to go back to the way we were. I'm moving to Amsterdam! I'll have to learn Dutch.*

"We are the screenwriters, directors and actors in our own lives," he said in a stage whisper, extending his arm out in my direction. I moved toward him for an embrace, just as he turned and headed to the bathroom. He undid his fly and started to pee in the impossibly low toilet. I looked away. "Hey," he called over his shoulder, "can you do those dishes before you leave? If I don't get out of here now, I'm going to miss the plane." He zipped up, grabbed his bags, and said, "I'll call you when I get to Schiphol."

He never did.

Chapter Nine

Chapter Nine

I'm going to get fired, I thought, speeding out of the drive to the house and onto the main road. *Or at the very least, ticketed for driving my Golf with the front-right headlight smashed out.* I hoped Rose could cover for me. With Edward gone, and me chasing after him, there was a distinct lack of cooks in the kitchen.

The snow was picking up, and my wipers were doing the best job they could. Keeping my eyes glued to the road, I reached for my bag so I could grab my phone, but it wasn't there. I'd made a split-second decision to run out of the house. At The Hall, we always left our keys in our cars in case rearranging was necessary. So now I couldn't even call Edward and tell him…tell him what? That I wanted him to stay? That even if the sex hadn't meant anything to him, it had to me? That I loved him? *Juliet, you've done it again.*

I smacked my freezing cold hand on the steering wheel.

"Come on!" I screamed. There was a car in front of me hesitating to make a turn. "I cannot wait for you forever!"

I started to take calming breaths, but quit immediately when I felt tears coming on. WWPD? What would Posy do? Well, for one thing, she'd be pissed off instead of sad. She surely wouldn't be blaming herself. She'd tell anyone who'd listen what a bastardly bastard-bastard her ex-man was for abandoning her.

Right then, that was exactly what I was going to do, starting with Edward himself. Finally clear, I moved forward, speeding to my destination. The train hadn't left the station. I gunned it into the car park, and my wheels skidded sideways out from under me on an icy patch.

Slow and steady, Juliet, I told myself. *You've got to make it through this in one piece.* I pulled the car into a spot and turned off the engine. Running up to the platform, I could hear the wheels starting to turn. Treading carefully, I peered in every window, looking for Edward's face. One window, another, then the next. Then I saw him, staring out the window opposite me. But he looked sad and distracted.

Then he turned toward me and locked me in his gaze, green eyes cutting through the veil of the falling flakes. He didn't smile. As the train pulled out, he mimed writing a letter. He got smaller and smaller until he was gone.

I stood on the platform staring at the space where he'd been, until I realized everyone else was gone. Was that it? Was that all I was worth? Snapping back to my senses, I shook off the snow that had been piling up on my hair. Shivering, I walked down the stairs to my car, holding tight to the railing. My kitchen clogs didn't have much traction.

I got back on the road to Thornton Hall, driving slowly and deliberately this time. I felt a fool. Hadn't I learned a thing from chasing down Stephen? You can't make a man want you if he doesn't. Edward's face said it all. Even though I was alone, I blushed to think of how he hadn't smiled. Only that he'd write me a letter. He didn't even want to hear my voice. Thank God I'd forgotten my phone. Anything I might have said would only have made things worse.

Time to shut off your heart, Juliet, I told myself. *Once again, here's what being spontaneous and taking a risk will get you. Stephen, Ben, and now Edward. Three strikes and you're out. Lesson learned. Now you know who you are. A cat lady like Mother.*

As I crossed the gate to Thornton Hall's drive, I looked forward to the warmth and solitude of the kitchen. I'd make homey apple pies, and maybe I'd eat them all by myself. Slowing to a near stand-still, I eased over the cattle grates. Still loud, but I hoped the falling snow would dampen the racket. I crossed my fingers that no one had noticed my absence. I couldn't bear telling the truth of where I'd been. *Especially not to Jasper,* whispered an unwelcome voice.

Anyway, I was back at the Hall. It's always better to be where you're wanted.

Sneaking in the back door, I stomped the snow from my shoes in the mudroom and checked the big clock above the washer and dryer as I walked through the laundry. I'd been gone just short of half an hour.

My bones practically reached out toward the heat from the Aga, and the smell of the loaf in the oven (had Rose thrown it in?) made my stomach growl. I'd been living in my head. I'd forgotten about my body.

Terrence blew in from the dining room, grousing under his breath, "Why am I in charge of organizing the bird-spotting trans-port and gear while Chizzy the Interloping Butler attends the table? Last time I checked, this was *my* house. I hope Mr. Roth will be quite comfortable with a pebble in his Hunter wellies."

He stopped and took a look at me. "Where have you been?"

Chisholm swung into the kitchen right behind him. "The Viscountess of Brearley requires preserves," he announced grandly, using Lady Ambridge's full title.

"You mean Lady A wants some jam?" Terrence snapped at him.

"At Clarence House, we refer to the guests of the house by title." Terrence rolled his eyes.

Chisholm had only ever worked in two places – for the Queen Mother at Clarence House and for Jasper Roth. Like Terrence, we staff all found him pompous and eminently mockable. However, the rest of us just sucked it up and got on with our jobs. Working alongside him took twice the energy we normally expended and we suspected he acted as a spy for Roth.

Mr. Chisholm indicated the apple mixture as he flew by with a jam pot on a silver tray. "Is that for the expedition to Cotswold Water Park?" he said, frowning.

"Umm, I…" I'd lost all track of what I was supposed to be doing. I was grateful for all the commotion.

"Mr. Roth has asked me to ensure that the hamper contains a bottle of Frank's Red Hot Sauce, a jar of marshmallow crème, and a balloon whisk." With that, he turned and left the room. I'd learned a long time ago not to ask questions.

"Between your skiving off and Chizzy's hissies, my day's been twice as hard as it needed to be," Terrence complained, stalking out of the kitchen.

Rose rushed in past him, excited. "Ah there you are, Juliet! Were you in the cellar? I've just heard Mr. Roth announce to the table that he has a Christmas surprise! My money is on a new arrival. That would certainly put some pep in The Painter's step! I'd love to see him jolly again. Wouldn't it just be grand? A new life at The Hall."

For a nanosecond, my stomach flipped. I guess I'd imagined that Lady Penelope and Roth had a marriage of convenience. Or that Lady Penelope was too nerve-addled, drunk, and medicated to fulfill that side of the nuptial contract. *God, Juliet, they're married. What do you think goes on between them? Are you jealous?*

"If that's the case," I said, in what I hoped was a professional and detached manner, "I hope Dr. Dearden is going to suggest the Lady rethink her psychiatric meds." A ball of something sour was rising up in my empty stomach. "I couldn't help noticing at meals that she sits glassy-eyed with plates of food going cold in front of her," I answered.

"It's a simple nerve tonic," defended Rose. "You make it sound like she's ready for the rubber room! He's been giving her the same things for decades…maybe added one or two in the last few years.

Go easy. She didn't want to join the party for breakfast, she just wanted to walk the grounds."

Walk the grounds to Edward's cottage? I thought.

"Poor lamb, she deserves a bit of peace. If she's in a family way, she'll need double the rest and quiet. It's just a matter of time now until the young couple takes over the big house. The hour is ripe, I'd say. Happens with every ancestral estate. Mr. Roth might stop traveling so much and put the focus on family, where it belongs, if you were to ask me."

Focus on the family! The phrase "*I know I'm married at the moment*" tickled inside my head.

"And The Earl and Countess could move to Home Farm…"

It seemed inevitable that one day The Earl and Countess would move to an only-slightly smaller house on the massive grounds, to live out their old age, while the younger folk started, and raised, a family in The Hall. Word on the street was Roth already saw himself in the master suite. After all, his money could buy many things, but not legitimacy as far as the born aristocracy were concerned. Owning the house would be a step in the right direction.

I crossed into the dining room to stir the compote and refresh the butter; Roth was presenting to his guests what we staff have come to call "The Cheese Dissertation."

"…and the Hoja Santa comes from Dallas. I have to smuggle it past customs, but I still prefer it to the Chabichou du Poitou or the Roves des Garrigues that we have brought in from France." Lady Penelope gazed past him, without much expression. The Earl sat at the head of the table, resting his chin on his fist, eyes closing. Occasionally, he handed bites of cheese under the table to Rex. Lady Ambridge, looking particularly like William Shakespeare this morning, but with slightly more hair, was absorbed in *The Times* crossword.

Five minutes into the lecture on all things cheese, The Earl cut in. "Rose," he said gently, as she passed by the table, "nip into the kitchen, if you'd be so kind, and see if there's a bit of mousetrap?"

I saw Rose smile the faintest smile at The Earl. Mousetrap, of course, is English slang for the cheapest cheddar cheese there is. I smiled to myself, enjoying his quiet power play against Roth.

Suddenly, Lady Penelope snapped to life. "Did you see that? Anyone? Juliet's just used the tongs from the seafood to rearrange the scones! I'm highly allergic. You could have killed me."

"I beg your pardon, Your Ladyship, but I certainly did not!"

"Are you arguing with me in front of my guests?" she asked, eyes blazing.

"No, Your Ladyship, I…I…I'm just trying to say I'm well aware…" I hadn't touched the seafood or bread platters since I'd entered the dining room.

"What if I'd eaten one of those pastries? Your *recklessness* could have cost me…"

"Now Penny, if anyone's dying around here, it's me. I'm old as Methuselah, and my liver's weak," intoned the Painter. "Another hazard of fine English bloodlines. We're like pure-bred dogs. The more we mate with each other, the weaker and sicker we get. Ah, here's my cheese! Thank you, Rose," he said, taking the cheese plate directly out of her hands. "We should make it a point to mate with mutts, mix it up, I say," he exhorted with a twinkle in his eye.

Rose clanged a serving spoon a bit too loudly on a platter. "I beg your pardon," she said loudly.

"My Dear," the Countess began, with a nervous glance toward Rose, "I'd prefer you didn't broach such grim topics at breakfast. No one is dying any time soon. Not you, and not Penelope."

"Juliet," The Painter said calmly, signaling his wife to stop talking. "Please carry the shellfish platter to the kitchen and send Rose in for the scones."

"Your Lordship…" I began, whispering next to his chair.

"Just remove the fish, please," he said. I knew there was no point in defending myself, but I was fuming. I know he's her daughter, but he'd never been rude to me before! *Is he being cold to me because he thinks I'm sleeping with his son-in-law? Because I most certainly am not! And now I'm not sleeping with Edward either!* Suddenly, I felt punched in the gut. For a moment, I'd forgotten about Edward, and now regret was crawling down my collar and making my spine tingle.

"Don't die, Hugh, old boy. I like your paintings too much," Lord Ambridge said good-naturedly.

"He never painted me," Lady Penelope mumbled.

Trying to appear composed, I stacked anything near the platter, including forks, knives and serving spoons, on top of it. I didn't want to stand accused.

"Penny, my daughter," said The Painter, "I rarely painted you because you wouldn't sit still. But you can't say never. What about the red one?"

"That's abstract," she said.

"That's my art. That's how I saw you in that moment," he said. "Besides, many surprises might occur before I leave this mortal coil."

I began stacking scones, determined to remove all reason to charge me with negligence in one fell swoop.

"Heavens!" Lady Ambridge said to The Painter. "I insist that you don't die. End of topic. Now, I suggest we all fortify ourselves with this delicious breakfast and prepare to clap eyes on a few wintering pintail and smew. I do not intend to die this outing – I'll see all the birds on the list or I'll eat my hat."

"Just watch her," whispered her husband. "It may happen."

"No need for that," said Roth. "I'm paying Juliet here an arm and a leg to cook you whatever you can dream of. Use her. I plan to."

I stopped, mid-scone clearing. I was furious. *You are married, and you're wife is pregnant,* I wanted to shout. I resumed my job, hands shaking. *Calm down. Stay professional.* I needed to eat something, sit down for a minute.

"At any rate," said the Countess. "Fresh air and the sight of some wild budgies will refresh body and mind, right, my shiny Penny?" she said, walking up behind her daughter and giving her a little squeeze. "All this morbid talk has upset you. Think light thoughts, like I always say." She looked twenty years younger than her age, her face relaxed and serene. "Happiness is a choice."

I began crossing the room with both arms full, determined to get out quickly.

"I must spray my boots one final time," said Lady Ambridge, spittle flying from her overbite. She really did resemble a horse. "It rained so much this fall that the topsoil's unstable. Stray from the path, and you're up to your ankles in soft mud."

Stick to the easy path if you know what's good for you, I thought. *Happiness is indeed a choice.*

"Well, then, I'm off to finish dressing," said Lord Ambridge, standing. "Say, Juliet," he turned to me. I was forced to pause and balance all my platters. "Can you have that Daphne bring another coffee to my room?"

"Certainly, Sir," I said, thinking it odd that he'd requested her specifically. Maybe he'd forgotten Rose's name.

I pushed gently through the door back into the kitchen and found Isaac and Rose sitting at the farm table.

"I was just about to take a quick cup of tea and Isaac sat down to show me his painting. Would you like a cup?" Rose said, rising.

"More than anything." I dumped my platters and took a chair. Isaac pointed to a fat shrimp, and I nodded. He popped it into his mouth. "Rose, can you make sure no seafood leaves this kitchen again till I'm safely back in London?"

"Whatever's happened?" asked Rose, setting a cup in front of me.

"Lady Penelope just called me a murderer."

"Oh, I'm sure she didn't. She just gets confused easily."

"This picture is lovely, Isaac," I said. "Did you do a poinsettia especially for Christmas?" It's hard to say if Isaac suffered brain damage from falling in the pond. Maybe he wasn't going to cure cancer, but he certainly could paint. It reminded me of that old saying about how when a door closes, another one opens. I felt protective and proprietary around him, and it stung a little. I wished I had a little brother to protect.

"There's one on my porch. Jane put it there."

Rose piped in proudly, "Painting comes natural to him. He's been drawing since he could hold a crayon. Almost like a photograph, isn't it? He doesn't do faces, since the accident. Strange… but he did a group of trees that the Earl hung in his study," she boasted.

"Larch, willow, pine, spruce, oak, apple. Hugh shows me how," said Isaac. Only Isaac could get away with calling the Earl Hugh.

"Yes, he takes interest in Isaac's art. Bought him his first brushes, taught him to stretch a canvas. Tried to teach Lady Penelope, too, but she didn't take to it." Rose told her. "The priest displays several of Isaac's flower paintings in Our Lady, Help of Christians' Church social hall. Isaac and Jane were both baptized there, and they married there. You remember the reception here on the grounds… very generous of the Earl and Countess. Oooh, speaking of which, I'd better clear the table," she said, swinging into the dining room.

"Jane was a beautiful bride."

"Like one of the ladies from the oil paintings in The Hall, here," Isaac said.

It had been springtime and we staff had put up a marquee on the lawn. Edward and I made canapés, which were passed around by some young girls hired from the village, and there was a cold picnic. The Painter had made a toast to Isaac's happiness and had actually gotten a bit teary. I remember thinking at the time that it was exactly the kind of wedding I wanted – simple, homey and unpretentious. Not Ben's style at all.

Ben! I'd nearly forgotten about Ben this morning…I wonder what that said about our relationship…but now the heavy stone was back in my chest. We wouldn't be marrying and I wouldn't be a bride any time soon.

"Everyone's entitled to make a mistake," Rose always says. *What if that's all this was with Ben? A mistake? One act of poor judgment? What if I'm being a hothead, and throwing away my chance at being part of a couple, warts and all?*

Was being a couple important? Mother never married. Aunt Suze and her partner, Ruth, live in separate houses, next door to one another. Their nod to marriage was putting 100 surnames in a hat, drawing one out, and both legally adopting it.

But what if Ben was the one? Edward sure let me know that he's not.

Being double-dumped had splashed my rose-colored glasses with mud, and I felt physically low. "Be in the moment," Aunt Suze always preached. Right, there was a task at hand. I couldn't control men, but I could control how well I did my job. Edward's leaving was an opportunity to impress the guests and to really put my stamp on the meals this holiday. *That's it, Juliet,* I told myself with a mental pat on the back, *Why not try being a man instead of wanting one. Throw yourself into your work, and cut off your emotions!*

I set a couple of theoretically crustacean-tainted scones on the table for the staff, and got busy cleaning and packing the hampers for the birding lunch. Terrence, Chisholm and Seamus would be out for the day, driving passengers, setting up and waiting at table. I was heating water for the gallons of tea I'd be putting in thermoses.

"Well, you can pack a tad more lightly" Rose sighed as she swung into the kitchen with arms full of dirty dishes. "Lady Penny's gone above to rest."

"She obviously needs it," I grumbled. "She's a mess."

"Juliet!"

"I'm surprised Roth didn't demand she go out with them."

"When she said she was feeling poorly, all the guests jumped to tell her to go lie down, then Dr. Dearden said, 'I was there when you came into this world, and I'd be remiss if I didn't continue to keep you safe,' and he ordered her to bed. The old ways are the best ways, I like to say. Her husband couldn't really argue with the doctor. And in her condition…"

"Rose, we don't know what her condition is or isn't," I snapped.

"Nobody said she's pregnant yet."

"Nevertheless, she's asked for hot tea and sherry in her room. I'll run her a steaming bath then come back for it."

"I thought pregnant women weren't supposed to drink alcohol or sit in hot water," I said. *Besides, isn't she tanked already?* I thought.

"Honestly, what tosh young women have in their heads these days. For the last three months of her confinement, my mother had a rare steak and a pint of Guinness in the bath every night and I'm as sound as a horse."

Never having been pregnant myself, I didn't feel qualified to argue, so I made yet another cup of tea and poured a snifter to set on a tray. "Anyway," I said to Rose, "I'll bet the baby will be gorgeous and born with dark curls like her father." There, that was an appropriate wish for their happiness. See Rose? I don't hate her.

"You never know who God will make a child resemble. It's always a mystery. Isaac, better get tonight's firewood moved into the house. The snow's picking up and the job'll just be harder later. Ah, wouldn't a white Christmas be just the thing?" Rose said.

Isaac wiped his mouth on his sleeve and rushed out the back door with a little wave. On the one hand, you could say it was kind of the Painter and Countess to give him a job and a cottage. On the other hand, they'd gotten a hardworking, able-bodied man to work for them who knew their estate like the back of his hand and was loyal as family.

Daphne pushed open the door and peeked into the kitchen. "I need to mind the fires. The ones in the bedrooms will be dying by now," she said. "Have you seen the extra matches?"

"Bottom cabinet, on the left, behind the paper towels," I told her, gesturing with my foot because I was elbow deep in sausage-grease-and-suds water. Daphne rooted around for a minute, then said, "I can't find them. Could you lend a hand?"

Great. A housemaid who needs a housemaid.

I dried off and got on my knees, practically crawling into the cabinet. I strained to reach the back shelf, and just managed to nip them with my fingertips. I felt a cold breeze on my back as my chef's coat rode up.

Terrence blew in and squealed, "Aaaah! Put that thing away! Chef Hill, when the Pussycat Dolls are hiring, they'll ring your agent."

Mortified, I snapped into a sitting position. I'd completely forgotten that this morning, in lieu of my usual white cotton panties (the sensible thing to wear doing kitchen work), I'd put on a hot-pink thong with a gold-plated star sewn on where the "T" sat on my spine. They were a gift from Posy, meant to be taken to Ben's for the holiday trip. I felt like twice the idiot since I had to admit to myself that they were bought for Ben, and I'd worn them for Edward, who was now lying in wait, biding time until he ran off to the Casbah with Lady Penelope. Or maybe Rose was right and he had a sweetheart at home and at this very moment they were drinking wassail and Christmas shopping.

Fucking Edward! Double fucking Ben!

Terrence soon forgot about me and my lingerie when he saw the bottle of sherry out on the table. "Ooooooh. And a very merry early Christmas to me!" He took a coffee mug from the cabinet and poured himself a large shot. "Lady Daphne? Fortification?"

"Do you mean a drink? If it's OK, I guess a little splash won't harm anything…"

"Course it won't. It should be written into our contracts!"

"What contract?" Daffy asked, befuddled.

"Never mind," said Terrence. They both downed their mugs. "Chef?" he asked, pouring out new measures for Daphne and himself.

I hesitated. "Maybe half a pour…" He pulled down another mug. I never, never drank on the job, but after Lady P's nasty accusation, and whatever the hell happened with Edward, my nerves were jangled. It now suddenly seemed like an overly prudent rule. These days, it's like my brain was a Siamese twin. *Next I'll be doing tequila shots and singing karaoke in the drawing room.*

"Over the lips and through the gums," said Terrence. He downed his second mug. Daphne imitated him, smiling shyly.

"Easy," I said, "that's the good stuff." I could feel the warm liquid hitting my blood.

The door swung open and Lady Penelope strode in, and we all jumped to attention. She glanced at the brandy bottle. She made a big show of sniffing the air. "Is it teatime already?" she asked me icily.

"Lady Penelope," Rose jumped in. "I thought you were resting."

"I came to remind Juliet not to contaminate utensils with shellfish in the kitchen as well as the dining room." Daphne guiltily lay a shrimp as big as a baby's arm down on the platter. "Is that staff lunch?" Lady Penelope asked, knowing we'd never have anything half that expensive. "Supervise her. If she even touches something of mine with soiled hands, I could become extremely ill."

"I'll be sure to advise Chef and the rest of the staff about your allergies, Lady Penelope," Rose said. "No need to trouble yourself. Now, I'll be up with refreshment for you in a jiffy, and I'll see that it's served on sterile china."

"I am sorry I let Edward out of my sight. He's the only one who can really attend to my needs, you know," Lady Penelope said as she left the kitchen, nearly colliding with Chisholm, coming through to the kitchen, laden with binoculars, birding vests, backpacks and cameras, hanging from his neck and strapped to his back. He was wearing a plaid hat with earflaps. "Beg pardon, Your Ladyship," he said, standing to one side. He took one look at the bottle and at my coffee mug, and tsked, "At Clarence House, we never popped the cork till after Her Majesty was asleep."

"Well, anyone would have to be asleep with you and your cork anywhere near them, eh?" quipped Terrence.

"You'd do well to avoid his bad influence," Chisholm told Daphne. "Mind your Ps and Qs and you could be working for royalty someday."

"Take his advice," Terrence said. "No one knows old queens like this old queen." They both pushed through the door, and got stuck, shoulder to shoulder, before dislodging themselves and propelling out together, leaving the door flapping vigorously. I poured another shot into my coffee mug, and downed it quickly. *You really need to eat something, Juliet,* I thought as the warmth of the liquor relaxed me.

Daphne stood wringing her hands. "Beg Pardon, Miss."

"I'm Juliet, not 'Miss.'"

"All right. Juliet. Can I ask you a question?"

"Sure," I said.

"Do you think Lady Penelope is a bit, well, like… batty?"

"What do you mean?" I asked, though I knew exactly what she meant.

"You know, I was, like, clearing up in The Ambridges' room – Rose told me to – and I ran into her in the hall and then Lord Ambridge came out and she, like, gave me a look. I wasn't doing anything wrong in there, I swear it!"

"I think you're imagining it, Daphne," knowing very well she wasn't. "The Lady is kind of delicate. She also takes, um, medicines for different health issues," I said, not wanting to gossip with someone who wasn't part of the house. "So, my advice is just be polite to her, let Rose attend to her when it's possible, and take what she might say to you with a grain of salt." *Like I do when she accuses me of not knowing my job in front of a room full of people,* I thought bitterly.

"I guess you're right," she said. "She really scored when she landed Mr. Roth, though, didn't she? I mean, he's really hot and she's, well, she isn't hot in the slightest."

Eager to stop this conversation in its tracks, I told her, in my best advanced-aged and auntie-like manner, "Passion isn't always what makes a strong partnership. It's far more often about compatibility and both Mr. Roth and the Lady are very intelligent people." *Said the lust-mad night vampire who recently ate the permanent chef alive,* I finished in my head. *Geez, Juliet, talk about hypocrites, you're parroting Mother to this poor girl, when just last night you behaved like Ted Kennedy at Mardi Gras.*

"Take my advice," I told her, suddenly feeling stronger in my convictions. Either the brandy or Mother was urging me to give a "do as I say, not as I have done" speech. "Find a man like Seamus. He may not ride a motorcycle, or look like a model, or have his way with you in the pantry…"

"What?"

"But that type of man will be solid, and sane, and will keep you from making a fool of yourself." I looked earnestly into her eyes. "You need that. We all, do, don't we?" I realized I was slurring a bit. "To be saved from ourselves?"

"Yeah, I get it. I totally see what you mean," she said, with a look of concentration on her face. "It's like, about your mind and reading the papers and all." She was nodding resolutely and backing away. "I'm going to make sure there are no glasses left in the library."

"Wait! Don't forget Lord Ambridge's coffee," I said. "Put sugar and milk on this tray."

"You don't have to tell me how he likes it," she said, slipping out the door.

Chapter Ten

Emboldened by the brandy, I stole out the back door, looking from left to right. If anyone saw me on the path, I'd just walk to Dove's Nest. Nice and easy. Like I was going to get my hairbrush, say. Or dry socks. Everything in the kitchen was under control, and everyone on staff seemed to be attending to this or that.

At the last possible minute, I veered right instead of left, and headed for Edward's. With one last glance behind me, I sped up and popped in through the door. I knew what a big risk I was taking, leaving my post and snooping around where I had no business, but I wanted an answer.

Everything was neat and tidy. The dishes were in the sink, the throws on the sofa were folded and draped, and peering around the corner, I could see that the bed was made. It was dark in the cottage, and I didn't dare turn on the lights, but I could see a white envelope on the bed, illuminated by a swath of light from between the curtains.

Just then the front door opened wide, and I heard hard heels clacking across the wooden floor of the entranceway. I turned the corner into the bedroom and slid quietly toward the closet. I wedged myself inside without opening the door more than a crack, for fear it would creak. I sensed before I saw that it was Lady Penelope.

She flicked on the light. Without making a sound, I pulled a raincoat around my face, with one eye, surveying the room. She ran her fingers over a stack of folded sweaters on the shelf above the headboard. Pulling a wooly tan one from the stack, she buried her face in it, inhaling. My shoulders were cramping from hunching over. I squinted hard, trying to read the handwriting on the front.

I willed her to leave before she saw the letter, but no such luck. Still holding the sweater, she picked up the envelope, pocketed it, and walked out leaving the lights on. I could hear her walking around the rest of the cottage, opening doors and drawers. My only option was to deal with my discomfort and wait.

"There you are? Where have you been?" asked Rose.

"Lip balm. Had to go to my cottage," I didn't look at her. "Then I got some more eggs from the barn."

I'd managed to slip back in and now stood at the sink, washing piles of dishes I'd gotten behind on. Isaac made trips back and forth, carrying logs from the woodpile to the mudroom, and Chisholm and Terrence interrupted me periodically to get this or that for the picnic hampers. Thankfully, Jasper Roth was focused on micromanaging the packing of the Land Rover and the people movers. He'd sent in a few requests for odd things like a lemon zester and white vinegar, but at least I didn't have to be in the same room with him. My nerves were shattered enough.

My mind felt fuzzy from lack of sleep. Or maybe it was the brandy. Or maybe it was just jealousy. At any rate, I found it hard to concentrate on my work. I couldn't wait till the party was out of the house…new guests were arriving tonight, after dinner, so in addition to a sit-down meal, I had to plan the "kind of a rolling food thing" that Mr. Roth had ordered. A cook to order service for as soon as they arrived. Whatever they wanted, I had to deliver. And I was furious that Edward wasn't here with me. For so many reasons.

Most of tonight's dinner was already prepared – a crown roast smeared in mustard was roasting slowly in one of the ovens. There were, of course, Brussels sprouts to go with it. A little green looks nice on a platter, and the English believe sprouts are wed to beef in a holy union. I had already prepared popover tins for individual Yorkshire puddings. I like doing them this way because they each form a hole in the middle, making a nest for the gravy. And because excess was the order of the day, I also had mashed sweet potato, roasted root vegetables, and butternut squash soup. I couldn't believe I'd pulled all this out of my ass considering I'd been in and out of the house all day stalking Edward. *Effing Edward!* Tears were springing to my eyes. *God, I'm so uncomfortable!*

Pulling it out of my ass reminded me why chefs never wear thongs. I felt really stupid. All through high school, on Mother's advice, I'd been careful not to be the "done and discarded" girl. Now, at age 28, I was exactly that. Three times over. The thong stood as a brutal reminder. And because I'd already disappeared twice, I couldn't even go back to Dove's Nest to get a nice pair of white cotton panties to put me out of my misery. I swiveled my hips to make an adjustment, but it only served to twist the thong further into my delicate lady parts. I sighed.

"Are you ill?" Rose asked, picking up a tea towel to dry china.

"No, I'm fine." Even I could hear how sad I sounded.

"Juliet, love, I can't help noticing that you haven't mentioned that fellow of yours once since you've been here," Rose opened. "I'll just put on the kettle."

"Nothing to tell, really," I caged, taking out milk and pouring it into mugs. Tea would be soothing. "I decided he wasn't right for me." *Immediately after I discovered he cheated on me.*

"And then? You jilted him at Christmastime? He must be smarting."

"I'm sure he'll survive."

"Being cold and hard isn't like you," she said calmly, popping tea bags into the mugs.

"Well he made me this way!" I slammed the sugar bowl down

on the table. *Which he?* I wondered though.

"Remember love, no one can make us do anything."

"Well, he *hurt* me!" It was the first time I'd said it out loud and suddenly, I was bawling. *You're a hot mess, Juliet.* The whole story of Amanda's panties was forcing its way out past the big, barking sobs.

Rose kicked into mother mode. She shoved me through the kitchen door leading to the staff dining room. As it swung open and shut, I saw her strategically placing a cutting board piled high with lemons, a bunch of fresh cilantro, and a chef's knife on the corner of the kitchen table visible through the dining room's swinging door. This implied that I was very busy slaving over fresh ingredients. She brought in our cups of tea, and a pot of peas, which we shelled as we talked.

"My poor dove," she said, throwing peas into her empty bowl. "I know it feels personal, but it may not be. Men make mistakes. Someday you'll realize it's nothing to do with you. A man can love one woman with his heart and brain and still find that his body's thinking something else," she said.

"Why wouldn't Ben's body think of me? Why would it think of Amanda if he loved me?"

"I'm sure his body thought of you plenty."

"It doesn't matter. I'm done with it all."

"Ah, go on, you're young. You'll have other fellas."

I just had another fella, I thought. *It only made things worse.* "Do you think Edward would make a good boyfriend?" I asked, dipping my toe in. Holding back information from Rose didn't feel right, but I wasn't ready to spill.

"Sort out one problem at a time. Have you heard Ben's side of it? You may be throwing out the baby with the bathwater."

"No, but..."

"That's the place to start. But I have a hard question for you, miss. Are you more upset about being duped or losing the man?"

"Well, losing Ben, of course. I loved him. I think...Maybe I still do. I mean, maybe I still should," I said, fiddling with the empty pea pods in the pot. And because loving Edward certainly wasn't doing me any good. *You don't love Edward,* I told myself, heart squeezing with fear at the thought, *it's the hormones and brain chemicals swirling around, confusing you. He was a rebound. He made a first-class fool of you anyway.* "Ben could be a good fit for me, right?"

Rose continued shelling peas.

"I mean, throwing your whole life away because of one mistake is foolish, right?" I asked.

"Only you can answer that. If he's the right man for you, it'll become clear."

Maybe the perfect man was a myth. Edward wasted no time showing me that. At least Ben had been willing to try to go the distance, to have a relationship. At least he never did unspeakable things to me, like Edward did, leaving my body and mind permanently altered, then skulked out in the dark of night. *But he never made my knees weak by nibbling the back of my...*

"Whatever!" I burst out. "There are no princes, after all. That's fairytale crap for starry-eyed young girls. Who gets a prince?"

"I suppose I do, in a manner of speaking. Seamus behaves well and takes care of me."

"Is he your one true love?"

"I love him dearly," she said.

There was silence between us for a moment.

"I'm really sad, Rose," I told her.

"The young won't believe this, but sadness never killed anyone." She sighed. "And I'm not sure you have a right to it."

"What?" I asked, indignant. "My boyfriend's been cheating on me! I'm not allowed to be upset?"

"You have all the choices in the world available to you. You're bright, you've had an education, you're healthy and you have a great gift as a chef."

"I don't know about gift..."

"Don't hide your light under a bushel! That insults God, my girl. It's a happy accident that I'm excellent at service, and that I like it, because that was my one and only choice. And as far as lust and marriage go…" She opened her mouth to say more, then closed it again and nailed on a smile.

"You met Seamus, had your son, and lived happily ever after," I finished. "Simple."

She sat still for a moment. "I wouldn't say simple." She stood up, and grabbed the shelled peas and empty pods. "Now, I'm giving you a cup of tea to carry back to your cottage. I want you to sit in a scalding bath and drink it, then lie down for half an hour. See if you can hear the voice inside speaking to you. No one's coming back any time soon." She kissed me on top of my head, and swung through to the kitchen.

Chapter Eleven

"I'm so glad you rang! Happy almost Christmas!" Posy sang through the phone. "Where are you?"

"Thornton Hall, where do you think I am?"

"Given that I didn't know you were headed there until the wind was at your back, I'd say it's anybody's guess. Besides, I thought there was no cell reception there because of the beautification council and the mobile phone towers, etcetera, etcetera."

"There isn't. I'm on the landline in the laundry room. Rose sent me for a nap, but I needed to talk to you. I had to hear your voice. I'm a little lonely. My mother is, well, my mother, but it's hard to be without family or my best friend right now. I didn't think things could get worse, but guess what? They have."

"Aww, that's awful," she said. "But I'm really glad you rang. Your timing is perfect! I've got sort of an emergency. You know how you told me you'd love to show me Woodstock someday?"

"Of course. Oooh, do you want to go back with me to The States after New Year's?" I asked. "That would give me something to look forward to. I don't want to go alone. We can talk about it right after Christmas."

"No, it can't wait. You see, Piers Conley-Weatherall had a deal to do his first ever cookbook, and word on the street is that the deal fell through."

"So? What's that have to do with Woodstock?"

"Hear me out. Piers hasn't wanted to do a book before now because he got burned by a publishing house that wanted him to do a slick, cheesy, paper version of his television show, with trendy picks of the moment like cake pops and seafood spumas and exotic beverage syrups. He wanted to do an illustrated version of his family's home cookbook, with heirloom recipes for simple foods, maybe with a few of his family's photos thrown in. He didn't want to include measurements…just a 'pinch of this' or 'a handful of that' or 'add as much pepper as your family likes.'"

"And?"

"I'm friends with his publicist's assistant, and he told me that Piers Conley-Weatherall is planning to fire his literary agent. I've done deals with this fab agent in The States called Pilar Steinberg. If she and I worked together, I know we could give him a book he'd be proud of. If I could just get to him for a word, I could convince him to do a deal with my publishing house. Can you see it? The first book of which I am sole editor of hitting the *New York Times* bestseller list?"

"That would be great, Posy. I hope it works out." In fact, I kind of didn't. I knew that was mean of me, though. I was feeling really jealous. Why does Posy always land butter-side up? And why does she have to steal my hero? She'd never even heard of him until I made her watch his show. I knew I was being childish, so I swallowed hard and pasted a smile on my face. Aunt Suze's book says that if you smile on the phone, people on the other end will hear it through the receiver.

I needed to get her opinion about Edward. Should I track him down and let him have it or should I play it cool? "Listen, I have to ask you something…"

"Me first! You are not going to believe this! I have an unbelievable scoop that will help me pull this off. Piers Conley-Weatherall is doing a press junket and he'll be in New York City tomorrow to cook on the *America Today Show*. My source tells me that his driver is taking him to your aunt's house immediately after so he won't have to be alone on Christmas."

"My aunt's? She didn't tell me. Last week all she could talk about was some big blowout she'd had with my mother and how they're not speaking. Mother's not speaking to me right now, either. She called me a 'hash-jockey' and I hung up on her." I wished I hadn't.

"My publicist friend said Piers and Aunt Suze got really close with all the life coaching, and now they're friends," Posy charged on, not answering me. "When I spoke to her, she told me it's true – they're really tight."

Did she just call my aunt Aunt Suze? I felt my mouth drying up. "You spoke to her?"

"I rang her and invited myself for Christmas! Can you believe the cheek? I hope you don't mind, but I told her that you said to call."

"I live for Piers Conley-Weatherall. Remember? I turned you onto him."

"I know," she said. "Isn't it brilliant? And now I'm spending Christmas with him. I can tell you all about him. I'm working out the dates and flight arrangements now."

I got an itchy feeling, like I was just another one of Posy's networking contacts. The pain of feeling suspicious of my best friend was too much to bear on top of everything else. As Posy rambled on about what she'd be packing, and ground transportation from JFK to Woodstock, I remembered the day we met. The day Stephen left me.

Alone, feeling untethered to the earth, I ordered one expensive, foamy coffee after another as my last hurrah in the City of Lights. I was girding my loins to check into a hotel for a few nights while I searched for flights back to Kentucky. Even though no one in the café knew I'd been dumped, my cheeks were aflame. On some level, I'd felt like I deserved what I got, and that may be the worst feeling a person can have. Without warning, my nose started streaming blood and I was forced to staunch the flow with my white cloth napkin. It was bizarre, like someone turned on a faucet.

"I need something stronger than a coffee. You look like you do, too. D'you fancy a glass of wine? I say I never drink alone, but I've been breaking my own rule lately," said a girl with a plummy English accent. I looked up to see Posy Wase-Bailey, nearly my twin, tall, with creamy skin and dark hair. Her eyes were red-rimmed and puffy. She was wearing a blindingly day-glo Lilly Pulitzer dress, and a wide, lime-green headband, which I later found out to be ironic. I felt ugly and conspicuous in my now-stained t-shirt. *Why didn't you just find some McDonald's to sit in?* I chastised myself. I couldn't really talk with a bloody cloth on my face, so I just nodded.

She gestured to a waiter and said, "Une bouteille de vin blanc, … Chanson, Vire Clesse." Then she sat herself down at my table.

"Hey, we could be twins!" she said.

Does she not notice that I'm bleeding from my face?

In a way she was right. There was a resemblance, aside from the fact that she was super-chic and I looked homeless. We're both really tall, and chesty, and not at all Paris-thin. The big difference is that my hair is a wild, unruly wig of chocolate-brown twists that cannot be tamed by clip nor spray, while hers is stick-straight and nearly jet-black, worn in a neat, Louise Brooks-style, chin-length bob with very short bangs. She says it's her "brand". We drank that bottle of wine, while she urged, interrogation-style, that I unburden myself of the tale of my mistreatment at Stephen's hands. I was so nervy from the shock and coffee that I blurted it out in a continuous stream. She interrupted from time to time, crying out, "That bastard!" and "That *absolute* bastardy *bastard!*"

After more wine, I told her he'd been my first lover.

"No." Pause. "Way." She blinked. "There is no way that is true. You have got to be kidding me. Ever?"

"Yes."

"That utter *bastard*," she said darkly, her eyes narrowing to slits.

I took in Posy with some suspicion, and thought, *What does she want from me? Could this pushy, boundary-less creature be a con artist or an intercontinental serial killer? Am I going to wind up as a story on* 60 Minutes? But by the time the second bottle had been upended, I had a much more *laissez-faire* attitude about the threat she might pose. Turned out, despite Posy's refined table manners, she was a sloppy drunk and talked more loudly than was strictly necessary. For some reason, this made me trust her.

"No more about me," I finally managed. "Why were you crying?"

"Oh, it's silly, really. I'll be fine." She suddenly looked small. I sat very still and waited, the way Mother always did with me. "Most people are afraid of silence," she always said, "and will say anything to fill it." It's a shrink trick.

"Well," she said, "I suppose it's that I'm lonely." She took a moment and clamped her lips together. "I'm feeling sorry for myself." She tried to smile but her chin got quivery. "I said goodbye to a friend this morning."

"A boyfriend?" I asked.

"Well…" She signaled for the waiter, who wasn't even on the floor. "I should order a meal, probably, but I don't feel like eating." She stared off into the distance for a minute. "And would you believe today's my birthday?"

"Happy birthday," I said.

"Not bloody likely. Not a soul remembered. I hate being in Paris alone. I'm so utterly, utterly alone. Wow," she said, opening her eyes wide, "that sounded dramatic even to me." She fiddled with her wine stem. "God, you must think me a mess."

"My aunt – she's well, kind of a life coach – told me that sometimes it's OK if my mantra is 'I'm doing the best that I can, and that's good enough.' She told me to go around practicing it…to say it at my job, to my teachers, when someone in the supermarket gets pissed because I'm pushing my cart too slow. You should give it a try."

"I like it," Posy said. "Sounds like it shuts people right the fuck up."

"We're a pair, aren't we? What are we going to do?"

"We'll just keep moving forward. "

"What if I feel sorry for myself?"

"My aunt would say that you should stage a reinvention."

"Reinvention?" she said knowingly. "Is your aunt that life coach woman from *The Eva! Show*?"

"Yes," I admitted.

"I'd kill to meet her. She may be the only one who can help me."

"Cheer up, you could be me. I just got dumped and I'm homeless."

"I'm a heartbroken and I don't have any real friends."

"I'm poor and I don't have a father."

"I'm lonely."

"I'm lonely."

She looked at me hard, and nodded her head. "Get your bags, you've pulled."

"Pulled?"

"S'what we say when we're taking someone home for the night. It was a joke. What I mean to say is, you're moving in with me."

"That's crazy!" I told her. "You don't know me…"

"I've always been a risk-taker."

Suddenly, all I wanted was to be packed up and leaving Thornton Hall, on my way to my aunt's for Christmas. With Posy. She was still talking about carry-on luggage this, and ski parka that. *Does she even care that I'm heartbroken?* How had I gone from toasting my engagement around the tree with my future in-laws, to slaving away for people who want to fire me while my best friend has dinner with my family?

"Jubes, are you still on the line?"

"I'm here."

"Can you give me sizes for your aunt and her partner. Her name's Ruth, right? I want to bring prezzies. Are they more the angora scarf or the softball glove type?"

"I don't know," I said. Deflated, I gave her height and weight guesses. "Hey, know what?" I said, taking a final stab at getting back on track. "I didn't know if I was imagining the spark between me and Jasper Roth, we had this talk, and now his wife is breathing down my neck and…"

"Jubes, sorry to cut you short, but I have to ring off and book these tickets now so I don't get shut out. Thanks for listening! Love you loads. I'll give your best to Aunt Suze. Happy Christmas!"

Pushing out the back door, I ignored the cold and the snow falling on my head.

"Get back, Rex," I said, pushing him backwards with my foot. He gave a high-pitched yelp and ran away from me, toward the kitchen, nails scrabbling on the stone floor of the mudroom. "Sorry, boy! I didn't mean to be rough!" Ignoring me, he pushed his snout through the kitchen door. I may as well tattoo Friendless Orphan, Who Even Dogs Hate on my forehead. I could not believe my best friend was stealing my aunt and my idol.

I couldn't stop imagining how Aunt Suze and Ruth would embrace the dynamic, career-driven Posy who was singing the hell out of her heartsong with no man to weigh her down. They'd sit around Aunt Suze's Amish-carved harvest table, drinking wine and swapping stories of how their inner guides brought them to complete fulfillment while Piers Conley-Weatherall whipped up a family-style meal. They'd sit with their organic, agave-sweetened, fair-trade cocoa in front of the woodstove, and realize that Posy and I had been switched at birth, like in that Prince and the Pauper story.

"It's too late to switch back, Posy, but know you're one of us," Aunt Suze would say meaningfully. "But as long as we have to keep Juliet, can you make sure she gets her degree and stops being dumped? It's getting embarrassing."

"Don't be too hard on her. You can't expect everyone to be as gorgeous, focused and popular as I am," Posy would say. "Did you know I speak flawless French?"

Piers Conley-Weatherall would wipe a tear from his eye, and tell her, "I've got four children of my own, but I'd swap any one of them for you."

Focus on your job, Juliet, and what you're here for. Tomorrow will be another day. If nothing else, you've got your reputation to protect. At the very least, no one can accuse you of not being a good chef, so be a good chef. I dragged myself to Dove's Nest, and barely managed to set my alarm clock before I fell into a hard, dreamless sleep.

Chapter Twelve

When I arrived back at the kitchen, Rose was just clearing lunch dishes from the kitchen table, where Terrence and Daphne were finishing sandwiches.

"I convinced them I needed to come back ahead of the crowd to get the house in order. Left Chizz to pack up the gear and shepherd the birders back from the frozen tundra. And just in the nick of time! I can't feel my feet!" I glanced down to see that he was wearing a pair of pink marabou mules where his tuxedo slippers should have been.

No sooner than I'd tied on my apron, the birding party descended on the house. All hands were immediately on deck to collect snowy boots, coats, gloves and hats, to fetch slippers, warm fleeces and throw blankets, and to pass out bullshots – hot Bloody Marys with beef consommé in the place of the tomato juice. The family and guests were installed in the drawing room with cocktails and canapés.

"The snow is still coming down. I wonder how the roads are," said Rose. "It's a good thing Dr. Dearden and the Ambridges kipped here. I hope the last arriving guests don't have trouble driving in all the snow. It's likely to spoil the shooting party tomorrow." Rose was sitting at the table, wearing white gloves as she polished the silver. She took great pride in handling the house's beautiful, antique silver and it always gleamed like it was new. She kept a special box under the kitchen sink with baking soda, toothbrushes, chamois cloths and white cotton gloves, reserved solely for this chore. "But there's nothing as romantic as a White Christmas. I'd have loved a Christmas wedding, myself, with a white gown."

"Yes," sighed Daphne. "I'd have a gown like Kate Middleton, all sleek and sophisticated, not a bit tarty, and my groom would wear a morning coat, and have curly brown hair like Prince…"

"Prince Jasper of Rothdale?" Terrence teased. "Below stairs, they all think the lords are going to make them into ladies, don't they?"

"I don't think that! And I was going to say Prince *William*."

"Terrence!" Rose said. "Stop teasing the poor girl. All *domestics* are not lying in wait for some lord or rich man to save our lives."

"I don't know," I said, innocently. "Maybe I could be Princess Juliet and still futz around in the royal kitchen from time to time if and when the mood struck me."

Just then, we heard a loud shot, and we all went running to the window. The Painter and Isaac were standing under a giant oak tree, rifles in hand. We watched as The Painter said something to Isaac, who stood back, then aimed his sight at the top of the tree. The old gun blasted another ear-splitting shot, and Isaac and The Painter stood stock-still. Several seconds later, a large clump of mistletoe fell to the ground a few yards away. Both men threw down their rifles and did some version of a victory dance, which ended in a handshake-hug. Rose backed away from the window, smiling and wiping her hands on a dishcloth.

"I'll never get used to guns," I said.

"Here in the country, you'd better try. The Painter's an excellent shot, and I must say, nothing compares to fresh game. Isaac is going as a gun for the shooting party tomorrow."

Minutes later, Seamus and Isaac came in the pantry door and through to the kitchen, Seamus had taken The Painter's firearm and was carrying an armful of wood, and Isaac was carrying a rifle and the bunch of mistletoe.

"Are those things loaded?" I asked, cowering.

"That they are," said Seamus, "but we always engage the safety. Here, Isaac, I'll put that away," he said, and Isaac handed his father his gun.

"The Painter said that the mistletoe that grows on oak trees has magical powers and good luck. If it gets me a kiss from my Rose, I'd say he was right," said Seamus, winking at his wife and walking out through the mudroom. Isaac handed the bundle of mistletoe to Rose.

"Thank you, Isaac. Daffy, will you cut sprigs of this and hang it in the doorways?"

"Should I do it upstairs and in the library, too?"

"Yes, all over," said Rose. "And give the leftovers to Barry. He's been putting up decorations outside this morning. On second thought," she said eyeing the white maid's blouse straining over Daphne's chest, "bring the rest to me and I'll give it to Barry." Behind her hand, she whispered to me, "No good sending a lamb to a lion."

Daphne all but grabbed the mistletoe from Rose's hand. "Oh, I'll cut ribbon and tie it on, and maybe add some jingly little bells. Trust me, this will look perfect!" she squealed as she ran through to the main hall. "I'll do a special arrangement for Mr. Roth's office."

"And visions of sugar daddies danced in her head!" said Terrence.

"Leave her be, Terrence. Not everyone has a scheme, you know," said Rose.

"It's the age-old story of the maid and the master, from where I'm standing," he replied.

"Maids don't always want masters!" said Rose sharply.

Mr. Chisholm swung through the door with a tray of empty glasses.

"Speaking of Christmas spirits, ladies and gentlemen," said Terrence, "I give you the Ghost of Christmas Past. Or as I like to call him, 'The Ghost of Christmas-That-Is-So-Last-Year.' Honestly,

I haven't seen a tuxedo coat like that since the Corn Laws were in place."

"Juliet," said Mr. Chisholm, ignoring Terrence, "Would you please mull wine? And as I'm working, would you pour me a virgin cocktail?"

"I'd say any cocktail you drink is a virgin cocktail," Terrence said, elbowing me. "Surely no one would touch you with a ten-foot pole. Certainly not his own pole."

"Terrence! Mr. Chisholm has earned a cold drink," said Rose. "Now, Isaac, help me carry this tea service and the rest of the silver out to the dining room. Mind that you don't use your hands… that's right, pick it up with a tea towel."

Before long, I glanced at the clock. Dinner was ordered for 6:30 and I was right on schedule. The kitchen was warm and smelled delicious; I could hear the laughter of some of the guests from the hallway. "It's our cue, Rose," I said, putting frilly panties on the bones of the crown roast and surrounding it with lightly browned vegetables and brilliantly green Brussels sprouts. I handed a gravy boat to Mr. Chisholm. It smelled like everything you'd want on a winter's day – aromatic richness and warmth. I placed an antique silver ladle alongside it on the platter and nestled a long sprig of rosemary in for garnish. Terrence swooped in with a covered basket of burlis — an intricate Swiss bread favored by Lady Penelope who went to boarding school in its home country – and Seamus followed up with the Yorkshire puddings. I paraded in after and placed a platter of perfectly browned, roasted potatoes. My trick is scoring them with a fork before drizzling them with beef fat for maximum crispness, then finishing them with a liberal handful of rock salt. Lady Ambridge literally smacked her lips and rubbed her hands together like a cartoon character as I put them down. I walked back in to the kitchen, puffed up as a lord.

I was proud. This meal was the direct opposite of the fussy menus in hip London restaurants, but it was what Christmas-y evenings called for. Home. Family. Comfort. And I did it solo, improvising with what Edward had laid in.

Ha, Edward. Looks like I don't need you for cooking, or in my bed. And I damn sure don't care about you!

Only, the truth is, even just thinking his name had my stomach doing a little flip.

Through the door, I heard a deep "hurrah!" from Lord Ambridge, and knew that I'd been spot on in choosing a Yorkshire pudding and not something like spaghetti squash coulis finished with a reduction of lemon and pomegranate. I sighed, relaxed now that dinner was on the table.

"Ah, the roast has gone down a treat," said Rose. "Truly. You're a genius, my dear. I'll say it again, the way to a man's heart is through his stomach, and you should see how the gentlemen out there are tucking into that meal. And, er, Lady Ambridge." I smiled at Rose, and pulled out the industrial-style hose from the deep kitchen sink and began showering water into the greasy roasting pan.

"Well, at least I have one trick for keeping a man!" We laughed together and it felt good.

I wondered what my mother would think of the gorgeous meal I'd created from nothing. I had a peaceful feeling inside, knowing that despite her ways, she'd be proud. Looking out the window, I saw crystals of snow in the outside lamp by the kitchen window. It was simply beautiful. I felt content. I put Ben and Edward, and even Posy, out of my thoughts. I was finally a little excited about Christmas.

****

When we had a full house, Jasper Roth launched into full host mode, and there was a sizzle of tension in the air at the guests' arrival. The minute people arrived by car, he wanted champagne buckets filling and refilling, more logs for the fires, lemons and limes for the bar, canapés ready to go, and so on and so on. He'd had Barry bring in all the best he had in the hothouse, and the place looked, and smelled, like a florist's – or a funeral parlor.

I'd just gotten the kitchen fully cleared up from dinner, when Kaylie Hart and Jacques Lacoste rang the bell. I could hear Jasper in the hallway as he alternated between barking orders at Terrence – "Take these bags up to the Regent's Room" – and gushing all over his guests – "Hey Beautiful, good to see you."

Through the swinging door, I could just see him kissing Kaylie Hart. "Brutal traffic on Fridays, right? Are you guys freezing? Jacques, wait till you taste my chef's food… it'll give new meaning to the phrase 'rave review'. Were the roads icy as hell?"

I walked out into the hallway to spy, pretending to need a chafing dish that was stored in an oversized, antique piece of furniture featuring a giant mirror and an umbrella stand. Jasper Roth had just helped Ms. Hart out of her Dr. Zhivago-style, full-length gray fur coat with a high collar, piling it onto Daphne, nearly smothering the tiny girl. Underneath, Kaylie was wearing tight satin leggings with high-heeled leather boots and an asymmetrical, off-the-shoulder lace top, belted around her nonexistent hips. Her dark, curly hair was tumbling over her shoulders from beneath a gray, fur cloche, which she declined to remove. Jacques, well known as an "it" boy and the most respected food critic in Paris, had on yellow-lensed Gucci aviator sunglasses and a leather outfit that implied he might leave any minute to either downhill ski or drive a racecar at high speed.

There was sinister and comical jostling between the butlers to see who would "win" and carry bags to the assigned rooms. The butler twins and Rose were at the top of their game – a forgotten toothbrush was replaced, wet shoes were exchanged for lambswool-lined house slippers, and hot toddies were handed round. Next, I knew towels would be placed on the towel warmers, pajamas would be laid out, beds would be turned back, and pillows would be jelly-babied. I'd always thought jelly babies on pillows was an especially weird custom in grand English houses. Couldn't they just do chocolates, like the Hilton? Especially since the mice often nibbled off the corners, or carried the candy away completely, if the guests were late to arrive.

"Not those bags, leave those there," Roth fussed at Mr. Chisholm.

"What else do you guys want to drink? Come into the library!" he said warmly. "Meet the others…"

He was two sides of the same coin, and I felt no one knew that better than I did.

"Terrence, get Seamus to garage the car."

"Chisholm this is the wrong ice."

"Terrence, can you get Juliet moving with the canapés?"

"Chisholm, fresh lime juice, not bottled."

"Kaylie, you're hardly wearing anything, let Terrence get you a fleece. Or do you want a shawl?"

"Are the blinds drawn in the Blue Room? Rose, the blinds!"

Mr. Roth didn't need to yell – Rose was always one step ahead of his wishes. Despite her close-to-the-ground girth, Rose could glide like a dancer into a crowd of guests and hypnotize them into following her lead. She had, by studying over the years, learned to be a lady, and The Painter treated her as such. He silently made it clear that he did not approve of the way Roth dismissed her.

I was still busy with the post-dinner washing up, with Daphne's help, and was sending out tray after tray of canapés and aperitifs. I was on deck to serve dinner on folding tables for the newly arrived and late-night sandwiches for the established guests.

"You've been summoned," Terrence said to me, as he swung into the kitchen with an ice bucket, which he swiftly dumped into the sink only to refill it immediately.

I rarely went anywhere besides the kitchens and dining rooms of houses. At Thornton, however, Jasper Roth always required at least one "parade the chef in front of the guests" session. I knew the drill. He set himself up to look like a solicitous and generous employer who took an interest in his staff, using me as his trophy to impress.

I popped into the loo off the staff dining room, took the clip out of my hair and brushed it. I freshened up my lipstick and took stock of my appearance. *A bit tired*, I thought. I noticed that I had gravy on the front of my chef's jacket so I tossed it in the corner hamper. The old stone house was chilly and I was cold in my tank top, away from the warm kitchen. I kept a stock of fresh jackets folded in the bathroom cupboard, but there were none left.

I opened the door to the main hall and ran smack into Jasper Roth's chest. He took me by the shoulders and held me back at arm's length. He didn't speak for what felt like a longer time than was comfortable and instead made a noise in the back of his throat that was a cross between a sigh and a hum. I was aware of his strong fingers, warm against my cold, exposed skin.

"Is that what they're wearing in the kitchen of The Hall these days?" he asked, his eyes dancing.

"You should visit the kitchen occasionally, *Sir*, and then you'd know."

"I like it when you call me sir."

"Jasper!" Lady Penelope called from down the hall.

"I'm, uh, on my way to the laundry for a fresh uniform," I gently freed my wrist and took a step back. "You called me into the library?"

"Yes, Dr. Dearden wants to compliment you on dinner and I want Kaylie and Jacques to meet you. They may come to Nantucket this summer, so you'll see them again then."

I won't be a chef by summer, I thought wistfully, thinking of grad school.

"I'm half-ready to tell you to come to the library in that," he said, continuing in a low voice. "You make me look good."

My face flushed hot. "My food makes you look good. I'll be right in to greet your guests. And your wife." The bare skin on my chest was covered in goose bumps, from the cold and the way his eyes ran over it. "I'll just get a jacket," I said, in what I hoped was an authoritative voice, and walked toward the laundry room.

Pulling on new chef's whites, I took a deep breath, and headed for the library. I walked just through the door and stood still, waiting to be spoken to first.

"This is great, Jasper, the house, everything. You know," Kaylie Hart said to Lady Penelope, "Jasper's hardly invited me anywhere since I got famous. I mean since I was *really* famous. Anyway," she said to Mr. Roth, "now we're bosom buds again, you should come to my house in Marin. You and Penelope, I mean."

"Juliet!" Mr. Roth said in a warm and hearty voice. "Come in." He didn't stand. I knew how to play my part. I walked to the side of his chair, clasped my hands in front of me and waited to be interviewed.

"So, Juliet" said Mr. Roth, "Dr. Dearden was praising your roast. He asked what your secret is." People are always asking chefs what our secrets are. The secret is that I know how to cook, but people always want a dramatic answer so they'll be in the know.

"I sear it in herb-infused oil on the stovetop, start it in the oven at a very high heat, then lower the heat to finish it for a long period, never opening the door. My roasts were a great favorite at both Brady House and Kempton Castle." I let that dangle in the air, knowing Roth's desire to keep up with the Joneses and his reverence for true English bloodlines.

"I'll have our chef try that," said Lady Ambridge. "I've rarely seen my husband eat so many helpings of anything. Of course, I'd like him to go vegetarian, but he was like a lion falling on your roast!"

"Eet zeems your chef ees not only lovely, but knows her craft," said Jacques.

"Before Juliet came to Thornton, she worked in a ton of great places, and they all ate her up with a spoon," Roth said. "Who wouldn't?"

I tried to throw him a sharp look, but when I met his eyes, I melted. He was sitting sprawled out, legs open wide, arm draped across the back of his chair. He was taking up a great deal of space and looking like he owned the place, which he kind of did. I stared at my shoes. Was it my imagination or had he just been looking at me with naked appreciation in front of a roomful of his guests? For half a second, I let myself imagine what it would be like to be sitting on his lap, snuggled into his soft cashmere sweater against the cold. I could almost smell his scent just thinking about it. I'd rub my cheek against the stubble on his jawline and instead of waiting for him to kiss me…

I was jarred back to my station when the Countess asked, "For what other families have you worked, dear?"

This was my cue to name-drop about all my rich and famous employers and throw in "juicy tidbits". I had a litany of well rehearsed "insider information" that would satisfy without betraying confidences. That composer insists on well done filet mignon (blasphemy!), that Hollywood actress demands that star fruit be served at every meal, despite the season, and that football player has me cut his fettucini into one-inch strips because "he doesn't like to twirl." I always get appreciative raised eyebrows and Jasper Roth puffs up with pride, showcasing my little act.

"Chefs are the new models. Hot, hot, hot. You should have one of those chef shows!" declared Kaylie Hart. "You could dish on everyone. You're good looking enough, but you might have to get a breast augmentation…and wear a sexier outfit."

"My word," said Lady Ambridge.

Kaylie was talking at a high volume and sloshing a rocks glass filled to the brim with what appeared to be either water or vodka. My money was on vodka. Jacques sat next to her in a deep wing-chair, bouncing his crossed leg as he gazed openly at Kaylie's chest, not the least bit embarrassed. "I'm friends with Piers Conley-Weatherall, you know. Jacques here knows him from the food world."

"Piers and I are old friends," confirmed Jacques.

"I did an episode of his show, you know, Low-Cal Thanksgiving? We hit it off. It's weird, with your crooked smile, you remind me of him. Or maybe it's just that chef coat and your crazy hair." I didn't know whether to be flattered or insulted. On the one hand, he was an idol of mine, on the other hand…crazy hair?

"I don't want Juliet on TV, I want her cooking for me," said Mr. Roth smoothly.

Then you'd better get your passport ready to follow me home to America, I thought.

"You'll have to come back when we have our senior chef, Edward," Lady Penelope said. "He's excellent. Never piles on the rich foods," she said throwing me a dismissive glance. "Meticulous with cleanliness. We're devastated he isn't here, but I have it on good authority he'll be popping the question to his lady love soon." She looked like the cat who swallowed the canary. "It's hard to imagine keeping a man like Edward tethered, though, wouldn't you say? One must give such a man a long lead, in my opinion. If you don't try to pin someone like Edward down, he'll circle back to you when he's had his fill of what's common."

Popping the question?!! I screamed in my head. That was it. Not only was *Ben* not asking me to marry him, but my red-hot lover *was* asking someone – someone who was also not me. Not that I wanted to marry him. Or Ben. Did I? Feeling swoony, I fell lightly into a sitting position on the ottoman next to Jasper Roth's chair. Realizing I had just sat down with guests, I sprang to my feet.

"Juliet, are you quite well?" asked the Countess.

"Fine, thank you," I said, though I was certain I was not. I couldn't really remember the last time I was. *As soon as this gig's over, you're on a plane back to The States to finish your degree,* I told myself. *Who do you think you are with all this international bed-hopping, star-fucking, adultery-tempting, billionaire-world chefery. Mother was right.* In my head, I tested out my new heartsong – the phrase I had to say to myself again and again so I would believe it – *I am a scientist and a therapist.* I was too distracted to make it stick.

"…and steer clear of the media, I say," The Painter lectured. "Trust me, a nice quiet life with someone you love – maybe alone in a little cottage – where you can walk the streets in peace, in a sunny country, anonymous…" he trailed off, lost in his fantasy.

The Countess looked pinched. "Anyway, we'd be quite crushed to lose Juliet," she said, the portrait of grace.

"I don't plan to be on TV," I said, though I declined to tell them what my plan actually was. I was a chef, at least until the end of this Christmas holiday. "I enjoy being in charge of a kitchen, and I love my agent, who has booked me with Mr. Roth, *one of* my favorite clients." I reminded everyone of the fact that I wasn't his private chef.

"Juliet is superior," said The Painter. "And she's pretty as a picture." He smiled kindly at me. I certainly didn't feel pretty next to Kaylie, the toned and stacked starlet. "That Conley-Weatherall fellow could do worse than to have her as his *sous-* chef."

"Quite so," agreed his wife, smiling graciously at me. "Lovely and capable." Her compliment made me blush, as she was, even at her age, a true beauty. If Helen Mirren and Catherine Deneuve were rolled into one elegant and fine-boned lady, she would almost hold a candle to the Countess.

"And she makes an excellent raclette," said Lord Ambridge, his face contorting as he Swissed-up the pronunciation, which appeared difficult for him, given his level of drunkenness. "One must never drink water with raclette," he lectured slowly, taking care to enunciate his consonants. "Only very warm tea, or alcohol if you are a drinker," he continued, glancing sidelong at Kaylie, who was slugging back the remains of her vodka. "It interferes with the digestion of the cheese and has been known to cause death when cheese balls form in the stomach."

"Well, eef one as to die, ee may as well die by fine cheese or a fine woman," Jacques said, leering through hooded eyes. "When you ave a female chef, there is dan-zher of death both ways, eh?"

"She's a smarty-pants, too. She studied psychology, so she's a keen observer of human behavior, right Juliet? You better be careful, Jacques, she can tell when a man's trying to overcompensate." Roth turned his body fully away from Jacques and said,

"Kaylie, you must be starved. What can my Juliet here make you?"

"*Your Juliet* could bring me another brandy," snapped Lady Penelope. I stood frozen to my spot. Strictly speaking, fetching her drinks wasn't in my job description. Daphne, who shouldn't have been serving in the room rushed up, her white cap pinned cockeyed on her head. Before Terrence could outrun her, she lowered her body into an awkward curtsey, and said "Allow me, Lady," sounding exactly like Eliza Doolittle. She looked extremely pleased with herself. Terrence ran from the room, strangling on his laughter. I thanked my lucky stars that Mr. Chisholm was not present to hear that faux pas, and made a mental note to teach Daphne to address the Earl's daughter as "Your Ladyship and never 'Lady.'"

Too focused on her drink to care, Lady Penelope accepted the offer and tossed two pills to the back of her throat, chasing it with the drink.

"Nothing wrong with warming your bones, I always say," Daphne said heartily. I winced inwardly, and tried to signal her with my eyes.

"Jasper, I don't want to eat," said Kaylie. "Maybe another cocktail?" she said, holding out her glass, which Mr. Roth jumped up to grab, motioning for Daphne to leave the room. She got in one last half-curtsey before she was banished. "And don't have Juliet analyze me!" Kaylie said to the room. "My shrink in L.A. said I'm an 'oversharer' and that I have 'compulsive disclosure syndrome'. I'd never make it as a spy, they'd just have to tickle me and I'd spill the beans, right Jasper?"

I watched all the various lords, ladies and gentlefolk stare at the wall, look at their laps, and pretend to re-button their sweaters. The English, no matter how tanked, are not a people who speak freely about personal issues, and nearly everything out of Kaylie Hart's mouth triggered cringes. Jacques, who didn't seem to notice the awkward reference to Kaylie's ex, smiled in Franco-oblivion.

"You guys have to eat. C'mon! Jacques, what would you like?

Anything you want! Juliet will make it."

I held my breath at the thought of what Jacques Lacoste, sophisticated international food critic, might casually toss out. If he named braised kidneys in a cherry-chocolate sauce, or a pineapple upside-down cake with sweet chili syrup, I'd have to scrounge around for the ingredients and whip it up.

"Well, all thees talk of cheese…maybe a bit of fruit, a bit of bread, a bit of cheese…"

I exhaled, but didn't relax.

Jasper Roth never let guests off the hook as far as drinking alcohol or eating went. He handed Kaylie another full glass and sat down. His wife held her now-empty glass toward him and smiled. He cast her an annoyed look, and took away her brandy glass. He replaced it with one of sparkling water.

"Jacques, how about steak frites? A food reviewer can't refuse to taste my chef's offerings! Don't forget, Juliet knocked around Paris. You can challenge my girl and see if she can do it up to French standards."

"By all means," said Lady Penelope, setting down her water glass and helping herself to the brandy on the sideboard, "let his girl service you. Pardon. I mean serve you…" She wobbled back to her seat, sloshing brandy onto the centenarian rug. Terrence, back to collect empty glasses on a tray, raised his eyebrows at me.

"Sure, sure," Jacques said. "Please, Zhuliet, I like when it says 'Muuh.'"

Kaylie hooted. "He means moo! He's telling you he wants it rare! Did you know that all animals in France speak a different language? Isn't that precious?"

Steak frites was good. Steak frites was manageable.

"Kaylie, what're you going to eat?" asked my boss.

"I don't know…bring me a salad."

"It's *snowing* outside, you can't eat a salad!"

I jumped in, knowing this would go on for days. Starlets don't eat meals, and they rarely eat in front of other people. But I knew Mr. Roth wouldn't let her skip being fed with crystal, linen, and china on a tray in front of her deep, leather chair. Before he suggested something intricate like a whole roasted snapper with lobster sauce or stuffed duck breast, I decided to offer some suggestions of easy-to-make dishes, since I knew they'd sit uneaten anyway.

"Could I suggest a pasta with a light white wine and basil sauce?" I said.

"Oh my *God* no! Carbs are like cyanide to me!"

"Perhaps, then, we should move the scotch to another room?" slurred Lady Penelope.

"Penny, perhaps you'd like to lie down..." suggested the Countess, sensing trouble.

I cut them all off. "In that case, Ms. Hart, an egg-white omelet?"

"Yeah, that sounds great," she said, waving me off. She was far more interested in her drink and flirting with her host than she was in having me in the room.

"A plain omelet?!!" roared Mr Roth. "C'mon! What do you want in it? Anything! I have truffle, fois gras, white asparagus, mushrooms, prosciutto, ten kinds of cheese..."

"Cheese?" she spat at Roth. "Are you trying to pick a fight with me? I don't know," she said, waving her hands. "Anything. Mushrooms...asparagus, no, um, mushrooms...I don't care." She was flustered and clearly didn't want to be having this conversation. "It doesn't matter. *Mushrooms.*" She turned away from me, obviously dismissing me to go and make the food she wouldn't be eating for dinner. I waited for Mr. Roth to signal me and he nodded. I was released.

Chapter Thirteen

Back in the kitchen, Seamus was seated at the table, eating a ham sandwich on brown bread with Branston pickle and drinking a cup of tea. "Juliet, since you're up, would you be kind enough to hand me the salad cream?" he asked.

"Anything for you, Seamus," I said, crossing to the fridge. Terrence and Daphne were sitting with an almost-empty bottle of Chianti between them. Rose was tidying up dishes.

"Where's Chisholm?" I asked, as I pulled out a pan, the butter and some eggs.

"He's standing at attention right outside the library," said Terrence. "He told me that's the way they did it at Clarence House. I suppose Her Majesty enjoyed being surrounded by erect men."

"And I've sent Isaac home to his Jane. He'll be up with the sparrow for the shooting party tomorrow morning," said Rose.

"Anyone want steak frites or a mushroom omelet?" I asked around the kitchen. I realized I hadn't eaten in a very long time. In general, I liked to sit down and savor whatever I was eating, but chefs often made do on a bite here, or a slice there.

"I'm drinking my midnight snack," said Terrence.

"Would it be too much trouble to ask you to fry me an egg?" asked Rose.

"None at all. My pleasure," I said, and I meant it.

I quickly cut potatoes for the pommes frites and grabbed a steak to toss under the broiler. I looked in the bottom of the pantry for mushrooms, but there weren't any. *On to Plan B*, I thought, grabbing asparagus and spinach instead. "Terrence," I said, "no mushrooms for the film star."

"Let them eat cake, right mate?" Terrence answered.

"Will you tell Ms. Hart that the vitamin E in spinach is a skin youthener?"

"Is it? Fry me up some to rub on my turkey neck!" he said, pulling out the skin on his throat like a wattle.

I set a plate of eggs and toast with a spray of sliced fruit down for Rose and made trays with the omelet, steak and potatoes to take into the library. Terrence stood and took it from me. "Ha, got it first. Terry, one. Chizzy, zero!"

As I cleaned up what I hoped would be the last round of cooking for the night, Seamus excused himself and asked to take Rose home with him.

"With all this snow, I wonder if the shoot'll be scrapped for tomorrow," he said. "Maybe we'll all have a nice lie-in," he chuckled, shrugging on his coat, and handing Rose her wrap.

"I wouldn't hope too hard," Rose answered. "If I know Mr. Roth, wild horses couldn't stop it. Good night, dear. We'll leave you to it," she said as she closed the back kitchen door behind herself.

Suddenly, I heard footsteps pounding down the long hall.

"Incoming!" whispered Terrence as he flew through the swinging door from the hallway. Right behind him was Jasper Roth, with fire in his eyes. Daphne sucked in her breath, stood up from the table and, inexplicably, saluted.

"Juliet! Explain to me why there are no mushrooms in this kitchen? We are sitting on 1200 acres of land, Lord and Lady Ambridge run a goddamn organic produce farm within driving distance, there are at least 10 vehicles in the garages, including a snowmobile. I put mushrooms on the list. Are you an idiot?" he yelled.

Terrence and Daphne scuttled through to the staff dining room and disappeared in the blink of an eye, Daphne with a look of stark terror on her face.

I was furious. This is how he was going to talk to me after all I'd done for him? All the service I'd given him, all the plans I'd cancelled to be available for him, the ear I'd lent when he had no friends to talk to, all of the excuses I made for him, saying he was a good person deep down.

"Listen to me carefully, Jasper," I said in a quiet voice, filled with warning. I'd never called him by his first name, not even during the times in Nantucket and Aspen when we'd had spontaneous intimate talks. "I will leave here this minute. I will walk back to London in the snow if I have to." All of the Ben-and-Edward mania I had tamped down inside me was percolating. "I will leave you with a house full of hungry guests." Roth looked like I'd slapped him. I could feel myself spiraling out of control, and even as I was ranting, a part of myself was calmly observing my behavior from the outside. *Juliet,* my inner voice told me, *take a deep breath and stop talking.*

"The last man who called me an idiot is at the top of my list of people I could kill with my bare hands," I spewed on, ignoring my voice of reason, "and right now, you're second. I mean third. Maybe fourth, if you count Stephen."

That seemed to jar him out of his stormy mood and he looked genuinely confused and curious. "Who's the last man who called you an idiot? Edward?" His ice-blue eyes were losing their fire and clouding with confusion.

"What? No…why would Edward have called me an idiot?" I demanded.

"I don't know. Because he's the boyfriend you were always sneaking off to MacGregor's cottage with?"

"I never sneaked off to MacGregor's cottage with Edward! Where did you hear that?"

"Well. Or maybe because he's always been crazy about you, and you stayed aloof, acting like you were too good for him, maybe? You do that, you know. Or because everyone in town saw you two cavorting in and out of cafés?"

"We did not cavort! When we were in town, it was because we were shopping for the Hall, and stopped for a cup of tea." Even as I said it, I knew it wasn't true. Every lunch felt like a date, and every sneaked pint at the pub was a prelude to my sleeping with him. I'd been lying to myself because I was with Ben. True, I'd never acted on it before this trip, but I wouldn't have wanted Ben to see videotapes of our times together.

"Or how about this: Because he was jealous of me?" said Jasper Roth.

How was he so right about everything? Did he also know I was attracted to him?

"Jealous of you?" I laughed, acting brave. "You must think every woman who comes near you wants you to take her to bed." I regretted saying the words, because an image of him lounging on his richly brocaded and overstuffed bed, wearing nothing but the royal-blue silk pajama bottoms I'd seen delivered from the dry-cleaners sprung to life in my mind. I drove it away by focusing back on my indignation.

"And may I ask, what does anything between me and Edward have to do with you?" I could not believe I was getting so fresh with my boss. Of course I'd been bluffing…but now I might *have* to walk back to London in the snow. "Don't pin it on Edward when he's not here to defend himself. Maybe *you're* the one who thinks I'm a tease," I heard myself saying out loud, "but here's news for you…you're married and you shouldn't be thinking about me at all." He stared at me hard. "And it was Ben who called me an idiot!" I couldn't stop myself now. "You…idiot!"

"Who's Ben?"

"Are you joking? Ben is my boyfriend. *Was* my boyfriend! The one I told you about over bottles and bottles of wine I shouldn't have been drinking with you in Nantucket. Do you ever, *ever* listen to me when I talk to you? I thought you cared about what I said. That's what I get for imagining I'm special."

"You are special."

My pounding heart let me know I was in dangerous territory. "I didn't mean special, I meant I thought you cared about me. Not about me, the things I say. When we talk. Whatever! It's my fault, all of it. I thought you were a good guy underneath. When you confided in me about wanting a family, and maybe children, I thought I was seeing the real you. I even imagined you were a hero for staying with your wife, supporting her through her illness, even though," I dropped my voice to a whisper, "you told me you didn't love her. But I clearly, *clearly*, and I mean *clearly* have no judgment when it comes to men. Someone should cloister me with nuns. I'm not safe on the street!"

"Why would you say that?"

I hesitated. "Because I fell for it."

"Juliet," he started, but I cut him off.

"And then I watch you here, on this turf, strutting around acting like you're the ruler of God's dominion, showing your bad manners and ill temper to the world. All that time in Nantucket, when your wife was – sorry, but not in her right mind."

Jasper winced.

"I'm not trying to be cruel. But however you want to say it, she was not there for you. And you leaned on me. And like a fool, I lapped it up. I guess I wanted to be a hero or something."

Jasper's face softened. "Is that the only reason you sat up with me those nights, drinking wine and sharing dinner?"

"It doesn't matter. I was with Ben. And you were married. *Are* married."

"I don't want to talk about Ben. I want to talk about us. Look me in the eye and tell me you didn't think about sleeping with me after we kissed that night, here, in the drawing room."

"That was hardly a kiss," I protested. My face burned in shame. It had been a kiss, if I were honest with myself. *Stupid, stupid,*

Juliet. Who drinks a whole bottle of wine with her boss in a dark, quiet house after midnight? Good thing Rex had gotten spooked and started barking. I'd scared myself at how close I'd come to crossing the line. "It was a peck goodnight," I said lamely.

He flashed a charming smile. "Do you kiss all your clients goodnight, or is it just me you can't resist?"

"You know, it's really a good thing I'm quitting being a chef." My outrage was back. "Going back for my psych degree is the right move, because I need my head examined, because for five minutes in Nantucket I stopped thinking you were an asshole!"

Fuming, I sat down on a kitchen chair. *Fire me* I thought. *I dare you.* I looked out the window at the falling snow and the drift that was piling up on the sill. I should have known better than to ever get personal with someone I work for – or maybe with any man, for any reason. The less of yourself you put out, the less of it gets taken away.

"Hey. I'm sorry," he said after a few seconds. "You're right. I'm the idiot. And I remember you telling me about Ben now. I listened, I really did. I didn't know you broke up. I'm sorry about that. It's getting late, and it's no excuse, but I guess I'm tense about entertaining. Forget the mushrooms…"

"It's not about the mushrooms. So we had no mushrooms. The kitchen was stocked with 587 items and I forgot the 588th! Big deal! By the way, I was supposed to be an assistant here. Your wife dismissed the man who did all the planning and ordering, remember? I'm not supposed to be the boss of everything…"

"No, I am. I'm the boss, and I'm the one who sent Edward away."

"Oh my God. Why?"

"He was just in the way." He looked down into my eyes. "Don't you see?"

"I think you'd better call the agency and replace me." I felt an incredible emptiness in my chest. I stared at the swinging door.

He pulled up the chair next to me, but I looked away. He took his hand, cupped my chin and turned my face to his. He smelled like bay rum and wool. My stomach flipped at the memory of his scent, which was homey and comforting. I'd expected him to smell cold and steely, like expensive cologne with a name like *Wall Street* or *Tycoon*, but no. When he'd held me in his arms, he smelled and felt like a real man.

"Hey," he said softly. "Don't leave. I don't expect you to forgive me, but I'm sorry. Not about Edward. About the way I spoke to you. I was just blowing off steam. Who else cooks like you, can talk about art and politics, and knows what makes people tick? Who else pegs me for the jerk I am?" He smiled. "Not the guys at the office. Certainly not my wife. Why do you think I keep asking for you?"

"Don't insult your wife to me," I said with a warning look. "We both know why that's a trap. You ask for me because I'm one of the best at The Gastronome's Trust and because I don't quit when you bluster around or swear at me. And because I'm funny and you're not. And because you like it when I take charge." I looked at him. "You may think you're the boss, but it's not always true."

He raised his eyebrows.

"Who else takes charge of you?" The question hung in the air. His eyes locked with mine and he wouldn't turn away. It was a game of chicken, and nervous, I gave up first.

"Of course you fear me," I said, breaking eye contact and making a joke of it. "As a chef, I could poison you and get away with it!"

He laughed, then his face turned serious, like he was choosing his words carefully before opening his mouth. He reached over and put his hand on my cheek.

Just then, Chisholm swung through the door. His face temporarily registered alarm as he saw Mr. Roth seated in the kitchen, whispering close to me. In a move stolen from the beefeaters at Buckingham Palace, he did a hop-step, pivoted on his heel and marched out without ever breaking his stride.

Roth reluctantly stood up next to his chair.

"You're right, you are funny. You do make me laugh. And

you're gorgeous, my God, look at you. If I had met you first, I'd have used all my guns and money to…"

I stood up, and crossed my arms over my chest.

"Shut up! Stop it right there. I'm not playing the 'my wife just doesn't understand me' game with you. Really, I'm the house's chef and that line of B.S. is for dumb and desperate girls. Secretaries who sleep with their married bosses…"

"Pardon me, Sir," Terrence said, opening the door half an inch but not coming through, "but her Ladyship requests your presence."

"Tell her I'll be right there," he said. The door eased shut. "Do me a favor," he whispered. "Don't quit. I just want to finish this conversation, once and for all. Can't we do that?"

"No. I think we shouldn't. If what you have to say doesn't involve whether you want fish or fowl served at dinner, I think we should avoid talking."

"You'll find the ice right through here in the freezer, Daphne!" Terrence shouted as he stomped down the hall, clearly warning us that he was about to enter the kitchen. I stood up from my chair and moved to the sink to fold a dishtowel.

"Right Terrence, the freezer!" she shouted back, you just knew she was winking very obviously. "And we definitely were not drinking the good wine from the cellar!" she yelled.

I rolled my eyes as Jasper Roth swung out the door, just as they came in. We heard him walking back to the library. Even though I'd just put up a wall between us, I had to admit to myself that his abrupt departure stung.

"So what's up?" asked Terrence. "Chizzy told us the master was in the kitchen and not to disturb him. I read between the lines and figured Santa was making plans to go *up* the chimney this season."

"Terrence, you are so beyond ridiculous I don't know what to say to you," I told him, trying to steady my breath and sound calm.

"Mr. Roth stopped looking angry," Daphne said. "He looks kind of sad. Maybe I should take him a treat to cheer him up?"

she said excitedly.

"Why do you keep mentioning treats?" asked Terrence. "He's not a toddler. He's not a lapdog."

"Leave him alone," I told her.

Mr. Chisholm came into the kitchen holding a tray with the dishes from Kaylie and Jacques' meals on it. As I'd predicted, the omelet was untouched.

Rex poked his snout through the door from the laundry room. "Hey, you're in luck. C'mere, Boy. Rex!" The dog came all the way into the kitchen and I set the omelet down on the floor in front of him. As I watched him bolt down the omelet, I thought of how I ended up here.

You've gone from being a top chef in London at the Ivy to making late-night snacks for a dog. Good work, Juliet. Taco Bell can't be far off.

"It's best to know one's place in all matters, whether it be in habit or relationship," Chisholm said to me archly. "Your advice to 'leave him alone' is spot on." He picked up one packet of Sweet and Low, placed it on his large, silver tray and left the kitchen.

As much as I disliked Mr. Chisholm's stuffy, old-English pompousness, what he said made me stop and think. *Who am I, exactly, and what is my place?*

Maybe I was simply my mother's daughter. A middle-American girl, probably single, with a quiet therapy practice in the town where she was born. I found myself wishing she'd tell me what to do. I needed someone. *OK, Mother. You win. I'll call you for Christmas and you can sketch out my life.*

Chapter Fourteen

"Seriously?" I said to my travel clock, slapping it off the bedside table and knocking it to the floor. It felt like I'd just closed my eyes. 5:45 a.m. A pre-dawn jumpstart in the kitchen had seemed like such a good idea last night when I'd set the alarm.

My fire had died and my cottage was freezing. I pushed back the sash on the window and saw snow still falling in the gray half-light of the early morning. I quickly washed and dressed, and pulled my long coat over my chef's whites, eager to get to the main kitchen to make coffee. My old wooden door opened against a drift. I crunched into the snow that was already deeper than my ankles. Sprinting across the yard to the back door leading to the kitchen, I kept slipping on the cobblestones as I went. There on the step, dusted with snow, was a red, wooden basket of mushrooms and a brace of pheasant.

I carried them in, put the mushrooms on a low shelf in the pantry and made sure not to lay the birds out on the corner of the table where they could be seen from the hall... since the family and guests were going to Peabody Park after breakfast, I thought I'd make pheasant pie as a treat for staff lunch. I grabbed a bowl of cranberries from the refrigerator, a bowl of unshelled walnuts and a burlap sack of flour, arranging them on the corner of the table. *There, that looks duly Christmas-y.*

Rex was lying in his dog bed. I bent down and stroked his ears. He was whimpering softly. "Wake up, boy. Are you having a nightmare?" He heaved himself up, and padded across the wooden floor, his claws clicking. He drank from his water bowl like he'd just walked out of the desert. I followed him through the pantry to the mudroom, and stood outside while he did his business. "Oh, Rex. That doesn't look right!" I told him as he squatted and sprayed the walkway. "Poor boy. Sorry you're sick, but if you have diarrhea, could you at least go closer to the woods?" He followed me back to the warm kitchen and fell back onto his bed. I offered him a biscuit. He sniffed it and left it lay.

I started a pot of regular coffee and made myself a cappuccino with the sleek and expensive Nespresso machine Jasper Roth loved so much. Edward had sold him on it, bringing in the brochure, leading his boss to it like a duck to water. By the end of the conversation, Mr. Roth was congratulating himself for having thought of it himself. I thought about Edward. It was strange that we'd been so intimate and now I'd never see him again. I had a hollow feeling deep down and low in my belly.

It was quiet in the large, old kitchen, and starting the intricate breakfast preparations was a breeze with no one underfoot. Snow was coming down with a purpose. I hoped the shoot wouldn't be cancelled, I wanted solitude. I needed the family to leave for the afternoon. My body took over the prepping and cooking and before I realized it, I had pans sizzling on the stove, various batters prepared in mixing bowls, fruit simmering, and dozens of eggs cracked. I started peeling potatoes over the sink, staring out the window at the falling flakes and letting my mind wander in the quiet. For the moment, I felt happy.

Are you happy, Juliet? I asked myself. I kind of was.

Maybe I was just born to drift. To roll with the punches. And what if, just what if, I wasn't not an uber-intellectual? Right now, I was really happy to just peel potatoes and look out the window.

"Oh, allo. Could I get a coffee? I'm feeling ze cocktails thees morning." Jacques walked through the door from the staff dining room. He had on a gray and burgundy silk dressing gown, with a fleur-de-lis pattern on it, and a black silk eyeshade pushed up onto his forehead, like a headband holding back his hair. Gesturing backward toward the staff room with his thumb he said, "I found myself in a strange dining room. I was a leetle lost."

"I know the feeling," I said

"*Comme?*" he asked.

"Never mind. Would you like cappuccino or filter?"

"Whatever ees strong," he told me.

"I'll have it sent to your room. Would you like anything else?"

"Non, non, I weel seet," he said, and pulled out a kitchen chair. I felt awkward having him in the kitchen, especially when I was alone. I set about making two cappuccinos, his first and mine second.

"You are a real chef, I sink," he said.

"Thank you. I appreciate that, especially coming from you."

"Zo, your boss is kind of an asshole, non?"

I stiffened. While I didn't technically disagree, I was an employee at The Hall and I wasn't used to kicking back with the guests and biting the hand that fed me. Smiling a terse smile, I set the cup of coffee in front of Jacques.

"Sugar?"

"Non, I take my sweetness elsewhere. You don't zee that to be true, about Jasper?" he asked.

I took a stab at answering him. "Um, do you mean because he was flirting with your girlfriend?"

"Non, non. I don't care about that, of course! Zay were lovers, now zay are not, maybe zay weel be again. C'est la vie. I just mean how…how do you zay, *uptight,* he is. And he treats you like a dog who dances, eh?"

"I'm treated very well here," I told him, trying to be both professional and loyal to the house. *Kaylie and Roth were lovers? When?*

"But ee gives me fine food, ee gives me a zoft bed and ee is

169

taking me to shoot, I cannot complain. Life is to enjoy, non?" Jacques took his cup and stopped, mid-swing out the door. "An observation? Ee does not care what Kaylie thinks of heem except he wants that she desires heem, naturally. But weeth you, ee ees hungry. Non, not hungry…ehm, *angry*."

"Why would he be angry with me?"

"Not weeth you, about you. Because you don't act like ee eez a man." He walked out the door and I heard him padding in his socks down the runner in the long hallway.

Rose and Seamus came through the back door carrying pitchers of juice that they rushed onto the sideboard in the dining room.

"Good morning! Aren't you the early bird?" said Rose, brushing the snow off of the top of her hair carefully, so as not to collapse it.

I turned on the electric kettle. Seamus and Rose were strictly tea drinkers. They made it clear that they didn't dabble in coffee. Without a word exchanged, Rose started carrying out platters of cold items, setting the table and arranging chafing dishes on the buffet.

"I'll just make Sanka for Lady Penny. And give me a pitcher of water, Juliet. She has to take her vitamins before she goes to the coffee morning with the ladies. I have to lay out warm clothes, since it's likely to be freezing in the bothy. She really shouldn't be dragged out in her condition."

"Has she announced…?" I started.

"Having lunch outdoors in the snow when there are roaring fires inside! Nonsense! Why they're carrying on with the shooting party today, our Lord only knows."

Terrence blew in the back door and began folding napkins and taking down the serving bowls and platters.

"Well, at least she's taking her vitamins. If she's pregnant, that's a good thing," I said. I slugged down the rest of my coffee in one swallow.

"She might be, but I meant her nerve pills. She depends on them. The poor dear. Ever since she was a girl, she was nervous.

She likes to be alone. We were truly stunned she married at all. When she was little, she almost wouldn't play with Isaac. You'd think they'd have been thick as thieves, but no…"

I had to hold my teeth shut to keep from saying, "*She's a spoiled, crazy bitch, and it looks like she's a drug addict to boot!*" I really would make a crappy therapist. The woman obviously needs help.

Trying to take the high road, I asked, "Does she have many friends outside the family?"

"She ran that gallery in London before she married, but it didn't work out. She has a difficult streak. She's one to hold a quiet grudge. She can go from day to night in the blink of an eye. Though she's close with Edward, I suppose."

"What do you mean she's close to Edward?" I asked lightly.

"Oh, you know, he's the chef she takes when she travels. He's the one to bring her meals and whatnot. They've always spent a fair amount of time talking in her room. She wasn't very happy that time he'd gone traveling for six months, that's certain. I think she thinks of Edward as a brother."

Brother…that doesn't seem right. Oh my God, are she and Edward lovers? I wondered. *If so, what was all that about his hometown girlfriend?*

"It's true," said Seamus. "I've hardly seen her open up to anyone the way she does Edward."

"When The Painter sent her off to school in Switzerland," Rose continued, "she begged to stay home. I know her father thought that going to school at Downe House would toughen her up and bring her out of her shell. It must have been hard on him, doing that for her own good. The Hall would have been very quiet indeed all those years, had Isaac not been here. The Painter often said so."

"Children make a home merry," Seamus said. "Welcoming a child is a blessing. I hope Lady Penelope gets to feel the joy I've felt. Ever since Isaac was little, I've found no greater joy than peering into those bright eyes of his."

"When he was a boy, his eyes were like flashlights in a dark room, I swear it. Of course, I have blue eyes, but not like those. Mine are darker blue. Isaac's are like ice."

"Good morning," said Chisholm, coming into the kitchen. "Mr. Roth is at the table and has requested a double-shot cappuccino with no foam. Has anyone seen Daphne?"

"I assume she's stoking the fires," said Rose. "I haven't yet seen her this morning."

"You're coming in late," said Terrence. "Have you spent your morning writing Chizzy plus Jasper in little hearts in your diary?"

"As I'm here to support the needs of Thornton Hall, I'm choosing to ignore the underbutler," Mr. Chisholm said, directly to Rose.

"Underbutler!" yelled Terrence. "You and that American are practically Locusta and Agrippina, the way you're eyeballing the throne. Face it Mizz Chizz, I'm the butler and I rule The Hall. If you can't stand the small square footage back in Roth's tacky flat, you'd better get yourself rehired by the royal family."

Mr. Chisholm went red in the face. "My days in service to Clarence House are in no way…"

"Isaac," Rose said loudly, cutting him off, "have you prepared the gear to take for the shoot?"

"All done, Mum," he said.

"I'll just double-check and tie up any loose ends," said Seamus, exiting the back door.

"Isaac, if you have a free moment, can you help me pluck these birds?" I said, gesturing to the brace of pheasants half-hidden under towels on the butcher block.

"Ah, sure he will!" said Rose. "He's an expert! But Isaac," she said, "you'll need to wet pluck as these are fresh and haven't been hung. It's crowded in here with all of us doing breakfast. Take the pheasants back to Rose Cottage and do it in my kitchen. That way you won't bother Jane. Use the big copper basin under the sink for scalding water."

"I'm making pies, Isaac, so don't worry about tearing the skin.

You can do it quickly, it doesn't matter," I told him. Pheasant skin is thinner than that of other game birds. When you want the birds to look pretty on a platter, plucking can be painstaking work.

Isaac picked up the birds and went out the back door.

"If he has time before the shooting party leaves, I'm sure he'll bring them back gutted and cleaned," Rose said. "Where's that Daphne? I need her to start taking costumes out of boxes."

"Costumes? What costumes?" I asked, but Rose was already through the door. I picked up a giant platter of sausages and carried it through to the dining room. Roth was seated at the foot of the table, poking furiously at his iPhone.

"Chisholm, I thought you set this up to control the Flood Street house."

"I did, Sir," said Chisholm. "You're able to turn on and off the lights, work the security system, the sound system…all remotely. May I, Sir?" Chisholm took the phone, touched it a few times and handed it back. "There you are, Sir," he said.

"Great. Make sure my warm silk underwear is laid out, will you?"

"Of course, Sir," said Chisholm, walking out of the dining room.

I was arranging the sausage platter on the sideboard, turning on the electric hotplates beneath. The silence hung in the air.

"Hey," he said.

"Yes, Sir?" I answered.

"Oh, so you're 'sirring' this morning, huh?" he asked.

I sighed, and wiped my hands on a towel. "I'm your chef. What am I supposed to do?"

"You're more than my chef. Let me explain…"

Kaylie Hart burst into the dining room, wearing skin-tight, pink velour bell bottoms with the word "Juicy" printed across the rear end, and a form-fitting white knit turtleneck.

"Morning, Glories!" she trilled. "Black coffee," she said in my direction. "Sweet and Low on the side. Jacques isn't coming down. Can you send him up a croissant or something?" Annoyance flickered across Jasper Roth's face. If he was laying a spread, he intended for everyone to enjoy it, whether they liked it or not. "Juliet," he said softly. "Send him a full English breakfast on a tray."

Lord and Lady Ambridge filed in behind her and took their places at the table.

"Oh what a beautiful Mooooor-niiiiiing, Oh what a beautiful Daaaaaaaaay," sang Ms. Hart, in full voice with her arms extended, as though she were singing in a large Broadway theater. I had to give it to her, though. She really had pipes. She was practically blowing the walls off the place. Anyone who hadn't been awake surely was now. The Ambridges smiled at her, but with a hunted look behind their eyes. You could see them assessing her as if she were an exotic jungle animal.

"You know, Kaylie," Jasper Roth said, cutting through the awkwardness. "Suleiman Pictures just acquired the rights to that hot new book *Geek Party at the Circus.* The role of the trainer's girlfriend has your name written all over it."

"Is that why you asked me here? You know I don't decide those things. You'll have to talk to the team."

"If you're gonna play hard to get, we could just move forward with Reese." He turned his back to her. "Ambridge, tell me about your market share. I've been reading some hot stuff about the dairy in *The Wall Street Journal.*"

"Hold on," Kaylie broke in, "I didn't say I wouldn't do it. If the timing's right, I'll think about it."

"I can't make a firm offer, but it's good to know you're interested."

"You just asked me!"

"We're waiting to hear back from some people. Scarlett's people like the idea. Angelina's have some questions."

"I should know better than to take you at your word, Jasper. It's like you said in *Forbes*, you're always looking for a bigger, better deal."

"You read *Forbes*?" asked Lady Ambridge through a mouthful of waffle.

"Morning, Helena," said Lord Ambridge, as the Countess took her seat.

"I'm a morning person. People hate that about me," Kaylie announced. "I know you always did, Jasper," she stage whispered to Mr. Roth as Lady Penelope came through and sat next to her husband. Everyone noticed that she was a little wobbly getting to her chair and didn't make eye contact with anyone. Ultimately, her gaze rested on *The Veiled Madonna*.

"Penelope, that painting is wild! If my skin looked like the girl in the picture's, I'd run around naked all the time, too," Kaylie said, gesturing at *The Veiled Madonna*.

"I had the unique experience of seeing both *Stone Cold Foxes* and *Remembrances of Autumn*. Judging from your work, it seems that that's exactly what you do," said Lady Ambridge.

There was a collective sound of people around the table sucking in their breaths and the words hung in the air for a second.

Kaylie burst out in a snorting laugh. "Muriel, you are a hoot! '*Exactly what I do!*' You are too funny!"

Everyone exhaled and laughed nervously.

"I'll just send Rose through with more coffee," I said, though no one was paying any attention to me. As I crossed behind The Painter's empty chair, I wondered why he wasn't at the table.

Back in the kitchen I took out the mixer, sprinkled the table with flour and started to make dough for the pies. Out the window, I spied The Painter fully dressed in a plaid, wool coat, hat and gloves. He was walking the land, occasionally stopping to look down beneath the snow or to kick the ground. The snow was picking up to the point that his hat with the earflaps was already turning white. Occasionally, he'd dig around under one of the trees, using his gloved hands.

Rose came through with an armful of empty platters. "They're tucking it away this morning, to be sure. I always say that cold weather and snow make a body want to eat. It's times like this I want nothing but dripping sandwiches and deep-dish pies."

Or to dive under the duvet with a sexy chef, I thought involuntarily. *But I guess that ship's sailed.*

"I should have saved the grease from the sausage pans for you," I said, shifting my attention back to Rose. "But here's what I can do... I'll make the lardiest, creamiest pheasant pies with sweet peas you've ever eaten and lay them in front of you with hot, milky tea!"

"That's my idea of heaven on earth. Paradise would be complete if I could take to my bed with a down quilt, afterward," she said. "But there's no rest for the weary."

"Tell me about it! If I were rich like this, I'd sleep in, take hot baths in those giant pools they call baths, and lay around on the sofas reading novels. You'd have to threaten my life to get me to traipse around in the driving snow to shoot at wildlife or to eat a winter picnic in the bothy when I could by the library's fire with a butler's tray."

Daphne came through the door like she was shot out of a cannon.

"Oh, nice of you to stop by," Rose said, glancing at the kitchen clock.

"I'm sooo, sooo sorry. The logs were all, erm, damp and it took forever to light the fires upstairs. Especially in the Ambridges' room. Is breakfast done? Do I need to take in coffee considering the ladies are having a coffee morning later?"

"The 'coffee' at the coffee morning will be more like high-octane booze in mugs. Don't worry, everyone's had hot drinks this morning," I said.

"They won't feel a bit of the cold in that drafty bothy after filling their bellies with cake and sherry, that's a fact," said Rose. "A reminder, Juliet. Seamus and I have to go to Mass today or at midnight tonight since we'll be working on Christmas. Maybe sooner's better than later, the way the snow's coming down. Come along, Daphne. You can dust the library." Daphne followed Rose out the door, taking the furniture wax and a white cloth in hand.

The intercom telephone rang and Terrence rushed in to pick it up.

"All right. Be there in a flash," he said into the phone. "I'm going to Rose Cottage to pick up the birds…Isaac's got them finished."

"Have him bring them over," I asked.

"Well," he said carefully. "No sense making a spectacle out of a few game birds, so I'll bring them by discreetly."

"I'm not following you."

"Technically, shooting on an estate is poaching. And all I'm saying is, if a few little birdies drop into one's pie, where's the harm?"

"Where did they come from?" I asked, narrowing my eyes at Terrence.

"Ahhhhhh, sweet myyyyyy-stery of life at last I've fouuuuuuund yooooooooou…" Terence sang, as he went through the mudroom and out the back door.

I could hear pairs of boots clomping in the hallway and the low, indistinguishable murmur of conversation through the solidly closed door. The party was finally leaving! Shortly after, Terrence rushed in from the cold, carrying a large roasting pan covered with a bath towel, dropped it on the table and pirouetted out the swinging door.

I was taking vegetables and bundles of fresh herbs out of the crisper and laying them on the counter. As a house present, Lady Ambridge had brought that beautiful gift basket stuffed with sprigs of organic rosemary, chives, cilantro and basil and jars of curds, preserves and chutneys. Looking out the window, I saw The Painter, still kicking at the ground. Isaac had joined him and was holding a green, wooden peck-sized basket with a handle. The two of them seemed quite companionable and content.

As I was cutting onions, celery and carrots into chunks, at last there was quiet. I listened to the silence. I took a minute to hide in the bathroom. After all the morning's excitement, I felt an adrenaline let-down and was suddenly very, very tired. I washed my face and brushed my teeth with the spare toothbrush I kept in the main house, then simply sat alone for a minute.

Daphne was pouring hot water over a tea bag. "I found some apples and other stuff on the porch. Couple of buckets. Something that might be turnips – I can't tell. I don't really eat vegetables. And some potatoes. I put it all away."

"Oh, good. I wonder what else is out there?" I said, walking through the pantry and laundry room. Rex heard the door and heaved himself up from his dog bed in the corner by the kitchen library.

"Why are there apples on the porch in the middle of winter?" Daphne asked, following on my heels. Rex followed on her heels.

"Oh, they come from the apple store, out back. They go there when they're picked in the fall. Who knows who left it? Maybe MacGregor, maybe Barry…maybe Isaac."

Daphne pushed past me and opened the door. "By the way," she said, "I have something for you…Oh look! Someone left eggs. I love me a boiled egg."

"Good. I'm glad I don't have to go to the henhouse in the snow." Rex pushed past us and took off at a gallop. I dove to grab his collar, and missed. "Rex! Come back, boy! Rexie!" I yelled. He eventually disappeared into the white. "Crap!" I said, grabbing a coat off one of the mudroom hooks. "I'll have to go after him."

"Let me!" said Daphne. "I've been cooped up for ages. I'd love to get outside." She took a man's oilcloth coat off of one of the hooks. "These are all massive!" She tried to shove her feet into a pair of boots by the bench. "Let me just go up and get boots I can wear. I'll be back in two shakes."

"Well, let him out for a minute or two. He's got a sick stomach, if you know what I mean."

She pushed in front of me, and ran toward the kitchen, and I heard her climbing the stairs.

I checked on everything in and on the Aga, then made myself yet another cappuccino. Turning on the ancient transistor radio, I fiddled with the dial until I found a station devoted to Christmas carols. It was tough to find music, as even the smallest stations were caught up in the Winter Storm Warning and emergency broadcasting mode. The big stations were giving constant updates, with facts and figures from the highly technical StormTracker Dopplers and Radar Sensor 5000s. The tiny, local station featured one lonely DJ whose car wouldn't make it out of the lot, so he just looked out the window between songs to report that the snow was still coming down.

"God Rest Ye Merry Gentlemen" came on. It was my favorite. I moved my cutting board to the table and sat down to chop, with my feet up on the chair opposite me. OK, my life isn't totally perfect, but I'm about to serve a killer meal that's going to make everyone swoon and swear I'm the best chef who ever lived. I'm sitting in the warm kitchen of a Merchant/Ivory-style house with some people I'd call friends. I've manifested this! For a change, I decided to take Aunt Suze's advice to live in the moment. It sounds dippy, but for right then, I felt like I was where I was supposed to be.

Chapter Fifteen

"Juliet! Juliet, where the hell are you?" screamed Jasper Roth, coming through the back door.

Where I was, was seated at the staff dining table with Rose, Daphne, Barry and Jane about to dig into a hearty lunch. Jasper Roth came in and we all froze, as if he were seeing us naked. I'd bet he'd never once set foot in the staff dining room.

"Hugh's ill and the dog is dead!"

"Ill? What are you talking about?" I asked.

"Was anyone shot?" Jane asked, frozen to her chair.

"Oh my god, Daphne," I said softly, nudging her over to the corner. "Tell me you brought Rex in," I whispered. She looked at me with eyes like headlights. "I meant to…" she said to me softly. Her face was flour-white. The phone rang. I motioned with my head that she should go pick it up.

"Where's Isaac? Is everyone else all right," said Rose in a high-pitched voice, standing up from her chair.

"Everyone else is fine. We're going to need lunch," Mr. Roth said to me over his shoulder as he exited the room.

We were all on our feet immediately, running into the kitchen and out the back door. The snow was getting heavier and it was hard to see three feet in front of your face. We were struggling to keep our eyes open. Rose spied Isaac and Seamus and made the sign of the cross.

"Thank you, Sweet Jesus," she said in a breathless whisper.

"I can't fathom this snow up to my knees," said MacGregor. "Make way, if you can," he said, trudging through the heavy snow. "What's going to happen when all this melts?" he mumbled to himself.

"What's going on, then?" shouted Barry the gardener to Seamus, who was marching through the deepening snow, laden with gear. "Shall I call a medic? Was someone shot?"

Emerging through the snow came Isaac and Chisholm, carrying Rex's limp body, followed by Terrence and Dr. Dearden, practically dragging The Painter between them. Jacques was close behind, struggling to haul in the lion's share of the gear. "Zo upzetting, *triste*," he said to us.

"What happened, Terrence?" I asked, half-terrified to hear. We were all still standing in the falling snow, stock-still, waiting for an answer.

"It was unreal. We had trouble seeing because of the snow — shouldn't have been out there in the first place. The first time the birds were driven, all the guns shot. The Painter was looking up, waiting, trying to see if he'd hit. A few seconds later, a pheasant dropped from the sky and smacked Rex square on the back. He fell to the ground like a brick. Dearden was starting to improvise CPR on the poor hound, but his ribs were broken. Next thing, The Painter collapsed. Dearden thought he may have had a mild heart attack from seeing his dog die in front of him. On Christmas Eve! So Dearden began mouth-to-mouth on The Painter, but he sat up and started wailing."

"Terrible, terrible!" Rose said, "Lord bless him. But there's no point in the rest of you getting pneumonia. Everyone back inside," she said, herding people in through the mudroom. "Come in, and warm your feet, I'll make hot drinks. Daphne, get blankets and boil the kettle. Mr. Chisholm, pull the chairs up to the fire in the library and make a tray of brandies," Rose ordered.

The next half-hour was a blur of activity as Mr. Roth, Jacques, and Lord Ambridge were stripped down, redressed, seated in the library and given stiff drinks. Terrence was assisting Dr. Dearden with The Painter in the Regency Room on the first floor. The Countess had been sent for and brought in. Needless to say, the other ladies, who'd already been drinking in the drawing room, were beside themselves. There was a lot of hubbub on the other side of the swinging door and I could hear murmurs of "Who let the dog out?" and "Did he suffer?" and "Should we call the vet?"

Oh my god, I killed Rex.

"Lunch is going to be on the table soon," I heard Jasper Roth shouting over the voices of his guests from the hallway. Lunch!

I walked into the staff dining room, picked up the pies from the table and put them back in the oven to warm.

"Sorry, guys. Say goodbye to your hot meal. I'll make sandwiches in a little bit." I was still having trouble taking a deep breath. Would I be blamed for Rex?

"Well, isn't that a dainty dish to set before the king?" cried Terrence, coming into the kitchen. "Taking the food right out of our mouths, and on Christmas Eve. Union! Union! Union!"

"Shut up, Norma Rae," I hissed. "The Painter nearly died, and Rex did! Will it ease your pain if your egg and cress is given to you with a side of 18-year-old Scotch?"

"Serving it in crystal tumblers would lessen the sting."

"How is The Painter?"

"Dr. Dearden said it's best to let him rest and simply observe him for now. He's given him something, I don't know what. They may still call an ambulance. If you ask me, it's just a panic attack. Whose heart wouldn't stop for a few if his pet got whacked by a projectile game bird? Dearden's started passing tranquilizer tablets out to the ladies like they're Smarties. I'd say the ham isn't going to be the only thing glazed over round here."

I heard the Countess's voice in the hallway, so I poked my head through the door. "Was His Lordship felled by the bird that he, himself shot, Your Ladyship?" I asked her. "Do you think it was just shock?"

"God's sake, Juliet, leave my mother alone! Can't you mind your own business?" said Lady Penelope, pushing past. "My father would be fine right now if he hadn't been suffering indigestion from all that fatty food you've been shoveling into him! If you please, just stop poking your nose where it doesn't belong. You're only the chef. This has nothing to do with you."

"In a way, Your Ladyship, it does." I swallowed hard. "You see, when I opened the door, Rex ran out, but Daphne told me she'd go…"

"You let my father's dog out?" she demanded.

"Technically, yes, but I sent Daphne to get him. It was an accident." I felt sick.

"Just stop talking! You're upsetting my mother," said Lady Penelope.

The phone on the hall console rang and Terrence sprinted past me to answer it. "Thornton Hall," he said quietly. "Oh, hello Edward. Now may not be the best time… All right then, just a moment. Juliet." He held out the phone. Reluctantly, I accepted it.

"Yes." I said shortly. I had to admit that I was aching for answers, but what good would it do for me to hear them at this point? He'd left me, hadn't he, with nothing more than a wave from the train. Posy's advice when Stephen had bolted had been right. You can't keep a man if he doesn't want to be kept.

"Jubes," he said. His warm silky voice melted the edges of my resolve. "You haven't tried to call me."

"I know when I'm not wanted," I said, trying to sound resolute and not pathetic. It didn't work.

"I asked you to phone, in my note."

"I didn't get a note." My mind flashed back to the envelope on the bed. I recalled the feeling of sneaking around his cottage, grasping at straws. My heart sank. *Juliet, do you want to spend your life rifling through men's drawers on the hunt for other women's panties? You chased Stephen across the globe, you turned a blind eye to Ben's true nature, and now this. It's time to stop playing games.*

"Then let me explain now..."

"Is that Edward?" Lady Penelope asked, snatching the phone from her hand. "A little privacy, please! Terrence, take care of Mother."

Terrence offered his arm to the Countess. She shook her head and continued walking to the Regency room, where The Painter was, and Terrence high-tailed it through the oak door. Stung, I noticed that she didn't even look up at me. The Countess had never been rude to me before. It hurt that she might think I was at fault.

I thought I heard Edward's voice, small, metallic through the receiver, saying "Juliet," but Lady Penelope clamped it to her ear. For a moment, I had the urge to grab it out of her hand, but I realized it was best to let go.

"Penelope, here," she said into the phone. "Hang on," she said, covering the mouthpiece with her palm and eyeballing me. "Don't you have duties?" she hissed.

"Yes, Lady Penelope. I have a job to do," I said loudly enough so Edward might hear. Firm in my conviction that all this with Edward had to be over, I zombied my way into the kitchen and got back to the task at hand.

"Don't mind them, Juliet. Everyone's just rattled. Dr. Dearden's given Lady Penelope some tranquilizers. I'm just getting some water. Where did Daphne go? I sent her for blankets ages ago," Rose asked.

"Daphne has a way of disappearing. Should the Lady be taking drugs when, she's pregnant?"

"Juliet, you're her chef, not her doctor," she scolded me.

"I know, but I did study biology and the anatomy of the brain at school. And I had a course in mind-altering pharmaceuticals. I'm just asking..." I dropped it. *Why was everyone having a go at me?*

"My dear, Dr. Dearden is right here in this very house. The roads are terrible, and decisions are being made about medics and hospitals. Seamus and I have even decided that we won't risk going to Christmas Mass. God doesn't want anyone to be unsafe in this weather. Lord Chinnerton's man was coming by to drop Christmas gifts, and he just slid off the road right in The Hall's own driveway," she cut in. "I suggested that we give him the other attic room but he was intent on walking back to Peabody Hall. It's getting icier by the minute."

"Rose, I was just…"

She looked really agitated. She closed her eyes, and said briskly, "It'd be a great help if I knew that the lunch I was promising them was on its way. I'll tell them half an hour."

****

I knew I shouldn't do it, but I picked up the extension and dialed Mother's cell from the kitchen landline. I was looking for comfort, but every call with her wound up feeling like a session.

"Doctor Edith Hill," came the efficient voice through the phone.

"Hi, Mother. It's Juliet."

"When you say 'Mother', I know it's you. Is there a reason you redefine our relationship at the top of each conversation?" I could almost hear her whipping out a notepad.

"What's all that noise? Are you out shopping?"

"Actually, I'm at the airport. I'm spending Christmas with Suze."

"What?" I was shocked. Mother hasn't done much for Christmas since I was little. She usually went skiing or went to the movies and ate Chinese with her Jewish friends. I was surprised at how hearing she was flying to Aunt Suze's made my heart lurch. "You hate flying at Christmastime. Anyway, I thought you and Aunt Suze were having a fight."

She was silent for a beat. "Doctor Levitt thinks our conflict is what's keeping me stuck. I'm up to three sessions a week. I hope you'll start analysis when you come back. The transition may be hard. There's no shame in seeking support."

"I'm glad to hear you say that. I called because, well, everything here is falling to pieces. I don't think things could get much worse."

"Of course they can't. You're working a menial job, cooking for strangers."

"Thanks for that comfort, Mother! I called for some cheering up."

"Don't you want the truth from me? I made a vow never to lie to you. Well, of course, I mean not to harm you with lies. There are, of course, times when a parent has to, you know. What I mean to say is, well. Just that." She paused. "I think they're calling for me to board the plane."

"Are you OK?"

"I'm fine," she said in a sing-songy voice that was not her own. "Just getting on the plane now."

"Mother! You are not getting on the plane! Don't you dare cut me off. Why are you being so weird?"

"I'll call you from Aunt Suze's, they've said to cut off all electronic devices. Hang in there! I'll text you Dr. Levitt's number in case you need to talk. Merry Christmas!" she said, and hung up.

So now Posy, Aunt Suze *and* Mother would all be sitting down to a Yuletide dinner cooked by my hero, and I'd be stuck here being treated like a leper.

It's official, I thought, *Christmas sucks*. I don't know which story about the joy of the season was worse – Santa's or the Baby Jesus's – but I knew I was pissed at both of them.

Chapter Sixteen

Like a robot, I checked the salad for signs of wilting, cut up a few more fresh vegetables and tossed them in, and continued my early preparations for tonight's dinner. I'd planned it to be simple but festive. I'd be serving Christmas goose with all the trimmings tonight as the Christmas Day meal was to be a traditional Hungarian extravaganza, an homage to Jasper Roth's childhood Christmases, the centerpiece of which was a spicy stew. I wondered how Daphne and the others were going to decorate and finish getting ready for tomorrow with the family and guests back from the shoot and underfoot.

As I was working, I realized none of the staff had eaten and began assembling sandwiches. Improvising, I threw together a soup using jarred chicken stock, pre-cut chicken breast strips, fresh garlic, herbs and a large handful of chopped spinach. The staff had had their hot pheasant pies pulled out from under them. The least I could do was give them something warm.

"I'm so sorry about Rex," Daphne said, slipping in the door. "Please don't tell on me. I'm so scared they're going to fire me. This is my big chance, you know."

"I don't know, Daphne. I can't think straight. Let's see how things shake down." I couldn't help thinking that she needed the job, and I sure as hell didn't, since I'd never darken the doorstep of Thornton Hall after the New Year.

"Oh, please. If you could just not get me in trouble. Rose is already watching me. I need to get back on her good side. Do I have time to start ironing and unpacking costumes before we eat?" Daphne asked, coming into the kitchen.

"What costumes?" I asked, but she was already out of the room.

"Terrence, what's going on in the library?" I asked, as he came in and flopped down across two kitchen chairs.

"Everyone's drinking for England. I guess they want to take the edge off the shock, but if you don't get some food into them, it's going to look like a wake in a Dublin pub out there. The Countess convinced Lady P to come down and sit in company, but that's a disaster in the making. She's alternating between snapping at everyone and hanging her head on her chest, crying. She's twice as bad as normal without Edward here."

"What do you mean?" I asked.

"Never mind, listen to this," he said gleefully. "She slipped on the melty snow in the hallway during the confusion and hit her head. She has a theatrical bandage wound round her skull. I like Dr. Dearden and all, but she looks like she's in a panto from the year 1900."

"Do you think he's a good doctor?" I asked.

"Let's put it this way," he said, pausing to think. "In his day, the old duffer was probably top-notch. He's a smart enough man, I suppose. But, I'd just as soon call 9-9-9, if you know what I mean. That being said, he has given me some lovely Ativan and Klonopin when I've had bad break-ups. And, anytime I get a cold, he'll give me penicillin or a Z-pak. The Painter's blindly devoted to him, and so're Rose and Seamus."

"There's so much to do before tonight's dinner. Why don't you tell Chisholm to go ahead and ring for lunch?" I said, taking the hot pies out of the oven.

As soon as I said it, I heard the tinkling of a little bell and the subsequent shuffling of people to the dining table. I began making lunches to take out to Jane and MacGregor. After all everyone had been through today, I felt a little extra kindness was in order.

Chisholm, Rose and Terrence began carrying in food and pitchers, and through the door, I could hear the muffled sounds of shouting and complaining from The Painter, and the higher-pitched sounds of women trying to soothe him. I heard my name in the commotion but couldn't make out what was being said. The door opened.

"The Earl requires a light meal," Chisholm announced. "Lady Penelope suggested a mushroom omelet."

"Meal? I thought he was fighting for his life! Does Dr. Dearden think he should eat? What should I make?" I asked.

Terrence burst through, shoving past Chisholm, and said, "Quick, cook The Painter a mushroom omelet. Can you believe he's out of bed and sitting at the table in his dressing gown? He asked if pheasant pie is your idea of a joke."

"Idea of a joke? Why, because of Rex? Should he be eating? Is this some kind of an English thing…feed a heart attack, starve a cold? Of course it's not a joke! I had pheasant pies! People needed food! I didn't think about *that* pheasant, and I didn't expect The Painter to be at the table! Last I heard, he was on his deathbed. Is anyone else upset about the pheasant pie?" I asked, rooting around, looking for the basket of mushrooms in bottom of the pantry.

"No, all the others fell on the grub, especially Roth," Terrence said. "He's pouring gas on a fire by demanding that everyone be in their rooms at six for the first of his Christmas surprises. Lady P just asked him if he has no respect for Rex's death, and Roth said, 'Sure, but we've still gotta eat!' Priceless! And you should check out Kaylie Tart! She's slurring her words and stuffing pie in her gob like it's her last meal. Coupla drinks and a valium and the old willpower's right out the window. We'll have to change the sign on her bum from 'Juicy' to 'Juicier.'"

Lady Penelope burst into the kitchen, saying tightly, "You've upset my father terribly. Chef Hill, I realize that you are an

American, but here in England, servants strive to go unnoticed! If you'll excuse me, I'm going to make my father a cup of tea in his favorite mug," she finished, pushing past me and flicking on the electric kettle.

"Your Ladyship, I'll be happy to make tea," I said, reaching for the mug.

"No!" she said, snatching the mug back out of my reach.

"It's my job to make it, Your Ladyship." *Leave!* I silently willed her. *Get out of my kitchen.*

"Just bring me the milk and sugar." I did as I was told and we all busied ourselves in various corners of the kitchen until she left with her steaming mug of tea.

"Watch your step with her, missy. She doesn't like you."

"I know. But she doesn't like anyone. I'm not special."

"You think so? I know women, in a way only a poof can. She's jealous of you. Watch your step."

"Jealous? You're crackers, Terrence. She's a titled heiress with a rich, handsome husband and I'm covered in bird fat, sweating through my chef's coat."

"Whatever you say, but her face is as green as that basket of mushrooms there whenever Roth talks about you. Or Edward. Or her dad, come to think of it."

"Yeah, because she wishes she were peeling onions and being called an idiot on Christmas Eve. I'm sure she'd trade places in the blink of an eye," I said. "Let me get The Painter his omelet. I seriously can't believe they're going on with the big dinner and party tonight. I think they're taking 'Keep Calm and Carry On' to a bizarre extreme. They should change it to 'Give Up and Lie Down.'"

I quickly whipped up an omelet with mushrooms and basil, and some dry, white toast – the way The Painter preferred it. "Terrence," I said, "can you carry this out and watch the kitchen? I want to run lunch out to MacGregor and Jane."

I packed two shopping bags with sandwiches, soup and some leftover cakes and scones from breakfasts over the last few days.

I put in some of the lovely lemon curd and blackberry preserves from The Ambridge Dairy gift basket. Bundling into my long coat, I made my way through the back door and out into the snow.

They just had to go bird hunting in a blizzard, didn't they? If anything "against all odds" was going to happen in my life, did it have to be canine death by wildfowl? It couldn't have been the lottery or finding out I have psychic powers?

The icy pellets stung the skin on my face and I had difficulty keeping my eyes open.

I crunched over to Isaac and Jane's cottage, and knocked on the door.

"Oh, hello! I wondered who would knock. Come in, come in," Jane said.

She was in her dressing gown with a blanket wrapped around her shoulders and on an old, comfortable-looking wing chair lay a cocoon of more blankets and some knitting.

"I didn't know you could knit," I said. "That's something I always tell myself I'll learn and I never get around to it. Can I see?" I picked up the small, thin needles attached to a tube made of soft yellow yarn. "Looks painstaking."

"Not really, when I knit, my mind wanders. It's not like at the Post Office where I have to like, concentrate, you know, to make change and put letters into the proper bins," she said.

"Well, I've brought you some lunch, since you've been ill." I didn't say anything about her the Earl's dog.

"You didn't need to trouble yourself. But it looks lovely, thank you," she said taking the food out of the bag and putting it in the kitchen. She looked at me for a moment, as if deciding something.

"I must admit, Juliet, I was surprised to see Daffy hired at the house," she said.

"Why do you say that?" I asked.

"Well, she lives above the post office, and I don't like to use a black tongue, but she seems a bit loose to me."

"Daphne? Oh, I don't think so."

"I don't like to make a thing of it, but she seems to go out with a lot of men."

"I don't know, Jane, sometimes we all get irritated when others act with freedom and abandon, when a secret part of us wishes we could too."

Projecting! I heard Mother's voice in my head. I was thinking of how Kaylie Hart irritated me, prancing around in her tight clothes and blurting out whatever was on her mind. I hated feeling jealous, and these days it seemed I was jealous of everyone.

"Oh, that's not it. I have loads of freedom! I'm head clerk at the Post Office and I get first choice of holidays. Isaac never makes me do anything I don't want to, I can sit and knit or work in my garden. Don't mention this around, but Hugh has offered Isaac and me money to take a holiday. He said we might want to go to Spain or somewhere. Spain! Imagine it! Seems like a lot of bother to us, but it's kind. Anyway, put what I said about Daffy out of your mind. Father Francis would say to look for the goodness in her. It's a shame we'll miss Mass," she said looking at the still-falling snow out the window. "I'd like to give Father his Christmas gift."

I looked at Jane, simple and sweet-faced, her straight, long hair pulled back off with a headband. She didn't seem to be yearning for anything. I was jealous that she didn't seem in the least bit restless.

I stood up and spontaneously leaned over her chair to hug her. She pulled back in surprise at first, then relaxed and squeezed me back. It felt good to be touched. I started to think about not being touched anymore, and I got misty. Maybe the Christmas season was getting to me. I was getting sentimental.

Out in the cold, I wiped my teary cheeks with the back of my hand and high-stepped through the snow to The Pond Cottage. I knocked, but MacGregor didn't answer right away, so I shuffled through a tall snowdrift to peer in his window to see if he was there. A pack of dogs suddenly started barking and I jumped back. Then, MacGregor's face appeared through the glass, and I let out a little scream. Recovering, I pointed to the door. "Sorry!"

I yelled, embarrassed.

"Hello, Miss Juliet," he said, not opening the door all the way. "Do you need something?"

"No, I just brought you lunch."

He looked perplexed and a bit wary. As I stood there thinking about it, I could see why. I don't think any of the staff ever visited The Pond Cottage, except Edward.

"Come through," he said, stepping aside reluctantly.

I looked around his cottage and saw that it was clean and spartan. Hanging from the ceiling above the kitchen sink were a salted, cured ham and a whole duck, with the head still on. There was no more furniture than was needed. In front of the fire, a beagle and a retriever lay in a heap on a round pile of quilts. In the one easy chair, a spotted spaniel sat up expectantly, whining and looking at me.

"Oh, cute dogs," I said. He cleared his throat. "It's horrible about Rex."

"Rex was His Lordship's favorite." He looked at me sidelong. "Accidents happen." The spaniel pawed the air. "She's not here to see you, Bud," MacGregor said. "Sorry about that, he hasn't seen a woman here since, well, since there was a lady coming round."

"What lady?" I asked.

"Never mind. He's just a man's man, that's all I'm saying. Dogs get used to a certain way of things."

We stood saying nothing for longer than was comfortable.

"Lots of snow," I ventured.

"Right," he said. "Thought winter'd never get here. Wet and warm, all through November. I hardly wore my coat. It's not natural, not good for the crops. Suppose it's all that global warmth."

"I guess so."

"I don't like it. It doesn't feel right." He stood still, offering nothing else in the way of conversation.

"Anyway, here's your lunch. I brought you some soup and sand-wiches," I said, looking around, intrigued. "Wow, look at that!" I said, crossing to a magnetic, wall-mounted rack filled with Sabatier knives. "Do you cook?"

"Of course I cook. How else would I eat?"

"It's just that these are really beautiful knives. I know they must have cost you a bundle. Most amateurs don't invest in knives like this."

"They belonged to Edward. He gave them to me when a girlfriend gave him a better set. The knives belonged to him, not the house."

"What girlfriend?"

"We don't get personal, like," MacGregor said. "But these knives were his to give."

"I didn't mean anything weird. I was just saying the knives are nice." I tried to keep the conversation rolling. *Let it go, Juliet. Edward is a thing of the past.*

"We have a few laughs and we watch each other's backs," he said. "Mates."

"Alright, enjoy your lunch." I smiled and made an effort to give off an attitude of non-threatening friendliness. "And you do know you can come eat with us anytime. It's Christmas, after all." I paused, waiting for him to accept the invitation. "Maybe you'll come to the house for tonight's meal and for The Queen's speech tomorrow?"

He didn't respond.

"Just so you know," he said gesturing to the meat hooks above the sink, "that boar meat hanging there is from a hunt at Peabody. Chinnerton's man and I had leave to hunt there. And His Lordship told me I could keep an extra duck or goose for myself from time to time." He shifted from one foot to another, waiting for me to answer him.

"I didn't think about it one way or the other," I told him truthfully. It was only his bringing it up that reminded me of the strange history and rules of poaching on an English estate. Terrence broke the whole thing down for me while I was making the pheasant pies. In the 1800s, the laws had been so severe that poachers were more willing to risk a gunfight with estate owners and managers defending their land than to face poaching penalties after being arrested. Men would go from poacher to murderer in the blink of an eye. From my point of view, though, MacGregor was the sanctioned gamekeeper, so I'd assumed he had authority over the spoils of the land. I was hopeless at keeping up with obscure English laws and practices.

"Right then," he said, crossing over to Bud and scratching him around the ears. "Thanks for the food," he said, looking at the dog and not at me. I took it as a dismissal and left.

On the way back, I detoured to Dove's Nest, just to be alone for a few minutes. I flopped down on my bed and let my mind go blank, savoring the delicious feeling of my body sinking into the warm quilt. I hadn't realized there was so much tension in my muscles. The more I let go in my neck and lower back, the more I was aware of the vague pain. I knew multiple factors were at work: Hard floors, repetitive motions like chopping and stirring, Ben, the fight with Jasper. Not to mention Rex. Aunt Suze always goes on and on about the connection between mind, body, and spirit. I began to doze and imagined Ben's hands on my body. I snapped myself promptly to attention, remembering that I didn't have that avenue of comfort and tension-release available to me. I felt my heart squeeze. I missed Ben.

My mind started to wander to all of the nice things about him – his body was long and tall, and it felt good to curl up next to him, when he got his hair cut, it felt like velvet. He was funny when he imitated his boss. Part of me wished he were coming to take me away.

Maybe we could get past this and get married. Don't lots of couples forgive transgressions? Surely there was forgiving going on between Roth and Lady Penelope. *Stop, Juliet. Roth and his marriage are none of your business.* If I forgave Ben, we could just go back to the way we were. I was tired. That sounded good.

I could teach him to do a few of the things Edward did to me…

I snapped my eyes open and drove the images out of my head. For some reason, the thought of Ben knowing about my sleeping with Edward felt very wrong. As much as I wanted to rest, I dragged myself back out into the snow. There was still so much of the day to get through.

Chapter Seventeen

"You missed all the uproar," Terrence said. He was scraping a plate into the trash. I recognized The Painter's half-eaten mushroom omelet.

"I was barely gone for 20 minutes. And how could there be *more* uproar? What happened?" I asked.

"More like 45! For one thing, Rose walked in on Daffy and Lord Ambridge getting off in the toilet off the staff dining room."

"Whaaaaat?"

"I tease you not. She walked in and I heard her scream, 'Jesus, Mary and Joseph! And on Christmas Eve!' Then she shut the door behind herself and the three of them were stuffed in there together for ages. There was yelling and crying from every vocal range on the scale! It was operatic! Daffy came out hanging her head and Lord Ambridge was bowing and practically kissing Rose's ring. I guess she let them off with a warning and decided not to spill the beans. Rose is in the laundry, ironing costumes for tomorrow and Daphne's being monitored by Chizzy. They're decorating the tree in the ballroom. After they decorate it, they're to wrap it in sheets so it'll be a surprise tomorrow."

"There's a tree?"

"Wait till you see! During lunch, Seamus and Isaac heaved in the first tree that the nursery had delivered yesterday morning and left out by the vegetable garden. They set the great hulking thing up and Roth immediately started shouting about how it wasn't big enough and it wouldn't do. So, Seamus enlisted Isaac and Chizz, and they went out and took a chainsaw to the tallest tree they could find on the property. And in all this snow! Took three of them to move it, and they had to open the tops and bottoms of the lead-glass French windows. It looks like bloody Rockefeller Center in there!"

"Where are all the guests?" I asked.

"Oh, they were shooed upstairs. The tree's to be unveiled tomorrow in a Hungarian secret ceremony."

"Secret ceremony?"

"Oh, all right, a traditional Hungarian party. Did anyone ever tell you you're no fun? Daffy and Chizz are covering the great, pine giant in *szaloncukor* – don't mock my pronunciation, I can't help it I've never been to Hungary on my poor butler's salary – which are these frilly decorative candies which he ordered for, like, a thousand pounds, from the top confectioner in that exotic and far-away land. I think usually the shindig is supposed to happen on Christmas Eve, but you know Roth is a big drama queen. You get a bigger bang out of Christmas Day, don't you? Legend has it that the angels and the baby Jesus bring the tree and the gifts. If you squint hard, you can sort of see Isaac as angelic and Jesus-like. The rest fall short of the mark, sadly."

"A lot happens around here when you turn your back for a moment," I said.

"Oh, that's not the end of it, by far," Terrence said. "P. S. – you're i-in trou-buuuul!" he said in a childish singsong.

"Do you mean more trouble?" I asked. "For God's sake."

"Oh, calm down. It's not that big a deal, I'm just on a roll. Well, first, you were gone from the kitchen and they were looking for you. Once Lady Ambridge saw The Painter's mushroom omelet, all she could talk about was the time she was a guest of the Swiss Count Amadeus the Third of Geneva and how they toured the

Cotswolds late one autumn with their party and stayed at The Crown Inn in Frampton Mansell. The inn served a dish of wild field mushrooms with wilted spinach in a creamy blahblahblah and couldn't she just taste it on her tongue now. Needless to say, Mr. Roth was about to have you whip one up. Lady A insisted she couldn't eat another bite and Chizzy, that gormless git, announced that you weren't in the kitchen anyway."

"Nice. I owe him one."

"Anyhoo, they were cackling back and forth and The Painter slammed down his glass and said, 'Keep her out of the kitchen! She's killed my dog and now she's trying to kill me with all this rich food. I'm going to die of indigestion!'"

"No way! The Painter said that about me! What was he doing at the table, anyway? Are you joking? I made him an omelet and dry toast! And he didn't even eat it all."

"Calm down. All's well that ends well…everyone jumped in and told him he was just upset and he needed a lie-down. He was just spouting off. Plus, his stomach wasn't right. Dr. Dearden took his pulse and looked into his eyes and throat. He even palpated his abdomen right at the table. Hot senior citizen, man-on-man, action, that," intoned Terrence. "I nearly pulled up a chair to watch. In the end, Dr. Dearie told him to take some flax seed capsules and drink some plain soda water. It doesn't mean anything. He's got a bellyache and he's embarrassed from the fuss – it would make Mother Teresa herself cranky."

"Maybe so, but that's the second time he's been angry with me. He's always liked my work in the past…I, I, just…" I was starting to lose my footing. *I'm a good chef, aren't I?* I could feel myself headed down a path on which I let Mother into my head. Luckily Rose came in just as I was sitting down at the table.

"Oh, there you are," she said. "Lovely!"

"Rose," I asked, "am I a good chef?" I hated myself for asking.

"The best, dear. Why?"

"I told her about the mad shouting at lunch," Terrence said.

"Her tough skin is soft today."

"I don't have tough skin!" I snapped. "Can't I want people to love me?" I'd said it without thinking. "You know what I mean. I think I really do have to quit."

"My dear," said Rose, "if you worry about these people's tempers, you'll never know a moment's peace. How many times have I carried a third cup of tea up a flight of stairs just to hear that is still wasn't 'lapsang-y' enough? Take it with a pinch of salt. The Painter thinks you're grand. He's having a hard day. Give him a wide berth."

"She's telling the truth, Juliet. Whenever he hears you're coming to cook, he says things like, 'Smart girl, that Juliet,' and 'That's a chef who listens when you talk,' and 'Damn, I'd like to hit that!' OK, I'm lying about that last one, but he does like you," Terrence said. "Why wouldn't he?"

"I don't know. It's irrational, but it makes me angry that he doesn't think I'm good. Everyone else does, I think. I'm solidly booked most of the time."

"Right then," said Terrence, "you're acting with your clients the way you act with men…If most of them like you, why are you focusing on the one who doesn't?"

"Who doesn't like me? Do you mean Edward? Oh. You mean The Painter, don't you?"

"You're on my last nerve, Cheflette. Drop it already," said Terrence.

"I know I'm being tedious, but I think I should just leave now. I'm quitting after the New Year anyway. I dread telling my agent."

A shadow passed over Rose's face. "Quitting what? Being a chef? Because of one bad day? Take it from me, it's not in the falling down, but in the staying down."

"I didn't want to make a big deal out of it, but I decided to go home and finish my studies."

"That, my girl, would be a real pity. Unless of course all you've ever wanted out of life was to be an academic."

I didn't answer.

"You'd really deny what you were born to do?" Rose asked. "I know I'm not your mum, dear. This might not be my place, but I'm going to say it. I finally thought you'd recognized who you are. I've watched you over these years, taking baby steps, looking a bit lost from time to time. But I thought you'd gotten over the wall with all that."

I turned my back on her. At the sink, I started running water into a deep pot.

"Here's a story I meant to tell you ages ago about Mr. Roth. He and Seamus were meeting about accounts, and when I was bringing them a tray, I heard them talking about expenses. According to budget, you were too expensive, but Mr. Roth said, 'Pay her what she asks, she's worth it, and she's the only chef I've had in five years who doesn't get on my nerves.' I agree with him. My heart would break if you went and buried your nose back in a book."

I felt like I might cry, so I changed the subject. "Edward got on his nerves?" I asked, setting the pot over a flame.

"Forget that part," said Terrence. He was right. Asking about Edward was just reopening a wound that I was trying to heal.

"The point is, people who do the hiring think you're good. When The Painter was going on just now, he was on pills and half-drunk."

"They gave him alcohol?" I asked, gasping.

"Sure. Bit of brandy'll always calm you," Rose said. "Medicinally."

"Someone needs to take that man to the hospital," I mumbled.

"Well, you'll need to go to the hospital to see a psychiatrist if you're thinking about quitting."

"Everyone was hitting the sauce pretty hard," Terrence went on. "Not to mention, pharmaceuticals were being flung about like it was Mardi Gras. The Painter broke out the really, really old Scotch, and I mean ancient, to toast the late Rex of Gloucester, and the men took the tribute quite seriously. Lord Ambridge was feeling his oats...or feeling Daf's oats, as it were."

"Terrence, let's not make evil twice by gossiping! As my mum always said, 'A good word never broke a tooth.' The fewer people who get hurt, the better. We all get one mistake." She paused and looked at me. "Don't we, my girl?" I looked away.

"But I'm watching that Daphne like a hawk. She'll learn how to behave like a young lady if she wants to work in my house. Just because you come from nothing it doesn't mean you have to act like trash. There's the wife to think about. Young girls today seldom remember that fact."

I blushed crimson, worried that she sensed my eyeballing Mr. Roth.

"Right, then. That's enough of all this, there's work to be done and we'd better make hay while the sun shines. Everyone is upstairs resting, except Lady Penelope, who's reading magazines in the drawing room. And for the love of heaven, she doesn't need disturbing, so keep your voices down."

I was even more tired now, from the post-panic letdown of The Painter's accusations. I loaded a capsule into the Nespresso machine and poured milk into the frother. I stood at the sink, still holding the half-gallon jug, looking out the kitchen window. It was gray outside from the heavy clouds and the still-falling icy snow, and because of the winter solstice, it was one of the shortest days of the year.

"I could go to sleep standing up," I said to no one, as a figure in a black hat, face wrapped in a scarf appeared out the window, in front of my eyes. I screamed a high-pitched scream and dropped the milk to the floor. Standing there, with milk dripping down the bottoms of my trouser legs, I heard myself still screaming the word "Yah!" in a stream that was growing weaker and weaker but wouldn't end.

"Shut up, you ninny! Lady Penelope's practically right next door and she doesn't need to be pushed that extra inch into the loony bin. What the hell is the matter with you?" Terrence said.

Rose ran in, saw the damage, grabbed kitchen towels and started mopping up the mess around my shoes, saying "Shh, shh, shh."

"I just saw, I don't know, some guy out the window. Right outside the window," I said.

"Well, was he wearing a hood, and carrying a scythe covered in blood?" demanded Terrence.

"No, it's just…it surprised me is all."

"Then keep your bleating to a dull roar!" said Terrence.

"Everything's all right. Just a little startle," said Rose.

"Skip the coffee. I'd say you're jittery enough as it is," Terrence said, pouring the coffee and hot milk into a cup, then drinking it himself. "Was it MacGregor? Barry?"

I felt silly. Of course it was one of the men from the grounds, and even if it weren't, where could be a safer place than Thornton Hall? The security system here rivaled Buckingham Palace's.

"Sorry," I said sheepishly to Rose and Terrence.

Daphne came through the door. "What's the matter?" she asked.

"Nothing to worry about," Rose said. "Juliet just had a fright. Where have you been? I need you to do the mirrors in the library and the conservatory."

"I've, uh, been with Mr. Chisholm.."

"You don't answer to Mr. Chisholm," Rose said. "You answer to me. Would you please do the mirrors? And use newspaper and ammonia." Daphne stood looking dumbfounded.

"Oh, come on, then," Terrence said, rolling his eyes. "I'll show you," he said, grabbing a stack of papers off a table by the door of the laundry room.

"Right," said Daphne, looking out the window. "Just let me nip up to my room. I have to do something. It's my time of the month, you know."

"You can keep any references to your coochie to yourself, Daffy. I'm like Oscar Wilde in that respect – everything below a lady's waistline is cold mutton to me."

"That'll do, Terrence," said Rose, shoving a bottle of ammonia at him. "Will you please start with the mirrors in the dining room while no one's in there?"

"A woman's work is never done, is it?" Terrence asked, doubling back for my cappuccino.

As the door closed, Rose grabbed sprigs of Rosemary, a bunch of carrots and a pile of turnips, and set them, along with a cutting board and chef's knife, on the corner of the table. There was no real cooking left to do, as I'd prepped the whole roast goose meal ahead of time.

"Right then, Juliet. You're jumpy as a cat. Dinner's cooked, the kitchen's clean. Everyone's napping off the lunch and spirits and I don't expect any demands except for the odd cup of tea, which I can handle. Why don't you go back to yours, shower off that milk before it sours and put on some fresh trousers?"

Chisholm came through the door, wearing an overcoat and hat, and pushed the button on the hot water kettle.

"I'm frozen through," he said, shivering. "Mr. Roth sent me out to the stable to festoon the sleigh with bells and pine boughs. I fell down twice on the icy path, making my way back to the main house. I can't imagine anyone's going to be sleigh-riding in this snow. You can't open your eyes and it's getting too deep for the horses."

"Was Daphne helping you?" Rose asked.

"I haven't seen her since after lunch," Chisholm said.

"Hmm," Rose said. "Well, never mind. I'll set her to work now. Idle hands are the devil's tools. Juliet, go get changed and rest for a while. Your nerves are stretched and I'm guessing it's going to be a long night. I'll call you on the intercom if anything changes. Seamus and I are going to the lounge. There's an on-air Mass at 4 o'clock. Doesn't hold a candle to Father, but it'll have to do in a pinch. We'll be saying a prayer for His Lordship's recovery. Now go, break time will be over before you know it."

"Thanks, Rose. If you have a spare minute, will you ask God if he can straighten out my head?"

"There's always time for a prayer. I'll send a special petition up to Saint Dymphna for you."

"Who?"

"She's the patron saint of the mentally ill."

"If the shoe fits," I said. "I'll take all the help I can get."

Chapter Eighteen

Lying in my cottage, warmed by the wood fire, and snuggled under the heavy quilt, I was drifting in and out of sleep. My flannel pajamas were so soft and warm it was like being hugged. Thinking about being hugged brought prickles of tears to my eyes.

I could almost imagine that I didn't have to go back to serve dinner and that I could just stay in bed for the night. I was clean from my afternoon shower, my sheets smelled like soothing lavender and it was fully dark outside. I could not have been more relaxed. Then I heard a crunching from the front step. A chill went through me. Everyone was busy, except maybe Jane and MacGregor, but they'd never come directly to my cottage.

My doorknob rattled. I heard a whoosh and felt cold air around my head. My blood turned cold thinking about the apparition in black at the kitchen window. Irrationally, I lay stock-still, as if a murderer wouldn't notice that there was a human-shaped lump under the quilt. I was like a little girl, afraid of a monster under the bed. I hadn't fully surfaced from my semi-sleep yet. My brain struggled to grasp the facts.

"Rose?" I said loudly, as if a brave voice would signal to the intruder that I was tough, despite my ball-like, undercover posture. Footsteps crossed my wood-plank floor. I was too paralyzed to open my eyes or raise my head from the pillow.

"Jasper?" I whispered.

"Jasper?" The voice asked back. "Why would Jasper Roth be coming to your cottage after dark?"

"*Ben*?" I screamed, jumping out of the bed and turning on the side-table lamp. "What are you doing here?"

"I told you I was coming."

"No you didn't!"

"You never picked up your cell. I left a dozen messages."

"You know you have to call the house phone. Cell reception here is crap."

"I did call the house phone! I talked to some young girl."

Daphne! I thought. *Utterly useless.* "It doesn't matter. Why are you here?"

"I came to see you. I almost didn't make it. I've been driving for nearly six hours. My car slid off the road the minute I turned onto the drive to the house. I left it there and walked the rest of the way. I had to drag my case through the snow. It must have been over a mile."

I stared at him. I felt myself blinking, over and over again, trying to understand the sight of him standing in my cottage at The Hall. For the briefest moment, my heart soared at the romantic gesture. Trekking through the snow to surprise me on Christmas. Then the memory of Amanda's earrings crept back in. "What the hell, Ben?"

"I thought you'd seen me through the window. I signaled to you. I looked for the back door, so you could let me in, but this bloody pile's enormous. And it's gotten unbelievably dark out here. I saw the cottages and figured you were back here somewhere. Lucky, I hit you on the third try. The first one I opened was empty, and the second had a girl sleeping on a chair like Goldilocks." He was smiling at me, looking charmed with himself. "And look at you in your sensible PJs." He gave me a salute. "I'm pleased to know you're not dressed for entertaining. That would make me mad with jealousy."

I shook my head to make sense of it and looked at the clock.

4:45. I'd have to be in to put dinner on the table any minute. Finally, my head was clearing. Any residual longing for Ben was melting away. I felt anger rising up through my gut, to my throat.

"What are you doing here? It's Christmas Eve, Ben. You could cost me my job. And in case you hadn't noticed, we broke up."

"No we didn't," he said.

"No we didn't?" I marveled. "What planet are you living on?" Blind with fury, I grabbed for my bed pillow and hurled it at him. "Yes, we damn well did, you son-of-a-bitch, bastard, idiot, jerk, bastard, jerk!" I hardly knew what I was saying and kept scooping up pillows and blankets and throwing them. Everything I'd felt when I found that envelope was bubbling like hot lava in my chest. I grabbed my fold-up travel alarm clock and cocked my arm back to throw it at his head. I realized just in time that this would most likely break it, and threw it down on the mattress instead. "Leave me alone!"

"Whoa!" he said, arms still up in front of his face to protect himself. "You really aren't yourself right now, are you?"

I ran into the bathroom and slammed the door so hard the mirror swung back and forth on the wall and the shampoo fell off its shelf in the shower. It was either that, or punch him. I was shocked at the violence my body was feeling. I've never hit anyone in my life, but there was a first time for everything. I was standing with my back against the door, panting like an animal.

"Calm down," I told myself. I had to be back at work, and I couldn't walk into the kitchen in this state. "Breathe," I said out loud. I felt the door against my back and concentrated on breathing in and out. It wasn't relaxing me. I realized I was a coiled spring, ready to pounce if Ben said even one word through the door.

OK, none of this makes sense, it can't be happening, so I may as well change my clothes and get ready to finish dinner for The Hall. When I walk out of this bathroom, there will be no Ben. I'm aware I'm in denial, but I haven't murdered anyone yet, and I'm managing to get dressed, aren't I?

Temporarily comforted, I took off my pajamas, pulled on the underwear and bra that were hanging on the hook, and climbed into a fresh jacket and pair of chef's pants. I swiped a freezing cold, damp washcloth over my face, and reapplied my lipstick, concealer and mascara. By the time I was rolling on deodorant and brushing my teeth, I'd practically convinced myself that I was alone.

I took a deep breath, raised my chin and opened the door. There, on my bed, with his coat and shoes off, lay Ben.

"I've really missed you," he said. He looked great. Better than great, if I were to be honest with myself. His hair was even shorter than it used to be, making him look very city-chic, and he was wearing a thin, steel-blue, fine-gauge-knit, silk turtleneck that made the colors of both his blue eye and his brown eye pop simultaneously.

I felt split in half. One part of me wanted to hurt him. I wanted to describe every nibble, fondle and thrust of what Edward did to me. I wanted to make him suffer the way he'd made me suffer. I wanted to see him twisting in agony. But I was shocked to realize that there was another part of me that wanted to pretend none of the bad things had ever happened – Amanda, the note, the earrings. That part of me wanted to crawl into the bed with him and pick up where we'd left off, to delete chunks of history. The lawyerly part of Ben was comforting, and sexy, and I still longed for protection. That part of me wanted a boyfriend at Christmas.

But he cheated on me.

"Juliet?" he said.

"I cannot deal with you right now, Ben. I have a houseful of people to feed. You aren't supposed to be here. You could get me in real trouble. When I get back, I don't want to find you here."

"Wait!" he said, as I stepped into my chefs Crocs and walked out the door. I closed it behind me and kept a steady stride, not looking back, willing him not to follow me. I was slipping every few feet and felt very cold, since I didn't bother to put on a coat. It was dark, but I could see the back porch light ahead of me, so

I aimed toward it, picking my feet up out of the ice-frosted snow with each step. Why didn't I wear boots? The snow was snaking its way up my pant-legs, past the tops of my socks and against my bare skin. I'd have to dig through the laundry room for a dry pair.

Maybe he'll just disappear by the time I get back. Suddenly, I found myself pitching forward, grabbing wildly at the air. My foot had caught on something on the path, and I was lying face-first in the show. I cracked my chin on the stone walkway and the fall knocked the wind out of me. I heard myself moaning as I raised myself to my feet, cheek scraped from the sharp ice crystals. I inhaled and my breath caught in ragged sobs. I had to pull it together. Was I crying because I was hurt, or because Ben was here?

Come on, Juliet. Put yourself on autopilot. You can't go back into the house a walking, raw nerve. Just six more hours and you can crawl back to your bed and hide under the covers. This will all be over soon and you'll be back in London, packing, ready to start a brand-new life back in the States, away from all these stupid Englishmen. And Jasper Roth.

I pulled myself to my feet, and steeled my resolve. I gingerly made my way along the slippery path. On the steps, I almost tripped again on a basket of spiky *marron de lyon* chestnuts, still in the casings. Was MacGregor trying to cheer me up? I picked up the basket and tried to balance it on my hip to open the door against the drift of snow on the porch. I kicked the door with my foot.

"It isn't locked! Entrez-vous!"

"Open the door!" I barked.

"Oh my, it's the Big Bad Wolf!" Terrence said.

"Here! Take this," I said, shoving the basket at Terrence.

"Ouchie! Is that your idea of a joke? Giving me a bunch of pricks?"

"I'm getting frostbite in my feet," I said. "Terrence. Get out of my way!" I trudged into the house, stomping the snow off of my shoes. "Take those to the pantry."

"You take them, Bossypants. I'm bleeding!"

"Fine, I'll send Chisholm to do it. He'll man up."

"That's a low blow, Madam," he said, holding the basket at arm's length. "By the way," he said over his shoulder, "you look like you've been dragged through a hedge backwards."

Ignoring him, I dug out a dry pair of socks from a basket in the laundry room and luckily came upon another pair of my chef's trousers, washed, folded and scented with lavender. *How many pairs can I go through in one day?* I sat down on a bench and took off my socks, then slipped off my wet pants, and crossed over to throw it all into the dryer. It was top-of-the line, sleek and intimidating, and required a rocket scientist to start it. As I was staring at the knobs and buttons, I heard a voice behind me say, "Well, we found your boyfriend. I guess that explains why you're standing around naked."

I whipped around to see Jasper Roth standing there nonchalantly, arms crossed and leaning against the doorjamb, as if he hung out here all the time.

"Seriously?" I said. "You're in the laundry room? Well, of course you are. Because I'm in an alternate universe. What happened? Did someone sell you a map of the servant's quarters?" My nerves were fizzing. "Did you come in here to get a good look at me in my underwear? Well, here I am! Have a peep," I said, holding my arms up in the air and sticking out my chin.

"Juliet, in my wildest dreams, how could I possibly know that you'd be standing in the laundry room in your panties? Or, for that matter, that they'd be white cotton, like a schoolgirl's?" He laughed, his eyes twinkling.

I harrumphed back to the basket of clean clothes, thanking the gods of undergarments that I wasn't wearing a thong, and grabbed my chef's trousers off the pile.

"Let's get back to business. What do you want?"

"Rose told me you might walk off the job. She also told me that you want to go back to the U.S."

I thrust my leg into my pants. "It's none of your business."

"It is if you leave me with a house full of unfed guests."

"That's all you're worried about. Your own skin."

"No, actually I searched the whole house for you so I could tell you you're the best chef I've ever had. Whether you ever work for me again, you shouldn't stop altogether."

"Well, that's very nice," I said, smoothing down my chef's coat.

"I mean it. Tell me you won't walk out."

"I suppose I can see this one job to the end." I couldn't meet his eye.

"After everyone goes to bed tonight, let's talk. OK?" he said.

"I'll think about it," I mumbled. I made my way into the kitchen, leaving Jasper Roth standing in the servant's domain. I bellied up to the sink to wash my hands when Rose walked up behind me.

"We've put Ben upstairs, my dear, in The Blue Room."

"What do you mean you've put Ben upstairs in The Blue Room?" I asked, blinking. "How do you even know Ben? He's not supposed to be here and he's not staying. Send him away," I said calmly, opening the door to the oven and checking the thermometer in the roast.

"At first he said he'd just sleep in your cottage, and I told him that wouldn't do, since you're not married," Rose said, as if I hadn't just spelled it all out for her. "Mr. Roth wholeheartedly agreed. He said it wasn't right for him to be in your cottage and that he certainly didn't want him in there."

My mouth dropped open.

"So I asked if we should put him in the attic room across from Daphne and Mr. Roth said, 'No, that's nuts, don't put him in a maid's room, give him a *room* room' so I got The Blue Room ready for him. Chisholm took him a cup of tea and told him to get in a hot bath, he was practically frozen solid," Rose said. "He said he didn't want to be any trouble and that he'd just take a dinner tray in his room, but Mr. Roth wouldn't hear of it."

I leaned against the stove with my hand on my hip, gawping at Rose.

it into the phone."

I grabbed the handset, agitated. "Hi Posy, I really can't talk now. Ben's here and I have to get food on the table."

"Ben's there? Why on earth is Ben there?"

"I really can't talk now," I said. I was still feeling pissy about her being with my family.

"You have to hear this," she whispered. "I'm outside, around back of Aunt Suze's house."

"Aunt Suze? Are you calling my mother 'Mom' now, too?"

"What's the matter with you?" she said, sounding hurt. "I'm calling to tell you something really, really big…"

"Congratulations," I said. "You used my family to seal a deal with Piers Conley-Weatherall. Now you'll be even richer and more in the media than ever. If you'll excuse me, I have to go wash a sink full of dishes so I can earn a living!"

"Jubes! What in the world…" I heard her say before I hung up.

Terrence raised his eyebrows at me. "That was rough. Are you turning into Joan Crawford before my very eyes? Maybe you should nick one of Lady P's calmy-downy pills."

"Just take those trays. I'll have more ready by the time you get back," I said, embarrassed. "So I lost my temper a little. She should know some people have to work for a living."

"Anything to get out of your path, Lucrezia Borgia," he said, swinging through.

I pulled clean gardening gloves from a drawer and got my tiny, sickle-shaped Chestnut knife and a pair of heavy-duty kitchen scissors from my tool roll. Standing over the sink, I tore the green, spiky jackets off the chestnuts. The only way to stay sane was to focus on my work. The creative part of my brain had independently formed a plan to make *marron glacé*, a traditional French Christmas treat involving sixteen different processes in a typically French cooking style. Some recipes for it take up to four days, but I was already figuring out ways to make it work through my own special alchemy.

As Terrence came back through with empty trays, I caught a glimpse of Isaac and The Painter talking in the hallway, standing practically toe-to-toe.

"You were born to it. You could take care of your family," The Painter said.

"I do now," said Isaac.

I kept peeling chestnuts, standing as still as possible, straining to hear.

"Ah, damn it Isaac. Just listen to reason. It's the Royal College of Art. I showed them your paintings. They think you have promise. I *know* you have promise."

"You're shouting at me."

"Just say yes, I've got to get to the loo. My stomach's acting up horribly. You're enrolled. It's all paid up."

"They could give you your money back."

"Blast my stomach! Aaaah…You are not hearing what I'm saying, don't go anywhere…I'll be back," said The Painter, as the door was swinging closed.

I was listening hard when Daphne walked through from the staff dining room, where she'd been setting the table for our meal that night.

"Here's a note from Mr. Flannery," she said, putting an envelope on the counter. A note from Ben? I'd figured he'd realized how pissed off I was and decided to leave me alone. I wondered – if the roads were clear, would he have left by now?

"Did you talk to him?" I asked casually, aware of an uncomfortable twist in my stomach.

"Only to say, 'Yes, sir,' when he asked me if I'd give you that note. Wait till you see our dining room!" she said. "I nicked bits and bobs from decorating The Hall and I made it really Christmassy in ours with holly around the candles and pine boughs pushed through our napkin holders. I can't wait to eat. What are we having?"

"I made us ham, with all the trimmings," I told her. I wanted to open the envelope but I didn't want to do it in front of anyone. I was afraid to read it, and I was angry that I was afraid. Why should Ben have power over me? My shoulders were as tight as a spring.

"Ham, yum, I'm starved," she said, reaching for a toast point piled with caviar. Without thinking, I smacked her hand with my wooden spoon.

"Ow, you really are an old schoolmarm, aren't you?" she said, rubbing her hand.

"Old schoolmarm?" I yelled. "Did Ben call me that?"

"No, I just did."

"Sorry."

"I already told you everything he said about you. By the way, you don't have to whack me you know!"

"I'm sorry, I just reacted." I shouldn't have smacked her, but I was annoyed that she'd pilfer from my kitchen without asking. Was I or wasn't I the chef around here? She should follow the pecking order. I hated that I tried to behave but no one else around me felt the need to do the same.

"You can't take the caviar is all," I said, trying to smooth it over. "It's worth nearly 200 pounds an ounce. Over there on that plate are some extras I made for us."

She grabbed a jalapeno hush puppy, popped it in her mouth and ran to the sink, spitting it out.

"Oy!" she said, running to the table to grab a paper napkin. "Are you trying to kill me?" she asked, spitting it out.

Isaac rushed through the swinging door, with a troubled look on his face and headed quickly thorough the kitchen and out the back toward the cottages.

"Isaac?" called Daphne. "Did you hang the mistletoe in the staff dining room? Isaac?"

He didn't stop.

"What's wrong with him?" she asked, grabbing milk from the fridge and slugging it straight from the container. I couldn't help making a disgusted face at her, and I heard myself saying "tsk, tsk." I suppose I really am an old schoolmarm.

"What?" she asked, wiping her chin on the back of her sleeve and walking out the door.

I picked up the envelope. The front said "Juliet" in Ben's symmetrical script. He rarely called me Juliet, almost always Jubes. The paper felt luxurious in my hand. The note was written on the luxe, heavy card stock stationery that was supplied in every guest room, alongside a silver mechanical pencil and pen set bearing the family crest. I tore open the envelope, and pulled out the card.

Dear J,

You know we belong together. You're the only woman for me. It was one mistake. Can you forgive it? I need to talk to you. Meet me in my room when you're through for the night. Please.

Love, B

My lower belly was full of eels. I'd expected an apology and a goodbye, not a plea to start over. Meet him in his room? It sounded so intimate. My heart drummed at the thought of sitting next to him on a bed, hearing him tell me why he loved me.

"Forgiveness isn't for good of the offender, but for the good of the harmed," Rose always told me. If I didn't show up to meet Ben, would I be depriving myself of the best thing that could ever happen to me? *What if Edward was my last hurrah before settling down?* a voice in my head asked. *Like Rose said, men are built differently. Is there room for one mistake?*

From the hallway, a woman screamed a high-pitched "*EEEEEEEEEEE!*" I stuffed the envelope into the pocket of my apron and ran to the door and into the hall, to see who was hurt.

"Ben Flannery?" I heard Kaylie Hart demand dramatically, in a smoky voice. "What the *eff* are you doing here?"

I stood there, half-in and half-out the door, wondering what that was supposed to mean, when Terrence came barreling down the hall, ice bucket extended out in front of him.

"Move!" he said.

I backed out of the way and held the door for him.

"Wrong ice again," he said, dumping the bucket in the sink. "I'm going to throttle Daphne."

"Terrence, what happened in there? Why was Kaylie Hart screaming?"

"Apparently, she knows Ben from New York. When she walked in and saw him standing there, she wrapped herself around him like a python."

"Knows him from New York? Are you sure? What did he say?" I asked.

"He looked simultaneously thrilled and embarrassed. He cleared his throat, and muttered and blushed a lot. In short, he behaved like an Englishman," Terrence said. "He blathered a lot about how privileged he felt to talk to 'The Roth' in person about, and I quote, 'his triumphs in business as the head of Roth Fund Management'. What an arse-kisser. You should see him with Kaylie all cozied up and chatting. It was just getting good when I got sent away for the ice…they were name-dropping like artillery bombers. Now I'll never find out whose drink Kevin Spacey dropped his hotel key into at the Oak Bar."

I took the goose out to stand on the counter so it would be ready just in time for carving. I thought Ben's life in New York was all boredom and staring at the gray walls of a cubicle. How did he cross paths with Kaylie Hart? I took out the hot canapés and arranged them on a tray. He moaned about how he never looked up from his stacks of papers and that every meal was a tuna sandwich wrapped in wax paper, eaten at his desk. My newly soft feelings toward him began to harden.

"Well, that's quite a coincidence," I said.

"No kidding! La Roth is not amused. He doesn't like anyone else to hold the cards, does he? He made a big show of cracking open a bottle of the Bollinger *Blanc de Noirs* and said, 'Oh, so you know our little lawyer? That's fun.' He made it quite clear who had the biggest, um, *bank account,* in the room."

"That must have chapped Ben's ass," I said, laughing. "He always gets edgy when Big Dogs alpha him."

"Jasper Roth certainly is a master at humping, that's for sure."

"How would you know?" I asked.

"Terrence can tell."

"I'd say 'Terrence' had better pick up this tray of hors d'oeuvres and get that bucket of ice to the party before he gets alpha-dogged by Mr. Roth himself," I said.

"From your mouth to Santa's ears," he said, "it's the only wish on my list this year. Speaking of dogs…" he said, stepping back from the doorway to let Chisholm through.

"I need a glass of Bromo-Seltzer for The Earl of Gloucester. Also, Mr. Roth has requested that the bell be rung. I trust dinner is ready?"

"Yes, it's ready and waiting," I said.

"The Painter's in a mood, by the way," Terrence said.

"Is it because of Isaac or because he's feeling ill?" I asked.

"What about Isaac?" Terrence asked. "Do dish."

Just then, Rose came in from the dining room, followed by Daphne. I felt a blast of cold air, and Seamus came through the back way. Out through the hallway, I heard the bell tinkle, and people's footsteps and voices growing closer as they headed toward the dining room.

"Where's Isaac?" Rose asked Seamus.

"I told him to keep to his cottage until staff meal," he said, giving Rose a meaningful look. "Perhaps he's ill."

I placed the goose on a centuries-old, heavy silver platter engraved with a swirly "G", and surrounded it with roast vegetables and fresh leaves of thyme. Chisholm swooped in to be the one to pick it up and carry it to the dining room. Everyone else fell into line as I put hot food into crystal and china bowls as the Christmas Eve meal was being served family-style.

There was a roar of approval from the dining room, no doubt in appreciation of the Christmas Goose. Suddenly, everything grew quiet and I was alone in the kitchen. I began running water in pots and generally cleaning up, thinking how bizarre it was that my ex-boyfriend was sitting in the next room eating the food I'd just cooked.

Terrence came in and said, "I just got trapped! I usually manage to slip out before any praying happens. I just got caught unawares by Lady Ambridge and was forced to 'be reminded of all of those suffering hunger, homelessness and despair this Christmas'. So much for holiday cheer. She won't be winning any Toastmaster's awards any time soon, that's certain."

Shaking my head, I went back to my pots and pans, when Mr. Chisholm came in to say, "The Earl of Gloucester requires an omelet and dry toast."

"He's the only bloody Earl out there. You don't have to keep mentioning Gloucester, unless you're getting a residual check from the town council for being its spokesmodel," Terrence said, coming in behind him. "The Earl's complaining that the goose and gravy and the creamed peas were too rich, and asked if you'd studied under Father Gourier. He's taking wagers on how long it would take for you to kill him, now you've killed his dog. He may have been joking. Sort of."

"I didn't kill his dog. By the way, goose and cream sauce wasn't my idea. That's what Mr. Roth ordered for tonight. Plus there's salad and roast veg on the table. Who's Father Gourier?" I asked.

"Père Gourier," Mr. Chisholm said with a crisp French accent, "was an eighteenth-century gentleman and French gourmand who took great pleasure in murdering his victims in a legally acceptable way. He dined them to death on the richest and most indigestible foods, causing them to perish from gout, strokes, fatty liver, and diseases of the wealthy."

"And The Painter called me Father Gourier? Because obviously, I'm trying to kill him. That's what I do. Insane," I mumbled. "Chisholm, why do you know all that about Father Gourier?" I asked.

"Because there's a book called *Culinary Quips and Foodie Facts* in the master loo, where Chisholm shouldn't be doing his beeswax," Terrence said. "Père Gourier is in the chapter about bizarre food deaths. I'm telling Mr. Roth that your fanny was on his throne."

"That is *not* how I am familiar with Gourier," said Chisholm, reddening. "If you must know, I heard about him at a 'Lunch and Learn' at The Westminster Ladies' Gourmet Society."

"Out of the frying pan and into the fire! That's even worse than prowling around above stairs, Mrs. Chisholm. Let's just set the record straight…you're a girl, aren't you?" said Terrence.

"You low-born, mongrel, cretin…"

"Stop it, you two." I said, pulling the butter and basil out of the Sub-Zero, "you're giving me a headache. There's too much noise and chaos around here, and apparently I have to make another meal since all anybody ever wants out of me anymore is an omelet! Maybe I should just get a job at a diner and start making corned beef hash on the side." I grabbed a sourdough Pullman and sawed off several thick slices for toast. "And don't blame me for killing Rex." I threw down the bread. "Blame that pheasant."

"There now, let's all be peaceful. It's Christmas, we're all safe and sound, we're due to sit down to a lovely meal and we have our health. We're surrounded by beauty…just take a look at the snow falling out there and the decorations. A row has no place in this season," Seamus said. "On top of it all, I'm drinking this lovely brandy, here."

Coming from anyone else, that speech would have prompted an eyeroll, but all our ruffled feathers were smoothed by Seamus' sincerity, so we continued working in silence. Daphne picked up the salad for staff dinner and took it in, Chisholm and Terrence went to check on the main dining room. I reached into the pantry and took four mushrooms off the top of the green basket and grabbed a jar of Ambridge's orange marmalade off the shelf. I'd put some in a monkey dish for The Painter and top it with a fresh cranberry and a sprig of mint. It would add some Christmas festivity to his pathetic omelet and no one could say that it was too rich.

It really bothered me that The Painter was blaming me. My ego was bruised on two levels – I hated being called a bad cook and I hated being accused. Period.

I inhaled deeply and grabbed a glass from the cupboard. I went straight to the wine cooler and took out the nice rosé wine I'd been dreaming about, opened it and poured myself a glass. Then, I switched on the little kitchen radio, making sure the volume was suitably low, and dialed around for some cheery Christmas music.

"Fine," I said, "if I'm making a Christmas omelet, it'll be the nicest Christmas omelet anyone's ever eaten."

"That's the spirit, love," Rose said. "Let's get these people fed and onto coffee and dessert in the conservatory so we can dig into that Christmas ham. I'm all for rich food. I'll have Daphne start carrying the puddings you've finished into the library and to set up the coffee service."

I'd been instructed to lay a dessert buffet. I'd made simple, homey desserts to match the meal and the holiday. There was plum pudding with cream, chocolate layer cake, Victoria sponge, peach crumble with vanilla bean ice cream, and because Jasper Roth can never leave good-enough alone, goat-cheese cheesecake balls rolled in crushed pistachios with celery sorbet.

"Good on ya for the glass of cheer, Juliet. A little Christmas drink and some music are just what the evening calls for. No one ever said work has to be work."

"Ben did." I remembered his lecture about work being called work for a reason.

"My old Da used to tell us, 'If you love what you do, you'll never work a day in your life,' and the man was a groom. He spent his days shoveling horse manure, but never a happier man there was. I feel the same. It's good to be content with what you have. Wishing things were different is a sure road to suffering," Seamus said.

I flipped the sautéed mushrooms in the pan and poured beaten eggs over them. I let it set, then sprinkled the basil on top, and plated it, piping hot, with a buttery gloss. "That's what my aunt Suze says," I answered, arranging toast and marmalade on a bread plate, "and I…"

Lady Penelope flung open the door, interrupting me. "I've come to check on my father's meal," she said. "His stomach is already upset, and waiting is making the situation worse. Here, give that to me," she said, snatching the two plates. She passed through the door to the staff dining room, instead of straight through to the hall. We all stood at attention for a second, poised to react.

"Leave her be," Rose said. "Don't take it personally. I'll just go through and wait for her in the main dining room to make sure everything's alright."

After she left, Seamus continued, "I can tell you're off-kilter, my dear. I'm not ashamed to tell you, I've seen my share of trials in my life, Juliet. One in particular, I remember." He paused, and a thousand-mile stare took over his face. "I'd come to a crossroads and I had to make a choice. Would I blame and punish the sinners around me or would I find compassion? Which choice would make me happier? I chose forgiveness, but it took time to scrub all traces of black out of my heart." He shook his head as if to clear it, and smiled. "But you can see the reward I've reaped. I'm content. It's a gift to myself in the end."

"You know, Seamus," I said washing out the omelet pan and setting it in the drainer, "you could have been a therapist."

"Ah, go on now," he said, looking pleased. "I'm just an old Irishman with a bit of common sense."

"You've brightened my holiday," I admitted, feeling quite moved.

"You're a star," he enthused, squeezing my shoulder. "You deserve brightness."

Terrence broke the moment by coming in to inform me that Lady Ambridge had seen the mushroom omelet and was once again rambling about the mushroom and spinach dish from the

Mansell Inn.

"Of course, Roth sent me right through to have you make it," he said.

"Make what? I'm not psychic! I don't know what she means," I said.

"Then you'd better find out, because they're sitting there waiting for it."

I was frozen in my tracks, realizing I'd have to go in to the dining room, where Ben was sitting, and give an audience to the guests. I ran my fingers through my hair, squared my shoulders and pushed through the door to the other side.

I walked into the dining room and stood by Mr. Roth's side, hands clasped behind my back, waiting to be spoken to.

"So Jasper, you're head of Roth Fund Management, of course, but I've read in *The Journal* that you're launching a new company and doing some private investing?" said Ben.

"Yeah, I bore easily. My new business is going to deal in riskier ventures. Art, film, technology."

"I've heard you have your fingers in pots in New York and L.A. What's the name of your film company again?"

"Suleiman Pictures."

"That's an area that interests me. I thought you were planning to spend more time in the U.K. Who'll look after your interests stateside?"

"I have eyes in the back of my head," said Roth, swiveling around to smile at me.

"I've recently spent some time in New York for Thompson Loyal," said Ben. "I had the opportunity to…"

"Kaylie, your glass is empty," Roth said, cutting Ben off. It took all my concentration to relax the muscles of my face into a neutral expression. I had a moment to glance around the room and I was able to confirm that Lady Ambridge's sweater was, indeed, hideous. I stole a look at Ben, who looked very smart in a dark suit and silvery-gray shirt, open at the neck. *Why would he have packed a suit to come and visit me at work?* A jolt went through my chest. Had he come here to ask me to marry him? I felt a little dizzy.

"Juliet?" Roth said. I looked around and realized that everyone at the table was staring at me. "Lady Ambridge complimented you on dinner."

"Thank you, Your Ladyship," I forced myself back to the present.

"Not at all, my dear," she said in her no-nonsense voice. "I take robust pleasure in watching someone handle fresh vegetables the way you do. Food is what life's all about. My life, anyway! Almost ranks above my children," she said, "certainly above marriage! Ha!" Every S that she pronounced sent a fresh shower of saliva across the table.

"It's a pleasure to offer meals in such a warm house and to such gracious guests," I said, turning my face away from Ben.

"So, Juliet, are you up to the challenge of Muriel's side dish?" he asked, eyes on fire, sounding like a game show host on The Food Network.

"Can you describe it, Your Ladyship?" I asked.

"Well, to begin, it was very rich, and I generally avoid rich foods," she said.

"Advice I wish our good host here would take," said Dr. Dearden, waving a hand at The Painter.

"But in Frampton Mansell, of course, I indulged at the Count's insistence. It appears I have another insistent host in Mr. Roth."

I was conscious of the time and was getting antsy to get this dish made and on the table before the meal was over. Terrence and Chisholm were circling to fill water and wine glasses, and to clear dishes.

"And would you be kind enough to tell me all you remember about the dish, Your Ladyship?" I asked.

"To start, it had wild field mushrooms, that much I know. The maître d'hôtel was very proud that his man had foraged for Agaricus campestris mushrooms that very day on the grounds of the Crown Inn. He and I talked extensively about botany. I was quite the natural scientist at school," said Lady Ambridge.

"I can see you dressed in one of those lab coats with glasses and rubber-soled shoes," said Kaylie. "Did anyone here ever see the movie *Honey, I Shrunk the Kids*? Rick Moranis is a scientist…"

"It also had spinach, slightly wilted and still very green," said Lady Ambridge, cutting Kaylie off. "It had a cream sauce, but it was more aromatic than what you've put on the peas. And the sauce had more body."

"Ooh, ooh, I know! It was eggs Benedict, but on spinach!" Kaylie said. Everyone ignored her.

"Would you mind telling me what the aroma was like?" I asked.

"It was pungent, and well, outdoorsy. That sounds odd, doesn't it?"

"Would you say it was smoky, Your Ladyship?" I asked. "And were the mushrooms sliced?"

"Yes, absolutely smoky. Woodsy. And the mushrooms were so thin, they were almost see-through."

"Perfect. I'll do my best. Advance apologies if I don't hit the mark," I said.

"I've never tasted a dish that you've cooked that hasn't hit the mark," said the Countess, raising her glass of sherry to me in a toast.

"It's true," said The Painter. "I'd also like to raise a glass to her." There was a general chorus of "To Juliets" and "Hear hears." I nodded my thanks to the table and smiled directly at The Painter, who was smiling back at me. I hoped he was sincere and that I was back on solid ground with him.

"Juliet has always been known…" started Ben, but I cut him off swiftly.

"That's very kind of you all," I said loudly, "if you'll all excuse me, I should start the dish."

"Yes, go! Let's see if your spinach is as good as Peter Luger's or The Strip House in New York," said Roth. "Or even this Crown Inn's."

By the time I got into the kitchen, Terrence and Rose had already taken out a cutting board and French knife, butter, flour, garlic, onions, olive oil, three saute pans and a baking sheet, a pile of mushrooms and had the spinach from the fridge in a salad spinner in the sink. They were flanking me like an Indy 500 pit crew.

"We pulled out everything we could guess you'd need," said Rose. "Daphne, go through and help Chisholm clear dishes and fill glasses. And mind you don't speak to anyone."

"Could someone grab the bacon from the meat drawer, and the raw meat cutting board? Also, that block of parmesan cheese and the extra-fine grater? I'm only cooking one batch now, but if you'll prep twice as much, I'll make another for staff meal right before we sit down."

"All that fat will go straight to my hips!" said Terrence.

"Nonsense," said Rose. "You don't count calories at Christmas."

The sauce would take no time, and luckily, thinly sliced mushrooms and spinach needed only to be heated for seconds, or they'd be overcooked. At my elbows, Rose chopped and Terrence grated.

The steaming, fragrant dish was ready in a flash. I finished the top with a grind of fresh pepper, and sent Rose through with it. I began prepping to make round two of the dish for our table. A short while later, Rose came back in.

"Lady Ambridge sends her highest compliments, saying that it's even better than what she'd had at The Crown. Everyone took a taste, except Ms. Hart, and after that, they passed the bowl till it was empty. The Painter seems to have perked up. He's off the Bromo and onto wine," Rose said.

"Wine seems like a bad idea to me," I said.

Daphne, Terrence and Chisholm were parading in and out, delivering dirty plates and platters. I was pleased to see that The Painter's omelet was completely gone, and only scraps of toast remained on his plate.

"Well, if they're finished, we can sit down to our meal," I said, transferring the ham onto a serving platter. "Someone tell Barry. He can't go home for his dinner because of the roads, so he'll be with us."

"I'll be sure to seat him far from Daphne, between Seamus and MacGregor. I daresay he won't be fishing under the table, sandwiched between those two," Rose said, whispering to me behind her hand.

"They're onto the pudding," whined Daphne. "Can we sit down now? I'm starved."

"Yes, go through and take a seat," said Rose.

"'Lead on!'" said Seamus. "'Lead on! The night is waning fast, and it is precious time to me, I know. Lead on, Spirit!'"

"I adore Dickens," said Chisholm, taking bowls from me.

"You don't have to drive the point home, you old Nelly," said Terrence, picking up the ham.

Before going into the staff dining room, I opened the door to the hallway and strained to listen to the family and guests. I could only just hear Kaylie's voice shrill above Ben's deep, booming laughter. I felt my cheeks color as I eased the door closed and went in to eat Christmas Eve dinner with the staff.

God bless us every one, I thought to myself.

Chapter Nineteen

"Oof, I'm stuffed like a tick," Daphne said, lifting up her shirt and sticking out the slight curve of her belly.

"Could you bear a little more stuffing?" said Barry. "Might want to work that meal off, if you know what I mean." Daphne gave him a filthy look, and he cackled to himself.

Macgregor averted his eyes and slunk out the back door, muttering "thank you" and "goodnight." I opened a kitchen drawer and took out a penlight.

"Don't you want a flashlight?" I asked, holding it out to him.

"No need. Know the property like the back of my hand"

"Stubborn. It's really icy out there," I said, putting it in my pocket. Jane was beginning to squirt Persil into a huge pot she was filling with water.

"Don't bother with that, Jane. We've got enough hands and you're not well. Have Isaac take you home and put you to bed," I said, taking over at the sink. I rolled up my sleeves and attacked the mound of dishes.

"Here, Janey," Isaac said, picking up Jane's shawl and holding it out for her.

My heart melted, and I couldn't separate out which feeling was poking me – not having a brother like Isaac, or not being part of a loving couple.

"All right, Isaac? You were quiet at dinner and I noticed you only ate two puddings," Terrence said. "You'll waste away if you keep that up."

Isaac smiled for the first time all evening. "Da ate three," he said. "He'll be fat as a hog." When the lines crinkled into place around his eyes, he almost looked his age. I laughed at the thought of the skeletal Seamus ever being plump.

"Telling tales on your old man," he clapped Isaac affectionately on the back and kissed his cheek. "There's my boy!" said Seamus. "Now go sleep off that good food and wine, tomorrow's a big day."

"Night," Isaac said, walking out, as Rose came back into the kitchen with an agitated look on her face.

"What's the matter, my dearest? Why isn't anyone cheerful?" asked Seamus. "Is The Painter ill?"

"He's fine, or at least he's the same as always. I just overheard the Lady and Mr. Roth fighting in the corner. Mr. Roth said he bought The Painter some grand picture by Roy Lichtenstein or some such, which, from what he was saying to her, looks like a page from the funny papers, and he plans to hang it in the dining room."

"And?" asked Seamus.

"It just raises my ire the way he's always poking his nose in where it doesn't belong. This isn't his house. The Painter doesn't want that picture, he doesn't want roast goose, and he doesn't want things to change!" Rose said.

"My dear, it sounds like you're taking this all a bit personally," Seamus said. "The only way to tolerate Roth is to let him roll off your back."

"You should see him in his own house," I said. "I have to staple my lips shut. Try to ignore him."

"The Earl can't let him just give the painting away. It's wrong," Rose said. "And it's wrong for Mr. Roth to torment him when he's not well and making his best effort to be cordial to the guests in *his* home despite the fact that he's suffering."

"What painting?" I asked.

"The painting in the dining room!"

"*The Veiled Madonna*?" I asked.

"Yes, *The Veiled Madonna*," she said sharply. "Is no one listening to a word I say? It hangs where he plans to put the new one."

"Why would he get rid of it? It has to be worth a mint," I said.

"It's priceless! Art muckity-mucks have been begging for it for years. Mr. Roth was in there cackling about how they'll endow it to the museum and maybe get a wing named after the family. But it's not his to give, to be sure."

"Stop troubling yourself, Rose, and let The Painter fight his battles with his son-in-law," said Seamus.

"Well he's not fighting the battle. He was so upset he excused himself up to his room before coffee," Rose said.

"Did he say he was upset?"

"Not in so many words, but I've known him nearly all my life," Rose said.

"Last I heard, he was saying he wanted to rest up for Christmas," said Terrence. "Maybe he's drunk?"

"His belly is plaguing him, and he's tired from all these guests. You might want to bring him some more tablets and a glass of fizzy water. He's not as young as he used to be. His eyes look tired and cloudy, to me," said Seamus. "Da used to say when the horses had that cast in the whites of their eyes, it was their livers that were failing."

"It's not because he's ill. He's furious about the painting, I can tell you what he's thinking."

"Well, I know better than to argue with a girl from the north side of Dublin," Seamus said. "Let's finish cleaning and get you to bed."

"I'm not the least bit sleepy," Rose said, chipping furiously at the layer of dried flour paste on the farm table.

"Yes, but I've got visions of sugar plums already, and I'll need someone to keep me company."

"I'm not fit company. I can't see my way to settling down at the moment."

"Ah, the beautiful girls always leave us begging," said Seamus.

"The guests and family have all gone above," announced Chisholm, coming in from the hall with a tray of empty glasses and coffee cups.

Daphne was right behind him with another tray. "This is the last of it," she said. "I already Hoovered in the library and turned off the lights. I'm knackered. I can't believe I have to be up at 6:30 tomorrow."

"Go on, then Daphne. And you lads, too," said Seamus, gesturing to Chisholm and Terrence.

"What? No cocktail hour on Christmas Eve? Does no one love Terrence anymore? Yo ho ho and a bottle of rum, that's what Father Christmas always says," said Terrence.

"If Father Christmas were a drunken pirate," said Chisholm, sneering.

"Well, have you seen his red nose and his jaunty boots? They're not exactly Uggs, are they?"

"All of you, go," I said. "C'mon, tomorrow's Christmas. Get to bed… 'll only be another five minutes here." There was a lot of shuffling, last-cup-of-tea making, and doubling back for handfuls of sweets as everyone disappeared out the back.

Eventually, I was alone in my lair. I had my eye on the clock as I cleaned. I knew I should go straight back to Dove's Nest when I was through but I could already feel the restless pull in my legs. I'd be climbing the stairs to hear what Ben had to say. I took his note out of my pocket and slumped over the counter to read it again, looking for clues between the lines as to what he might be planning to say.

"Don't mind me, just down for a cup of tea and some Bromo," said The Painter.

I started and jumped to attention, once again stuffing the note into my apron. "Sir, you should have rung. I would have brought it up to you," I said, flushing.

"No need for that," he said. "I've got two legs and I'm not one to let pain get the better of me." He sighed. "It has been a hell of a few days, though." He pulled out a kitchen chair and sat down.

"If you'd like to take a seat in the dining room, I'll bring your tea through. Would you like anything else?"

"Just the tea and powder. And more brandy, though I've probably had enough. I'll stay here…every now and again it's nice to sit in my own kitchen. And bring me some water. I'm so very thirsty."

There was an awkward silence while I heated water and placed tea in a strainer. Behind my back, I could feel the weight of him in the chair. I filled a teacup part way with hot water to take the chill off the ceramic.

"I'm sorry you've been ill, Your Lordship," I said.

After a beat, he said, "It's a terrible thing. I've tried to keep it to myself. I suppose she could see right through me. Rose, I mean. Ah well, things change and you can't get back what you once had."

Half-listening, I put a cup of tea in front of him, along with a snifter and a small dish with glass of soda dissolved in water. My mind was on Ben. I glanced at the clock. It was five to twelve.

He snorted. "I may be spending more and more time in this kitchen. Terrence told me that my son-in-law plans to get rid of my red-headed girl. She kept me company at dinner."

"Which red-headed girl?" I asked, wondering if he meant Daphne. He seemed confused and it was spooking me.

"In the dining room. The nude. The love of my life. He's giving it away and replacing it with a comic strip panel that'll make my eyes bleed. Maybe that's his plan – I'll move to a side chair and he'll take over the head of the table, figuratively and literally. But I suppose it's time. Someone has to eventually take the baton. Penny had to marry…and she almost got it right. Almost, but she never grasps a thing completely, does she? She married money and power but not blood. And certainly not love. To marry for love is a luxury rarely enjoyed! Well, my daughter's grown." He sighed. "I did my duty."

"I have to say, Your Lordship…"

"We never clicked, Penny and me. Always missed each other… sad, really. I rather imagined having a daughter who was, well, more like you. Bright. Capable. Stands on her own feet."

"I suppose I made a mistake sending her to Switzerland. She's crazy with melancholy over me. Girls don't thrive when they're not close to their fathers." He sipped his drink. "She's just crazy, some would say," he laughed. "You must know that, with all your training and whatnot. She has her quirks. But she was born into protection, by the luck of the draw. " He had a faraway look in his eyes. I leaned in closer to make sure he was all right. Now he had my full attention.

"There are so many rules in this life, but they're all imaginary. If I had it to do over, I'd ignore them roundly but I was a coward. The more times you don't live by the truth, the easier it becomes to continue living a lie."

"Sir, are you alright? I could call Doctor Dearden…" I said.

"I know how to fix Jasper. Once he gets rid of my girl on the wall, I'll use the empty space to put up one of those posters of a kitten clinging to a branch with a caption that reads 'Hang in There, Baby.' That's good advice for anyone." He laughed, and took a deep drink of his brandy. "Or maybe one of Isaac's paintings…"

He sat staring. "It's close in this kitchen. I'm sweating in the dead of December. Can you crack a window?" Even though I was chilly, I did as I was asked. The kitchen was cleaned and it was now midnight. Ben was waiting for me, but I couldn't leave, and it was uncomfortable to be in the kitchen with no work to do.

"I feel awful," he said.

"Let me wake the doctor."

"No, it's not that kind of awful. It's just…" His mouth was open and his lips were moving almost imperceptibly as he stared into the middle distance. I leaned in, trying to pick up what he wanted to say. "Never mind. We make our beds and lie in them. We come into this world alone, then die alone. Try to snatch joy where you can, my dear. I see that you're a good girl." I kept trying to follow him, but he wasn't making sense.

"Anyway," he said, pushing back from the table and standing up, "tomorrow is another day. And tomorrow and tomorrow and tomorrow." He smiled, tipped his glass at me, and finished off the brandy. "Thank you for this," he said, and walked through the swinging door to the hallway.

I listened to The Painter's footfalls on the staircase. I had to go past everyone's rooms to get to Ben's. Why hadn't he planned to meet me in my cottage? What a stupid plan! My anger at Ben flashed fresh. I gingerly pushed open the door and crept into the hallway. I'd only been upstairs by the bedrooms once, and that was to help one of the many wedding florists carry up boxes of fresh flowers.

Every stair had its own unique creak or groan. A third of the way up, I decided it was like pulling off a bandage and walked briskly and with intention. *Walk like you're one of the family*, I told myself, *then no one will notice*. People often forget the wisdom of hiding in plain sight. I'd done a psych study in college exploring this concept. If you want to tell a secret in a crowded room, my theory went, talk in a normal voice and don't whisper. Almost universally, the secret conversation was roundly ignored. Working on that premise, I walked briskly up the stairs and, to my relief, sailed under the radar.

Finally on the landing, I heard the deep tones of a man's voice to my left and tiptoed over to hear who it was, hoping to find the right room. I could just make out that it was Ben.

"Jacques doesn't care about that. He's French," I heard Kaylie say.

"Yes, but I'm English," Ben answered. "Listen, I just wanted to ask you to put a good word in for me with Jasper. I'd really like to be on his team at Suleiman. For now, I don't think our getting together is a good idea."

"You thought it was a good idea in the screening room at Tribeca Film Center."

"I know, but…"

"Anyway, it's sweet you came looking for me down the hall. But my publicist said I can't be in a serious relationship right now, so I don't want to hurt you."

"It's fine, it's fine. Kaylie, I told you, I didn't go into the hall looking for you. Right then, it's my bedtime, and surely you want to get your beauty sleep…"

"Am I ugly?" she asked in a horrified tone.

"Of course not. You're exquisite. It's just now's not the time or place. It was great in New York. But here, under this roof, it's tricky. Who wouldn't want you? You're gorgeous, you're hot, you're a big star…"

"I'm spiritual!"

"Yeah, course you are," Ben soothed, condescendingly. "Very spiritual."

"They say in Hollywood that I have substance. I'm a serious actress, you know."

"Right, yeah. And any man would be daft not to jump back into bed with you, but now's not a good time…"

Back into bed with you? I thought. So Amanda wasn't Ben's only distraction from the legendary stale sandwiches and mountains of paper files that were his version of Manhattan. He'd slept with Kaylie Hart!

Reeling, I turned around too fast and caught my rubber sole on the edge of the antique Persian runner in the hall. I went down face-first for the second time that day and smacked my already-tender brow bone. *You're not inhabiting your body,* I could hear Aunt Suze observing. Wincing in pain, I froze, terrified that Ben and Kaylie would open the door to find me there. Another door opened and Jasper Roth came out, quietly closing it behind him.

"Shh," he said, leading me by the shoulders not down, but up a staircase.

"I'm sorry, I…"

"Shh…" he said.

The attic hallway was very dark and he was feeling along the wall with his hand, while simultaneously steering and pushing me with his body. My head was throbbing. I heard a doorknob turn, then he opened a door and edged me through. I heard the rattle of a tiny chain and a fringed, silk torchère painted with orchids lit the room.

He sat down on the bed, which was covered in a nubby, ivory-colored chenille spread, and looked at me. He was wearing black cotton jersey pajama bottoms, a deep scarlet fleece bathrobe and nubuck, boot-shaped L.L. Bean Wicked Good Slippers.

"I'm glad you came looking for me," he said. "We needed to talk."

Our eyes were locked in what began as a staring contest, then I started really looking into his eyes, aware of our breaths rising and falling together in the silent room. The shadows fell on his high cheekbones and turned his blue eyes into spotlights. I could imagine walking the two steps to the bed, falling into his arms. What did I owe anyone? It would be so easy, and it would feel so good.

"By the way," he said, breaking the silence, "is that a paper wad in your apron pocket or are you just glad to see me?" His eyes crinkled into a smile.

My hand flew to the note in my apron, instinctively covering the bulge. I hardly knew what to say to him first. I sure as hell wasn't going to discuss Ben. "Um, I didn't come looking for you."

He eyed me levelly. "Then why are you up here?"

I didn't say anything.

"What's in your pocket?"

"None of your business."

We looked at one another for a long time, and neither of us spoke.

"Sit down," he said, gesturing toward the bed.

"It's one in the morning," I said. He sat there, very relaxed, breathing and watching me. Silently. I had to fight the urge to do what I was told. I stayed on my feet.

"You did a good job on the spinach thing," he said.

"Thank you."

"It was a stellar dish."

"Thanks," I said. I waited for him to say something else. He didn't. "Really?" I looked at him hard. "We're in the attic at midnight talking about spinach?"

"The Painter doesn't fully appreciate you."

"What do you mean?" I asked, panicking. I had just started to feel better in that department. After all, he'd toasted me at the table and we'd just had a nice, if weird, chat in the kitchen.

"You're more my thing," he said.

"If your *thing* is a top-tier chef who makes excellent food, then I suppose I would be," I told him. "In that case, I think I must be The Painter's thing, too. Who's thing wouldn't I be?"

"If you weren't looking for me, who were you looking for?" he asked. "Lawyer-boy?"

"Tell you what, at this point I'm not looking for anyone," I answered.

"O.K. then. I won't keep you," he quipped and I started to get up. "What's with you, Juliet? You know, I don't get it. I've got money and connections. A lot of people would love to be my friend."

"Is that what we are, friends?" I asked. "Because I thought I worked for you. I thought that's why I was standing in the kitchen cooking, while you and my ex-fiance were breaking bread with Hollywood's brightest star."

"Ex-fiance? You were engaged to that English prat?"

I was too embarrassed to answer. Because, of course, Ben had never technically asked me to marry him.

"Juliet, at some point, you're going to have to stop messing with boys who can't appreciate you," he said.

"What 'boys'?" I asked.

"Ben. And Edward."

"Edward's got nothing to do with it," I said, balling my hands into fists. It was bad enough that I'd been used and tossed aside, but did everyone have to know about it? "And I wasn't messing with him, as you put it." I crossed my fingers behind my back. *Until the night I got here.*

"C'mon, Juliet. So you were sleeping with a co-worker. I'm not going to tell your agency." He looked at me. "I was just surprised you were doing it behind Benny's back. Although now that I've met him, I'm less surprised. He's no match for you. You're out of his league."

"I really wasn't sleeping with Edward," I said weakly. It was hard to talk and think at the same time. Jasper just said I outclassed Ben. The whole time we were together, I'd been self-conscious about not looking smart enough, or grown-up enough. "I'd never cheat on someone I love." As soon as I said it, I felt like a fraud. *If Ben had seen spy-cam videos of your "almosts" with Jasper and Edward, would he find you blameless?*

"Penelope asked me for a divorce. I talked her out of it for now. The thing is, at this point, if I lose her, I lose the house."

"At what point? Is there another point down the road?" I asked him.

He sighed. "You see it. You see me, Juliet. To them…I don't know…I'm just an American. I guess water rises to its own level. They'll smile and do business with me, but my money's dirty here. Without all this…" he said, gesturing around to the house and the grounds.

I cut him off. "I don't want to know about your personal life," I said, though it wasn't true. "But you should know that I wasn't cheating on Ben with Edward."

"I have people in town who tell me things, they saw you two all over the grounds. I get reports. My wife walked in on a lovers' spat. I'm not angry, I just question your taste," he said. "He's a poser, just like this one."

"No, he isn't, and don't compare him to Ben. He's smart and funny and accomplished and kind, but I was not involved with him." I thought about Ben and how he cheated on me with Amanda and Kaylie. "Sadly, I was not involved with him."

"It doesn't really matter now. I sent him away."

"Your wife told me he begged to go home," I answered back furiously.

"I make the decisions, not Penelope."

"Tell me what happened."

"You know Penelope. She makes things up. Call it lying, or fantasy. The point is it's better that he left."

"Did you send him away so you could have me?" I was shaking, embarrassed to ask in case my guess was wrong, and terrified of his answer.

A door slammed shut across the hall. We both froze. "Daphne?" I called.

"Shh. Is that her room?" Jasper said quietly. He opened the door and gestured for me to go down the stairs. He didn't follow me.

I crept down to the bedroom level, then down the next flight and turned into the kitchen. It was dark as I passed into the mudroom. There were a hundred sweaters, jackets and coats hung up on the pegs. I grabbed a man's oilcloth coat from the rack in the laundry room and bundled into it. I stepped out of my clogs and plunged my feet into Jasper Roth's Caterpillar Colorado boots that he'd had pimped out with metal cleats. Two falls were enough for one day. I reached into the coat pocket automatically, looking for my flashlight. I felt a stiff, crumpled piece of paper, then realized the coat wasn't mine.

Sensing my way through the dark, back to Dove's Nest, I glanced through the falling snow at what I guessed was Ben's room. It was hard to tell, as the house was so vast. His lights were dim, but on. I looked away from his window and back toward my door. For a second, I wondered what he thought about my not showing up tonight. He was welcome to stay in the big house, with all its complications and unrest. For my part, I was quite happy to foray out to my own cocoon, to sleep in my own company, unjudged, in pajamas that pleased only me.

Chapter Twenty

The day was finally here, and Thornton Hall was the picture of the traditional English Christmas. Outside, the expansive acreage was as smooth and frosted as a sugar-topped layer cake, and clear icicles hung from every tree and eave. The sharp, icy snow was still plinking down lightly and even the weak sun's reflection on the whiteness illuminated the grounds to blinding.

Inside, Barry and MacGregor had been working behind the scenes to punch up the already spectacular adornments. The giant gingerbread house served as the centerpiece for the dining table. The ancient chandelier, once having sported dripping candles, had long-since been converted to electricity, and each arm was tied with green and gold velvet ribbon. Great silver bowls of walnuts and hazelnuts in their shells, with antique nutcrackers, now festooned every surface, along with every variety of orange, tangerine or mandarin that grows on earth. Even though it was just past nine, a kettle of mulled wine steamed on the stovetop and, despite the early hour, many cups had already been drunk from it. Stacks of mince pies were standing by to be offered around liberally throughout the day.

Breakfast had been served and cleared and I was working at a fever pitch to prepare Christmas dinner. I made a tray of toast and tea, with a side of Tylenol for The Painter.

Terrence had been up this morning. He told me The Painter had an incredible headache and had drunk about two liters of water in a sitting. Terrence declared it a monster hangover and had asked me to add a side of brandy to The Painter's tray for "a hair of the dog". He'd said everything was going right through the poor man, anyway. Though The Painter hadn't made it down for breakfast, he told Terrence to assure everyone that he wouldn't miss dinner.

"The man should rest," said Seamus. His brow was wrinkled with concern. "Have you gone to fetch the doctor?"

"He said he's seen the doctor enough," Terrence said. "Says he's fine and doesn't want a fuss."

"Ask him again," said Seamus.

"I'm his butler, not his mummy," Terrence had told him.

I made another tray with a coffee and a croissant. Jacques had also stayed resolutely above, but with no excuse. I wondered if that was his genteel French version of a pissing contest with his American host. Then again, maybe not. I admired how comfortable he was just being himself.

I'd stayed in the kitchen all morning, avoiding Ben, and had recruited servers for every dish and warming tray that had been carried through to the main dining room. Rose had just passed through and warned me to put away the sherry as Daphne had already taken the invitation to Christmas cheer too seriously and was beginning to giggle and slur her words at Lord Ambridge's side. "Lord Ambridge asked me to bring a cup of tea," she said, coming back through, with a slight jut to her chin.

"Anything for Lady Ambridge?" I asked airily.

"She's snowshoeing with the Countess." Out of the corner of her mouth, Daphne whispered, "She'd better stay away from the stable, or she may get more than she bargained for from one of the nearsighted stallions."

"What did you say?" I asked, incredulous.

"Never mind."

"Nothing for his wife then?" I repeated.

"They may not be back for ages, so no." Daphne paused and stared at me. "Unless you'd like to take it upstairs yourself? You know the way, yeah?"

I didn't say anything.

"Daphne," Rose said, "you'll carry the tea and I'll see you back directly so you can take another to Lady Penelope, then help salt the walks." Daphne went over to the corner of the counter where I was working and stirred a bowl of batter in front of me. My hair stood on end. I hated for anyone to touch anything I was cooking without permission. Right now, though, I didn't want a scene with Daphne. I subtly pulled the bowl toward myself and finished preparing Lord Ambridge's tray. Before I handed it over, I asked in a whisper if she'd collected any notes for me. I hated myself for doing it, but couldn't quash my curiosity about Ben's reaction to my not showing up last night.

"Which fella were you expecting a note from?" she asked very loudly in a high-pitched voice.

"Never mind," I mumbled. That was a rookie mistake. First, I needed to just forget Ben existed, and second, trusting Daphne was folly.

She picked up the tray and walked toward the door, pausing to look pointedly back at me over her shoulder. My scalp tingled and my hands went cold.

"Shameful, that girl," Rose said, not appearing to notice what had passed between Daphne and me. "And this early in the morning. Maybe if she'd eat a bite or two now and again, the drink wouldn't go to her head. Lady Penelope stayed behind from snowshoeing. I need to go press her blouse for the Hungarian Christmas dinner. Oh, by the way, Mr. Roth told me to remind you, as ever, to only use the noble rose paprika. To quote him, "I want this to be a Christmas dinner no one will forget.""

Shit! In all the pre-shopping and last-minute preparation, I'd forgotten to pick up the imported Hungarian paprika in London. The Gastronome's Trust had emailed me that instruction, along with the directions I didn't need, and my contract for this job. Even if we could drive to the store with the roads the way they were, nowhere local would have something so exotic. Plus, no shops were open on Christmas Day outside of London. I started frantically searching the cabinets.

Just as I had lost all hope, I found an old can in the back of a cupboard, featuring a whiff of dust in the bottom. I kept an eye on the door as I poured a plastic bottle of spice from the supermarket. I hated sneaking, it wasn't like I was committing murder. It was sort of a white lie, just like with the blue potatoes. Oh, and the store-bought pasta. And whatever I'd been doing with Edward when I was with Ben.

Just then, Terrence flew threw the door, screeching, "'That's not how we lay a table at Clarence House. That would not do for the Queen Mother.' Chizzy thinks she IS the Queen Mother returned to the earth. Let me just set a lavender, feathered hat atop her head and blow *God Save the Queen* out of my arse!" Mr. Chisholm was hot on Terrence's heels, proffering a butter knife in his white-gloved hand.

"This is soiled, Juliet," he said, laying it on the table. "Please inform Rose." He walked straight out the door on its next swing. Terrence picked up the knife and threw it at him, but the door volleyed it back and it struck the angry butler in the crotch. Doubling over, Terrence shouted, "I will take you down, you Nancy! Even the baby Jesus on Christmas can't save you!"

"Terrence! Lower your voice. You'll give Rose a coronary. Take this tray to The Painter as soon as you can stand up straight," I asked.

Still doubled over, he squeaked, "I should have had my bits insured through Lloyd's of London. I'm the John Holmes of Thornton Hall, but at least he got to lay down once in awhile. I've already been up to The Painter once this morning, with a hot water bottle and Tylenol. I may as well become his roommate. He told me he'd been feeling better last night, but was in the 'crapper' again – his words, not mine. He keeps bathing his face in cold flannels. He says he's clammy. I say he's hungover."

"He certainly didn't seem well last night," I said. "In fact, have you noticed…"

"By the way, brace yourself for a Yuletide smackdown," he interrupted. "Wait till you see the get-up Roth picked out for him. I unbagged the outfit and clutched my heart. The Painter said he'd rather die than wear it to dinner." He picked up the tray and headed out.

For the Hungarian extravaganza I was preparing, I needed to finish the stew, form egg dumplings, sauté pearl barley with onions, and make dilled carrots, stuffed cabbage, and fish in aspic. I was in my zone. And while attending to all of those dishes, I was still being called upon for nibbles, sweets, sandwiches, and a cheese plate for Jacques, who was presumably still lounging Frenchly in bed.

Rose came through the back, pale and moving slowly. She lowered herself into a chair by the kitchen table, and asked quietly, "Love, if it's not too much trouble, will you bring me a white coffee with lots of sugar?"

"You don't drink coffee! What's the matter, Rose?" I asked, concerned.

"Just knackered is all."

I put a capsule of the mildest coffee into the machine and watched the brownish liquid trickle into a mug, and poured milk into the frother of the Nespresso machine. I spooned sugar into the brew and topped it with milky foam. She took a sip of the coffee, and made an unpleasant face, but continued to force it down like medicine, till she'd drained the cup. "I must make sure all the shoe boxes for the costumes have been handed round." She took a deep breath. "Christmas Mass would have done me a world of good today," she said as she ascended to help the family and guests.

Seamus came through, and asked, "Do we have news from The Painter?"

"What sort of news?" asked Rose.

"Is he well?"

"You know how he is. Same as always. Brandy and aspirin, and he won't keep to bed."

"Is he any worse?" asked Seamus.

"Not that I've heard," Rose told him. "Find Isaac and have him bring in wood, and tell that Daphne she'd better be dusting and stoking fires! Off you go to find her."

"Yes, m'dear,"

I went into the dining room and began setting up the sideboard with hot plates and chafing dishes. The gingerbread house would need to be moved back to a side table, but it was at least a two-person job. I'd tried to lift it at one point, but it was surprisingly heavy. I reminded myself to ask MacGregor to organize that. As I set up, I glanced over at *The Veiled Madonna*, thinking about how it would be gone after today. Word was, among the staff, Mr. Roth was unveiling the new painting at Christmas dinner. I rarely had the time to really take in the Earl's masterpiece, but I was used to seeing it in the dining room.

It really was extraordinary. There was almost nothing in the background to offer perspective, just a simple, pearl-gray wash, and still she seemed to hover three-dimensionally outside the canvas. Her skin was lit from within, all peaches, strawberries and cream. The colors of the accent symbols were electric – the fireball orange of the wax seal on the letter, the biologically red envelope, the almost-embarrassing pinkness of the open rose between her legs. The most astonishing thing about the painting was that it conveyed yearning sexuality without benefit of seeing this girl's eyes or mouth. The black mantilla with the high comb in the back fell to her shoulders, covering her face and hair. Was it her posture that signified the ache? I couldn't put my finger on it. It was elusive, like the Mona Lisa's smile.

My son-in-law plans to get rid of the red-headed girl.

The Painter's words came to me as I gazed at the work. Why had he declined the opportunity to add a bold feature, like red hair, if that's how he saw her in his mind?

"I see you're looking at my father's painting," said Lady Penelope. She looked glassy and distant.

"Yes, Your Ladyship, it's quite remarkable." I started out of the room.

She kept her eye on me as she circled the table and very carefully pulled back one of the heavy, oak chairs and lowered herself into it. "So you think you know art, cooking and culture? It's commendable that a chef would be so well rounded. Edward told me you were quite something. He tells me everything."

"If you'll excuse me, Your Ladyship, I'll just get back to the kitchen and continue with dinner."

"Wait. Bring me a cup of tea."

"Of course. May I bring you something to eat? Mince pie? Some toast or biscuits?" I was thinking that some food in her bloodstream might steady her.

"No, I'm not supposed to eat. I'm meant to be skinny like Kaylie Hart, or at least sort of fit like you, according to my husband," she said eyeing me. "But as you can see, I'm failing miserably. It won't be the first point I've failed my husband on, and it's not likely to be the last. And I've failed my father. See? I'm in no way a boy, am I?"

I didn't answer.

"I'm not enough boy and I'm too much girl. How can I win? Bring me a Sanka…that's what I really want. And a great slab of mince pie."

I waited a beat to see if the rambling speech was over. This was more than she'd ever said to me in all the time I'd worked here put together. I backed out carefully, saying, "Of course, Your Ladyship."

No one else was in the kitchen, so I quickly pushed the button on the electric kettle and spooned instant coffee into a cup. I wished I hadn't run into Lady Penelope. I had plenty of work to do and, in addition to waylaying me, she was freaking me out. I sliced off a piece of the mince pie, plated it with a twist of lemon and a sprig of mint and carried it through.

"That's me, you know," she said.

I looked at the painting. I felt that she was watching me and waiting for a response. My gut told me it couldn't be true. "Your father does excellent work. You must be very proud," I said, choosing my words carefully.

"Father often painted me in the abstract and here he's hidden my face. He was always protecting me, you see." She picked up her cup with great concentration. A puddle was forming in her saucer. "He loves me very much."

"His Lordship is a great painter, and a good man," I said, twisting the bar towel in my hands.

"Yes, he's very partial to me but he can't show it. I don't mind not having the limelight when someone loves me. Knowing it is enough. I don't have to wave a flag about these things. Do you need to wave it in people's faces?" Her eyes changed from distant to fiery. Was she having some kind of episode?

Need people to know what? I wondered, trying to stay with her.

"I'm always happiest when I'm working hard and minding my own business, Your Ladyship." *Far away from you nutbags.* "Please let me know if you need anything else. I really should check the stew to make sure it doesn't scorch." I waited to be dismissed, as protocol demanded, itching to leave this conversation behind.

She had picked up her fork, and was eating her pie without looking at me. She seemed suddenly in a different world. I wondered how many pills she'd taken this morning. *Is this the full implosion? Or is she going to nosedive like she did in Nantucket?* I took a tentative step toward the door, waiting to see if she'd stop me. She didn't, so I just kept going until I'd reached the safety of the kitchen.

Chapter Twenty-One

"That is disgusting. Looks like cold and flu season on a plate," Terrence said, wrinkling his nose and inspecting a gray, gelatinous platter of fish in aspic.

"I didn't choose the menu. Blame Hungary. Roth wanted to share his childhood upbringing with his Hungarian grandmother." I lifted the heavy lid from the stew pot and the peppery steam bathed my face.

"Odd, if you ask me," Terrence said, "considering how he falls all over himself trying to play the part of an Englishman."

Suddenly, I felt protective of him. I pictured Roth as a child, simply enjoying who and what he was.

I'd heard a bell tinkle, then the guests tramping down the stairs and filing through to the dining room, a general hum of conversation filtering in from the hall. Rose slipped in the swinging door, shaking her head as if to clear the cobwebs, and sat down at the table with Daphne and Mr. Chisholm. "You'll never believe it," she said loudly and with conviction. "Truly."

Jasper Roth came in shortly after them, and we all leaped to our feet. He was dressed in full Hungarian costume, complete with a tasseled black hat, embroidered bolero-length jacket, white stockings and slippers with curled toes. Terrence inadvertently gasped and Seamus elbowed him sharply in the ribs. It was nice to see

Roth so engaged and happy. He was like, well, a kid at Christmas.

"That smells familiar." He stuck a spoon into the pot on the Aga, tasted some, and moaned appreciatively. "Thank you, Juliet. You've made me feel at home," then left.

We all stood silent until Terrence regained his composure and asked, "What? No tambourine?"

Chisholm shushed us all, and snapped to it. He picked up the fish platter and walked out proudly, as if he were presenting the prize pig. The rest of us flew into action, heaping food into bowls and onto platters. Rose and Daphne filed into the dining room and Seamus ducked into the washroom for a quick sprucing. I carried the stew pot in and set it on a giant trivet near Jasper Roth.

The dining room was quite a scene. Every single guest was in full Hungarian costume, including headwear. Kaylie wasn't yet at the table. Roth had pre-arranged and ordered outfits for everyone, and by the looks of the stony faces around the table, not everyone found the surprise festive. Lord and Lady Ambridge, stout and round, reminded me of a pair of salt-and-pepper shakers. Even the usually ethereal-looking Countess looked oblong and two-dimensional, as if the red and black of her outfit had stolen her cheekbones.

The Painter sat fingering his embroidered vest with derision. His skin looked pale against the black and yellow background of his frippery. He'd been ill in his room since breakfast and he looked especially small today, in that way the elderly can.

Lady Penelope, looking heavy and frumpy in her dirndl skirt and flats, took her seat. "Here, Daddy," she said, putting a glass of pale pink liquid at his place. "Drink this vitamin water. And you," she said, jutting her chin at me, "bring my father a mushroom omelet. You know this rich food isn't right for him." I nodded at Chisholm. I had just such an omelet plated and warming in the oven, lying in wait. Fool me once, shame on you. Fool me twice, I'll be cooking short orders all day with no rest.

Jacques helped himself to the wine on the table. He looked

amazingly sexy in the get-up, as if he were a model and it were the latest thing on the runways. As always, he seemed suspended in a perpetual shrug and raised eyebrow. I could almost hear his voice in my head, *"Eh, ee gives me good food, ee gives me a bed and wine, so I wear zee fancy dress. What ees zee differ-aaance? Life ees good, I am Frahhhnch!"*

"Terrence, fetch me a pillow, if you would. I've a backache I can't shake," said The Painter. Terrence made a smarmy face at Chisholm who was whisking in to deliver the omelet, apparently triumphant that he'd been singled out by name.

"Of course, Your Lordship," Terrence cooed.

"My dear, you've been doing entirely too much this holiday," said the Countess. "I'd feel so much better seeing you rest for the next several weeks. He won't sit still, you know." She smiled fondly at him. "And all of the unpleasantness with losing our darling dog."

"Quite so," said Dr. Dearden. "Symptoms of grief often appear in the body."

"Not to worry," said The Painter, wincing as Terrence slid the cushion behind his back. "Would you bring me a few aspirin and a neat whiskey?" Terrence nodded and walked out. "Tylenol doesn't seem to be making a dent, these days." Seamus gave a nod to Terrence, indicating that he would do it, and pushed through the door.

Ben was wearing an outfit that must have been pieced together from extra parts of the other men's costumes, leftovers or alternate sizes. In place of a jaunty hat, Ben had a swashbuckling black bandana tied around his head. The word "doo-rag" came to my mind. Unfortunately for me, he had on a white puffy blouse, tight pants and tall, black boots that gave him a whiff of the Captain-Jack-Black-by-way-of-Johnny-Depp look. The inadvertent hotness of it caused me physical pain for a sharp moment, as I remembered how all those tight muscles felt pressed against my body. Maybe I'd never seen stars with Ben, but now that my body had tasted honey, as they say, I had to agree that even a bit was worse than none at all. One taste, and now I felt like an addict. It was a good thing the splashes of brocade and embroidery girled him up a little, offering me some relief. He was raising his eyebrows, subtly trying to catch my attention, and I worked hard to train my eyes anywhere but on him.

I busied myself around the dining room, trying simultaneously to be invisible and look busy to justify my presence. Seamus squeezed past me with aspirin and a rocks glass on a tray. Terrence stared till he caught my gaze behind the guests' heads, and winked at me, knowing I had no business in there. I pretended to rearrange the aspic mold on the sideboard. Terrence came up beside me and pretended to arrange everything I had just arranged, but one beat later. I elbowed him sharply in the ribs for trying to make me laugh.

While Chisholm was at the table, presenting a wine cork to Mr. Roth, Kaylie Hart rushed in, cheeks flushed. Her shiny, dark hair was pulled back severely into a high ponytail, over which was fastened a French maid's headpiece that stood half a foot tall. She had on a gauzy white blouse and a too-tight lace-up vest, colorfully embroidered, which thrust her bosom out and nipped her waist in to full advantage. Instead of the drapery-weight skirt and flat cotton shoes inflicted on the other ladies, she sported a black, leather miniskirt and knee-high boots.

"My word!" whispered Lady Ambridge.

Jacques raised his eyebrows, and literally said, "Hawnh, hawnh, haaaaawnh!" like he was in a cartoon about being a Frenchman.

"I'm so sorry, Jasp, as you can see from the vest, a few of my sizes were wrong. I improvised with what I had in my bag. What fun!"

His hand, reaching to take the cork, stopped in midair and he looked at her, in awe. "Oh wow," he exclaimed. You could almost hear the subtext of *We used to have sex together*. He looked up and accidentally caught my eye. His face colored.

Daphne, who'd been standing quietly against the wall, whistled. Mr. Chisholm grabbed her by the wrist and dragged her out the swinging door.

"Here's a seat right next to me. Merry Christmas to you! There's a girl, sit right down," said Lord Ambridge, eagerly patting the chair next to him.

"Shall we say grace?" asked the Countess.

Just then, Terrence was swinging through the door with a basket of warm rolls, with Daphne on his tail. His eyes widened at the word "grace" and he practically lobbed the bread to the servant girl and ran back to the kitchen.

"Yes, Muriel, would you do the honors?" Lady Penelope said, and Roth slitted his eyes at his wife. She smiled a victory smile. Any plans he'd had for a grand holiday speech couched in the guise of a holy petition were crumpled into dust. For a rare moment, he'd have to abdicate center stage.

"Would everyone present please bow his or her head? Thank you."

"Beg pardon, if you'll excuse me," said The Painter, rising from the table and walking out of the room. The Countess's expression flickered quickly, but landed in an encouraging smile. She nodded to Lady Ambridge, who made a show of clearing her throat and inhaling deeply, as if she were going to blow up a huge balloon.

"Ahem… huuuuuuhn…. O, Lord, on this holy occasion, please shine your grace down upon us, filling our hearts with humility, and prudence. We sinners solemnly acknowledge that without your divine gifts, we would be little more than worms in the loamy earth…"

"What's loamy mean?" murmured Kaylie to Ben.

"Ssshh!" admonished the Countess.

"…and we ask your guidance in decision-making. Give us your shepherding hand and your commanding voice in our heads that we may advance down the path of righteousness and adhere to our marital obligations…"

"Ahm-ayn," said Jacques, reaching for the wine bottle at his elbow.

"It's not over," whispered Ben.

"…and may we be reminded that gluttony and avarice are black drapes on the soul, obscuring the light. And let us remember those who steal the companions or property of others, and who feel lust and avarice against their fellows…"

A tinkling and clattering grabbed everyone's attention briefly as Daphne, who had been tipsily dozing against a sideboard stacked with champagne flutes and crystal dishes, woke up flailing. She grabbed wildly to keep the stems and stacks from falling.

"Sorry," she said sleepily. "'S'all right. Carry on then."

"Oh ho ho," Mr. Chisholm murmured sadly, unable to hold back his dismay at Daphne's shockingly familiar address.

"Ho ho, indeed," breathed The Painter, coming back in to take his seat. "Oh, ho, ho, ho, ho…" he trailed off, coughing.

Miraculously, nothing had broken and everyone was forced to drag their focus back to Lady Ambridge and her lengthy holiday sermon.

"…ahem, lust and avarice against their fellows, and let us pray that they toe the holy line set forth by you, O Lord, and that we dampen our pleasure in this Christmas repast with thoughts of our mortal shortcomings, and that we, in the New Year, strive to be dogsbodies in your relentless work toward peace on earth. Amen."

"Amen!" Rose exclaimed, a beat before everyone else, her chest puffed up like a pigeon's and a bright shine in her eye.

"Amen," all the others muttered, seemingly reluctant to unfold their hands, lest the prayer continue to go forward.

After a moment's wait, Lady Penelope said, "Thank you, Muriel. That was lovely." Immediately all of us among the staff began buzzing back to our duties and the guests at the table began to pour new glasses of wine, unfold their napkins and converse with animation. I heard a muffled thumping down the hall and a scraping on the flagstones. It stopped and started again.

"I think I hear old Rex at the door," The Painter said dreamily. The Countess looked distressed.

"Daphne," I whispered. "Whatever that is, make it stop." She slid out the swinging door.

Terrence came back in with three more dusty bottles of the good wine from the cellar and set them on a buffet.

"More wine, Kaylie?" Ben asked her bosom.

"Yes, have another glass of Christmas cheer," urged Lord Ambridge.

"What the hell? I'm so good all year. One day of a bloated face won't end my career."

"It's not her face that's bloated," Terrence whispered, making booby gestures.

"Shh!" I hissed. It was like being in school with a naughty boy. He was determined to drag me down with him.

"To our host," Ben said, raising his glass. "A man of business at whose knee I aspire to learn."

"You can learn all kinds of stuff at his knee," Kaylie whispered to Lord Ambridge, who did a classic spit take, spraying his drink everywhere, and wound up coughing in his napkin.

"So sorry," he said dabbing ineffectively at the tablecloth. "Beg your pardon."

"Thanks for the toast, Ben," Roth said dismissively. "I always say that some people learn, and some people were just born knowing. Taking care of money and taking care of women come naturally to me. Juliet," he said, waving me over, "would you bring me a clean napkin?" I took one off the stack on the sideboard and brought it to him. Terrence raised his eyebrows. It was a breach of etiquette to order a chef around the dining room. Roth took it from me, holding my fingertips for a second before breaking his grip. "Best to know how to run with the big dogs if you're going to come off the porch."

Ben turned red, and looked from Roth to me, his face clouded with anger and confusion.

Just then, The Painter lolled to the side in his chair and let out a low, long moan.

"Darling, are you quite well?" the Countess asked her husband.

"Fine, fine," said The Painter, staring straight ahead.

"I know it's Christmas, Old Man," said Dr. Dearden, "but perhaps the early start with the spirits has been a bit much for you. Did you sleep last night?" The Painter's skin looked gray and papery.

"You're a killjoy, Dearden," said Lord Ambridge. "Let the man enjoy himself!"

"I'm fit as a fiddle," said the Painter, straightening up. "No need to fuss. Well, then. Look at this lovely table."

"Exactly," said Jasper Roth, as he raised a glass and held it in the air until the guests at the table took notice and raised their own.

"A toast. To my wonderful guests who have accepted my invitation to spend a happy Hungarian holiday at The Hall." He paused so everyone could laugh politely at his alliteration. "And to Ben," he said, his sharp eyes alight.

Ben attempted to laugh along good-naturedly, but it came out a seal's bark.

"Chisholm, go ahead and serve."

Mr. Chisholm lifted the pot and began circling the table, pausing to the right of each guest, allowing him or her to put a ladle of the soupy entrée onto his or her plate. Rose was removing cocktail glasses, replacing dropped napkins. Not to be outdone, Terrence picked up the roll basket and butter dish and began serving in front of Chisholm. Tension crackled between the two butlers.

Mr. Chisholm stopped at the right of The Painter, who held his hand over his bowl. Chisholm moved around to the Countess.

"Wait," said Roth. "You've got to taste it."

"I've an omelet, here. I can't eat spicy stew." He half stood up, but sat down again. "I don't feel myself all of a sudden."

"Well at least take some in case you change your mind," said Roth, smiling broadly. This was a man who knew how to hold an audience under the worst of circumstances and keep his cool. "Chisholm, please serve my father-in-law."

Chisholm stood perfectly still, a placid expression on his face. I knew he was having an out-of-body experience, having been in his situation myself. There is nothing more delicate for a servant than being given conflicting orders from two people with equally high status.

"This is a day that's special for so many reasons," said Roth. "It's a chance for me to offer hospitality to a bunch of people who make my table look good," he cast a glance in Kaylie's direction, "it's a chance to share old family traditions…"

"Whose family?" muttered The Painter. "Get out of my chair."

"Hugh? Sorry, all, I think Hugh's become ill." The Countess laughed lightly, but her eyes were frightened. "Hugh, Are you alright?" she whispered.

"… and it's a day for 'out with the old and in with the new,'" continued Roth, "as we bequeath *The Veiled Madonna* to the Tisch Institute of Art in Manhattan and hang my gift to my father-in-law in its place."

"I need the loo," said The Painter, looking wobbly. He stared at Roth. "Did you say you sent my Rose away? Send for her. Get her back before it's too late," he said rising.

"My dear," the Countess began, blanching, "you aren't making sense. Please, sit…"

Roth continued, ignoring them both. He stood up and walked to an easel in the corner. With both hands, he swooshed a cloth off a framed, brightly colored work of art. "So on this Christmas Day, allow me to say, 'Welcome, Mr. Lichtenstein…'"

"And goodbye Earl of Gloucester," said The Painter, falling face-first into his bowl of goulash.

"Daddy!" screamed Lady Penelope.

"Hugh!" screamed the Countess and Rose at the same time. The Countess sprung to her feet, and froze at her chair.

"Your Lordship!" cried Edward, dropping his knapsack and racing into the room. My heart did a little squeeze and I sucked in my breath. Edward? Was my befuddled brain superimposing a fantasy over this horrible reality?

"Oh my God," yelled Roth, pulling up The Earl by the hair. "Hugh! Hugh, can you hear me."

"Is he choking? You," Ben said, indicating Edward. "Do you know the Heimlich?"

"Turn his face to the side!" hollered Lord Ambridge.

"Edward! Thank God you're here. Do something!" Lady Penelope said, running to his side, and tugging on his arm.

"Edward?" I burst out. "What are you doing here?"

"I'll ask the questions," said Jasper Roth, throwing me a funny look. "Edward, why are you here? How'd you even get here through the snow?"

Ignoring both of us, Edward ran over to the chair and wrapped his arms around The Earl's chest, easily pulling him upright. Terrence had the presence of mind to dunk one of the thick, white linen napkins into a silver pitcher of ice water and wipe the stew off the poor man's face. "Dr. Dearden, if you want me to start chest compressions, I was trained in CPR in the service."

"Dearden, what's happening? Can you help the man?" blustered Lord Ambridge. "Did he choke on something?"

"Lay him on his back," Dearden said. Edward lowered him to the rug.

Seamus moved toward Rose and clasped her by the shoulders. I watched Daphne squeeze through the door to the kitchen, while I scooted over to the corner by the gingerbread house and stood still. Like everyone else, I waited. Every passing minute feels like an eternity when you're waiting for someone to take a breath.

Dr. Dearden was swiping out his mouth with two fingers. Edward knelt over him, taking his pulse.

"Is it a heart attack?" asked Ben.

"I think it must be a heart attack," said Seamus, looking from side to side.

"It's that painting," mumbled The Painter, drooling. "And the damn stew."

"Daddy!" yelled Penelope.

"He didn't even eat the stew," mumbled Jasper.

"Oh, Hugh. Oh, thank goodness," said the Countess in a sloppy, gasping cry. Lady Ambridge stood beside her shoulder-to-shoulder, soothing her and repeating under her breath, "It's fine, Helena, there there, he's alive."

I knew I should probably head back to the kitchen, but I was frozen to my spot, rubbernecking like one would at the scene of a car crash. Edward's momentum was comforting; he kept doing exactly what needed to be done. My body felt the urge to huddle near him.

"Boys, get him to a bed, and unbutton that collar," said the doctor, tossing the small, folded black hat from his own head. Edward picked the patient up, and carried him toward the door, while Jacques loosened his collar and belt. I couldn't help noticing how utterly manly Edward looked. Judging from Lady Penelope's face, it appeared she was thinking the same thing.

Dr. Dearden was on his knees, panting from the exertion. "Tell Rose to bring loose pajamas." Seamus hurried over to help the old doctor to his feet.

"Is it a heart attack? What's going on?" asked Kaylie, quietly for once.

"Edward, lay him in the Regency Room down here. I'll examine him there, now that he's breathing." Jacques ran alongside Edward, spotting him.

"Call 9-9-9, just in case," said Jasper Roth, looking straight at me. I ran into the kitchen, relieved to have a task to take my mind off Edward's surreal arrival. I picked up the extension and dialed.

"Emergency. Which service?"

"I need an ambulance at Thornton Hall."

"What is your emergency?"

"I'm at Thornton Hall. The Earl of Gloucester blacked out."

"We'll try to send an ambulance. The roads in your area are so bad, we've had two rescue crews go off the road. They're currently awaiting rescue services."

"You'll *try* to send an ambulance?" I asked incredulously.

"Please remain calm, Miss. We are doing our best. When our ambulance drivers become casualties themselves, situations worsen."

"One of the staff just arrived. The roads can't be that bad."

"By car?"

"I don't know," I admitted.

"Please try to stay calm. For the record, what are their symptoms?"

"I'm not sure. He was tired and had a headache. Last night he said he felt sick at his stomach and needed the bathroom. He said he had a backache, then he passed out."

"Could it be a poisoning?"

"I don't know! I doubt it."

"I can connect you to the poison control center when we're through here."

"We have a doctor in the house," I said.

"Do you need to be connected to poison control?

"I don't think so. Let me ask the doctor."

"We'll try to send a team. In the meantime, try to stay calm."

"You already said that," I said, and hung up.

I opened the door to go back into the dining room to report the news, and ran into Daphne coming down the stairs. "Where did Edward come from?" I whispered urgently.

"From the front door."

"Just out of the middle of the snowstorm by magic? Did a car drop him off?"

"He was just standing there. I meant to say ages ago, he rang again looking for you."

"When?"

"I don't really remember. Yesterday. Or maybe the day before. One of the times, Lady Penelope took the phone right out of my hand."

"Daphne!" I hissed. "Why didn't you tell me?"

"I have a very stressful job, in case you hadn't noticed," she said puffing up. "I have duties! I can't be expected to cater to your personal affairs! I gave you that note from Mr. Flannery, didn't I?"

"Yes, but you didn't tell me he phoned here ages ago, before he showed up!"

"I can't keep track of everything, can I? I'm a maid, not a secretary. And I did give you that note from…erm, well, there was another note. I thought I'd given it to you. Hang on, let me think…"

"Another note from Ben?"

"No," she stamped her feet impatiently. "Aren't you listening to me? A note from Edward."

The note! The one from his cottage. It was all I could do to keep from shaking her by the shoulders. "Well? Where is it?"

"I don't know," she said. "I had it one morning in the kitchen. I found it in Lady P's bedroom. White envelope that said 'Juliet' on the front. Hard to read if you ask me, he doesn't exactly have the best penmanship…"

"Daphne! You never gave it to me. Where is it?" I was furious at myself for wanting the note. I thought I'd closed the door to my heart against Edward once and for all, and here I was, like a fool, falling for the games again.

"I could swear I did! We were talking about veg and eggs and all, and then you made me take Rex out. So really, all that business with Rex has to do with you, not me…"

"Quiet! What happened to the note?"

"Maybe I left it upstairs when I went to fetch my boots. You don't have to shout," she said, looking hurt. "I'll look for it. I don't know what the big deal is," she mumbled. "It's not like 'don't forget to thaw the chicken' is a life or death matter."

"Is that what it said?" I felt myself skating on the brink of hysteria. "Did you read it?"

"No, even though it was open and all, and I could have, I didn't read your precious note from Edward!"

Jasper Roth came into the hallway. He looked from me to Daphne, and back again. "Is an ambulance coming?"

I took a couple of deep breaths to try to steady my voice. "9-9-9 offered to connect me to poison control," I whispered softly. "In light of the fact that Dr. Dearden is here, I told them I'd wait."

"They said he's poisoned?" said the Countess hysterically, coming up behind Roth. "When will an ambulance be here?"

"Your Ladyship," I said to her, "would you like to come along with me to sit in the library?"

"No, she won't 'come along' with you," said Lady Penelope, steering her mother away from me. Her pupils were big as saucers and she wasn't blinking. "Did you poison him?"

"*Did I poison him?*" I asked, horrified. "Of course not!"

"Helena, come along, dear," said Lady Ambridge, shuffling through, leading The Painter's wife through the door.

"Someone ask her what she's been feeding him! If she poisoned Daddy, there are measures to take," said Lady Penelope rapidly. "Could she be angry about her wage? You read about cases like this. Jasper, I believe it's possible she was trying to have an affair with him! The wrong sort of servant could get ideas about how to find a way in the front door, and being American, well…"

"An affair with your father?" I was agog. "Are you mad?"

"Why not? Who wouldn't you sleep with in this house? You hopped into bed with Edward, and he's deeply involved with someone else. And I suppose everyone knew about my husband even before I did, isn't that so, Jasper?" she was ranting hysterically now. "To say nothing of Lord Ambridge."

"Lord Ambridge?" I yelled, incredulous. "I can assure you that I have not laid a finger on Lord Ambridge!" Daphne stared at her shoes.

"Ssshh…ssshh. Let's stop all this, Penelope, you'll upset your mother," said Lord Ambridge, crowding into the hallway, and turning crimson. "Come with me. We'll talk in the library. Let's get you a brandy."

"No! I will not be taken to the library for a brandy. I'm not a child!"

After a moment, Kaylie sneaked through and headed up the stairs, walking for once, instead of sashaying.

"Everyone stop condescending to me!" Penelope said. "Where's Edward? I want Edward!"

"He's in with His Lordship, Your Ladyship," Mr. Chisholm told her. "May I escort you to the library? Or to your rooms, Your Ladyship?" he asked in a calm, coaxing tone, proffering his arm.

"Edward!" she called, ignoring the butler.

"Right then," bellowed Daphne, striding purposefully to the Lady and leading her by the hand. "Come on, then, Penelope. Come with Daffy now. Edward's needed to help your ol' dad. We'll just go into the library and have a stiff drink together. That's a girl," she said, dragging her along. "Come on, now. Good lass, Penny."

Mr. Chisholm stood slack-jawed for a moment, before recovering his butler's posture and gliding soundlessly into the kitchen.

Lord Ambridge harrumphed his way out, saying, "I'll be upstairs if anyone needs me. No call for a crowd just now." I could hear the speed of his footfalls on the staircase.

I looked around the room and realized that only Jasper Roth and I were left standing. Jasper motioned with his head for me to pass back into the dining room.

"9-9-9 said they can't get an ambulance here right away because of the icy roads. They'll keep trying," I told him.

"You and Ambridge?" Jasper Roth whispered, eyes glinting.

"Of course not!" I spat back. "For God's sake." He laughed for a second, then stopped. "You and Edward, though." he said quietly. "Go on, tell me."

I didn't answer.

"It doesn't matter." He walked toward me, and put his arm around the small of my back. Gently, he steered me toward the doorway. "Look up."

I did as I was told. We were standing under a bunch of mistletoe. "Just for a moment, can we forget about Penelope and Edward? Let's forget about everyone." He pulled me gently toward him, his strong hands on my shoulders. "We're Americans. We don't belong here." I could smell his bay rum scent and feel the warmth of his breath on my cheek as he whispered in my ear. "I think where we really belong is with each other." He grazed my lips with his, softly, testing. I wanted to relax into him, to escape. In that moment, all I wanted to do was to let him sweep me away in a deep, lush kiss. To be overtaken and to be taken care of. Still, something in me resisted. Struggling against his pull, I took a step back. "Jasper…"

Seamus came in, before I could speak. He was carrying a tray with a crystal pitcher of ice water and glasses. He put them on the table and stood back against the wall. Dr. Dearden poked his head through the door behind Seamus.

"He's breathing, thank God, and mumbling a few words," he said. "His vitals are weak. I have a few bags of saline in my kit to give him intravenously, that'll keep him stable. Damn these roads! It doesn't appear to be a stroke, Jasper, but it doesn't look good," said Dearden. "If it's poison, his organs will fail him and nothing short of a transplant can help, sorry to be so blunt. If it's a heart attack, well, it looks like the worst may be over for the present time." He sighed. "I just don't know." The doctor looked older than his years.

"Why does everyone keep talking about poison?" Jasper asked, exasperated. "Wait a minute, you don't think he tried to take his own life, do you?"

"Certainly not!" exhorted the doctor. "And I'm not pointing any finger of blame. Accidents happen…like, well…" he struggled to come up with examples, "for instance, cleaning fluid gets mixed up with mouthwash, or a lookalike plant or berry is eaten. For now, let's just hope for the best. I wish he were in hospital, but I'll monitor him until medics can get over the roads. Edward's working on a scheme to get help."

"What kind of scheme?" I asked. I knew I shouldn't be wasting the doctor's time, but I couldn't stand not knowing. I pushed open the door and craned my neck to see if I could catch a glimpse of Edward, but he wasn't in the hallway.

"He's on the telephone now. I'll just see what's developing then ring my colleague in Bath for some advice about keeping him stable," he said, disappearing out the door.

"Juliet," Jasper Roth said. I waited. "I have to ask. Penny's nuts right? You didn't give Hugh anything, right?"

"Give him anything like what?"

"Well, we were talking about poison…"

"What on earth could prompt me to poison the Earl? Really?" I stared at him. "If we're going off the deep end, did Rose poison him? Or your wife? Or you, for that matter?"

"Accidents happen. Maybe you made some kind of mistake? Like botulism or listeria?"

"I'm a top-notch chef. I can tell you without a doubt that I don't make mistakes like that. I'm a pro," I said, surprising myself with the conviction I felt in my words.

"Well, did he eat anything he's not used to? Maybe it's an allergic reaction?"

"He's only eaten omelets and dry toast for days."

He stroked his jaw and shook his head. "Sorry, I'm just trying to make sense of all this. Dearden's a dinosaur. What does he know? Listen, we're all freaked out here, but…" He sighed. Rose came in and stood off to the side, silently.

"So anyway," he said to me, "uh, I guess I'm going to have to go in there and talk to Helena and Penelope. And, so, um, the ambulance won't be coming till it clears up out there."

"Sir," Rose said to Mr. Roth. "I realize now may not be the time, but if you'd be so kind, I urgently need to have a word with you."

"Rose, I'm sorry. I can't deal with you right now."

"If you'll excuse me," I said, wanting to get out of there, "I'll go make sandwiches to bring into the library."

"I should check on Penelope," Jasper Roth said, and he walked out of the room.

Rose stood looking at the door swinging on its hinges, took a handkerchief out of her pocket and wiped her eyes. "I beg your pardon, Mr. Roth," she said to no one, "given the circumstance, there's no choice but to deal with me," she said. With a deep breath, she pushed the door open and walked out.

Chapter Twenty-Two

Frantically, I shook the coat, and rammed my hands in every pocket looking for the note. The coat had lay in the corner of my cottage ever since I'd heard Ben had slept with Kaylie. I pulled out the note card and held it in my hand. "Jubes," it said on the front. *Sorry to leave like this,* it began, with no salutation. *I'll explain everything as soon as I can. It's complicated. I can't write the proper words. Please call me on my cell. Edward*

I wadded the note and stuck it in my pocket. I'd hoped for clear answers. But all I'd got was evasiveness and excuses! It's Stephen all over again. Why hadn't Edward fought to stay? It was pretty clear that he'd had his moment with me and wanted a clean exit. Well, that seals the deal. However tiny my romantic hopes had been, I felt like a fool for wishing. I tried to harden my heart, but I got hit by such a longing feeling in my gut I had to sit down on the side of the bed. "He's not worth it!" I said out loud, attempting a heartsong in the style of Aunt Suze. I chanted it a few times but it didn't stick. The problem was my heart didn't recognize it.

It's over, Juliet. All of it. You'll be packing your bags and heading home soon. I closed my eyes and tried to visualize my successful career as a psychotherapist. "Manifest it!" I told myself. I concentrated, I really did, but all I could see were knives moving through crisp vegetables and sizzling pans of succulent cutlets. I realized that the feeling of loss wasn't about Edward, it was about cooking. I snapped my eyes open and stood up. "I'm a chef!" I said out loud. I ran to the mirror in the bathroom. "I'm a chef!" I said to my own surprised face, tears starting to sluice down my cheeks.

Why are you crying, silly? I asked myself. "Because that's my heartsong!" I shouted, hiccupping with laughter. I looked away, for a minute, embarrassed. "Hey you!" I said, looking into my eyes and pointing at myself. "Don't make fun of me."

I smiled. "OK, I won't," I answered.

"Good!" I said, nodding my head resolutely "Because we've finally figured out who we are!"

****

"Merry Christmas, Mother," I said, climbing up to sit on the whirring dryer. I had to find heat anywhere I could get it in England. "I have something important to tell you."

"Oh, Juliet," she said, sounding distracted. "I wondered if you were going to call today. You haven't talked to Posy, have you?"

"No, why?" I suddenly felt very guilty that we'd never made up after I hung up on her.

"I'd prefer that you didn't until you and I have had a chance to talk."

"Is she OK?" I asked, panic starting to surface.

"She's fine. In fact, everyone here likes her enormously. Did you know Piers Conley-Weatherall was coming to Suze's?"

"Yes, Posy told me. That's the whole reason she went." I felt a little of the old resentment bubbling up.

"If you knew, why didn't you tell me?"

"I figured you knew. You never even told me you were going to Aunt Suze's till you had one foot on a plane."

There was a terse silence. "I see your point." She paused again. "Juliet, are you sitting down? I have something to tell you."

"No, me first, Mother. And before you start lecturing, hear me out. I've come to a realization." The connection was crackly and

277

I thought I heard a click. "Mother, are you there?"

"Yes, I'm here."

"First of all, I don't need a man." Even as I said it, an image of Edward beckoning me under the blankets flickered across my mind. I pushed it away.

"I could have told you that. Is that your big revelation?"

"No!" I took a breath. "All right, here goes. I'm a chef!" I closed my eyes and waited for the backlash.

"I realize that."

"No, I mean *I'm a chef.* It's what I was born to do. It's like people say – it's in my blood!" I waited for a response nervously, but when none came, I soldiered on.

"In your blood…" She drifted off.

"Mother? You can wish things were different," I said firmly, "but this is what I am. It's like after searching my whole life, I've finally found out who I really am!"

A sob came hurtling through the phone line, loud and solitary at first, shape-shifting into a moaning wail. "Mother?" I said, my mouth drying up.

"I know you're a chef!" she cried. "I've known for a long time."

My heart sunk. "Are you really that disappointed in me?"

"No," she sobbed. "I'm that disappointed in myself."

I have to admit it. I was terrified. I'd never seen, or heard, my mother cry. Her naked expression of emotion knocked me off-kilter. "No, Mother, don't. You did your best," I soothed. "You've only ever wanted the best for me, and you've always been honest…"

"Juliet! There you are," said Mr. Chisholm sharply, disdainfully eyeing my cross-legged position atop the dryer.

"Hang on, Mother," I said, covering the receiver.

"Mr. Roth asked that the men in with His Lordship be sent a coffee tray and something to eat at once."

"Juliet," I could hear Mother's tiny voice calling. "Are you there?"

"Thank you, Chisholm. I'll be right in." He stood at attention, making it clear that he wasn't going anywhere without me.

Putting the phone back to my ear, I could hear Mother sniffling down the phone line.

"Mother…Mom…I'm so sorry, but I have to get back to work. It's too much to explain right now, but something huge happened here today…"

"Something huge, happened here today, too, and I need to tell you…"

"Juliet, if you'd be so kind," Mr. Chisholm prodded.

"Mom, I'm so sorry…"

"Wait! You can't go yet!"

Chisholm cleared his throat. "Mother, I have to…"

"Just promise me you won't talk to Posy!" she implored.

"Fine," I said, even though I felt guilty for promising. I owed Posy an apology, but I didn't have time to get into all that with Mother. Mr. Chisholm was making motions for me to hurry up. Uncurling my legs, I attempted a graceful dismount from the tall dryer. "I'll call you back when I can." I heard her blowing her nose and she was gone.

****

"Here's the first tray, Rose," I said, I said pointing to the exquisite sandwiches I'd assembled. Sliced goose and cranberry sauce with walnuts in pitas, pâté and frisse with a garlicky pesto on baguettes, and roasted peppers on hard rolls, smeared with stilton. I felt amped up, and alive. "I'll send Terrence in with hot drinks right away. By the way," I ventured cautiously, "is Edward still in with His Lordship?" Rose was miles away, and didn't even answer me.

I pulled down a bottle of whiskey for the toddies and a bottle of vodka for bullshots, excited that heat and alcohol might be a comfort. I put the kettle on to boil for tea and opened a brick pack of organic beef broth. Quickly slicing lemons and washing celery, I put clear-glass footed mugs on two trays and went down the line, filling each with the appropriate ingredients. No one had eaten since breakfast and these drinks were likely to hit hard. I placed a stack of cocktail napkins next to the glasses. My mind had already started fluttering to what I could serve next.

There was no sign of Terrence, or Daphne, for that matter. I picked up a tray myself and bumped the swinging door open with my hip. No one in the library was talking. Jasper Roth was pacing back and forth. Jacques and Ben were each sunk into the largest leather chairs like a pair of bookends, legs crossed, staring into the fire. Kaylie was curled up in an oversized chinoiserie easy chair, shoes in front of her, covered in a cashmere throw. Uncharacteristically, she was keeping to herself. The sun was setting and snow was only flurrying at this point.

Lady Penelope sat in the middle of a settee, glowering, with Lady Ambridge eyeing her watchfully.

I walked around the room wordlessly, holding out the tray to each person in turn. I didn't even mind serving. I felt a renewed sense of purpose and refused to get sucked into the drama. My job was to feed everyone. Simple! I was good at it. The relief of not analyzing people's motivations left me practically giddy.

"This is unacceptable," Lady Penelope grumbled, springing suddenly to her feet.

"Penelope, enough. We don't need the police, and even if we did, they couldn't get here over the roads. Let Dearden give you a shot of something to put you to sleep," Roth suggested.

"Put me to sleep? Am I a dog?"

"He meant no such thing," said Lady Ambridge. "We all just want to help."

"Well I won't rest until I get satisfaction."

"Now, now, Penny," said Lady Ambridge, raising her eyebrows behind Lady Penelope's back. "All signs point to a heart attack. I know it must be difficult to watch your father suffer. How about a nice toddy?"

"Everyone knows Isaac isn't right in the head!" spat Lady Penelope. "Maybe he did something to Father!"

"Penny! Stop that this instant. If you accuse him, you may as well accuse anyone here," said Lady Ambridge.

"Not just anyone. Isaac. For example, my husband may be a philanderer and a liar, but he'd never in a million years try to murder my father, would you?" Lady Penelope asked.

"You want to go there in front of everybody, Penelope?" said Jasper Roth. "I didn't think the English were allowed to behave like that."

"Let's stop mentioning murder," said Lady Ambridge, lunging for a bullshot. "It's preposterous. Your father's taken ill. This isn't some Agatha Christie novel. The best thing we can do for Hugh is to keep the atmosphere calm."

Rose came in with a tray of cake slices, and put them on the table next to a tray of untouched sandwiches. Her eyes were pink and puffy.

"If Daddy dies, a lot of things will be changing around here, mark my words," said Lady Penelope.

A tiny sob escaped from Rose and she coughed in a clear effort to suppress her emotion. She turned her back, pretending to arrange the sandwiches, and swiped her apron across her eyes.

"Rose," Lady Penelope erupted. "Stop crying this instant. Anyone would think you were his wife, the way you're behaving." Rose's look of shock pained me, and I turned away. From the corner of my eye, I saw her walk out of the room and smack into Edward.

"Sorry. Alright then, Rose?" he said. He came into the room, walked straight up to Lady Penelope and addressed her without waiting to be recognized. "I have a bit of good news," he said. "I've rung some of my mates at the base nearby. They've access to an Army Land Rover. We coordinated with rescue services and they're doing their best to get here soon."

"Oh, hurrah!" said Lady Ambridge, bubbling over. "You *are* a hero."

"Is that how you got here through the snow?" I asked. Everyone in the room stopped to look at me.

"Yes," he said, addressing me over the tops of the ladies' heads. "As a matter of fact, I called in some rather bold favors from one of my regiment mates to get back here. He brought me on a combat vehicle, that's now in a ditch up by the gate. My mate's fine. We've given him a room and a hot meal. I wish I hadn't caused him trouble, but…well, I thought it was important to get here."

We looked at each other in silence. The above-stairs folk shifted uncomfortably. It was unheard of for two servants' conversation to monopolize a room.

"How clever of you, Edward!" said Lady Ambridge, breaking the tension. "How terribly clever! Penelope, isn't it marvelous that he arrived in time to assist your father?"

"Very clever. Our family has always relied on Edward." She looked at him meaningfully. "I'd be lost without him."

"If you'll all excuse me," Edward said, looking around the room, "I need to get back to the doctor, and wait for the rescue team to ring." He walked close to me on his way out the door. "We need to talk," he whispered, grazing my hair with his cheek as he disappeared around the corner.

"Juliet, I hope my mother's been given something to eat," Lady Penelope said curtly. "And see to Edward's driver. Don't forget, Juliet, you are still on duty…"

"Penelope, won't you please just go lie down?" Jasper said, exasperated. "And behave in front of the staff!" he whispered.

I'd lost patience with this farce of "who's above and who's below stairs." The Painter, a man about whom the staff cared, had nearly died, and was still touch-and-go. We were all snowed in together. So what if we weren't on the guest list? We certainly knew him better than Kaylie Hart, who was allowed to snuggle up all puffy-eyed in an easy chair, being treated with delicate respect. How dare anyone impugn Isaac or shame Rose? Or yell at me, for that matter. Furious, I walked out without excusing myself.

To make up for it, I decided to concoct something fabulous for everyone behind the swinging door. We deserved comfort, too.

And since I'm a chef and not a therapist, I don't have to behave with professional respect around Lady Penelope's "condition". *Let's just call crazy crazy*, I thought to myself, *and Lady Penelope is Crazy-Crazy with a capital Crazy.* Enough with trying to get to the bottom of the reasons why people do the things they do. Time to break out the pâté and ancient bottles of port!

Chapter Twenty-Three

"Oh, beg pardon, Juliet," Seamus said, jumping up from the bookshelf. "I didn't know you'd come in to work." He headed toward the back door.

"You don't have to leave for me to cook, Seamus," I said, puzzled. "Have a seat, I'll get you some tea."

"No thanks, love. Got to run." He disappeared down the corridor and I heard the door to the mudroom slam. Once I was back in my domain, my muscles relaxed, and I took a deep breath. On my way to the fridge, my thigh scraped on the corner of a thin, hardcover book poking out from the shelf of the kitchen library. I bent over to rub my leg and tried to push the book in flush with the others. Noticing it was upside down, I pulled it out to reshelve it. The book's title was *Edible Wild Mushrooms — a Field-to-Frying Pan Guide.* I grabbed the book and stuck it into my apron pocket.

I began pulling food out of the Sub-Zero, and I had a flashback of Lady Penny pushing her way into my kitchen to make food for her father.

The thought made my muscles feel twitchy, like I had to get away from something. I sat down at the table then sprung back up again. I looked out the window to see that the snow had stopped falling. Something niggled at me. There couldn't be a poisoning, right? Where was everyone, anyway? I wanted Seamus or Rose or even Chisholm to talk some sense into me. Maybe Jasper's unpasteurized cheese was the culprit.

I opened the Sub-Zero and stared into it. The kitchen was stocked with the ingredients to make anything I could possibly want. What I really craved right now was a Lancashire hotpot, with a side of pickled red cabbage. I'd learned the dish from Piers Conley-Weatherall's holiday special and had made it many times for English families. It would take forever for the lamb and kidneys to cook till they were tender, but I was dreaming of the crispy, brown, sliced potato, laid on the top of the pot like tiles on a roof, dotted with butter chips and plenty of Kosher salt. It was a ton of work, but the staff would love having the steaming, savory dish set before them. It would be nice, though, for a change to have a steaming meal laid before me. I couldn't help wishing, for once, that I were the one being taken care of. Like when Edward had let me lie in bed, while he made me breakfast.

What if I'd given Ben up for Edward a year ago, when I'd had the chance? I wondered. The intrusive thought made me queasy and I tried to push it away. Would we be holed up somewhere, cozy for Christmas? Would he be making me a Lancashire hotpot in a snug house away from all this madness or would he have had his way with me and pulled a runner, just like he did this time? I hated the feeling of shame rising up in me. "*We need to talk,*" he'd said. *No, Edward, we don't* need *to do anything.*

I reached up to look behind a package of meat, wrapped in brown paper, and toppled a carafe of blood orange juice off the shelf, and it poured straight down the front of my white jacket. "Fuck Edward!" I yelled, blaming him for winding me up.

I quickly walked through the door to the laundry room, unbuttoning my jacket on the way. I took a fresh washcloth off the top of one of the piles, ran some warm water on it from the slop sink and washed the dark, sticky juice off my skin. I heard someone come through the swinging door into the kitchen and reflexively grabbed one of the white, Turkish towels stacked on a basket and clutched it to my front.

"Sir, may we go to your office? Or into His Lordship's study?" I heard Rose say from the kitchen. I slunk backwards.

"Look, Rose. I have five minutes."

"It's just that this is a delicate matter, and…"

"Spit it out, Rose. My head is going to explode."

"All right, then. The painting is mine. With the Earl in this state, I need to make it clear that the painting goes to me."

"What painting?"

"*The Veiled Madonna.*"

"Are you out of your mind?"

"It's my painting…It's me."

There was a long silence. I reached for a chef's jacket as quietly as I could.

"In the painting, I'm carrying Isaac. I fell pregnant by His Lordship."

"What are you saying, Rose?"

"Mr. Roth, I only want what was promised to me over 30 years ago. I was going to approach His Lordship, but then all this happened. I have to protect myself in case Hugh…in case His Lordship doesn't pull through." I heard Rose take in a deep, ragged breath. "He promised us a house for life, and a job. I only want what's rightfully my son's, not charity. I'll take care of Isaac for now, and when I'm gone, he'll have the painting and can sell it to support himself, if it comes to that. It's his insurance. For the moment, I'll wrap it in brown paper and put it away."

As I pulled one of my jackets from a stack of whites, I toppled a bottle of bleach and it made a huge clang onto the top of the empty washing machine. I held my breath.

"Isaac?" Rose called.

After a few seconds, Jasper Roth said, "You can't wrap it up in paper and put it away. I'm donating it."

"I'm afraid you can't," she said. "I'll find a way to put a stop to that."

"Is that a threat?"

"I'm in no way threatening you. Once again, I only want what's due to me and to my son."

"Jasper!" called Dr. Dearden, entering the kitchen from the hallway. "May we have a word? Come through Edward, that's right. Now Jasper, wouldn't you agree that your wife would rest easier in her room? As her doctor, I'm advising a sedative and bed rest."

"I'm in the middle of something Dearden! It seems to me that sedatives aren't making a dent. Penelope, why won't you go to your room?"

"I want to get to the bottom of why my father is really ill. I don't want to go lie down and forget about it," said Lady Penelope.

"Penelope, I realize you're upset about your father, but this is bordering on mental. No one tried to kill anyone. Stop stirring up trouble?" Jasper asked.

"May I escort you upstairs." I heard Edward's rich voice and strained forward. "Come with me," he soothed. "We'll get you settled."

That's right, I thought. *You go right ahead and settle her.*

"Man," Roth said, combing his hair back with his fingers, "this is all too much. Look Rose, I cannot deal with this right now."

I quietly pulled on my jacket and waited behind the door, picking up a stack of dishtowels so I could look busy if anyone came through. I heard the door swing open and Roth's footsteps going down the hall. "Penelope!" I heard him shout.

"I'm afraid this isn't over, Mr. Roth," I heard Rose say out loud, "but I have proof." I heard her footsteps disappearing into the hallway and I tentatively pushed open the door to the kitchen.

Terrence burst in, blustering, "What in the Hello Kitty did I do to deserve all this? I say we tunnel through the snow to the Pig Inn and keep drinking until all memory of this weekend has been obliterated." He flopped down and lay his head on the table.

"Seriously, I feel like I've been beaten with a club," I told him. Moving to the refrigerator, I took out three of Jasper Roth's sinfully expensive cheeses, butter, cream, milk and garlic. "I'm making mac and cheese, and I'm making it the way I like it. And I'm making a giant Lancashire hotpot. We can drown our sorrows in carbs and gravy. Alternatively, you can just keep on drinking."

"Prickly!" he said, rising to his feet. "I suppose now's not the time to ask you for a cappuccino." He reached up and took the good brandy from a high cabinet. I made myself a coffee, even though I'd had enough caffeine that day. I was already dehydrated and shaky, but it was either that or take a nap under the table.

"Terrence," I ventured. "Lady Penelope suggested I tried to poison The Painter and no one stepped up to defend me." I filled a huge pot with water to boil the handmade elbow macaroni that had been laid in from Danilo's pasta in the Landsdowne Road.

"She didn't suggest it, love, she accused you outright." He leaned against the counter, holding the brandy bottle by its neck.

"It's so absurd I feel like I'm on another planet."

"Well, they know the source is Mad Penelope and she's hopped up on goofballs and jealousy."

"What do you think of me, Terrence?"

"I've learned not to think too hard," he said, sipping his drink. "Live and let live. That's how we did in the bathhouses. Hold your head high and dare people to question you."

"You're right. I know that in theory. It's just hard to put into practice."

He pulled down a crystal tumbler.

"Don't you think I'm a good person?" I was grating cheese furiously into great, ropy piles on the cutting board.

"Does it matter what I think?"

"In theory, no. But you are a friend, so I'm asking you again."

"You're not asking what I think of you, you're asking what they think of you. Here's what I see: things have always been frosty between you and Crazy Lady P. She's never cared for your honing in on her man."

"I didn't hone in on her man," I said, aware that my voice wasn't exactly filled with conviction.

He took a deep drink and reached for a sandwich from a long-forgotten platter. "Either of her men." He eyed me seriously. "I'm frankly surprised the family had you back, save for the fact that Jasper Roth wouldn't rest till he'd slipped you the oyster you didn't order."

I grated off a large chunk of my cuticle. "Dammit!" I cried, sticking my finger in my mouth. "Is that what everyone *thinks*?"

"Who knows? Who cares? At the risk of sounding like a broken record, I'll say it again. Stop caring what other people think, Miss J. It's the recipe for happiness." He munched on his sandwich and watched me pull out the first aid kit and bandage my finger. "Anyway, why should you care if they did think it? So what if The Loony Lady's jealous that you, an indentured cook, could make her husband's eye roam? Or steal the delicious Edward from her clutches. Or whether or not slutty Daffy is furious that she could only pull the smelly and rotund Lord Ambridge with her smoking hot body when plain old Juliet has The Great American Titan sniffing around like she's a bitch in heat."

"Terrence!"

"Off your high horse. Old Terrence here spied you two in a clutch in the drawing room the last time you filled in for Edward."

"You may have thought you saw something, but as I've already told you it was just a conversation."

"Keep telling yourself that."

"Honestly Terrence, you've just insulted me six ways to Sunday and I don't even know how to begin to respond." My sluggish brain was beginning to catch up with everything Terrence was saying. "So are Edward and Penelope having it off?"

"I'm staying out of it," said Terrence, pouring himself another.

"Anyway, Roth is my employer, and it ends there! I am a professional chef not a concubine! And last of all, Terrence…'*plain old Juliet*'? Really? I may not wear a leather mini-skirt that could be mistaken for a belt, or push my tits into the faces of the lords I'm pouring tea for, but believe me, I know my way around between the sheets and can certainly be described as 'smoking hot'. Just ask… well… (I paused. I was going to say Edward, but I was working on erasing that chapter from my mind…) Ben!"

"I think I will," said Jasper Roth, smiling at me from half-in and half-out of the swinging door, apparently having just listened to my speech. I spun around in horror, groping blindly for a package of macaroni to put into the boiling water. I could actually feel the two hot red circles forming on my cheeks.

"Terrence, the Countess wants all the Christmas decorations down. She says she doesn't feel festive. Get Barry from out back and MacGregor. And ask Seamus if he's around."

"Right away, Sir," said Terrence, openly slugging the last of his brandy and standing up to leave.

"Take the bottle. Tell 'em all that the drinks are on me. Open whatever you like. It's been a hell of a day for everyone."

"Thank you, Sir. I will," he said, reaching back to grab the open bottle, and swinging through the door.

"Whatever it takes to finally get you alone."

I stood stirring my pot with my back turned, willing Roth to go away. He didn't.

"Is there something I can get for you?" I asked crisply, trying to find my way back to chef mode.

"Only if it's smoking hot…" he said.

"Mr. Roth…"

"Oh, knock it off, Juliet. It's Jasper. The world's been turned on its ear, we might as well just be ourselves."

I took down a huge copper pan from the rack hanging above my head and started to melt butter for my cheese sauce. My stomach was cold and empty, like I'd just swallowed dry-ice chips. I couldn't imagine eating a thing, but I kept cooking so I'd have something to do with my hands.

"I wanted you here for this holiday so we could finally have this out."

"Have what out?"

"And then Penelope hired Edward behind my back. I was lucky to get you at the last minute. Anyway, I've come to a decision. We're getting a divorce."

"And which cheater brought that on? You or Edward?" I asked stroppily.

"You're not listening. What about Edward anyway? What's he got to do with anything? The final straw happened when she accused me of having a fling with you. I told her I didn't."

Was Terrence wrong about Edward and Lady Penelope or did Jasper simply not know?

"I have never cheated on my wife…" Jasper continued.

"Right!" I laughed mirthlessly.

"No, listen to me," he said, snatching the spoon out of my hand and laying it down on the counter. He turned off the flame under the pan. "I have been a faithful husband. Period."

"I find that hard to believe. What about Kaylie?"

"Not since before I was engaged. Believe what I'm saying. You want everyone else to look past the obvious. Why can't you?"

"It's just that…"

"That I'm a loudmouthed, filthy-rich American businessman who keeps my body in shape and talks a good game with women? That's my image. That's why I'm alpha, why I'm rich. It's how the game is played. It's what makes me tick, and without all this," he said, gesturing around the room, "without the house, this family name, all I have is money. My parents are gone. I was an only child. Really, if you look at it this way, who am I? You're the only one I can admit this to. I'm lost."

He was going down that road again. *The road on which I'm the girl who understands the man, when his wife doesn't.* I picked up the spoon, and he grabbed it away from me, looking me hard in the eyes.

"Do you want me to say it out loud? I married Penelope for her connections, and for her father's name. Poor old Hugh. Does that make me a bad guy? Isn't that how the upper class do it here in Jolly Old England? It bit me in the ass, anyway. I tried something, and it didn't work out the way I'd planned. I'm not happy, and she's not happy."

I grabbed my spoon back from him and turned again to my pot, pointlessly stirring it with the gas ring off.

He searched for words. "I respect Penelope. I even care about Penelope. But she was never stable, and now she's gotten worse. In the beginning, we had the passion that comes with newness, and it was even fun sometimes, but now we live separate lives. Whatever it is she needs to make her, you know, peaceful or normal, it's not me."

"So you feel justified in cheating on her?" My back was up. "You don't have to lie. Ben follows your career and he read in all the papers that you and that girl from…"

"Ben's a twerp and I fucking hate the fact that he's ever had you in bed," Jasper Roth said, his eyes blazing. "If he tries to tell me one more story about it, I'm going to punch him in the face."

"What did he say?" I asked, horrified.

"I don't want to talk about Ben. I want to talk about us. Look me in the eye and tell me you didn't think about sleeping with me after we kissed in the drawing room."

"That was hardly a kiss," I protested. My face burned in shame. It had been more than a kiss, if I was honest with myself. *Stupid, stupid, Juliet. Who drinks a bottle of wine with her boss in a dark, quiet house after midnight?* I'd scared myself at how close I'd come to crossing the line completely that night. If Rex hadn't gotten spooked by that owl and started barking his head off, I'd probably be exactly the cliché I railed against. "It was a peck goodnight," I said lamely.

"Two questions. How many seconds difference is there between a peck and a kiss? And, in what world does the chef kiss her boss goodnight?"

I squeezed my eyes shut, willing him to go away, but he didn't.

He slipped his arms around me, his strong hands against the small of my back, pulling me into him.

"Tell me you're not thinking about kissing me right now."

I couldn't look at him. I closed my eyes just to avoid having to answer the questions in his eyes.

"In Nantucket, you told me I was different than any other man you knew. You had to have meant that as a compliment."

"I did, of course." I wanted to reach up and put my arms around his neck. It was so dangerous. "But I had a boyfriend and you have a wife." I forced myself to wriggle away. He tried to hold on, but I took a firm step back. "You're a fascinating man," I said, looking straight into his icy blue eyes, "but you're my boss."

"No, let's leave it at *man*. I'm a man, Juliet. I think you realized that in Nantucket and you didn't act on it because you're a decent person. And don't say you were drunk when we kissed, because you weren't. And don't say you only kept me company because you felt sorry for me, because you didn't."

****

It had been dangerous. And almost as stupid as following Stephen to Paris. I remembered us drinking really good wine and talking all night on his sea-salted, wraparound porch in Nantucket. Lady Penelope had come unhinged that week, going from manic to catatonic to manic, and had to be hospitalized for her own good. Even though I'd never been a fan of hers, I felt sorry for her.

Afterward, Jasper Roth had walked around with shadows on his face for three days. He'd cancelled all his guests, leaving just the two of us alone in the house. I'd had my bag packed, on high alert, thinking I'd be put on a plane out of there. I hadn't wanted to upset the apple cart by asking to go, but I also didn't want to be there. Instead, I'd walked around the house like a ghost, waiting for him to acknowledge my presence.

That third night, he came to my bedroom door.

"Juliet, I'm starving."

I made him some bay scallops with mashed potatoes and cranberry relish. I'd decided he needed something soft, warm and comforting. It was what I could offer.

"I've been alone enough," he said, rubbing his stubbly jaw. "Eat with me."

I'd felt awkward at first, sitting down at the table with him. We ate in the kitchen, with the French windows opened. The sky had started out milky black and dotted with stars. Once we started talking, we talked about everything. Art, our childhoods, religion, food, politics. Eventually, we moved our conversation outside and sat there long enough to watch the sun turn the sky pink and gold when day broke. For a while, I think we both forgot Penelope existed.

I'd been chilly on the wicker sofa, and he'd peeled off his worn, old Yale sweatshirt and given it to me. I should have just gone in. Knees to my chest, wrapped in that soft shirt that smelled like Gold Bond powder and bay rum, I had, indeed, noticed that he was a man. He sat close enough to me that I could feel the muscle of his thigh against my hip. I'd pretended to myself I was sitting that close for warmth. I also pretended it was normal for me to stay awake all night.

"We need another bottle of wine," he'd said, standing up.

"No, I'll get it," I'd said, standing up almost at the same time.

I don't remember who reached out first, but we wound up standing in an embrace for what seemed like hours. I looked up at him and he looked down, and our lips brushed. To this day, the playback of that moment in my mind is fuzzy. Was it a kiss or an accident?

"Let's go to bed," he'd said to me.

He walked away from me and up the stairs. I stood at the bottom, looking up at the landing, wondering if he'd meant "together". And then I'd remembered that it didn't matter what he'd meant, since he was married and I was with Ben, so I climbed the stairs and went down the opposite hallway, alone.

****

Blinking hard, back in the present, I reached for my spoon again, needing to get back to work, to find my feet, but Jasper grabbed my wrist.

"For just one minute, forget I'm your boss. You almost did in Nantucket, didn't you? Should I fire you right now? Or maybe you could quit, so we'll be on an even playing field. It may be all *Upstairs, Downstairs* in this country, but we're not them, and we don't have to play by the rules. I'm not the master and you're not the servant here."

"Servant! Do you think I'm just a cliché of a girl who pines for the master?"

"No, I think you're the kind of girl who can have anyone she wants!"

"Pfff!" I laughed. "People have said lots of things about me, but never that!"

"It's the truth. You're trying not to hear me." He balled up his fists in frustration. "It makes me *crazy* that you wanted that wet-behind-the-ears, butt-kissing, pimply-faced Ben."

"Is it me that you want right now, or do you just want to prove something to Ben?"

"Look at me! I don't have anything to prove. It's simple. I want you. You are complex, and funny, and sharp and decent, and soft, and just…you're just worth ten of Ben. I should give him what he's hinting at and send him to L.A. to work for my film backers. He belongs there." He leaned back against the counter. "I'm bored with my money. I don't need to conquer Europe. Let me just go back home and be a normal American. Whatever I have now is not enough. I need more. I need meaning." He reached out and cupped my jaw in his big, warm open palm, staring intently into my eyes. "I want you to be with me."

296

Turning my head to break contact with his hand, I pulled back and stared at him. "Are you out of your mind?"

"No, quite the opposite. I'm laying a reasonable offer on the table. I'm a sound bet."

"It's ridiculous that we're even having this conversation."

"I'm rich, I've proven that I can be faithful, and I'm still young enough to be healthy for years to come. I can provide for children. You'd never have to work again."

"But I love my work!" I said, with resolution. I really did love being a chef. My lungs felt tight at the mention of children. Even if Edward came back to me on his knees, would he want that kind of life with me?

"So you'll work. Lots of mothers do. We could stay in England, or you could establish yourself back home. With my contacts, it'll be a breeze. And when the kids come, you decide – you can be home or we could hire the very best help."

I started to feel boxed in, pressured. How could anyone make this kind of decision on the spot? "Maybe you don't always get everything you want. You're acting like it's a done deal and we're just tidying up and signing the contract. Five minutes ago, I was calling you Mr. Roth. Maybe you only want what you can't have."

"That's not what this is, Juliet. I've thought about this long and hard. I have it all worked out. You just need to give the green light."

"This is feeling like what Kaylie quoted from *Forbes*. Is this purely that you're always looking for the bigger, better deal?" I started washing an already-washed pot, to have something solid to hold onto.

"It's a clean plan." He walked up behind me and put his hands on my shoulders. "The rest of your life…mapped out and taken care of."

Taken care of? I'd just worked out that I didn't need a man, that I didn't need anything beyond my own skills as a chef. Then again, it seemed I was always trying to wedge in where I wasn't wanted. First with Stephen, then Ben, and it hurt me to think it, and with Edward too it seemed.

"Jasper!" I heard Lady Penelope calling from down the hall and footsteps were approaching. He stepped quickly away from me.

"C'mon, not now," he whispered. "In the kitchen," he called back, loudly. "Look, I have to take care of her for now. It's my responsibility. Think about what I've said," he added as he swung through to the hallway. "Will you?"

I didn't answer. I was out of words.

"Jasper!" she called again. He shook his head at me, and swung through the door.

Trying to blank my mind, I turned back to the stove and put another large block of butter into my pan. Cooking something would ground me and give me a reality check. I pulled a measure of flour out of the can and sprinkled it in slowly, browning it to make a roux. I poured in some cream and some milk and stirred constantly, adding large handfuls of cheese from my grated pile. With my other hand I started to melt butter in another pan, so that I could sauté garlic and breadcrumbs for the topping.

My mind wondered to a long shot of me walking down a vast aisle with Jasper standing at the end of it. There were endless pews filled with people staring at me in pure adoration. I looked good. I should, my dress cost a fortune. As I approached the smiling, confident Jasper, I looked to the side and saw Edward sitting with his arm around Lady Penelope's shoulders. She looked at me and said, "What's the matter, Juliet? Did you want to be the girl with the most cake? You can't have them all, you know."

Stop! I told myself, shaking the vision from my mind.

I uncovered one of the myriad Fortnum and Mason Christmas puddings sent to Thornton Hall as gifts, and hacked off a piece, stuffing it into my mouth, greedily taking in the sweetness, filling the void. *Slow down, Juliet, don't do anything till you figure out exactly what it is that you want.* I didn't know what I was feeling. My head, my heart and my stomach weren't talking to each other. I was thirsty, and as I often do, had gone all day without stopping to get myself a drink of water. Still, I just wanted to get this done.

Quickly, I mixed the cheese sauce into the pasta in two enormous baking dishes and topped them with my crumb mixture. I put all the pans and utensils in the sink and put the mac and cheese in to bake.

Daphne came into the kitchen, looking around shiftily. She set her jaw when she saw me.

"Have you seen Rose?"

"Not recently," I said.

"Good, because I…"

"Daphne, wash what's in the sink and take these dishes out when the timer goes off," I said. I grabbed a box of crackers and a bottle of wine off the counter. "Anyone who wants food can help themselves to that and the salad that's in here," I said, opening the fridge. "I'll make a hotpot later." I took out a wheel of brie and a wedge of Stilton. "If anyone asks, I'm taking a nap," I said, and I swung out the door, through the laundry room and out the back. It was dark out, and slightly warmer than it had been. I hurried carefully along the slushy path, quickly since I hadn't bothered to put on a coat.

I shut the door behind me, tossed my snacks and wine onto the table and adjusted the heating. I wished the fire hadn't died. It was quite chilly. Sighing, I untied my apron and it landed on the floor in a heap, with a thump. *The book.* I opened it up and began to thumb through it. There was a chapter heading for *Deadly Mushrooms/Poisoning Danger.* After the page featuring a photo of the *Amanita Verna,* or Fool's Mushroom, there was a ragged edge where someone had torn out a page. The next entry was *Boletus Satanas.* I put the book down on the table. Typical. It seemed like everywhere I turned these days, I was only getting part of the story.

Chapter Twenty-Four

There was a soft knock on my door.

Oh, come on. Jasper Roth was the last thing I needed to deal with at this hour, with my head such a mess. "Jasper…" I began, swinging open the door.

"Again, why would Jasper Roth be coming to your cottage after dark?" asked Ben. "Can I come in?" he continued, pushing past me. He looked at the table with the wine and cheese. "Were you planning to entertain?"

"Yes, I plan to entertain myself."

"Can I watch?" he asked, with a lascivious grin.

"Why are you here, Ben?" I asked tonelessly.

"You never showed up. I had to track you down since you never came."

"I did come. Apparently shortly after Kaylie did," I said, arching an eyebrow.

Ben's face clouded, then dissolved into relief. "Oh, that. We were just talking! Nothing happened between Kaylie and me."

"Not then, Ben, but it did in New York. You're a liar and a cheat. Now leave."

"C'mon, now, Jubes. I don't know what you think happened…"

"What I *know* happened. I heard you two talking."

"You misunderstood. Let's open this wine, and sit down, and…"

"It's over Ben. It's been an awful couple of days and now you're giving me a headache. Please leave."

His face hardened.

"I wouldn't be Miss High and Mighty if I were you. Looks like Jasper's been keeping you here in his love bungalow. Who's the cheater now?"

"It's time for you to leave, Ben."

"And according to the little housemaid, you've been very busy. Sounds like you've had a taste of something below stairs as well."

"What's Daphne been saying?" I asked, coloring. "Why would she even be talking to you?"

"Turns out for a glass of wine and a bit of flattery, she's anybody's."

"Tell me you didn't!"

"Not that it's any of your business anymore, but I didn't. I could have, though. Anyway, I suppose we're even. I had mine with Kaylie and you had yours with Chef Action Man."

"Never while you and I were together. By the way, you left Amanda Selmont off the roster." I shook my head. "But it doesn't matter. You're nothing to me, now. Please leave."

"Before I go, do me one last favor, darling," he said nastily, with a bit of silk in his voice. He pulled a Swiss army knife out of his pocket, flipped out the corkscrew and slowly began to open my bottle of wine. "Put in a good word for me with Roth. Since you two are so cozy and all." He popped the cork. "You know, he and I have gotten quite chummy ourselves. We discuss all manner of manly topics. I don't think he'd like hearing about Edward, do you?" He poured himself a glass.

"You can't tell him about that!" I said, flailing to find a reason why Jasper shouldn't know. "Just, well, please don't tell him."

"Roth's considering making me his legal counsel for his new L.A. film project." He gave a little self-satisfied grin. "I've been gunning to move to the States, and with you working at Thornton Hall, I had a prime opportunity for an audience with Jasper himself. With all that New York film work I did last Christmas, I'm a natural to run his venture."

"Is that why you showed up here? Is that why you packed a suit?" I had to stop and laugh. "I thought that you were going to ask me to…"

"To what? To marry me?" He poured wine into the lone glass on the table and leaned against the wall with his shoulder, swirling and studying it. "I considered it, but it could never work. If I'm going to break out in the States, I need a wife who'll host my parties, dress up, and make nice with the other wives. The way you put your career first and all that stuff about paying your own way…you behave like you're the man. Except in bed." He held up his glass to toast me. "Face it, the sex was really good fun, but did you actually see us together, long-term?"

"No, Ben," I lied. "I didn't." I thought of how I'd never met his family, how we didn't mix with his friends, and how I'd never been given a ring.

"And just for the record – the sex wasn't great," I said, aiming to hurt him.

He sniffed and shrugged it off but I saw a flicker of doubt in his face.

"Given the circumstances, Ben, don't count on me to recommend you to Jasper. If I told him anything, it would be that you're childish and not to be trusted."

"Don't think of it," he frowned, downing his glass of wine. "Or I'm going straight to Lady Penelope and telling her that the self-appointed Lord of the Manor is bending his lady chef over the butcher block. What you're going to do is tell him to hire me." He still held the knife in his hand.

"You're out of luck, Ben. I'm not caught. There's nothing between Jasper and me."

"Well, try to prove it," he said. "I'm a solicitor. I have a way with words and I can be very persuasive."

"But that's a lie!"

"Put in a good word for me to your rich American boyfriend and I'll play nice like we used to. In fact, I'm quite in the mood to play nice now. C'mon Jubes. One for old times?" He reached out and stroked my hair.

"No way!" I lashed out, pushing him away. "Not if you were the last man on earth!"

"Fair enough," he said, holding up his hands. "Let the record reflect that no force was involved. You can't blame a bloke for trying, but be smart, Juliet. As a team, we both stand to profit. Cross me, and the fun's over."

I opened my mouth but no words came out.

"Good talk." He relaxed his face into a smile, as he put his glass down on the table. "If you need me, I'll be in the library drinking impossibly ancient Scotch with your boss-slash-lover and paving the way for my future. But don't forget what I said, darling…I expect you to sing my praises."

He strode across the room and walked out the door before I could respond. I shut it behind him.

I glanced at my wine and snacks, and considered my bed. I was stuck. I couldn't decide what to do with myself.

There was nothing left to do but go back to work. The most solid thing I had to cling to was my being a good chef. By the time I had on a fresh set of clothes, I was ready to face whatever waited for me in the house. Except maybe Jasper. *You can't run forever, Juliet. Just tell him no*, I coached myself. *You don't even have feelings for Jasper Roth. Unless you do*, a soft teasing voice inside me whispered. I pulled on a pair of my softest, fuzziest socks, stepped into my clogs, and strode out determinedly into the now-dark night. Closing the door behind me, I reached into my pocket for my flashlight. It wasn't there. For a moment, I considered going back for it. *Never mind*, I thought, *I know I can find my way.*

Chapter Twenty-Five

Pulling the bubbly, cheesy casseroles from the oven, I inhaled their rich, complicated scent – the woodiness of the smoked cheese, the musk of the goat cheese and the tang of the cheddar. This was not your mama's mac and cheese. I was ravenous. Maybe I'd just eat a bowl of it…To stave off the hunger pangs, I made myself another strong cappuccino.

None of the family or guests seemed interested in much more than sandwiches. I had the macaroni, and if anyone else wanted something, I'd just cook to order – omelets, pasta, broiled fish. And they could eat this hotpot, if I ever managed to cook it.

I set my cappuccino on the table and pulled out the trashcan from its caster where it lived under the sink, and dragged it to the table so I could finally peel potatoes for the hotpot. I felt a little crackle in my apron. I reached in and pulled out Edward's note. I read it again before crumpling it up, and tossing it into the trash.

The door pushed open behind me. "Juliet," Lady Penelope said sharply.

Without thinking, I grabbed the paper wad and hid it in my lap, under the table. "Lady Penelope! I'm just peeling potatoes," I said, without turning around. "What do you need?"

"What I *need*, is for the chef we've hired to take care of my family!" said Lady Penelope. "Why are you lolling about?"

"Oh!" I said, jumping up, and turning around to face her. "I was told you were resting above." I put the paper behind my back.

"I'm back down, now," she said. "And I'm wondering where my mother's tray is?" She looked at me suspiciously. "What's that behind your back?"

"Nothing," I replied. "Just garbage."

"Show it to me."

"This?" I said, shifting the note to my left hand, and presenting the potato peeler with my right. "Oh, I mean, it's a potato peeler."

She sighed a nasty sigh, and started toward me. "No, your other hand," she said, roughly grabbing for my wrist.

"Hey," I said, instinctively blocking my body with my elbow. She's much shorter than I am and I ended up clipping her in the chin.

"Ow! Give me that!" she said, scrambling around behind me. Her nail scratched against my wrist. I dropped the paper wad and it bounced under the chair.

"Penelope!" Jasper cried, pushing through the door. "What are you doing?"

She stood up straight. "I'm checking to see where my mother's tray is! It's been half an hour! I think we have a right to expect our servants to do their jobs," she said, catching her breath.

I went to the sink, to wash out my cut. Jasper followed behind me, looking. "Are you all right?"

"Fine," I lied. "It was an accident." No need to stir the pot.

"We have two butlers, for God's sake," he said, turning back to his wife. She had bumped into my coffee and spilled it on the table. I stopped washing my wrist and got a bar towel. "You don't need to be in the kitchen," he told her. "Juliet, where's the tray?" he asked, annoyed.

"I didn't get an order," I said, adding "Sir" as an afterthought, for Lady Penelope's benefit. "But I can start one right away, if you let me know what the Countess would like."

During this speech, I watched Lady Penelope pretend to tie

her shoelace. She snatched the paper wad and stuffed it in her cardigan pocket.

"That Daphne's useless," Jasper Roth said. "Penelope, tell Juliet what your mother wants, and she'll make it."

"I'm sure Mother's fine for now," Lady Penelope said, taking Jasper by the hand and leading him through the kitchen. "Better to let her rest. She'll eat later."

****

The phone rang in the kitchen while I was chopping uniform, shingle-shaped slices from the potatoes. I waited, since it was customary for the butlers to answer it. I really wanted to get this in the oven. I couldn't remember the last time I'd eaten, and I was starting to get weedy. I tried to remember if I'd ever gotten around to eating. Feeling as though I could fall asleep on my feet, I slugged down the rest of the cold cup of coffee that I'd had sitting on the table. After five rings, the tension got to me, so I wiped my hands on my apron and picked up.

"Thornton Hall," I answered.

"Jubes? Is that you?" Posy asked.

"Posy!" I replied, surprised to hear her voice on the house line. "I can't believe you're calling."

"I can't either. You've been an utter jerk to me, but you're still my best friend, so I'll just have to give you a spank later. Right now, I've got more important business."

I bristled. She had no idea what I'd been through in the last several days, and she didn't even bother to ask how I was. "Do you need me to arrange for more contacts for you?"

"No, you massive baby, but I have one to arrange for you. First, I want to know if you can handle it. This is big. I mean life-changing big. You have to tell me if you really want the truth."

"I don't know," I said, honestly. I started to feel mild panic. "By the way, Mother made me swear I wouldn't talk to you. Why?" My

307

heart ramped up to pounding.

"I'll tell you why, but only if you're sure you want to know. It was your mother's place to tell you this, but she didn't, so I'll fall on the sword."

"Is it that bad?" I sat down in a kitchen chair, my mouth drying out.

"It's kind of fabulous. But big. No, huge. Yes or no?"

My brain actually hurt. *How could I answer? Kind of fabulous sounded good, but Mother was being so weird. Did I want to know the truth? The truth about what?*

"O.K. Yes," I managed to say, barely audibly, jaw clenched. I tensed up my body like I was about to get a vaccination.

"Here goes," she said, taking a deep breath. "You're flying from London to L.A. on December 27th to meet Piers Conley-Weatherall! He's having you on *Piers's Family Table* that week to cook something English and homey like Savoury Duck or a Lancashire hotpot!"

I blinked. "Why?" I felt a little woozy, and braced my hip against the counter for ballast.

"And don't worry, because I'm flying with him to meet you, you know, to make sure you have someone to support you. Of course he couldn't risk his reputation by having you on if you weren't a bona fide chef, so I put him in touch with that scary lady from The Gastronome's Trust," she said, "and he found out you'd worked for Liz Hurley. Of course he knows her from L.A. Then, we sat around and Googled different photos of you, and he saw the one of you on that yacht, and called you absolutely lovely and…"

"Posy!" I interrupted, my head starting to pound. "I asked you why he would have me, an unknown chef, on his television show. And why was it my mother's place to tell me?"

"Because you're his daughter."

I remember gulping to catch my breath, just before the lights went out. There was a loud clatter. Distantly, I heard someone calling "Jubes!" over and over. I wished they'd be quiet. It was so nice to just rest.

Chapter Twenty-Six

My head hurt so badly I couldn't turn my neck to look for a glass of water, but the pillow underneath it felt soft. It was too dark to see, anyway. My mouth was full of cotton balls. *Can someone get me a drink?* I was shouting in my head, but I could hear that it was only coming out a whisper.

"Shut up!" I heard through the door. "Stop talking to me. Jasper, tell her to shut up!" Lady Penelope whispered.

"That's as clear and honest as I can be, Sir. I've said what I've come to say, and I don't wish to upset the Lady further."

"Fine, Rose. We heard you. That's enough. Go," Jasper said. "Go find out if anyone's still awake. If they need food, tell Edward."

I want a drink of water! I thought as loudly as I could. *Tell Edward! No, don't tell Edward, tell someone else.* I heard Rose's heels clacking away from me on the wooden floor. *No! Come back.*

"The nerve of her." I heard Lady Penelope shrill. "With my father on his deathbed. I want Rose gone. Her and her whole family!"

"I know, calm down."

"Don't tell me to calm down! That moron is my brother, Jasper, my brother! I have to tell mother right now," I heard Lady Penelope say in a tight voice.

"No! Your mother's been through enough, today. Slow down."

I didn't really want to hear all this. Who knew what else they might say? Where the hell was I, anyway? With great effort, I moved my fingertips around. The sheets were like angel's robes. This was not Dove's Nest.

"So what am I supposed to do? Sit on my hands?" demanded Lady Penelope.

"No, it's a mess. She really wants the painting."

"Well, she bloody well cannot have it," hissed Lady Penelope. "I'm not bowing to her demands. I won't be blackmailed."

"It's not blackmail if she can prove he promised her the painting."

"How's she going to prove it if, heaven forbid, my father dies? I'll be damned if I just hand over *my family's* fortunes!"

"Just take care of it," Jasper said. "This is too much, just do what needs to be done. God, my head is so full. Listen, I know this is a bad time to bring this up but we really need to talk."

"You're bloody well right this is a bad time. In case you hadn't noticed, my father is in and out of a coma and *your chef* got drunk and passed out. It's a good job Edward turned up."

"I'm not drunk," I whispered. "Just sleepy."

"We can do this later if you want, but we both know it's reached a head. Once your father is stable, I'm going back to the States."

"You're asking for a divorce while my father is ill?" she shrilled.

"We can call it a separation. I'll support you in whatever way I can."

"Is it because there's someone else?"

I strained to hear the answer, but Jasper started talking in a very low whisper.

"I didn't mean someone else for you, you egomaniac." She paused. "I don't care if the whole house hears." Quiet. "And you? You've been trysting with that great, hulking kitchen hand for ages. I'm used to it!"

Great hulking kitchen hand? I'm not hulking! Jasper, tell her I'm not hulking.

"I was asking if you wanted a divorce because of my 'someone else'?"

"Penelope, at this point, I just want both of us to be happy."

"Aren't you going to ask me who your rival is?" she spat. "Don't you want to know who I have on the side?" I heard hard shoes on the wood, and Terrence said, "Beg pardon, Sir, Dr. Dearden asked me to bring this tray to Juliet."

Yay, water. Please let it be water.

"Can't you see we're having a discussion?" asked Lady Penelope.

"Beg your pardon, Your Ladyship, I'll come back."

"No, go ahead, Terrence," Jasper interrupted. "We're finished for now."

"For now," Lady Penelope said, and I heard her walking away.

A shaft of light sliced through the darkness as Terrence came in. "You put on quite a show. Jealous of all the attention His Lordship was getting, were you?"

"Water," I squeaked.

"Here you are, Camille." He lifted my head off the pillow and put a glass to my cracked lips. "Go slow. If you gulp it, you'll sick it up, then you'll have to suffer through Daphne while she strips your Heirloom bespoke bed sheets. Was this a stunt so you could see what the beds in the big house are like? But wait! You've already sampled Roth's. Of course the sheets in the attic might only be Charlotte Thomas, it's a bit downmarket up there. By the way, your mum has rung the house phone eight times. We didn't want to worry her, so we keep telling her you're busy. I didn't tell her you'd gotten the vapors like a proper, delicate English lady, and that you'd need to go to Bath to take the waters as soon as possible. You may want to ring her back at some point, though."

She knew who my father was, and didn't tell me. "I don't want to talk to her."

"Your prerogative. That Posy has rung a couple of times to ask how you are. She claims she heard your skull hit the floor. I think Edward spoke to her."

After several sips of water, my throat began to feel less parched.

"What else is going on out there?" I managed. "What time is it?"

"Edward's clearing up. Looks like all the drinking that's going to be done tonight has been done. I hope there's still wine left in the cellar! We've safely passed the 4-drink per person minimum, and it's barely a vicar's bedtime. Daphne's washing up the good crystal in the sink by the bar. Most everyone went up early. Judging from the sounds I heard coming from the Tapestry Room, Jacques and Kaylie are shagging away their grief and worry."

"You can't be so sure it's Jacques in there with Miss Hollywood."

"Do tell! Now Roth is giving it to the guest?" he squealed, slopping water onto my front. "Sorry."

"No! It's Ben. Maybe."

"Better her than you, missus. If you wind up getting back with him I'll deny that I said this, but he's a loser. Not to mention I overheard him bragging to Roth about having you over a judge's bench in the courtroom."

"He didn't!" I gasped, which sent me into a coughing fit. "I mean, he really didn't."

"He was talking shit. Hot-looking and all, but definitely a douchebag."

"Terrence!"

"Sorry, I've been binge-watching old episodes of *The Sopranos*. But, if the shoe fits..."

"So, no more food for me to make?" I asked.

"Girl, you passed out on the kitchen floor. I'd say you're off duty. Edward took over, and told you to stay in bed. My advice? Don't do drugs on the job."

"Shut up. You know I don't do drugs. I must have been dehydrated. Plus, I had tons of coffee today on an empty stomach." Not to mention the shock of finding out I had a real father, with a real name, and a real face. Suddenly, I was furious at Mother and started to hyperventilate. It made me dizzy. "And you can tell Edward that he doesn't get to tell me what to do."

"Don't get ratty with me! I'm just the messenger."

Rose poked her head through the door, and said, "Terrence, Dr. Dearden needs you to help Mr. Chisholm with some personal care for His Lordship."

"Righty-hoo, I'm off to show Madame Chizzypants how it's done. Enjoy your rest, clever girl. Full salary plus staff service. Why didn't I think of passing out during the busy season? If anyone asks you to get back to work, just tell them you're seeing double."

Rose swept past Terrence and sat on the side of my bed. "How's our patient?"

My eyes welled up. "Not good, Rose."

"There, there. You probably wish you had your own mum here."

"No Rose, I actually don't. I never want to see her again." Two hot tears rolled down my face and landed on my chapped lips, stinging them. My head really hurt.

"Ah, you don't mean it."

"I feel terrible," I said, turning my face to the side.

She looked concerned. Taking the damp cloth off the tray, she wiped my forehead and asked, "Still shaky from your fall? I'm sorry to have to ask this, love, but Dr. Dearden put me to the task. Could you be in a family way?"

Not only was I on the pill, Edward had also been very responsible about protection. "No, definitely not," I rasped. Without warning, more tears followed the first two. Being pregnant by Edward could have been nice under different circumstances. I felt so alone. "I'm sorry," I said. "I don't even know why I'm crying."

"It's perfectly understandable. You're suffering from exhaustion. It's been a long, trying day for everyone. I know I'm not myself, either. His Lordship's illness has left me in shock, though I suppose I'm no different to anyone else here." She poured out a cup of tea from the tray, propped up my head with some extra pillows, and held it to my lips. I sipped.

"But aren't you different?" I asked her gently. "Just a little?" I greedily drank some more.

"So, what did you hear?"

"What do you mean?" I asked.

"I've been in this house such a long time, it's a part of my body. I can feel in my bones when there's someone in the next room and I can tell everyone's footfalls apart with my eyes closed. You were in the laundry when I was talking to Mr. Roth."

I was gobsmacked. "If you knew I was there, why didn't you stop talking?"

"I knew it was you, my dear, and it'll all come out in the wash soon enough," she sighed, and put the cup back on the tray. She looked older than usual. "Sometimes, things have to be dealt with before you're ready. In some ways, I suppose it's good to have your hand forced occasionally."

"That's true," I agreed, my mind wandering to Edward.

"Still, I saw Hugh's death flash before my eyes. I hadn't quite realized we'd all gotten so old. That, I was not prepared for. Not at all." She looked away from me, her eyes watery.

"Rose, I'm so sorry."

"Ah, it's nothing…" She wiped her eyes on my napkin.

"Rose," I said gently, "I hope The Painter recovers one hundred percent. But just in case he doesn't…how do you plan to prove the painting is yours?"

She switched on the lamp and added another pillow to the ones behind my back, propping me up. Reaching into her apron pocket, she pulled out a faded, pinkish envelope out of her pocket and put it into my hands. "Are you well enough to read?" I nodded. The letter was open, with an orange wax seal, hanging from the triangular point. "Read it," she said.

I handled it carefully, as bits of paper were crumbling off. I slid out the letter from inside, and unfolded it.

My Darling Rose,
My poor words cannot describe the way in which you have electrified my soul and left my heart untethered to this earth. When a subject is too big to speak about, I paint

about it. I'm deeply sorry that my portrait of you on the beach in our beloved Barcelona – now, the holiest of places to me – has upset you. After your reaction to your portrait, I wrapped it and asked my old friend Chinnerton to store it at Peabody with his dusty wine bottles. In the future, when I paint you (and I cannot stop myself from doing so) I'll hide your face from the world, as you're hiding it now. I won't do this from shame, because I'm not ashamed of what we have, but because you have asked me to, and I can deny you nothing, Mi Corazon. These portraits, pale idols representing an angel, are yours, and only yours. I want to give to you, if you'll only receive.

I know I have your answer, but I cannot accept it, and so I ask again, will you marry me? If you cannot accept a divorce, I can seek an annulment. I have the highest regard for my wife, as you do, and wish her to bear no pain, but there are times in this brief life when mistakes should be corrected in the pursuit of pure joy, which to my mind is the godliest of all pursuits for us mere mortals. I've been blessed with so much through an accident of birth…let me elevate you, crown you in laurels and walk behind you, kissing the hem of your cloak. And if you won't allow that, let me cast off my coronet, and walk beside you clad in rough-hewn indigo garments.

Only say yes, and the choice is yours to make – be lady of my manor, and we'll raise our child in great halls filled with our laughter, or flee with me to Spain, and we'll raise our child as gypsies do, filling the open air with sounds of our joy.

Only say yes…

My eyes were misting, and the words had become blurry on the page. "Here," I said, offering it back to her. She held out a box of tissues, and I took one and dabbed my eyes. "Do you think he'll recover?"

"Let's hope it was just a mild heart attack. As ever, I'm offering my pain up to Jesus. Those who count their blessings are the happiest on this earth. I've a decent husband, a son who brings me joy, and good health, touch wood."

"That sounds nice."

"It is nice. Family is the most important thing, my girl."

"About Seamus…"

"Are you asking me if he knows about Isaac? That he does. But Isaac knows nothing. Neither does the Countess, and, for the time being, I'd be grateful if you'd help keep it that way." She felt my forehead and pulled the duvet up higher on my chest. "Sometimes happiness is about making a choice and committing to it. Those who are content with what they have are truly content. Longing for something different is the road to heartache."

"Should I have married Ben and made the best of it?"

"If you don't mind my saying so, I don't suppose Ben's your chance at happiness, either. I don't think he ever was."

"I know, it's just hard to let go." I was talking about Ben, but Edward's face kept blurring with Ben's in my mind. "There was a time when it felt like Ben and I were meant for each other, like we were one person." I shook my head. I didn't have the words to describe that transcendent period, frozen in time, even if it had proven to be false.

"I've walked down that road," she said, her eyes twinkling. "I've never said this to a soul…for a while, that feeling was heaven. And then it passed. I've had a wonderful life with a wonderful man who treats me like gold. So I'd say I'm happy. Now, our only concern before our time is up is taking care of our child."

I thought about Seamus, and how he loved Isaac. I got a pang for The Painter. Had it hurt all these years to know he had a son whom he couldn't claim? "Is that what all parents want?" I asked, thinking about Piers Conley-Weatherall. Why didn't he fight for me? I felt an endless, ancient loneliness. My father hadn't fought for me, nor had Stephen, Ben, or Edward. Would Jasper?

"We parents all make mistakes. We suffer dearly when we fall short where our children are concerned." She looked at me plainly. "Try not to judge your mam too harshly." I stared at her. "After Edward carried you in here…"

"Edward carried me in here?"

"After you'd fainted, I picked up the phone and talked to your Posy. She was worried sick and asks that you ring her as soon as you're strong enough." Rose drew the heavy, brocade draperies over the floor-to-ceiling window. "She told me about your dad."

My dad, I thought. It was like learning a foreign language.

"When Edward fetched me to undress you, she asked to be put on the phone with him, for an update on your condition."

"She's really nosy," I said, pouting.

"Sounds to me like you've got a good friend in her," Rose said. "She explained the whole thing to Edward as well."

"Why? What business is it of his?" My cheeks burned. I didn't want him knowing my secrets.

"I suppose she thought he'd be of some help," Rose said, kissing my cheek. "She has your best interest at heart. Edward asked to see you. Shall I send him in?"

"No!"

Rose picked up the tray, and moved toward the door. "I'll tell him you're resting, then. The doctor may be in to check on you. Sweet dreams, my chicken."

The door eased shut and I struggled to keep my eyes open in the blackness of the room. Finally, I gave into the stupor. I dreamed about stepping off a plane onto a blindingly sunny runway, Piers

Conley-Weatherall waving me over to a barbeque where he and Santa Claus were grilling. As I approached, I noticed that they were using grill tongs to lay on suckling pigs that looked alarmingly like babies. I shoveled them off the hot coals with my bare hands, and Edward ran forward and grabbed my blistered hands, telling me, "No, no!"

"No, no," I heard myself screaming, frantically pulling my wrists, trying to get free. My heart was motoring in my chest.

"Jubes, it's me. You're all right. Shh! It's Edward. Ouch, stop, it's me."

As I surfaced and landed in my body, I realized I was clawing at someone's face, and I struggled to focus. Edward was sitting on the edge of my bed, trying to hold my hands, while protecting himself from my blows.

In the dim glow of a flashlight laying on the nightstand, I could make out Edward's worried expression as he stared into my eyes. I realized I was still in the West Room of the big house. My arms were cold, and I saw that someone had dressed me in a long, sleeveless white nightgown. I was sitting on the train and struggling to sit all the way up without using my hands.

"Damn you!" I said, furious and pumped through with adrenaline, but wobbly. "You scared me! What are you even doing here? I told Rose to keep you out. Get off of me, you…you liar." I was batting at him furiously, but I could tell my reflexes were slow.

"Don't blame her," he said, dropping my wrists. "She told me you didn't want to see me. And I'll leave if that's true."

"Then go. Just like you did last time." I was starting to fully wake up. Some of the sluggishness I'd felt when Rose left was wearing off. "Go to Penelope! She's probably waiting for you."

"Are you still dreaming? You're talking nonsense."

"I'm not, no. I've pieced it all together. You've been sleeping with Lady Penelope for ages. Like she says, what's the point of trying to tether a man like you?" My mouth was dry, but I couldn't stop talking. "And I was foolish enough to believe your line about pining for me all that time. Typical of me to leap into bed first and ask questions later. I just hope you changed your sheets from when you had the mistress of the manor in between them!"

"That's ridiculous! Jubes, you're delirious."

The door to the bedroom swung on its hinge. "Hello?" I called. "Rose?" Edward and I both stayed very still and listened. I thought I heard feet padding around the corner. "Check." I said to Edward. He pulled the door open the rest of the way, and shined his flashlight down the hallway. "No one's there," he said. "Look, I seem to be upsetting you, and I'm sorry for that, but I did want to see how you were. Terrence said you're in bad shape. I hope it's not because of me. I want to talk, but you're ill."

"Don't flatter yourself," I tried to scream, but it came out a wordless rasp, and I started coughing. Edward grabbed a glass of water, and brought it to my lips, cradling my head in his arm. As I sipped it, I felt the muscles of his bicep against my ear and smelled his familiar spicy-sweet scent. With great effort, I pushed the duvet back so I could sit up, untangling my long gown from beneath me, and got a rush of freezing air around my bare arms. Within seconds, I had goose bumps all over, and I was aware that, under my thin, white lace nightie, my nipples could cut glass. I caught Edward looking, but to his credit, he looked away. As he pulled the glass from my lips, I relaxed backward, turning my face toward his chest, thinking, *Why don't you just slide under the duvet here, and we can…* "It's time for you to go!" I said abruptly.

Edward scrambled to set the glass down without spilling it while simultaneously disentangling his arm from my neck. "I'll leave you, but one last thing…Posy told me about Piers Conley-Weatherall being your dad and all, and I promised her I'd keep an eye on you to make sure you're coping with all of it. We're both really worried that you haven't rung your mum."

"Oh are both of you worried? You and Posy are tight now? You have secrets together and make promises behind my back?"

"Juliet, you're being completely irrational. I don't know what to say."

"Why is that not a surprise? I guess manly, sexy, hero seducers are too cool to form sentences, or…or to even write coherent notes, because your brain is too busy thinking about all the women you're going to trick into bed next? Who won't you seduce? Is Posy next?" I knew I was being insane, but I was so tired, and so wounded. And so hungry. "I'm hungry," I whined.

"At least let me make you something to eat," he said. "Then you can send me away. Or maybe, you'll let me tell my side of the story and not send me away. Either way, it's not fair of me to make you decide anything whilst you're ill. I'll bring you a tray," he said, turning to leave.

"Fine, go," I said softly as he pushed the door gently shut. "You're good at that." I pouted and humphed. "See if I care."

But I did care, that was the problem. Cutting Edward out of my heart was going to take a great deal more effort than cutting Stephen or Ben out had. *Or Jasper*, a voice whispered in my head. Jasper! Who said Jasper was in my heart? *Oh my God*, I thought. Even if he wasn't strictly in my heart, I had to admit my interest. My skin started to prickle, and my breath quickened as I recalled the last conversation we'd had. Say what you will about him, he'd at least had the balls to show his hand. There was an offer on the table. "I'm a sound bet," he'd told me.

Do nothing for now, I thought. *Just shove him to the back of your mind and you figure him out when you feel better.* I let out my breath, and tried to relax.

I lay there in the semi-dark and willed myself to go back to sleep, but it was no good. My muscles were straining toward the door. I sensed Edward working in the kitchen. I could picture him competently and skillfully slicing this and sautéing that, his chef's coat's sleeves rolled up to his elbows, exposing the tattoos on his forearms. My cheek remembered the scratchy shadow on his jaw. *Stop it*, I coached myself. *You've made up your mind. Edward was a fling, that was that, and now you have bigger fish to fry, like truly*

*diving into cheffing for the first time in your life. Oh, and meeting
your dad.*

I eased myself up to a sitting position on the side of the bed,
my brain struggling to find equilibrium, clanging painfully against
the side of my skull. Good God, it was cold. Honestly, it was like
the English didn't care to distinguish indoors from outdoors. I was
so uncomfortable. I scooted myself forward and down, plunking
silently onto the wood floor from the height of the house's ancestral
oak bed. Slipping on the ultra-luxe, hotel-style bathrobe and fluffy
house shoes that had been left for me, I peeked out into the hall
to make sure no one was there.

*Go in there and calmly tell him that you're leaving, and that he
can finish the stint,* I pep-talked myself. *Then, plan never to see
him again after tomorrow.*

****

I eased the door to the kitchen open and saw Edward standing at
the Aga, with his broad-shouldered back to me. He wasn't wearing
his whites. He had on jeans that fit him achingly well, and a long-
sleeved, crew-necked thermal shirt like a second skin. It looked like
he'd recently had a haircut and I couldn't help remembering how
the short hair up the back of his neck felt like velvet. He turned
around at the sound of my footsteps.

"Oh, hello you," Edward said, knitting his brows as he put the
lid on a saucepan simmering on the stove. "You shouldn't be up
and about. I told you I'd bring you something." He rushed to pull
out a chair, motioning for me to sit down.

"There's no need. I'm perfectly capable of cooking for myself,"
I said, trying to step around him to get to the Sub-Zero. And I
could have, had the floor not dropped out from under me, sending
my belly on an upswoop, like I was riding a roller coaster. Maybe
I shouldn't have gotten out of bed. "I'll just sit for a moment,"
I managed to say, my mouth drying up, "then I'll fry an egg or

something."

Before I knew it, he had slipped his arm around my waist and kicked the chair around to catch me as I floated downward and back. "Whoops."

"Sit still," he said, squatting in front of me and looking into my eyes with concern. "I'm going to go wake up Dearden."

"No, I'm fine!" I told him. "Really. If you'd just bring me some water and some Tylenol, and I need a cup of coffee for this headache." I pressed my palms flat on the table to steady myself.

"Let's stick with tea for now, shall we? I think you need something gentle."

"What I need, Edward," I said greedily gulping the glass of cold water he set in front of me, and plonking it down decisively on the table, "is to have a frank chat with you."

His eyes twinkled. "A frank chat? All right, then," he said, chopping garlic, and swooping it into his saucepan with the blade of a French knife, "by all means, fire away."

"OK, then." I cleared my throat. "Here's the thing." I fiddled with salt and pepper shakers, moving them apart, then together, then back apart. "I want to get past what happened between us and go back to being friends."

When I glanced up, he was staring at me intently. "Is that what we were?"

I ignored him and plowed on. "We're both adults here, so let's call a spade a spade." I sneaked another look at him. He was standing with his arms crossed, leaning back against the cabinet, his eyebrows raised in what appeared to be amusement. "What happened between us was sex, pure and simple. Physical, animalistic sex that was the result of being forced to rub up against each other in too close quarters."

"That's romantic." He turned his back on me, working at the sink.

"We're not talking about romance, Edward. That's my point."

The kitchen was quiet except for the sounds of water running and dishes clinking in the sink. I finished my soup, and drank the glass of water I'd been given. I felt much more like myself, but I was bone-tired.

Eventually, Edward came and sat at the table. I decided to let him talk first, which required force of will. I strained forward, anticipating what he was going to say.

"Juliet," he finally began. "We have a lot we need to sort out. I have a million things to say to you, but I'm not going to just at the moment."

"Are you afraid I'll make a scene in front of Penelope? I won't."

He laughed softly. "I'm not worried about that. You're weak right now. It's something I've never seen, which is why I'm sending you back to bed. And I'll handle the kitchen tomorrow…"

"It's not your call to make. I'm head chef. Besides, I'm fine!"

"I knew you'd say that." He looked at me for a moment. "You act too strong for your own good. It wouldn't kill you to let someone take care of you, just a bit."

"I don't need anyone." I stood up and pushed in my chair.

"I know that, too." He smiled wistfully. "Shall I walk you?"

I tried a smile, but I felt hollow inside. "I'm fine on my own."

Chapter Twenty-Seven

It was barely 5:30 when I pulled out the juicer and set the pot of fruit on the burner to stew. I'd awakened at around 4, unable to sleep since I'd napped so much. Quietly, I stripped the bed in the West Room and sneaked back to my cottage to shower and change. I felt so fresh and awake, it was like I'd made up the whole fainting episode.

Outside, the air was warmer and the snow was turning to slush. I'd never thought of myself as Scrooge, but I was glad to be putting Christmas behind me. Thank God the Countess had asked that the decorations be pulled down. I looked forward to seeing the guests off and leaving myself. *Except there's the question of what you're going to do about Piers Conley-Weatherall?* my inner voice niggled. *And Jasper.* How I wished I could just go back to my little flat in London and wait for a phone call to book me somewhere anonymous, in a house where no one knew me and my only worry was whether to wow them with a 21-dish *rijstaffel* like I'd learned to do in Amsterdam, or stick to traditional French and serve boeuf bourguignon followed by pots du crème.

I stepped into the pantry to grab some onions and potatoes, and when I came out, Seamus was kneeling in front of the bookshelf. "Good morning," I said. "You're up really early."

He stood up quickly, looking something into the stacks.

"Morning," he said, standing up quickly. "I'm surprised to see you. Shouldn't you be in bed?"

"Are you looking for this?" I held out. *Edible Wild Mushrooms – a Field-to-Frying Pan Guide.* He accepted the book.

"Can I make you something to eat?"

"I don't want to trouble you."

"Tea and toast?"

"That'd be grand." He shuffled a bit, then sat at the table. "As long as you're up, could I bend your ear with something that's been on my mind?"

"Anything. What's the matter?" I flicked the switch on the electric kettle and put a pullman of brown bread on the cutting board. I grabbed a bread knife off the magnetic knife bar and cut the mealy loaf into fat slices, then laid out the nice Irish butter and marmalade. Backtracking to the pantry, I looked for the basket of mushrooms. "Seamus," I said. "I know there were mushrooms in there. Do you know anything about that?"

"I'll just start, then. You seem to know a fair bit about psychology and all, so I wanted to ask ye if you think it's possible that someone could try to harm someone without realizing they were doing it."

"You too? Seamus, I did not poison The Painter, if that's what you're getting at!"

"No, no, not you. I was asking about myself. Something's eating me up inside." He sighed loudly. "You'll not find your mushroom basket in there. I came in early and took them out because they were poisonous."

"Poisonous!"

"I didn't want any harm coming to those that were handling them. It seems as though I foraged them." He was staring into the distance like he was trying to remember something from long ago. "Only I don't see how I could possibly have made a mistake. I've been gathering mushrooms all my life. I looked them up in one of these books on foraging. I think they're the Destroying Angels."

I stayed very quiet, setting a cup of tea in front of him, listening.

He paused, looking into the distance. "I know you heard the story about Isaac. I thought I'd forgiven Rose and Hugh long ago. Could it be that deep down a man's a man, and some dark part of me wanted to protect what's mine? Is there a part of the brain that can't help killing a rival? A waking dream, like."

"Are you asking me if you subconsciously tried to kill His Lordship?"

"I suppose I am." He looked tortured. "If I did, I'll need to confess and turn myself in."

"Even if you'd wished The Painter harm, how could you have known he'd be the only one who'd eat the mushrooms?"

"It doesn't add up, rationally. I see that. MacGregor taught me everything about mushrooms, and he's a master forager. He'd never make a mistake like that. He told me something, though. Said that the dog had liver disease, like my Da's horses had, and that poison will get you in a heartbeat if your liver's bad.

"I heard Dr. Dearden telling Mr. Roth that The Painter took medicine for hepatitis C," I said, setting a plate of toast in front of him.

"Did he say that, now? Ah, shite," he said, sucking in his breath. Tears sprung to his eyes. "Ah, damn it all. Dear God, have mercy on me." He pushed the plate away.

I stayed quiet for a moment. Finally, he shook his head and said to me, "Forgive me. Rose has that illness as well. Hepatitis. Lord, will the pain never stop?" he asked, eyes toward heaven. "Just hearing that puts a picture in my head. Forty years since, Rose is devoted to me, and the man is on his deathbed. Still, here I sit weeping like a baby. We've always had to be careful, Rose and me, like, you know, with…marital relations. This may be more than wants telling, my dear, but I'm in for a penny, in for a pound. Father Simon gave his blessing to our using protection. He knows the whole story about Isaac not being my blood son. He called me a modern-day Joseph." A lovely smile spread across Seamus' face. "He told me since we as a family were doing God's work by keeping and cherishing Isaac, that our Christian duty as parents was fulfilled. He said my life was as important as any God might provide. It's a pickle, but we took him at his word. He suggested we never share the conversation with the bishop, though. I suppose I tried to pretend to myself that Rose was born with the hepatitis or maybe that she got it in a public toilet. It hurts, having it spelled out that she and Hugh…"

"Seamus, I may not be a certified therapist but I think I'm pretty clear on a couple of things. First, as much jealousy as you might have living under the surface, you'd never intentionally harm anyone. Stop punishing yourself."

"I don't know, Juliet. It's why I'm asking you. I'm ashamed that I never came forward to say I left the basket on the porch. Tell me from the point of view of a psychologist, did I wish to see him dead?"

"Seamus, wishing something and making it happen are two different things. Our thoughts are not our actions. That's why humans have free will. And I strongly doubt you wanted him dead, even if you were jealous. Rose loves you, and is proud that you're Isaac's father…"

"But I'm not!"

"Yes, you are," I told him firmly. "Always have been. One thing I can tell you from my psychology studies is this: the most important thing to a baby is bonding with a loving caretaker who sees to his needs and shows him the world is a safe place." I thought about my mother. Maybe she wasn't fuzzy and warm, but she had always been devoted to me, in her way.

Seamus smiled. "The night he was born, Dearden brought him out as soon as he was bathed, and put him in my arms. Only the doctors and nurses were at the birth in those days, but as soon as I could see him, I did. I stood outside the room, waiting and praying. I held the little bundle and looked into his eyes and well, I fell in love. Those are the only words for it. I fell in love. It was the grandest day of my life altogether."

"Isaac is lucky. I wish I'd had a father like you."

"Rose told me about your da. I know it's not my place to say, my dear, but I hope you'll go hear what the man has to say. Speaking from experience, I'd wager that finding out you're his child was like a gift from God." He pointed a finger at me. "I see your face getting all hard-like. Don't be angry with your mother. You'll see as you get older that life's filled with hard choices, and we're all just human, doing the best we can."

"I'll try to remember that," I answered. "By the way, didn't that book spell out that if it was poison making The Painter sick, he'd be – God forbid – dead by now?"

"That's what I took away from it."

"It's a coincidence. The poor man had a heart attack. It looks like he'll be fine. Let it go."

He got up and gave me a squeeze before setting his dishes in the sink. "You're a good girl. Thanks for the chat. Since no one else is up yet, so would you mind holding the ladder while I put fresh batteries in the staff dining room smoke detector?"

****

"Can I get you something?" I asked Lady Penelope, who was pouring boiling water into a teapot when I got back to the kitchen.

"No, you cannot. Since no staff appear to be doing their jobs, I've had to serve myself," she said, putting the pot on a tray. Her pupils looked like Little Orphan Annie's. "I told Edward this morning to stay in bed since I assumed you'd be here doing what you were hired to do."

Stay in bed?

"I just stepped away to hold a ladder for Seamus," I told her. "I'll be happy to get you breakfast. If you'd like to go sit down, I'll bring the pot out to you." Her movements were so erratic, I was worried she'd spill it. "Do you want me to wake Dr. Dearden?"

She gave me a withering look. "No, I do not! I had to get up early

331

and run this house! Mother wanted the decorations down yesterday and the job's not done yet. I had to wake that lazy Isaac and put him to work, under my supervision. What would my parents do without me? As the saying goes, when the cat's away, the mice certainly do play!" She stalked through the swinging door and I heard her heels clicking down the hall toward the drawing room.

What was she even doing up at 6 in the morning? Was she sneaking out of Edward's cottage after a night of reunion sex? *None of your beeswax, Juliet. Time to pull the band-aid off once and for all. After tonight, Edward is dead to you.*

Since I was on my own for the breakfast shift, I kicked it into high gear, setting up chafing dishes and lighting cans of sterno, frying meats, and I decided to start lunch and dinner prep. Edward probably had a menu in mind, but too bad, if he was going to sleep off his post-Penelope sex haze, it was my kitchen. After all, possession is nine-tenths of the law. In America, anyway. Who knew what they did in this country where women weren't even allowed to inherit estates. No wonder Lady Penelope was cuckoo.

I rolled out some white-flour dough, and made a stack of thin, circular pancakes that I would stuff to make dumplings, and put them aside on the table. I pulled out a huge, wooden cutting board and placed a goose on top. I carefully tunnel-boned the huge bird, making sure to leave on the wing tips and leg ends, using Jacques Pepin's technique. *Voila,* I thought to myself. *I have excellent knife skills, if I do say so myself.* The thought cheered me as I proceeded to bone and skin a duck and a chicken, which would be layered and rolled inside the goose. *Let Kaylie be Ben's Hollywood wife. Screw him. She doesn't eat, so she doesn't cook. He can survive on diet soda and take-outs. I'm paid good money to make royal roasts like this one in condos, villas and chalets around the globe. And my little flat is cheerful, if a bit empty. I've got a best friend.* I felt a little squeeze in my heart when I thought about Posy and how I'd almost ruined our friendship with my suspicion. Thank God she refused to let me push her away.

Plus, on my own, I can lay around in my flannel pajamas to my heart's content. Who knows? Maybe someday I'll find a man who's driven wild by flannel pajamas with a bacon, egg and frying pan pattern on them.

A picture of Edward and me, drinking coffee in our matching flannel pajamas popped into my head, and I smiled. Suddenly, it was crowded out by a short movie of me drinking coffee in my pajamas with Jasper Roth in his black bathrobe. "Stop!" I yelled aloud.

"Sorry," I heard Isaac say softly behind me.

I whipped around to see him holding a fat, pimiento-stuffed Spanish olive, and looking guilty.

"Oh, Isaac, I wasn't talking to you."

"There's no one else here," he said, matter-of-factly.

"I was talking to myself. I didn't hear you come through. Take all the olives you like. There are more in the fridge."

"May I have a cup of tea? I'm cold." He looked sleepy and rumpled.

"Of course you can," I said, crossing to switch on the electric kettle. "But I'd better make it here and bring it in to you. Lady Penelope's waiting for you in the drawing room."

"Could I have a piece of toast first? I'm hungry."

"OK, but let's be quick. Lady Penelope is in a bad mood." I sliced some bread and stuck some in the toaster. Keeping my steady pace, I found the larding needle in the bottom of the utility drawer. I had thin strips of chilled pork fat prepared in the fridge to marble through the roast. This could be labeled an act of Caligulan debauchery in this age of the fat-free meal, but it's a technique that has never failed to bring me the highest praise for my long-cooked meats.

The fat would add richness and flavor and ensure that the outside skin of the goose would crisp up to perfection. Some people used the more modern, tubular type of larding needle or *lardoir,* which was essentially an injection, but I preferred the old-fashioned method I was taught by Henri in Paris. I used a long, antique needle with an inch-long eye that looked like a funhouse version of a darning needle. Then, I literally sew the fatback into the poultry meat. Barbaric, but with a sublime result.

Grabbing the popped-up toast, I buttered it, and set a plate in front of Isaac. "You really need to hurry."

I heard footsteps in the hall, and turned to the door, alert and at attention.

"Juliet, make me a Sanka."

"Of course, Your Ladyship. I'll have it sent right in."

She walked very carefully over to the farm table and placed a hand on the corner, steadying herself.

"No, I'll wait."

Uneasy, I rushed to make the instant coffee.

"My husband doesn't approve of my having Sanka, even though it brings me pleasure." She slowly pulled out a chair across from Isaac and sat down. My heart sank. I wanted her out of here.

"I heard from Chisholm that people thought 'the Christmas surprise' was that I was pregnant. I suppose people think I'm getting thick around the middle. No, I'm not with child, as they say. That moment in time has passed. May as well eat what I like."

"What can I make you to eat, Your Ladyship?" I asked cautiously.

"Give me what he's having. What's good for the gander is good for the goose, isn't that what they say?" she asked with a sharp edge in her voice. "That's what Jasper should be saying, anyway," she mumbled. "Plus, I'll have cheese and mayonnaise on it. There's no need for me to watch my figure. I have a real man who appreciates me for what I am." She stared at me, acting wobbly. "Do you watch your figure, Juliet? Do you have a man appreciating you?"

Wench! I thought. Go have breakfast in Edward's cottage and leave me alone.

As I sliced bread for her sandwich, I glanced at Isaac to see if he was paying attention. He, eating his toast, didn't seem to be listening.

Her tone was unsettling and I sensed I should tread carefully.

"I'm on my own at the moment, Your Ladyship," I said lightly "I'm content with my work." I spread a thick layer of mayonnaise on the bread, and laid on slices of emmentaler cheese.

"Work, yes, but you mustn't forget family. Is your family important to you, Isaac?"

I didn't like where this was going. "Won't you let me bring this into the drawing room?" I asked. She shook her head no. I moved aside some of the dishes I'd been working on, and sat her sandwich and cup of coffee in front of her.

"Isaac, I asked if your family was important."

"Yes, Your Ladyship," he replied, still engrossed in his toast.

"Home is where the family, is, right Isaac? Doesn't matter where as long as you're together?"

"I guess," he said, looking up worriedly. "I like it here. I told that to your Da when he wanted me to go."

"Where did my father want you to go?" She pounced like a leopard. I silently prayed for someone else to wake up and appear in the kitchen.

"Isaac, have you finished your breakfast? Maybe you should start taking decorations down in the drawing room?"

"He wanted me to go to the Royal College of Art," Isaac explained. "Said I was just like him, talented-like with painting, and he thought I could get famous like he did. I said no, I was happy here. I paint just because it's fun."

"He said you were just like him?" she asked in a tense voice. "If anyone is just like him, it's me."

"Your eyes are brown," Isaac said looking at her carefully. "His Lordship's are blue."

"Isaac, go into the drawing room. I need the table space to make lunch…"

"Just know this, when you're all sent away, your mother is not taking my family's painting."

"What painting?"

"Go into the drawing room, Isaac. It's time to take down the decorations," I said, trying to impart calmness to the atmosphere.

"I never had my tea," he said.

"You'll have to skip tea this morning," I said firmly. "Please do as Lady Penelope says."

I worked at the sink, worrying about Isaac. Even though my fondest wish was to be in a car headed away from Thornton Hall, Rose's family weighed heavily on my mind. I started making a fresh pot of tea to take in, just as an excuse to look in on Isaac. I hoped that someone else would wake up and come in soon. Lady Penelope was proving herself to be bat shit crazy, and I didn't want to be the only one in charge of managing her. Edward must be more whacked out than I ever imagined in order to put up with her. It just proved I dodged a bullet.

The Earl just had to recover. Until his absence, I hadn't realized what ballast he provided for this house. He certainly kept Jasper humble. *Oh God, Jasper.* There was no avoiding it. I'd have to face him today, one on one. I glanced at the clock. 6:40. He might be in the shower. My brain went rogue and conjured up an image of him, wrapping a thick, scarlet towel around his midsection, his gym-toned arms bare and beaded with water, his dark hair slicked back...

I had to get my head on straight. Jasper had made me an offer. I had to do the grown-up thing and give him an answer.

****

By 7:30, the sun had come out strong and bright, working double-time to melt the white blanket of snow into slush. The estate looked tarnished with tufts of dead grass peeking out of the now track-worn snow on the grounds. Out the window above the sink, I saw Lady Ambridge, stout and shapeless in her riding togs, high in the saddle of Thunder, Thornton Hall's most challenging mare. I had to hand it to her – clumsy as she was on her feet, she had an excellent seat. Both horse and rider looked ecstatic. Lady Ambridge, it seemed, was better suited to plants and animals than people.

Neither Terrence nor Chisholm had shown up in the kitchen, so I backed out the swinging door to deliver a tray with the pot of tea and digestive biscuits myself. Even though I dreaded the awkwardness that was bound to crackle between Edward and me in the kitchen, I wanted him to report for duty so I could slip out and speak to Jasper while Lady Penelope was still busy with the decorations.

"You oaf!" I heard her scream, as I was rounding the corner to the drawing room. She was lying on the floor with her robe askew. "I think you've broken my ankle! Juliet, ring the police at once."

"You slipped! I didn't touch her, I promise, Juliet. I was up on the ladder, and she was by the tree."

"Really! Whose word will everyone believe? Juliet, fetch Edward to get me up."

"Juliet, the Lady was stumbling, all sleepy-like, and she tripped."

"Isaac, just go get someone to help." He ran from the room. "Here, let me help you to a chair."

"Don't touch me!"

"Then would you like me to get you a hot cup of tea until someone else comes to help?"

"Just let me die here on the floor. Isn't that what you've wanted all along, you crafty bitch?" hissed Lady Penelope.

"Penny!" gasped the Countess, appearing at the door. She was in her dressing gown, which was unheard of, and her hair was down around her shoulders. She looked delicate as porcelain. "Oh, my dear, what have you done this time?"

Isaac rushed in with Dr. Dearden.

"I told you to get Edward, you idiot!"

"What's happened, Penelope?" asked Dearden, kneeling to examine her leg.

"Isaac attacked me! He came up right behind me and pushed me down. I'll see to it that he doesn't take my family's painting and that Rose doesn't take my father!" She ranted.

"I didn't touch her. I swear!" said Isaac.

Terrence and Chisholm scooped her up on Dr. Dearden's orders – against her protestations – and deposited her on the sofa. Dearden removed her shoe. "Don't try to move your foot."

"I'd as soon see Daddy dead as fraternizing with that…that…. low-born family! This is *my* house, Daddy is *my* father and Edward is *my* lover!"

"Hoo boy," whispered Terrence, backing toward the door.

"Penelope! Hush! You don't know what you're saying," the Countess said. "How many muscle relaxers have you taken this morning?"

"She slipped I swear it!" Isaac exclaimed.

"You may as well hear it now, Mother. Edward and I have a special relationship. There! It's out in the open. I haven't told Jasper yet, but we're divorcing. You can blame Juliet for that, if you like. She seduced him and they've been sleeping together behind my back for ages."

"Penelope!" shouted the Countess.

"Sorry to interrupt, Penny," said Dr. Dearden, looking embarrassed, "but you'll want to remain still. Your ankle is broken."

"Everything's broken!" she screamed.

"Your Ladyship," I said to the Countess. "I have to speak up for myself regarding Mr. Roth. I have never slept with him."

"And it's one of my greatest disappointments," Jasper said, striding into the room, dressed in jeans and a turtleneck. He stared me right in the eyes. "One I hope to remedy."

I was planning to have this out privately, but leave it to psycho Penelope to steal my moment and become the center of a huge scene.

"Jasper, you'll be happy to know I'm leaving you. You're now free to rut with whomever you like! If you hurry, you can cheat on your girlfriend Juliet with your girlfriend Kaylie. She's probably waiting for you in her bed!"

"No, I'm right here," she said as she walked in. Her hair was damp and pulled back haphazardly in a clip. "Black coffee," she said to me, standing in the doorway. Her sparkly, silver turtleneck was sheer enough to show a hint of nipple, outrageous for a night out clubbing, and utterly unacceptable for breakfast time at Thornton Hall. "Why's everyone yelling?"

"Because you and that other slut slept with my husband, that's why!" shrilled Lady Penelope, trying to twist her ankle out of Dearden's grasp. "Ow!"

"Ben," Kaylie pouted, turning around to grasp his hand and pull him in from the hallway. "Tell them I'm not that kind of girl."

"She hasn't slept with Jasper for ages," Ben said. "Kaylie is a one-man woman, and now she's with me."

Seeing smug Ben standing there in his non-proposal suit, as a guest in this house where he didn't belong, with a woman he cheated on me with, was just beyond the pale. "Why don't you and your Barbie doll go pack and get ready to go? This family's been through enough without having to host you."

The Countess gasped.

"Wow," Ben said, holding up his hands in mock surrender. "Lighten up, babe. I have to warn you, Jasper, man-to-man... when Juliet's feeling stressy, you want to steer clear." He crossed into the room to stand next to Roth.

"Don't talk about me like you know me."

"Come on, babe," he said, laughing disingenuously, in a fake attempt at bonhomie. "We've got your number, right, Jasper?" he winked. "And we still think you're adorable."

"Adorable?" I fumed. "Ben you're a patronizing jerk."

"Juliet, the cat's out of the bag. See, Jasper?" he smiled. "Adorable. And, as I'm sure you well know, a few 'stress-reduction' maneuvers and she's right as rain."

"Ben, you're embarrassing yourself. My advice is to stop talking and leave now before Jasper realizes what an ass you really are."

"Play nicely, Juliet," Ben said flicking a glance Jasper's way, "no one wants any dirty laundry aired in public. It would make our hosts uncomfortable to hear personal stories on either side of the fence." He shot me a warning look. "Especially yours."

"Say whatever you want. It won't be true. Liars *lie* is what I'm finding out. I'm sure the source will be considered," I said, walking right up to him and getting up in his face. I knew I was burning bridges with my career by acting out in front of the family, but I couldn't hold it in.

"Right Jubes," Ben drove on. "And your word as a PMS-ing cook who'll sleep with anybody really counts against mine as a respected lawyer from a top firm!"

"Ben, you're the only man I've slept with since college, and it was a mistake."

"Oh, go *on!* I know you were shagging that poncy Edward."

My face went up in flames.

"Surely you saw that right under your nose, Jasper? And now you've dropped your chef boy toy like a hot rock for someone with a bigger bank account! Fair enough. I guess the best man won, right Jasp?"

"Flannery, that's enough," Jasper said.

"I should say so!" said the Countess, frozen to her spot.

"I don't blame *you*," he said to Jasper. "It's her I've got the problem with. We hit a rough patch, so you just hightailed it out of town and fell into the next bed offered to you?"

"Ben, cut it out," Jasper said.

"Rough patch? You cheated on me! And it's true. I was so mad with rage about Amanda that I showed up here and had my way with MacGregor, Barry, Terrence, Chisholm, *and* Jasper! And guess what?"

"What?" Terrence cried, leaning forward.

"They were all better than you! And I never thought about you, even once, because you are awful!"

"You nasty little slag!"

"No one knows slags better than you, Ben. First Amanda, then

Kaylie."

"Hey!" said Kaylie from the hallway.

"Funny, one minute you didn't like 'cold, skinny bicycle girls', and the next minute you're practically Lance Armstrong riding that one like you're about to win the *Tour de France!*"

"I don't eat carbs," Kaylie explained to the room, matter-of-factly. "That's why I'm skinny."

"Skinny or not, they were willing to throw their backs into it, and toss on a little lacy underwear from time to time." Ben sneered.

"Shame they didn't get a big payoff for all their efforts! You're about as skilled as a pizza delivery boy!"

Ben moved forward, and Jasper shot up behind him and put his hand on Ben's shoulder. "Take it easy," he said.

"You wouldn't know good if you had it, you cold fish," Ben spat at me.

"We don't care to hear anymore about your disgusting, down-market coupling!" interrupted Lady Penelope. "The issue at hand here is that Rose is trying to steal my family's painting, and she sent Isaac in to rough me up. If no one will ring the police, I'll do it myself," said Lady Penelope. "You two," she said, indicating Terrence and Chisholm, "walk me to the hallway."

"No," said Dr. Dearden. "Go check on Hugh." The butlers walked as fast as they could from the room, determined to overtake one another without bursting into undignified runs.

"Your problem, Jubes, is that you're absolutely frigid." Ben shook his head at me.

"Knock it off, Ben," Jasper said, pushing him back, out of my space. Ben shrugged off Jasper's hand.

"I've thrown you back in the pond, and you're not getting any younger. You're lucky if you get a man to bed you out of pity."

"I'm warning you, Flannery," Jasper said, balling up his fists. "Quit while you're ahead."

Daphne rushed in saying, "Someone needs to check on His Lordship! He won't stay in his bed. Come on, quick." Dearden rose from his post at Lady Penelope's ankle, and the Countess leapt to her feet. They followed Daphne out of the room.

"Jasper, this is between me and my girlfriend," he said wagging his finger at me.

"I'm *not* your girlfriend!" I told him, shoving his hand sideways out of my face, accidentally bending his finger.

"Ow! You bloody cow."

"Ben, I said that's enough!" Jasper said, taking a step toward Ben and raising his fist.

"Nice, Jubes, now you're going to have your lover beat me up? I thought you wore the pants!"

Instinctively, I pulled my hand back to slap him and he grabbed my wrist to stop me. Jasper wheeled around, shoving Ben hard, sending him stumbling backwards against the paned glass of a curio cabinet, cracking the façade and shaking up all the porcelain knick-knacks inside.

"Ouch! Shit," Ben said regaining his balance. "You're going to fight me over Juliet? You can do better than her. Knock it off, Jasp," he added, putting his flat palms against Jaspers shoulders, shoving him in a challenging way. He stumbled backward against Isaac, who was standing there, poised to do something, but looking like he didn't know what.

"Isaac, back away," I commanded. "Go sit in that chair. As for you, Ben, I might have enjoyed sex with you if it had ever lasted more than ten minutes," I yelled from the sidelines. "By the way, I lied. I hated that hotel with the mirrored ceiling in Amsterdam! You spent the whole time looking at your own smug face!"

He started toward me, and Jasper blocked his body. All of the sudden, they were banging against a heavy cherry wood console in a wrestling match.

. "If you're looking to hold onto a man like Jasper, you'd better learn a few more tricks of the trade," he yelled at me, all the while trying to keep Jasper from pushing him over.

"Say another word and I'll slug you," Jasper barked breathlessly, still trying to wrestle Ben to the ground.

"C'mon fellas, let's break it up," Edward said, jogging into the room, wearing his kitchen whites. He tried to pry Ben and Jasper apart. It embarrassed me that I was so happy to see him.

"Thank heavens you're here, darling," Lady Penelope said, shouting to Edward over the din. "No one will walk me to the phone. Come here and give me your shoulder."

"Jasper, this isn't between you and me," Ben said, breathless. "I need to talk with Jubes alone. Juliet, you're coming with me," he continued, twisting away from Edward's grip and reaching out to take my arm. I ducked and swerved, as Jasper put his body between Ben's and my own. Edward grabbed Ben's arm, as Ben tried to reach around Jasper, and wound up butting him in the skull with his shoulder.

"Damn it, Ben," Jasper said, grabbing his own head and trying to punch Ben in the stomach.

"Mr. Roth," Edward said, blocking the punch. "Time to cool off."

"You stay away from me, Edward," Ben said, shoving Edward backward.

Edward regained his balance and grabbed at Bens' arms. Jasper cuffed Ben on the ear, and set his body into a boxer's stance.

"Stop it, all of you!" I yelled.

"Shut your mouth, Jubes," Ben said.

"That's it!" Jasper said as he pulled back his arm and swung, just as Edward threw his own punch, and I lunged forward in rage, my arm cocked back. Someone's fist connected with Ben's jaw with a sickening click. Ben staggered from the blow, falling backward across the coffee table and onto the settee where Lady Penelope was struggling like a bug on its back, trying to get up alone.

"You punched me!" Ben yelled at Edward, a trickle of blood appearing at the corner of his mouth. "I'll sue you!"

"No, I did," I said, gritting my teeth and cradling my throbbing fist in my other hand.

"You deserved it," Jasper said, standing above Ben. "You need to leave, now. Just go."

"Look, Jasper," Ben said, laughing nervously and holding his jaw. "This isn't between you and me. Why don't we take a breather? We'll have a drink, calm down, and then we can talk about Suleiman's legal needs."

"I said leave."

"Come on, Ben," Kaylie said, pulling him by the arm. "I just this minute decided not to do that film Jasper offered me…"

"I didn't offer it to you. We're still waiting to hear from some bigger names."

"Anyway," she sniffed, "I'm going to do that picture with Trojan. *Swimming in the Ganges*? It's got Oscar written all over it. Ben, when we get to L.A. I'll walk you in to the offices and insist they hire you. I'll tell them I need you near me 24/7 or I can't function."

Edward let out a low whistle. "Good luck on that, then, mate." I laughed, and Edward smiled at me.

"Now everyone has stopped behaving like animals, would someone please help me to the phone? I have to call the police. Ben, you can stay. I'll need a barrister to advise us. You can stay in The Blue Room, but that Kaylie needs to go. Next thing you know, she'll be seducing Edward." She tried to roll off the sofa.

"Whoa, Lady Penelope," said Edward, leaping to his feet to support her. "You shouldn't be standing on that ankle. Besides, isn't that very painful?"

"No, I took something for it when I woke up," she answered. "And Edward, the cat's out of the bag, you can just call me Penelope now."

"But your ankle wasn't broken when you woke up," Jasper sighed. "Terrence!" he called out into the hall, "fetch the doctor."

"I don't want the doctor. I need to use the phone! It's none of your business what I did or didn't take. We're getting a divorce."

"If I may say something, Lady Penelope?" Edward asked.

"It's Penelope. Yes, please say something. No one will listen to me."

"Calling the police isn't wise. Everything can be worked out privately," he glanced at me and raised his eyebrows. I shrugged. "Seems like everyone has forgotten that this is Thornton Hall.".

She started to speak, but Edward sat down next to her and put his finger over her lips. "Please rest easy, Your Ladyship." Edward said. "Your father had a heart attack." He held her hand solicitously. "Calm is the order of the day. Everything will be discussed behind closed doors. Look, here's the doctor to check on you."

"I'm very happy to report that Hugh has gained strength overnight. He's weak, but he has color in his cheeks, and I'm no longer worried about his breathing or circulation."

"Blessed be God," Rose said, following just behind him, Isaac holding her by the shoulders. "So the suspicion of poison is out of the question?"

"Heavens, yes. For the first few hours, I couldn't rule anything out, but he's on the upswing," Dr. Dearden said, mopping his forehead with a handkerchief. The doctor looked weaker than his patients.

I whisked over a chair and the old man sat in it. I poured him a glass of water from the pitcher on the table, as I was making a mental note to tell Seamus to clear out any and all mushrooms, and to take care doing so.

"I don't know why Juliet is getting off scot-free. Even if I can't prove she's a poisoner, at the very least she's a homewrecker."

Exasperated, Jasper said, "Penelope, you just announced to God and everyone that you've had an affair with Edward."

"Just one second," Edward said. "Mr. Roth…"

"Shh, Edward," said Lady Penelope, taking Edward by both hands. "We'll discuss this behind closed doors."

"Penelope, as your doctor, I'm advising you to go to your room to rest. Once you're safely in bed, I'll be up to wrap your ankle."

"I'll go upstairs, but before I do I want to clean house. Juliet, Rose, and Isaac, pack your things! You are no longer employed here!"

"I may be at death's door, but this is still my house," The Painter said. Everyone turned to the doorway. He was making his way into the room, gripping a walking frame with both hands and being held up by Mr. Chisholm and Seamus. "And Penelope, you're still my daughter, and I can turn you over my knee if need be. So stop all the nonsense, at once."

"Hugh! For heaven's sake, you should be in bed!" Dearden said, rising to his feet. I gently coaxed him back down into his chair.

"I'll go back, when I've had my say." The two men helped him to an armchair. He took a deep breath. "First and foremost, I want to clear Rose's name. The painting is hers. I gave it to her. Sorry Jasper, I know you've promised it to the Tisch. I'll dig you up a bit of something else. If I recover from this, I'll deliver it personally to glad-hand them a bit and smooth it over."

"You will recover from this, Hugh," said the Countess, eyes moist.

"Quite right," Dearden agreed. "Not a doubt in my mind."

"Hello?" We heard footsteps running down the hall. "Anyone?" Jane ran in, hair uncombed, wearing house shoes and fleece pajamas. Everyone turned to look at her. "Oh, thank heavens," she said, coming to a halt. "Beg pardon, sorry, I didn't mean to interrupt. It's just that I woke up and Isaac was gone, then I couldn't find anyone else in the house, not even in the kitchen, and I got a fright."

"Not to worry, Jane," The Painter said, "I'm glad you're here."

"Janey, sit down," Isaac said softly. "You can't get worked up." He took her hand and led her to a soft wing-chair.

"In case I don't make it, I'd like to say something that I should have said ages ago."

"Of course you're going to make it, Hugh," Dearden said. "You've come through the worst of it, and there's an army emergency vehicle on the way, thanks to Edward over there. We'll have you in hospital in no time."

"With your permission, Helena, my dear?" He looked at his

wife, eyebrows raised.

She nodded at her husband.

"What do you say, Rose?" he asked, eyes full of softness.

Rose looked at Seamus, standing by The Painter's side. He paused, and then nodded resolutely.

"I'd like to tell you all that Isaac is my son."

"No I'm not," Isaac said.

"Isaac, dear, let him speak," Rose said. There was a reverent tone in the room, and no one dared say a word. I sneaked a look at Isaac, who had stood up and was breathing rapidly.

"Ssh, Isaac," Jane told him, reaching for his hand. "Listen."

"That's right, you're not his son," Penelope said. "I'm his only child. Mummy, stop this."

"Let me make it clear that I'm not his father…that honor is Seamus's alone. Isaac, I wish we'd told you privately, but secrets have a way of telling themselves, even after decades of trying to keep them silent. I'm telling you now because I want to assuage any fears about your not being provided for."

"There was never any question about his being provided for," Seamus said, clearing his throat.

"Of course not. What I meant to say is that all members of your family will be housed on the estate until your deaths, if you choose to remain here. Additionally, Rose, I'm giving you *The Veiled Madonna*. You should have had it all along. That and the whole series."

"What do you mean by whole series?" She met The Painter's eyes.

"In Chinnerton's cellar, wrapped and preserved, are six other paintings of which you are the subject. I'll phone and you can pick them up when you like. Helena, I apologize for not telling you about them." She gave a terse nod and blinked tears out of her eyes.

"Those must be worth a fortune. My father's paintings are supposed to be handed down to my child," Penelope said.

"Oh, are you pregnant too?" Jane asked, smiling.

Everyone waited. For a tense moment, I wondered if Penelope's baby was Jasper's or Edward's.

"No," Penelope said shortly. "I'm not pregnant."

"Whew!" I said involuntarily, then faked a coughing fit to cover it.

"What Jane's saying is that *she* is," Isaac said.

"That's wonderful news," said The Painter, his face lighting up in a smile. "Isaac's going to be a father."

"Yes, Sir. Janey's pregnant. We were waiting to tell until we found out if it was a boy or a girl."

"Now that the first cat's out of the bag, I may as well tell you," she said, smiling radiantly. "It's a boy! I had a test to make sure everything was all right. They rang me with the results right before Christmas. I suppose people think I've just gotten pudgy!"

"I think you're beautiful," said The Painter. "Seamus, looks like you're going to be a grandfather. Congratulations."

"Same again to you," Isaac said, shaking his hand warmly.

The phone rang in the hallway, and Mr. Chisholm took off like a flash, presumably to beat Terrence to the punch. I heard footsteps and Terrence stopped at the doorway, hands folded primly in front of him. "Juliet, you have a telephone call."

"Uh, thank you Terrence," I said. Without meaning to, I stole a look at Edward, who was looking right back at me. I thought, So busted.

"I'll take it in the laundry room." Self-consciously, I walked out, making sure that my posture was good and my clogs didn't bang too loudly on the wooden floor. I was thrilled to get out of that room. *Who's calling me?* I wondered. I found myself hoping it was Edward for a split second before I realized he was in the house. It felt so good to walk into the spacious, high-ceilinged hallway and to leave the chaos of that claustrophobic room behind me. I needed some space to think.

Chapter Twenty-Eight

"Juliet Hill, give me one good reason for not ringing me in the last 24 hours! We have all been worried sick here!" Posy said as a greeting.

"Hello, P!" I said, smiling so hard my face hurt. "Oh, I am so happy to hear your voice." I had such a longing to be with my best friend at that moment, and my heart sung as I remembered I was about to be, very soon. "24 hours, hell. If I told you what had happened here in the last two hours you'd pass out." I hopped up on the dryer and kicked off my clogs.

"Speaking of passing out, I've gotten updates from your Edward, and your mum, and I wonder if you ought to be in hospital."

"He's not my Edward."

"Hmm," she said. "Anyway, your mum spoke to Rose or Seamus or whoever. She's been worried sick."

My mother. I hadn't spoken to her at all since I found out about Piers Conley-Weatherall. Since I found out about my dad. I shifted, crossing my legs under me. It was chilly in the laundry room. I unfolded a giant towel and draped it around my shoulders.

"Jubes, are you there?"

"Oh, yeah. Sorry. Here's the deal – it was never anything serious. Combo of dehydration, too much coffee, and shock of your news."

"Sorry, but you had to find out sometime. Better to find out in a house filled with four-poster beds and hot-and-cold running servants than alone in your flat. Are you OK now?"

"Don't worry, I'm fine."

"At any rate, I'm glad you got all that sorted with Edward. I can't believe you thought he was having it off with that old batty lady. How's his dad, by the way?"

"I don't know how his dad is. Why would I?"

"I figured he told you about organizing a care home for his dad, right? About how he had to get that one near his aunty so she could look in on him every day? After your man Jasper paid him his full wages and sent him packing, Edward used the time to sort out his family troubles."

Oh. My. God.

"Jubes? We must have a really bad connection. Can you hear me?"

I couldn't, really. Not with the world crashing down around my ears. Edward didn't plan to seduce me and flee. It *was* complicated! I'd been so stupid.

"I'm here," I managed.

"So, are you really down that you won't see him until July? Don't worry, long-distance relationships can work. I can really see Edward holding up his end of the bargain. And the time will fly with your being in L.A. with me. I still can't believe the agency approved my transfer to the other branch. I'm bi-coastal, baby! Oooh! And did I tell you? They made me a full-on editor! Junior, of course, but still! The Piers Conley-Weatherall deal clinched it for me."

I couldn't process it all. "No, you didn't tell me. We haven't spoken, remember? And I haven't even spoken to Edward. What's happening in July?"

"Edward's next contract is up. His agency placed him on that yacht, with that Greek family…what's their name? Look on mo'money.com. They're 8th richest in the world. Anyway, in July, he'll be done, so he'll come straight to L.A."

"And why would I be in L.A. in July?"

"Weeelll, I know we haven't officially asked you yet, but we have a plan."

"Who's we?"

"Your mum, Aunt Suze, Piers." She paused. "Maybe Edward a teeny bit."

"I'm beginning to think you shocked me like that on purpose, so you could nefariously take control of my life while I was incapacitated."

"Just hear me out. One of Aunt Suze's clients is staying in a London hotel but needs a long-term sublet. Did I tell you Aunt Suze thinks you should open your own restaurant there? She knows some guy who has a building. Anyway, we told Mona…"

"Who's Mona?"

"Stay with me, Jubes. Focus. Mona is your new sub-letter. We told Mona that she could pick your car up at Birmingham International and you'd text her which lot once you got there for your flight."

"My car?"

"It's perfect! Don't you see? Mona is 52, an investment banker, and a recovering alcoholic! Her profile is genius! She'll look after your car and house-sit your flat, and she'll pay you nearly twice your rent because her company is footing the bill. That'll give you an income in L.A. You won't need to pay rent there, because you'll be staying with me, of course, just like the old days in Paris!" she squealed. "I have missed you so much, and now I won't be alone in L.A. Aunt Suze says I need to embrace my fear, but I'm thinking baby steps."

"First of all, I have a job here…" I began.

"No you don't. You don't have anything booked past the New Year. We spoke to The Gastronome's Trust."

"You what?"

"We did a conference call when Piers called for a reference, remember? He needed to vet you before you cooked on his show.

By the way, your scary boss isn't as scary as I used to think. She had some ideas about booking you private work in L.A. She said you may as well be there as here, as far as she's concerned. She and your mum got on quite well during the conference call."

"This is too much. I really don't know what to say." I was going to meet my father. I lay down across the top of the washer and dryer, pulling my knees to my chest.

"Come on, then! Where's the girl who left university and followed a sizzling piece of tail across the ocean? The girl who wore the coconut bra and the feathered headdress to the Carnivale-in-Paris bash we went to with the gays? You nearly got frostbite when you jumped into that fountain."

"And to this day, ouzo has never touched my lips again. Look, even if I do agree to come to L.A., Edward's not in the picture. We broke up. I mean, we were never together. We're not together."

"Hmmm." I could hear her thinking. "Well, you can work that out on the way to the airport. His flight out isn't until 10:30 tonight, and yours is at 5:50, but he said he'd just get a snack and read the papers."

"He has a car here."

"His aunty is taking the train out there to get it. Seamus agreed to meet her at the station…"

"How do you even know Seamus?"

"…She'll need it to go back and forth from the care home, and Edward won't, since he'll be out on the yacht."

"Maybe you should forget being a book editor and become a production coordinator. You are really, really nosy. And bossy."

"But you love me." I could hear her smiling through the phone. "Oh, there's one more thing."

"What?"

"Your mum can't face talking to you over the phone. She feels really horrible."

I bristled. "She should."

"Aunt Suze suggested she fly out and talk to you in person. She wanted to come to London, but Edward told us that things there are hitting the fan, so she'll meet you in L.A. instead."

"When?" It was more than I could handle. "You know what? No. Tell her not to come."

"C'mon Jubes. We all had a lot of good talks. She's really proud of you, you know. She may not have told you, but she certainly crowed to us."

"Hmph."

"She asked me to ask you if it was alright if she came in a few weeks, instead of right away. She's getting that award from the Freudian Society, but she said she'd cancel on them if you wanted her right away."

My heart softened. "No, tell her that's fine." It actually *was* fine. At this point, one thing at a time was all I could deal with. I could imagine myself getting on a plane, but beyond that, I couldn't imagine what would happen. "I'll see her in L.A."

"Woo hoo! In L.A. We are going to have so much fun. Listen, I have to ring off, I have a zillion loose ends to tie up. Ring me when you're about to board the plane. I'll be there to pick you up in sunny Los Angeles!"

"Posy, you wear me out," I said, putting a towel under my head for a pillow.

"I love you, too. Byeee!"

I closed my eyes and lay there for a while, listening to the soothing buzz of the dial tone. Eventually, I was startled out of my peace by the alarming beeping sound that tells you the phone's off the hook. I scrambled to switch it off, and noted the silence. I guessed that Penelope and The Painter had been taken off in the ambulance, and the Countess had gone with them. I also guessed that Jasper would be packing to leave. Sighing, I pushed myself off the dryer and stood on my feet. I had to talk to him. If anyone knew what it was like to be a last-minute thought as someone was fleeing the scene, it was me, thanks to Stephen.

I headed in to look for Jasper, but found my feet carrying me to the kitchen. *OK, Juliet,* I said, letting myself off the hook for the time being, *you can cook first, but he's next on your list.* Maybe I couldn't wave a magic wand and fix the family, and maybe I couldn't even clean up my own messy corner of Thornton Hall, but I could cook. Back in the kitchen, where I was most comfortable, I felt hopeful. I got to work, excited to provide some much-needed holiday cheer.

****

I pulled the fragrant roast from the oven, my face bathed in herb-scented steam. With a couple of sherries under my belt, and some distance between myself and any man I'd ever laid lips on, I was feeling far more relaxed.

"I got Seamus and Isaac to sneak the gingerbread house into the staff dining room," Daphne said, coming through the kitchen. "Look at me, I'm one of them Christmas spirits." She was draped in paper chains and was holding branches of berry-festooned holly in each of her hands. Maybe the sherry had gentled me down, but I had to say, she looked very pretty.

"Take it through, Daphne, but don't get caught. We don't have permission for any of this, and there's been enough drama around here to last a lifetime."

"They made us skip Christmas! I dare anyone to complain about this little party."

"There's really no one around to complain. I'm so relieved that the rescue vehicle managed to get The Painter to the hospital."

"I'm doubly relieved that old Lady Penelope broke her ankle, so she had to go too," Daphne said, putting the holly on the table and pouring herself a drink.

"Daphne!"

"As if you aren't jumping up and down that she's out of your hair. She was crying when she left, she was. Edward carried her out to the ambulance and they were having some kind of a big goodbye. I brought her coat, so I could try and overhear, but all I heard was him talking about how he was sorry and how she needed to understand. I saw him walk back to his cottage after that."

"Where's the Countess?" I asked.

"She rode in the ambulance, too. And Lord and Lady Ambridge hitched a ride and asked to be dropped at the end of their road, since it's on the way."

Terrence came through, lugging a wooden box filled with bottles. "Delivery!" he sang, putting it down on the table. I peered in. Through the dust, I could make out that it was the good stuff. "Terrence!"

"Oh, please. After this holiday, do you think anyone's going to be taking inventory? I'll put it in our dining room. I've laid the table with the good crystal and china. If anything gets broken, I'll say Ben broke it during the fight."

I knew I should be a bigger woman than this, but I had to ask. "What happened to Ben?" I wondered if he was still in The Blue Room, like Lady Penelope had ordered.

"Oh, it was a sight. He and that Kaylie Hart were in the hallway, and Ben asked Mr. Roth when the car was coming for them. Mr. Roth said, 'What car? I want you off my property.' He told Ben that if he left that very minute, that he'd call for one, but they'd have to meet it at the gate! Can you fathom it? Off they went together, through the dirty snow, her in her spiked boots, sinking into the turf. Ben was dragging her hundred pieces of Louis Vuitton along with his own case. I could hear her carping at him till they were out of earshot!"

Seamus came through with a punchbowl, and asked Daphne, "Where did you want this, lass?"

"Set it on the sideboard, Seamus. Juliet, now that there's wine, get a big pot for mulling. And Seamus, did you get the mistletoe from the compost pile?"

"Isaac is hanging it round now."

"You're pretty comfortable being the boss, aren't you?" I teased

Daphne, setting a pot on the stove for the wine.

"Someone has to take charge if we're going to have any sort of Christmas!" she said. "Time is ticking. Mr. Roth hasn't come out of his room since the ambulance left, and the rest of the family is in casualty. Apart from the staff, the only person left is Jacques."

"Oh, it's Jacques now, is it?" asked Terrence, as he dusted the bottles.

"Well, it was 45 minutes ago when I was scrubbing his back in the shower."

"Respect," Terrence said, bowing to her. "And I thought I was a fast worker."

"Kaylie left him. He needed consolation," she said, opening the swinging door to the staff dining room. "I did what any good person would do at Christmas. I brought him comfort and joy," she said, disappearing with her decorations. "Set an extra place for him at the table."

Knowing that a food critic from above-stairs would be sitting down with us forced me to get my skates on. "Terrence, I'll have dinner in an hour. Will you set up chafing dishes and whatever else is needed in the staff room? And will you ask Mr. Roth when he'd like to dine?" I realized that if Jacques planned to slum it with us, Jasper would be on his own.

"Already done. Roth told Chizz he didn't want to eat."

I was worried about him, but said, "Let me know if he changes his mind."

****

Everyone cheered as I carried in the turkey. The table was heaving under the weight of the myriad, mismatched dishes that had been cooked and not eaten over the course of the last few days. Between the ham, the hotpot, the mac and cheese, and the variety of side vegetables, cheeses, pâtés, and home baked breads, there was sure to be something on the table to suit every guest.

I took my seat. I'd offered Jacques the seat at the head of the table, but he'd passed it to Isaac, in honor of his becoming a father. I suspected he really wanted to sit next to Daphne, to take advantage of the last hours they'd have together as an unlikely couple. It felt like a family dinner. All the servants were there, including MacGregor. All the servants except Edward.

Seamus made a lovely Christmas toast and Rose said a prayer that included petitions for the health of The Painter and Penelope, and gratitude for Jane's pregnancy. We went through the bottles Terrence had brought up from the cellar and sent him for more. It was as warm and congenial a holiday meal as you could ask for. The only hiccup was when Terrence kissed Chisholm's cheek under the mistletoe, declaring "Ho ho ho, you know that smooch is all you ever really wanted for Christmas." I managed to smooth the ruffled butler's feathers by listening to him describe the tablecloths at Clarence House for the entirety of the main course.

By the time I sent in the mince pies and cakes, all of us round the table were so content and relaxed it was as if the troubles of the last few days had never happened.

Stuffed and sleepy, I finally dislodged my rear from my chair, declaring "If I don't start the dishes now, I'll never get them done." Standing, I picked up a platter in each hand, and arrived at the door just as Edward was coming in the room.

"I thought I'd lend a hand clearing up," he said, in his soft chocolatey voice. His cheeks were ruddy from the cold, but he wasn't wearing a coat. In his low-slung jeans and leather boots, tight black thermal top, and his wooly red cap, he looked like a model from an outdoor gear catalogue. The funny thing is, I knew Edward, and I knew he'd simply thrown on the clothes for practicality. It was purely accidental that his outfit featured his gold-flecked eyes and showed off his athletic torso. Blocked from the kitchen, I stood still and waited for him to make a move.

"But you didn't even eat!" Rose cried. "Come, sit, we'll make you a plate. At least have some dessert."

"Wait!" Jacques cried, tipsily. "You haf trapped our chef underneath zee meestle-toe. You are entitled to a Christmas kiss."

"Mistle-toe! Mistle-toe!" Terrence had started a chant.

Edward's eyes asked me permission. Without my consent, my eyes told him yes. His cool, supple lips pressed against mine, softly at first, then more insistent. I leaned into the kiss, feeling my lips part, welcoming his tongue into my mouth. I melted into his taste, memories of our bodies together in his cottage swirling through my sleepy brain. One of the plates slipped from my hand and bounced off the rug.

"Ooh, the china," Terrence cried, jumping up to pick up the mess.

I pulled back, in a daze. Edward had never closed his eyes. He was looking at me, looking into me. I felt I needed to say something, but no words would come.

"Well, you haf no need for dessert, I'd zay," Jacques offered. "Zee chef herself seems to have been sweet enough."

Everyone jumped up to help clear, while I stood there, holding a lone plate. People were swirling around me and past me, cheerfully buzzing about the meal. Edward smiled, his eyes crinkling at the corners. I handed Rose the plate. "I'm a little dizzy," I told her, pushing through the door to the hallway. "I'm sorry, but I don't think I'm able to tidy this up."

Breathless, I headed back to the solitude of my cottage.

Walking out for what I was sure would be the last time, I closed the door to Dove's Nest. In the past several years, no matter who my clients had been, I had always figured there'd be another stint at Thornton Hall just around the bend. Now, I wasn't so sure. I picked up two of my cases, just as Rose was hurrying down the path.

"Leave those be," she said. "I'll send Seamus to carry them to your car. I've been looking all over for you."

"Does someone need me?"

"No, I just wanted to tell you goodbye. Edward asked me to

tell you that he'd listen from his cottage, and when you're ready, to sound your car horn."

"Rose, I never would have left without saying goodbye to you." I left the bags, and linked arms with her, walking up the slushy, wet path to the main house. "How's Isaac dealing with the news?"

"He's emotional, I won't lie to you. Seamus is with him now, they're having a private chat in Rose Cottage. He'll come around. Besides, there's not much could dampen his happiness about the new baby. Nor mine!" she said, giving me a squeeze. "I'm going to be a granny!"

"Congratulations," I said to her, holding the door open.

She made a beeline through the mudroom and laundry to the kettle and asked, "Do you have time for one last cup of tea?"

"A really quick one. I have one or two things to take care of," I said, thinking about how I was going to find Jasper. I took a seat, happy to be still for the time being.

She set a steaming cup of tea in front of me and poured in the milk. Without asking, she put in a spoon of sugar. "For shock," she said. I didn't argue.

I ached at the thought of leaving Rose. She has a perfect right to her nickname "Mum to the World." How many times had she pampered me, when the family wasn't on the grounds, by preparing staff meal? I always loved her fried breakfast, with eggs and black pudding, English bacon (which seems a lot more like ham than bacon to us Americans), grilled tomatoes and fried mushrooms, with a side of beans on toast. I'd devour it with two frothy coffees, a welcome, stark contrast from the super-haute cuisine Jasper Roth always wanted served at The Hall.

And her shepherd's pie, with ground lamb and a mashed potato crust. Despite, or because of, all my French training, it was only Rose who taught me not to confuse it with cottage pie, made with beef. The pie, along with a stout, had thickened our blood against cold English winters in the perpetually chilly stone mansion. My mother helped me, in her own manner, but Rose had always mothered me in traditional ways.

"What am I going to do without you?" I asked, choking up a little.

"You'll write me notes. I always love having something come in the post. Seamus has been thinking about getting on email. Who knows? Maybe we'll come to London to see you on a holiday."

"I can hardly believe I'm saying this, but I'm moving to L.A. Temporarily."

"Even better!" she said. "I could work on my suntan!" She smiled a huge smile, and her rosy cheeks looked rosier than ever.

Laughing, I stood up and gave her a tight, solid hug, and she gave it right back to me. "We'll meet again soon," she said, standing back and holding me by both hands. "I'll never forgive you if you don't come and see my grandson before he's up and walking."

"I can't wait," I said sincerely. I gulped down some of the tea. It's warm, thick, sweetness was just what I needed.

"Before too long, maybe you'll have a baby of your own to bring with you."

"Well, it'll only have one grandmother, so you can be honorary number two!"

"Has Piers's mother passed on? There might be a great grand-mother" she asked.

"Oh," I said, drinking my tea. "I have no idea." I'd forgotten to think about all the other relatives that come along with my having an actual father. I didn't have room in my brain to consider it. "Doesn't matter. You'll be its granny anyway," I said, standing up. "I hate to leave you, but I'd better get going. Tell everyone I'll miss them."

"Even Barry?" she twinkled.

"Maybe not him."

"Get a move on," she said, looking at me shrewdly, "You have a lot to take care of. Goodbye, m'dear, and see that you ring me when you arrive safely."

"I promise," I said, swinging through the oak door and walking out of Thornton's kitchen.

Chapter Twenty-Nine

Chapter Twenty-Nine

At the top of the stairs, I realized I'd been tiptoeing like a thief. *Don't be ridiculous, Juliet. The job's over, he's not your boss anymore. He's just a man, and you're just a woman.* Maybe that was the wrong phrase. *How can I be standing here, about to close the door on the offer of a future together and still be thinking about how sexy he is?*

I took a deep breath and stared at his door. I felt calm, just having asked myself that question. *Because he is sexy, that's why, I told myself. And you can think so, but that doesn't mean he's "the one". And knowing that is part of being a grown-up. Look how much you've learned since Stephen. So do the right thing, Juliet. Be a woman.*

I knocked firmly, lifted my chin, and waited for an answer.

"Leave it by the door," said the familiar, growly voice.

"It's me," I said. "Juliet."

For a while, I could hear myself breathing as I listened for an answer. Finally, I heard his footsteps, and he opened the door, saying nothing, looking at me eye-to-eye.

"Jasper, I just wanted to say I'm sorry."

"About what?" he asked neutrally, putting me on the spot, giving away nothing.

"If I led you to believe that I…"

He cut me off. "You don't have to let me down easy. I saw

something I wanted. I didn't get it. End of story."

I was stung. "Really? That's how it was?"

"If that's not it, then how was it?" he asked me, not moving an inch from the doorway.

"I don't know," I said, honestly. "I know that you were married and that made it wrong," I stammered, trying to form a thought on the spot. "I know that we have some kind of understanding. We connected, right?" I felt bare. "Didn't we?"

His face relaxed. He looked at me for a long time. "Yes, we had that."

"Good." Warmth spread over me, and a kind of relief. I was surprised that his acknowledgement meant so much.

"If things were different, I would have enjoyed being your rebound girl."

He smiled.

"You know, my mother's a psychiatrist, and she always advises waiting a year after a break-up to begin a new relationship."

"So I should call you in a year?" he asked.

"That's not what I really meant to say!" I said, waving my hands around. "I meant..."

"Relax. I was teasing." He reached up and grabbed the doorframe with one hand. He was waiting for me to end this, I could feel it.

"I'm just sorry," I said.

He smiled sadly. "Me too."

"Could I kiss you goodbye?" I asked.

"I'd like that," he said. "I'd like it if you'd kiss me." Holding onto the doorframe with both hands now, he closed his eyes, and parted his lips slightly.

I slid my arms around him, pressing my chest to his. I kissed him lightly on the ear, drinking in the smell of his cologne, of his skin. His body melted into mine, but he didn't embrace me. Rubbing my cool cheek against his warm one, scraping against the hints of his beard, I brought my lips to his, grazing at first, then pressing. I allowed myself to linger, to feel the hint of his tongue with mine before gently pulling away. "Mmmm..." he said. He didn't embrace me, never let go of the doorframe. I unwrapped my arms from around him, and stepped back. He opened his eyes.

"So, tell me, are you with Edward?"

"I don't know."

"He's lucky to even have a ghost of a chance. Look, if you need me, for a reference or anything, you're not gonna find me here. Obviously." He shuffled in his pocket and handed me a card. You can reach me at the Suleiman office and they'll give you my home and cell numbers in L.A." He held it out to me.

"What do you mean, L.A.?" I asked.

"Los Angeles. There's nothing for me in England anymore. I called my people last night, they found me a place for now. After the divorce, people on this side of the pond won't want to know me. That's business. That's the way it works." He stared at the card in his hand. "Take it."

I reached out and took it, and put it in my pocket. "Thanks," I said. *Don't tell him, Juliet,* the voice in my head warned. I thought it had a good point. "I have to go, I guess," I said, backing away.

"Give London a kiss for me."

I didn't answer. I turned and walked halfway down the hall.

"Really?" he said, softly.

I walked back to him, arms out, and this time, he opened his. He pulled me into an embrace and we rocked ever so slightly for a minute or two. Finally, I broke the moment, and pushed him away.

"Good luck, Juliet," he said, as I turned and walked away. "I hope you find a bigger, better deal."

****

Sitting in the driveway, I gripped the steering wheel to keep my hands from shaking. Time was ticking; I'd have to blow the horn soon. Unless you counted the combined 15 minutes when Edward peeked in on me in my sick bed and gave me soup in the kitchen, we hadn't been alone since we'd made love.

OK, *Juliet*, I coached myself. *You made a very adult decision to step away from Jasper. Good girl.* I reached around and patted myself on the back. Not that I could ever imagine sharing the intimate details of that friendship with my mother, but if I did, I know she'd applaud my logic and restraint. *As for Edward, he's going away for six months. Independent, smart women don't get involved with unavailable men. Besides, why would you need to commit to a man when you've just made a commitment to yourself?*

"A Commitment to Myself," I said out loud, and laughed. It sounded like one of Aunt Suze's books. Funny though, like a good self-help book should, the idea of it made me feel calm and powerful. I *did* make a commitment to myself. I wasn't going to live my life Jasper's way, or to try and woo Piers Conley-Weatherall. Scary as it was to think about, he'd have to take me for what I was, and if he didn't like it, well…I'd lived this long without a father. Most remarkable to me was that I wasn't going to live my life Mother's way, either. I'd decided, I'd told her, and the world didn't blow apart. A little part of me actually believed that she was proud that I defied her. *OK, so maybe you're living your life a little bit the way Posy wants you to –* I broke into a smile just thinking about my best friend *– but let's call that a choice.*

I checked the dashboard clock. 11:45. Edward had expected to hear me honk 15 minutes ago. *You could just back out, quietly, Juliet,* I thought. *Drive to the filling station and phone for a car for Edward. Soon he'll be onboard a yacht in the middle of the sea and you won't have to deal with him.* My body flooded with relief at the idea. Suddenly, I was itching to be away from Thornton Hall and to put Edward behind me. "Here I come, California!" I shouted manically. "Here's to a fresh start!"

I took off the handbrake and turned to look over my shoulder so I could back out. Just as I started rolling, I stopped, slamming the car into park, and laid on the horn. I couldn't do that to him. It had hurt too much when I thought he had done it to me.

Edward swung the door to his cottage open and I watched him walk down the couple of steps from his porch, grinning his lopsided grin. His lovely, familiar, one-of-a-kind, lopsided grin. He had on a brown, corduroy field coat and dark-wash jeans, and his carry-on bag was slung diagonally across his chest. *Oh my God, his chest,* my mind poked me. Between the distractions of having found out I had a father, watching one of England's oldest families unravel before my very eyes, I'd glossed over how attractive Edward was. And if I'm honest, by attractive, I mean insanely hot.

He approached the passenger side and raised his eyebrows. Staring up through the window at his dancing, green eyes, I hit the button, unlocking the door. He chucked his bags into the back seat and buckled up. He smiled, settled himself in, and didn't say a word. Backing out into the circular part of the drive, I stole a glance at him. With his legs lolling wide apart, and his elbow resting on the ledge of the window, he looked perfectly calm and relaxed. The bastard.

OK, I thought, *two can play that game.*

I took a stab at harnessing my thoughts, trying to turn them away from Edward. *Pretend he's not even in the car,* I told myself. *Embody grace and ease.* Instead I focused on improving my posture, endeavoring to project the very image of serene togetherness. Unfortunately, my thoughts rebelled when the car bounced over the noisy cattle grates, sending Edward's knee over into my territory to graze my leg. All my nerves crackled. I concentrated on keeping my face placid as I remembered what his muscular legs looked like, naked and taut, wrapping around me.

"Steady!" Edward said, just as I heard the loud spray of gravel pelting the side of my car. "OK, then?"

"I'm fine," I told him, in what I hoped was a nonchalant tone.

"I could drive, if you like. After all, you've really been through it."

I bristled. "You've got a lot of nerve thinking that you're so special you could mess with my head. Honestly," I said, dishonestly, "I've hardly given you and your disappearance at single thought."

"What I meant to say is that it takes time to get over…"

"There's nothing to get over. It was a fling, pure and simple." I smiled a tight smile to show him how absolutely fine I was with it. I could feel my lips twisting awkwardly. I checked myself in the rear-view mirror. Yikes! I looked like a circus clown. I breathed in and out and went back to trying to look serene.

"Jubes, what I meant to say is that it takes time to get over having been ill. You did pass out, after all. If you feel off, I'd be happy to drive."

I brought the car to a gentle stop at the end of the estate's long drive. I did feel woozy, for whatever reason, and as much as I hated to relinquish the wheel, it didn't make sense to take a risk. Not to mention, no matter how many times I'd driven on the wrong side of the road, it was still a challenge for me. I unbuckled, and climbed out. "All yours."

As he walked around the front of the car, and I walked around the back, I quickly touched up my lips with the gloss I had in my jeans pocket. *To prevent chapping,* I told myself.

I buckled in and fished around in my bag for my water bottle. My mouth was dry and my hands were sweaty. "All set?" Edward asked, and I nodded.

Oh, man! I thought irritably. *All men look sexy driving, but come on!* I couldn't catch a break. He'd shucked off his coat and he was wearing a tight, white Henley, all buttons undone at the chest, and it pulled tautly over his buff upper body. Over that, he had on a thin, dark, patterned vest that looked cut and measured for his chest. Its scalloped armholes accentuated his broad shoulders and stood away from his body around his stomach, reminding me how trim it was. He expertly held the wheel with one hand and maneuvered the stick shift with the other, lounging back like he owned the place. *Bastard!*

He looked over at me, and smiled. *Wow,* I thought, suddenly relaxing.

I noted that it wasn't a sleazy smile. It was not a manipulative smile, a flirty smile, a triumphant smile, or even a condescending smile. It was just a smile, and it was sincere. It was a smile that smashed through all my rigid rules and my need to play games. It was a smile that reminded me of other smiles: Edward smiling in the kitchen when I showed him how to make a Kentucky Hot Brown, the smile he gave me when he jogged past me calling me a pansy on an early-morning run, a smile when we clinked glasses at Isaac's wedding. His smile when he lay above me, gently stroking my hair, after we'd destroyed his bed.

Stop playing games, Juliet, my inner voice counseled me. *You can have everything you want, if you just let it happen.*

In that moment, speeding down the M5, stone fences and picturesque barns on offer for my viewing pleasure, I believed it. It was like my heart was a helium balloon, pressing upward in my ribcage, lifting me out of my seat. Take a chance.

"Edward," I ventured. "The night I was with you was the best night of my life." I was dizzy with terror, but it all had to be said. "It hurt so much when you left."

"You hurt me," he said so quickly, it was as if he'd already learned his lines for this play we were in. It was like he'd been waiting to get it out. "You assumed the worst."

I felt stupid, but my insecurities got the better of me and I plowed on. "Do you swear you weren't sleeping with Lady Penelope?" I asked, melting with fear.

"Never. Not once," he said firmly. "Did you sleep with Roth?" he countered.

"No." He nodded.

"You could have called me," I said.

"I did. And I wrote a note," he said. "You could have tracked me down."

"I didn't think you wanted me to. Look, I chased a man once and it didn't end well. Your note didn't explain anything!" I was getting agitated.

"I'm a soldier and a chef, not a writer!" he fired back. "What did you want me to say? That I took the money Roth offered me because I needed it. Because my father needed it? That I was frightened I'd lose my only parent?"

"Yes! That's exactly what I wanted!" I shouted, embarrassed, but plunging on. "I wanted reassurance! I wanted to know that I meant something to you!"

"And I suppose you wanted me to write that I loved you!" he yelled, eyes glued to the road, hands gripping the wheel.

"I did! I did want you to write that. I wanted you to write that you love me and you always have!"

"I do love you, and I always have!" he shouted.

"I love you, too!" I shouted back. I was on the verge of crying, but suddenly I was laughing, a huge, rolling belly laugh that I couldn't have stopped if someone had offered me a million dollars.

Edward was laughing too. I was worried he'd crash the car, and wanted to say so, but every time I tried to speak, I ended up saying, "Haaaaaa… haaaaaa… haaaaa" like a wounded animal instead.

He must have thought the same thing because, when I could force my eyelids open, I saw that he was turning onto a side road, and slowing down the car.

"Juliet."

"Just…stop…just…stop…" I managed to get out.

We sat there, pulled to the shoulder of the road, wiping our eyes, and gasping for breath. In front of us was a sign for the Stonehouse Court Hotel. Far in the distance, there was a building that looked like a modest castle. Every time we looked at one another, we tripped the wire, and sent each other back into hiccupping, stomach-squeezing laughter. This had gone on so long, I was wondering if we'd ever be able to stop by ourselves.

"What did you say?" he got out in a whole sentence before he started laughing again.

I was starting to wind down to the realm of involuntary giggles and tears. "I said I love you and I always have."

He gave a couple of final laughs, and went quiet. My laughing turned to heavy breathing, and we looked at each other silently.

"Do you mean it?" Edward asked.

I knew that I did. I knew it even when I was with Ben, even when I was considering Jasper. "Yes."

He leaned forward and softly put his lips onto mine. Oh, yes. With each peck, graze, nibble and flick of his tongue, he reminded me what I'd been missing, until we were melting into one another. He undid his seatbelt, and reached over to undo mine, never stopping the contact. At some point, I surfaced from the reverie with my hands under his untucked shirt and the clasp of my bra undone. "Edward," I moaned breathlessly, "it's broad daylight. We should stop." We straightened our clothes, and sat back, each in our own seats, panting.

"In case anyone asks, I'm your boyfriend," Edward said. He looked at me sidelong. "If that's alright with you."

"It's perfect with me."

"Can you wait?"

"Wait for what?"

"For me to finish on the yacht, so we can be together."

"Oh," I flushed, "I thought you meant…"

"Oh," he answered. "Oh!" He looked at his watch. "The hotel is five minutes in the distance. Let's see, 12:40 now, check in by 1 o'clock, check out by 2:15, and back on the road in time for a pre-flight 2 hours."

I must have looked surprised, because he quickly said, "Oh, I didn't mean to be rude. Never mind. Forgive me?"

"I'll forgive you," I said, hurrying to buckle my seatbelt, "if you can move that check-in time to 12:45." I looked at him from under my lashes, feeling my body begin to heat up. "By 1 o'clock, I want you to be showing me how much you mean it."

"Oh I mean it," he said, putting the car into gear, and gunning it toward the inn, "and I intend to keep showing you for a very long time."

The End

Acknowledgements

I'm deeply grateful to my editor Charlotte Ledger for snatching up my book with such enthusiasm and fresh-faced, forward-thinking positivity. Thank you for making my book better. I'm proud to have your fingerprints all over it!

A big thank-you to the HarperImpulse team: To Kimberly Young, the fearless leader, to Katie, the digi-marketing star, to Richard, the behind-the-scenes mover and shaker, and to Alex, the unparalleled cover designer.

Thanks to my agent Sharon Bowers for her wise input, and for treating me like a big fish in this very big pond. She's a good woman to have on one's side. Thanks, too, to Jennifer Griffin of The MBG Literary Agency for lending an ear, and offering advice.

My gratitude goes out to my friend and fellow author, Michael Harwood, who provided me inspiration. I am fortunate to have had your honest critiques and sincere cheerleading. Your practical approach to the brave new world of publishing has benefited me. I hope you have found, and will continue to find, my support half as valuable.

Deep thanks to my mother. Reading a book in peace was her favorite thing to do. Thanks to my sister-in-law Anni, the sister of my heart. And to my grandmother, Rose, who found everything I did delightful. Knowing that made all the difference.

Thank you to Rose and Wolf, my brilliant and bright-eyed darlings. You have made me who I am, and you exist in every thought I have, and every word I write.

And finally, to my funny, handsome, and menschy husband Sam: thank you for taking this ride with me.

www.ingramcontent.com/pod-product-compliance
Lightning Source LLC
Chambersburg PA
CBHW010631100726

47900CB00011B/2780